# *The Riders*

TIM WINTON was born in Perth in 1960 and was educated in Perth and Albany, Western Australia. He is the author of thirteen books, including novels, a collection of stories, non-fiction and books for children. His first novel, *An Open Swimmer*, won the *Australian*/Vogel Prize and is available in *The Collected Shorter Novels of Tim Winton* along with *That Eye, The Sky* and *In the Winter Dark*. His previous novel, *Cloudstreet*, won the Banjo Award and Miles Franklin Award in Australia and the Deo Gloria Prize in England. He lives in Western Australia with his wife and three children.

ALSO BY TIM WINTON IN PICADOR

*Blood and Water: Stories*

*Shallows*

*Cloudstreet*

*The Collected Shorter Novels of Tim Winton*

An Open Swimmer    That Eye, The Sky    In the Winter Dark

# *The Riders*

# TIM WINTON

PICADOR

*This book has had many patrons. Earliest work was done with the aid of the Literature Board of the Australia Council and the Marten Bequest. My heartfelt thanks to Joe Sullivan and the sound of his boots on the gravel every morning a long time ago, and also to Denise Winton and Howard Willis for their patience, their expertise and their very real help.*
*This is a work of fiction and all characters are imaginary.*

First published 1994 by Pan Macmillan Publishers Australia
a division of Pan Macmillan Australia Pty Limited

First published in Great Britain 1995 by Picador
an imprint of Macmillan General Books
25 Eccleston Place, London SW1W 9NF
and Basingstoke

Associated companies throughout the world

ISBN 0 330 34336 X



1 3 5 7 9 8 6 4 2

A CIP catalogue record for this book is available from
the British Library

Printed and bound in Great Britain by
Cox & Wyman Ltd, Reading, Berkshire

*for Denise*

*Wasted and wounded*
*It ain't what the moon did*
*I got what I paid for now*
*See you tomorrow*
*Hey Frank can I borrow*
*A couple of bucks from you*
*To go*
*Waltzing Matilda*
*Waltzing Matilda*
*You'll go waltzing Matilda with me . . .*

Tom Waits, 'Tom Traubert's Blues'

# I

*On Raglan Road on an autumn day*
*I saw her first and knew*
*That her dark hair would weave a snare*
*That I may one day rue . . .*

'Raglan Road' (traditional)

# *One*

WITH THE NORTH WIND hard at his back, Scully stood in the doorway and sniffed. The cold breeze charged into the house, finding every recess and shadowy hollow. It rattled boards upstairs and lifted scabs of paint from the walls to come back full in his face smelling of mildew, turf, soot, birdshit, Worcestershire sauce and the sealed-up scent of the dead and forgotten. He scraped his muddy boots on the flagstones and closed the door behind him. The sudden noise caused an explosion in the chimney as jackdaws fled their fortress of twigs in the fireplace. His heart racing, he listened to them batter skyward, out into the failing day, and when they were gone he lit a match and set it amongst the debris. In a moment fire roared like a mob in the hearth and gave off a sudden, shifting light. The walls were green-streaked, the beams overhead swathed in webs and the floor swimming with trash, but he was comforted by the new sound and light in the place, something present besides his own breathing.

He simply stood there firestruck like the farmboy of his youth, watching the flames consume half-fossilized leaves and twigs and cones. There in the blaze he saw the huge burns of memory, the windrows of uprooted karris whose sparks went up like flares for days on end over the new cleared land. The walls here were a-dance now, and chunks of burning soot tumbled out onto the hearthstone. Scully jigged about, kicking them back, lightheaded with the stench and the thought of the new life coming to him.

The chimney shuddered, it sucked and heaved and the rubbish in the house began to steam. Scully ran outside and saw his new home spouting flame at the black afternoon sky, its chimney a torch above the sodden valley where his bellow of happiness rang halfway to the mountains. It really was his. Theirs.

IT WAS A SMALL HOUSE, simple as a child's drawing and older than his own nation. Two rooms upstairs, two down. Classic vernacular, like a model from the old textbooks. It stood alone on the bare scalp of a hill called the Leap. Two hundred yards below it, separated by a stand of ash trees and a hedged lane was the remains of a gothic castle, a tower house and fallen wings that stood monolithic above the valley with its farms and soaklands. From where Scully stood, beneath his crackling chimney, he could see the whole way across to the Slieve Bloom Mountains at whose feet the valley and its patchwork of farms lay like a twisted shawl. Wherever you looked in that direction you saw mountains beyond and castle in the corner of your eye. The valley squeezed between them; things, colours, creatures slipped by in their shadow, and behind, behind the Leap there was only the lowest of skies.

He wasted no time. In what remained of the brief northern day he must seal the place against the weather, so he began by puttying up loose windowpanes and cutting a few jerry-built replacements out of ply. He dragged his tools and supplies in from the old Transit van and set a fallen door on two crates to serve as a workbench. He brought in a steel bucket and a bag of cement, some rough timber, a few cans of nails and screws and boxes of jumbled crap he'd dragged halfway round Europe. By the fire he stood a skillet and an iron pot, and on the bench beside some half-shagged paperbacks he dropped his cardboard box of groceries. All the luggage he left in the van. It was a leaky old banger but it was drier and cleaner than the house.

He lined up his battered power tools along the seeping wall nearest the fire and shrugged. Even the damp had damp. The cottage had not so much as a power point or light socket. He resigned himself to it and found a trowel, mixed up a slurry of cement in his steel bucket, stood his aluminium ladder against the front wall and climbed up onto the roof to caulk cracked slates while the rain held off and the light lasted. From up there he saw the whole valley again: the falling castle, the soaks and bogs, the pastures and barley fields in the grid of hawthorn hedges and drystone walls all the way up to the mountains. His hands had softened these past weeks. He felt the lime biting into the cracks in his fingers and he couldn't help but sing, his excitement was so full, so he launched rather badly into the only Irish song he knew.

*There was a wild Colonial boy,*
*Jack Dougan was his name . . .*

He bawled it out across the muddy field, improvising shamelessly through verses he didn't know, and the tension of the long drive slowly left him and he had the automatic work of his hands to soothe him until the only light was from the distant farmhouses and the only sound the carping of dogs.

By torchlight he washed himself at the small well beside the barn and went inside to boil some potatoes. He heaped the fire with pulpy timber and the few bits of dry turf he found, and hung his pot from the crane above it. Then he lit three cheap candles and stood them on a sill. He straightened a moment before the fire, feeling the day come down hard on him. It was sealed now. It was a start.

He put one boot up on a swampy pile of the *Irish Times* and saw beside his instep:

> BOG MAN IN CHESHIRE
>
> Peat cutters in Cheshire yesterday unearthed the body of a man believed to have been preserved in a bog for centuries . . .

Scully shifted his foot and the paper came apart like compost.

It was warm inside now, but it would take days of fires to dry the place out, and even then the creeping damp would return. Strange to own a house older than your own nation. Strange to even bother, really, he thought. Nothing so weird as a man in love.

Now the piles of refuse were really steaming and the stink was terrible, so with the shovel and rake, and with his bare hands, he dragged rotten coats and serge trousers, felt hats, boots, flannel shirts, squelching blankets, bottles, bicycle wheels, dead rats and curling mass cards outside to the back of the barn. He swept and scraped and humped fresh loads out to the pile behind the knobbly wall. The norther was up again and it swirled about in the dark, calling in the nooks of the barn. Stumbling in the gloom he went to the van for some turps, doused the whole reeking pile and took out his matches. But the wind blew and no match would light, and the longer he took the more he thought about it and the less he liked the idea of torching the belongings of a dead man right off the mark like this. He had it all outside now. The rest could wait till morning.

Somewhere down in the valley, cattle moaned in their sheds. He smelled the smoke of his homefire and the earthy steam of boiling spuds. He saw the outline of his place beneath the low sky. At the well he washed his numb hands a second time and went indoors.

When the spuds were done he pulled a ruined cane chair up to the hearth and ate them chopped with butter and slabs of soda bread. He opened a bottle of Guinness and kicked off his boots. Five-thirty and it was black out there and had been the better part of an hour. What a hemisphere. What a day. In twenty-eight hours he'd seen his wife and daughter off at Heathrow, bought the old banger from two Euro-hippies at Waterloo Station, retrieved his tools and all their stored luggage from a mate's place in North London and hit the road for the West Coast feeling like a stunned mullet. England was still choked with debris and torn trees from the storms and the place seemed mad with cops and soldiers. He had no radio and hadn't seen a paper. Enniskillen, people said, eleven dead and sixty injured in an IRA cock-up. Every transfer was choked, every copper wanted to see your stuff. The ferry across the Irish Sea, the roads out of Rosslare, the drive across Ireland. The world was reeling, or perhaps it was just him, surprised and tired at the lawyer's place in Roscrea, in his first Irish supermarket and off-licence. People talked of Enniskillen, of Wall Street, of weather sent from hell, and he plunged on drunk with fatigue and information. There had to be a limit to what you could absorb, he thought. And now he was still at last, inside, with his life back to lock-up stage.

The wind ploughed about outside as he drank off his Guinness. The yeasty, warm porter expanded in his gut and he moaned with pleasure. Geez, Scully, he thought, you're not hard to please. Just look at you!

And then quite suddenly, with the empty bottle in his lap, sprawled before the lowing fire in a country he knew nothing about, he was asleep and dreaming like a dog.

# *Two*

SCULLY WOKE SORE AND FREEZING with the fire long dead and his clothes damp upon him. At the well he washed bravely and afterwards he scavenged in his turp-soaked rubbish heap and found a shard of mirror to shave by. He wiped the glass clean and set it on the granite wall. There he was again, Frederick Michael Scully. The same square dial and strong teeth. The broad nose with its pulpy scar down the left side from a fight on a lobster boat, the same stupid blue that caused his wonky eye. The eye worked well enough, unless he was tired, but it wandered a little, giving him a mad look that sometimes unnerved strangers who saw the Brillopad hair and the severely used face beneath it as ominous signs. Long ago he'd confronted the fact that he looked like an axe-murderer, a sniffer of bicycle seats. He stuck out like a dunny in a desert. He frightened the French and caused the English to perspire. Among Greeks he was no great shakes, but he'd yet to find out about the Irish. What a face. Still, when you looked at it directly it was warm and handsome enough in its way. It was the face of an optimist, of a man eager to please and happy to give ground. Scully believed in the endless possibilities of life. His parents saw their lives the way their whole generation did; to them existence was a single shot at things, you were a farmer, a fisherman, a butcher for the duration. But Scully found that it simply wasn't so. It only took a bit of imagination and some guts to make yourself over, time and time again. When he looked back on his thirty years he could hardly believe his luck. He left school early, worked the deck of a boat, went on to market gardening, sold fishing tackle, drove trucks, humped bricks on building sites, taught himself carpentry and put himself through a couple of years' architecture at university. Became a husband and father, lived abroad for a couple of years, and now he was a landowner in County Offaly, fixing an eighteenth-century peasant cottage with his bare hands. In the New Year he'd be a father again. Unbelievable. All these lives, and still the same face. All these goes at things, all these chances, and it's still me. Old Scully.

He was used to being liked and hurt at being misunderstood, though even in Europe most people eventually took to Scully. What they saw was what they got, but they could never decide what it was they saw – a working-class boofhead with a wife who married beneath herself, a hairy bohemian with a beautiful family, the mongrel expat with the homesick twang and ambitious missus, the poor decent-hearted bastard who couldn't see the roof coming down on his head. No one could place him, so they told him secrets, opened doors, called him back, all the time wondering what the hell he was up to, slogging around the Continent with so little relish. Children loved him; his daughter fought them off outside crèches. He couldn't help himself – he loved his life.

As mist rolled back from the brows of the Slieve Bloom Mountains, the quilted fields opened to the sun and glistened with frost. Scully swung the mattock in the shadows of the south wall. The earth was heavy and mined with stones so that every few strokes he struck granite and a shock went up his arm and into his body like a boot from the electric fences of his boyhood. His hands stung with nettles and his nose ran in the cold. The smoke of valley chimneys stood straight in the air.

In the hedge beside him two small birds wheeled in a courting dance. He recognized them as choughs. He mouthed the word, resting a moment and rubbing his hands. Choughs. Strange word. Two years and he still thought from his own hemisphere. He knew he couldn't keep doing it forever. He should stop thinking of blue water and white sand; he had a new life to master.

The birds lit on an old cartwheel beside the hedge to regard him and the great pillar of steam his breath made.

'It's alright for you buggers,' he said. 'The rest of us have to work.'

The choughs lifted their tails at him and flew. Scully smiled and watched them rise and tweak about across the wood below, and then out over the crenellations of the castle beyond where he lost them, his eye drawn to the black mass of rooks circling the castle keep. A huge ash tree grew from the west wing of the ruin and in its bare limbs he saw the splotches of nests. He tried to imagine that tree in the spring when its new foliage must nearly burst the castle walls.

He went back to his ragged trench against the cottage wall. The place had no damp-coursing at all, and the interior walls were chartreuse with mildew, especially this side where the soil had crept high against the house. The place was a wreck, no question. Ten years of dereliction had almost done for it. The eastern gable wall had an outward lean and would need buttressing in the short term at least. He had neither power nor plumbing and no real furniture to speak of. He'd have to strip and seal the interior walls as soon as he could. He needed a grader to clear centuries of cow slurry from the barnyard and a fence to keep the neighbours' cattle out of his modest field. He needed to plant trees – geez, the whole country needed to plant them – and buy linen and blankets and cooking things. A gas stove, a sink, toilet. It hardly bore thinking about this morning. All he could manage was the job at hand.

Scully went on hacking the ground, cursing now and then and marvelling at how sparks could still be made off muddy rocks.

He thought of the others, wondered how long he would have to be alone. He wasn't the solitary sort, and he missed them already. He wondered how Jennifer and Billie would cope seeing Australia again. Hard to go back and go through with leaving it forever. He was glad it was them. Himself, he would have piked out. One foot on the tarmac, one sniff of eucalyptus and he'd be a goner. No, it was better they went and finished things up. He was best used to get things ready here. This way he could go through with it. Scully could only feel things up to a certain point before he had to act. Doing things, that's what he was good at. Especially when it had a point. This was no exception. He was doing it for Jennifer, no use denying it, but she appreciated what it had taken for him to say yes. It was simple. He loved her. She was his wife. There was a baby on the way. They were in it together, end of story.

He worked all day to free the walls of soil and vegetation, pulling ivy out of the mortar when the mattock became too much. He ran his blistered hands over the old stones and the rounded corners of his house and smiled at how totally out of whack the whole structure was. Two hundred and fifty years and probably not a single stone of it plumb.

Ireland. Of all places, Ireland, and it was down to Mylie Doolin, that silly bugger.

Scully had originally come to the Republic for a weekend, simply out of respect. It was the country boy in him acknowledging his debts, squaring things away. They were leaving Europe at last, giving in and heading home. It seemed as though getting pregnant was the final decider. From Greece they caught a cheap flight to London where they had things stored. The Qantas flight from Heathrow was still days away, but they were packed and ready so early they went stir crazy. In the end, Scully suggested a weekend in Ireland. They'd never been, so what the hell. A couple of pleasant days touring and Scully could pay his respects to Mylie Doolin who had kept the three of them alive that first year abroad.

Fresh off the plane from Perth, Scully worked for Mylie on dodgy building sites all over Greater London. The beefy Irishman ran a band of Paddies on jobs that lacked a little paperwork and needed doing quick and quiet for cash money. On the bones of his arse, Scully found Mylie's mob in a pub on the Fulham Road at lunchtime, all limehanded and dusthaired and singing in their pints. The Paddies looked surprised to see him get a look-in, but he landed an afternoon's work knocking the crap out of a bathroom in Chelsea and clearing up the rubble. He worked like a pig and within a few days he was a regular. Without that work Scully and Jennifer and Billie would never have survived London and never have escaped its dreary maw. Mad Mylie paid him well, told him wonderful lies and set them up for quite some time. Scully saved like a Protestant. He never forgot a favour. So, only a weekend ago now, Scully had driven the three of them across the Irish midlands in a rented Volkswagen to the town of Banagher where, according to Mylie, Anthony Trollope had invented the postal pillar box and a Doolin ancestor had been granted a papal annulment from his horse. That's how it was, random as you please. A trip to the bogs. A missed meeting. A roadside stop. A house no one wanted, and a ticket home he cashed in for a gasping van and some building materials. Life was a bloody adventure.

He worked on till dark without finishing, and all down the valley, from windows and barns and muddy boreens, people looked up to the queer sight of candles in the bothy window and smoke ghosting from the chimney where that woollyheaded lad was busting his gut looking less like a rich American every day.

# *Three*

SCULLY HACKED GRIMLY AT THE CLAGGY GROUND, his spirits sinking with every chill roll of sweat down his back as he inched his way along the last stretch of trench in the mean light of morning. He was beginning to wonder if maybe this job was beyond him. After all, he was no tradesman and he was working in a country where he knew none of the rules. And he was doing it alone. Every time he saw that forlorn heap of clothes and refuse out behind the barn he'd begun to see it as his own. Would it happen? Sometime in the future a lonely pile like that marking his failure? Man, he was low this morning. He wasn't himself. He watched a blur tracking uphill across the ridge. A hare. Funny how they always ran uphill. It dodged and weaved and disappeared into fallen timber.

Dogs barked in the valley below. He rested again, leaning on the smooth hickory handle of the mattock, and saw a car, a little green Renault van, labouring up the lane. Scully threw down the mattock hopefully and slugged across the mud in his squelching wellies to the front of the house where, thank God, the AN POST van was pulling in cautiously. He wiped his hands on his mired jeans. The driver killed the motor and opened the door.

'Jaysus,' said a long, freckled shambles of a man unfolding himself like a piece of worn patio furniture. 'I thought it was the truth all along.'

Beneath the postman's crumpled cap was a mob of red hair and two huge ears. Scully stood there anxiously.

'So there's someone livin back in Binchy's Bothy.'

'That's right,' said Scully. 'My third day.'

'Peter Keneally. They call me Pete-the-Post.'

Scully reached out and shook his freckled hand. 'G'day.'

The postie laughed, showing a terrible complement of teeth.

'Would you be Mister F. M. Scully, now?'

'That's me.'

'You're the Australians, then.'

'One of them, yeah.'

'By God, you're famous as Seamus around here already. Jimmy Brereton down there by the castle says you saw this place and bought it in less time than it takes to piss.'

Scully laughed. 'Close enough.'

'Signed the papers in Davy Finneran's pub, no less.'

'Yeah, did it on the spot. And they say the Paddies are stupid.'

The postman roared.

'My wife had . . . a feeling about the place,' said Scully, needing to explain himself somehow, knowing that no explanation could sound reasonable enough for what they had done.

'Well, I suppose that's nothin to be laughin at, then.'

Scully shrugged. 'It does seem stupid at certain moments of the day.'

'Ah, but it's a fine spot up here, high and away. And you're very welcome.'

'Thanks.'

Scully scraped mud from his boots and looked now at the pale envelope in the postman's hands. The two men stood there poised awkwardly for a moment.

'Thirsty work, no?'

After a long moment Scully realized the man needed a drink.

'Don't spose you fancy a nip?'

'A nip?' The Irishman squinted at him.

'A dram,' said Scully. 'I know it's early.'

'Ah. Weeeell, it is a bit sharp out still.'

'I've got some Tullamore Dew inside.'

'That's a mornin whiskey alright,' the postie said with a wink.

They went inside by the fire and Scully threw on a rotten fencepost. In the pale light of day the interior was foul and dismal.

'Excuse the mess.'

'That Binchy always was a dirty auld bastard, rest his soul. This is the best I've seen the place.'

'I'll get there.'

'That you will, Mr Scully.'

'The name's Fred. Everyone just calls me Scully, even the missus.'

'Well, if it's good enough for her . . .'

'They still had all his clothes and everything in here.'

'Ten years, so. It just laid here rottin. Got to be people were nervous of it. Still, the Irish love to frighten emselves half to death.'

'I would have thought his family might have come and taken his things.'

'There is no family, poor man. He was gardener to the castle like his father before him. Everyone's dead.'

'Including the castle,' said Scully. 'When was the last time anyone tended to that garden?'

'Oh, it was burnt back in the Troubles. No one's lived in it since. The lords and ladies went their way and the Binchys stayed in the gardener's bothy. It was left to them. Binchy and his Da grew some spuds and did a bit of poachin. They liked to drink, you might say.'

'Oh, here.' Scully dug the bottle out of his cardboard box and poured a little into tin cups.

'Cheers.'

'*Slainte*.'

The whiskey ran hot all through him. He only really liked to drink after dark.

Scully looked anxiously at the pale envelope in the postman's hand. It was a telegram, he could see it now. He curled his toes inside his boots.

'Your wife had a feelin, you say?'

Scully squirmed, lusting for the telegram, glad of the company and a little embarrassed about his own presence here. He couldn't imagine what the Irishman must think of him.

'Yeah. Yeah, she just went all strange and said this is it, that she felt she'd been here before, like *déja vu*. She had this odd feeling that this is where we should live.'

'She's Irish, then.'

'No. There's no ancestral pull. People talk about things like that but . . . no, nothing.'

'Well, you are. With a name like Scully.'

'Well, bog-Irish maybe a long way back. Desert Irish by now.'

'Ha, desert Irish!' The postie stomped his feet.

The fire hissed and spat. The walls steamed and the house smelled like a locker room hosed down with fish blood. Scully looked at the black work cracks in the Irishman's fingers.

'D'you know where I could hire a cement mixer? I thought there might be a place in town.'

'Ce-ment mixer? Conor's your man.'

'Conor.'

'My brother from Birr. He's the electrician, but he does a bit of this and that, you know.'

'Terrific. Maybe I could get a phone number, or something?'

'Be damn, I'll bring it meself tomorrow,' said Pete-the-Post slamming his cup down on the battered mantelpiece. 'In that little green machine out there, piled in on the mail of the Republic, no less.'

'Look, don't go to any trouble.'

'No trouble at all.'

Scully watched the postie lick his lips, as though tasting the last of the whiskey on them, with eyes shut to the wan light bending in through the window, and he wondered if he'd ever get his telegram.

'Rightso, time to go.' The postman whanged himself on the cheek with the heel of his palm. 'Ah, nearly forgot – something from the Dublin Telegraphs.'

He handed over the envelope and Scully did his best not to snatch at it in his excitement.

'Good news, I hope. Never liked telegrams, meself.'

'Thanks,' said Scully, stuffing it in his pocket and following Pete-the-Post to the door.

'See you in the mornin!'

As the van pulled away, motor racing horribly, Scully tore the envelope open and the telegram in half so he had to stoop to the mud and fit the pieces together.

HOUSE ON THE MARKET. AGENT ASSURES QUICK SALE. PACKING NOW. BILLIE AT YOUR MUM'S. WILL BE BACK

BEFORE CHRISTMAS. USE TELEGRAMS TILL PHONE ON THERE. JENNIFER.

A light drizzle began to drift in. Rooks and jackdaws came and went from the castle keep down in the misting hollow. Scully shifted from foot to foot, inexplicably deflated.

It was good news. It was contact, confirmation. But so damn businesslike. What was the result of the ultrasound? How was everybody? What did the wide brown land look like? Was it summer, real acetylene summer? And did she miss him half as much as he missed her? Though it *was* a telegram. You couldn't exactly get hot and sweaty in a telegram.

He stuffed the paper into his pocket. It was actually happening. They could stop moving at last and make a home somewhere, the three of them. Maybe she's right about magic in the spur of the moment. Could be she's been cautious and sensible too long. It was her new thing, cutting loose.

It was her prevailing outlook ever since they came abroad, but he had to admit he liked her just as well the old way. She was like a sheet anchor sometimes, a steadying influence on him, on everyone around her. Made people laugh, that sensible streak in her, but it also made her someone of substance. Jennifer wasn't just a good-looking woman, he once told her wincing parents, she was someone to be reckoned with. God, he missed her, missed them both. Their brown, swimming bodies and birdcall voices – even the sound of their sober, womanly peeing from behind a closed door. He missed dumb jokes with Billie and the warped games of Monopoly that she strung out endlessly with her insistence on 'the true and right and proper rules'. Seven and a half. She was a bright kid, and all fatherly pride aside, he knew she was different from other kids. She felt things strongly. She was fierce, precocious and loyal. She took shit from no one and saw things so clearly at times that it took your breath away. Now that he thought of it, he'd spent more time with her than he had with Jennifer. He missed their companionable silences. They understood each other, him and Billie. He wondered sometimes if Jennifer saw it, the way the two of them moved together in a crowd, in a boat, at the breakfast table. It was almost as though they each recognized themselves in the other. It was weird, like a gift. Jennifer was always busy, but she must have seen it.

Late in the afternoon, heaving and gasping, with the walls finally clear of soil and stones, he sat down for air on a stump behind the barn and saw Binchy's things piled out there, reeking of turps. He rattled the matches in his pocket but left them where they were. Why spoil the moment of triumph? He tilted his head back and let the sweat run through his matted hair. Tonight he'd boil up some water and take a real scrubdown. He'd rig up a bed from an old door and some bricks. The flags were too cold to sleep on another night. 'Live like an animal,' his father used to say, 'and you'll start thinkin like one!' Scully laughed at himself. This was like the tree houses of his boyhood, the *Robinson Crusoe* factor, the steady search for creature comforts. A cup of tea would render him human – he knew it.

After dark, scrubbed and fed and hugely satisfied, Scully went walking, a mere shadow moving through the ash wood with the wind tearing at the bare crowns of the trees above him. He was sore and happy, his hands still stung with nettles and his boots were full of stones. He saw the lights of farmhouses down in the valley, and wondered what they did at night, these farming families. He hadn't introduced himself yet. This was the furthest he'd been from the house since he arrived. But there'd be time. The night hardened with cold. The black mass of the castle loomed below. Scully sucked in the metallic air and watched the trees in turmoil, listened to their mob violence raging above him against the sky. When he turned and looked back uphill he saw the three candles burning in the curtainless window. The wind bullied at him, ripping through the cold wet of his hair, but he stood there a long time in the wood below his field, just watching those three candles twinkling in the empty house.

IN HIS DREAMS THAT NIGHT Scully ran through long grass between walls and hedges uphill with lights gathering behind him and only the cover of grass and night before him. On he ran, never stopping to see what it was behind him, blindly going on into darkness.

## *Four*

SCULLY JERKED AWAKE. A motor idled outside. It was light already. He wriggled from his stained sleeping bag and went to the window but could see only his ragged reflection in the frost. He opened the top half of his front door, felt the fierce cold, and saw a filthy grey truck slipping and yawing down the icy hill with its tailgate flapping. Diesel smoke hung in the air. He went out barefoot across the frozen ground and saw two tons of builders' sand heaped against the barn wall.

From around the bend on the hill came the little green van.

'Boots are the go, Mr Scully,' said Pete-the-Post getting out to unlock the back doors. 'On a mornin such as this, it's definitely boots, don't you think?'

Scully grinned, curling his toes on the unyielding mud. He helped the postman unload the cement mixer and several bags of cement.

'Cheaper than airmail, it is.'

'I really appreciate this,' said Scully.

'There'll be a load of blocks here within the hour, and meself'll be by at one o'clock to start into it.'

Scully blinked.

'Well, you'll be needin a hod-carrier, I expect.'

'Well. I. Haven't you got the post to do?'

'Diversify, Mr Scully, that's my motto. We're in the EC now, you know.'

'The EC.'

'This is the new Ireland you're lookin at.'

'Really?'

'No, it's the same auld shite, believe me,' the postman said, laughing, 'but don't go tellin!'

THAT MORNING SCULLY CLEANED THE COTTAGE out properly. He shovelled and scraped and swept until its four simple rooms were clean enough to move through without grimacing, and then he rearranged his equipment into an orderly system. He crawled across the upstairs floors on all fours, marking boards that needed replacing, and he went grimly through the barn, finding ancient bags of coal, cooking implements, some quite decent wood, and another wide door he sat on blocks to improve his temporary bed. Out behind the barn he looked again at Binchy's things and took from the heap a small, black rosary which he set above the mantel on a nail in the wall. Beside it he stood a stiff black-and-white print of the three of them, Jennifer, Billie and him, that a friend had taken one freezing day in Brittany. He stared at it a good while, remembering the day. Their Parisian friend Dominique had the Leica going all weekend. She took so many photos they got blasé and began to pose. This one was in the cemetery at St Malo. All of them were laughing. Jennifer's black hair falling from beneath a beret. His and Billie's like matching treetops, just mad foliage from the same forest. It was a good photo. They hung together as a shape, the three of them. Just behind them was the circled cross of the Celts, its carved stone knotted with detail, the entwined faces of saints and sinners. It was beautiful, so handsome it made the three of them look dignified. Dominique knew her business. She could take a photo. They'd miss her. Half of what you did in travelling was simply missing things, sensations, people. He'd missed so long and hard these last couple of years he could barely think of it. And he still had some longing ahead of him, the worst kind, until Christmas.

He touched the photograph once. Coal burned lustily in the grate. The house began to steam and dry. Scully went out to survey the gable wall.

## *Five*

THE DOOR SLIDES TO ON THE LOWING, dungspraying cows as the man in the cloth cap turns to see the scaffold up against Binchy's Bothy and two figures beneath it like trolls atop the hill. The sky is the colour of fish, a Friday colour beGod, and the bare trees stand forlorn. It's Pete-the-Post up there with that woolly young bastard with love in his eyes.

He fingers in his waistcoat for the damp fag he's been saving. The stink of silage burns at the back of his gullet and he lights up to beat it off.

It's love alright. Jimmy Brereton, bachelor unto the grave, recognizes a man doomed by love, snared by a woman. You could see it the day they turned up in that thresher of a Volkswagen. Her with the hair out like a black flag and her hands on the smooth stones of Binchy's wall as if it had a fever pulse, and him, hairy as anything on Christ's earth, waiting on her with eyes big and hopeless as a steer. The shackles of marriage, of doilies and lace curtains and mysterious female illnesses staring him in the face, and him cheerful as you like, and sheepish, sheepish like a lamb unto the slaughter, poor booger.

Jimmy Brereton kicks the shite from his boots and watches a while. He wishes they'd come down and bulldoze that eyesore nuisance of a damn castle out of his high field while the government's asleep in Dublin. It's a danger to one and all. In a big norther stones and rubble come belting down out of the keep, and a man can no longer leave his cattle in there out of the weather for fear of having them brained with Celtic history. He thanks God and Arthur Guinness he sleeps well enough at night not to worry himself sick about the things he's seen here over the years. Things that make the hairs on your arms stand up, like every poor bastard mortared into the walls and fed to the pigs and tilled into the cellars of that place is stirring. Sometimes you hear voices on the wind and stones falling like men to the ground. Bawlers, stinks, a bedlam of rooks, and lights from the mountains, streams of them that he doesn't look for anymore. It's not madness or drink in all of this, though he bothers the bottle mightily. All the valley people are chary of the place. He remembers standing right here with his own Da watching the priest from Limerick bellowing Latin at the keep and waving his candles at no one in particular. No Brereton, man or child, would be up there after dark at that nasty fooker of a place. It's a blight on his land, and it's made him an early retirer, a six-pint man at sunset. But he's not unhappy. Things might have turned out worse. He might have married Mary Finneran in 1969 instead of backing out like a man with spine. He might have a brother like Peter Keneally's instead of no family to speak of. He might be up the hill there with those two mad boogers trying to save the long lost and working like black monkeys.

Sheepish, that's him. That woolly booger with the hod on his shoulder and the love in his eyes.

Jimmy Brereton retires indoors to the company of Mr Guinness.

# *Six*

JUST ON DARK, Scully and Peter Keneally laid the last block of their rough buttress and stood blowing steam on the makeshift scaffold.

'That's got her,' said the postman. 'Tomorrow we'll render it!'

Scully laughed and leaned his brow against the gutter. The man could work. They'd hardly spoken all afternoon and now the postie seemed determined to make up for it.

'So, where did you learn to throw blocks like a Paddy?' said Peter.

'London, I spose,' said Scully looking down the valley. It was beautiful in an eerie, organized, European way.

'Jaysus, throwin blocks for the English!'

'No, an Irishman, actually,' said Scully climbing down.

'I went to London once.'

'Once is enough.'

'Oh, you got that right.'

Pete clanged the trowels together and they headed for the well.

'I worked with a gang of Offaly boys,' said Scully. 'Hard

men, I spose you'd call em. We did cash jobs, you know. Jobs light-on for a bit of paperwork, you might say.'

'Like this one, you mean.'

Scully smiled. 'Let's have a drink, I'm freezin.'

At the well, as they stood washing the mortar off their arms, Peter hummed a tune, low in his throat. In the dark he sounded like an old man, and it occurred to Scully that he had no idea how old the postie might be. Abruptly, the humming stopped.

'What was her name again? Your wife?'

'Jennifer.'

'They say she's a beautiful girl.'

'Geez, they're quick around here, aren't they?'

The postman wheezed out a laugh. 'But are they liars?'

'No, they got it right.'

'Then you're a lucky man.'

'Mate, she's a lucky woman.'

They went in tired and laughing to the swimming warmth of the hearth, and Scully poured them a porter each and they sat on a chair and box to listen to the whine of the fire. Scully wrote out a telegram message on the back of an envelope: GOOD NEWS. ALL WELL HERE. KEEP IN TOUCH. LOVE YOU BOTH. SCULLY.

'Telegram? I'll send it for you.'

'Would you?'

'You got snakes there in Australia,' said Pete thoughtfully.

'You bet. No St Pat out there.'

'Poisonous snakes, eh?'

Scully grinned. 'Dugites, taipans, king browns, tigers. A tiger snake once chased me all the way down the back paddock.'

'Are they fast, then?'

'I was on a motorbike.'

'Aw, Jaysus!'

'Snakes and sharks,' said Scully, hamming it up. He handed Pete the soiled envelope.

'And Skippy the bush kangaroo, beGod!'

Scully laughed. 'Not as unpredictable as a Paddy, though. Those Irish boys in London were a wild bunch, I tell you. Talk about take no prisoners.'

'Offaly boys, you say?'

'Yeah, the boss was from Banagher.'

Pete licked his lower lip, uncrossing his legs slowly. 'Banagher.'

'Yeah, you probably know the bloke.'

Pete swallowed. 'Could be.'

'Bloke called Doolin.'

'Mylie,' the postie breathed.

'You know him, then?'

'Jaysus, Mary and Joseph.'

'Silly bugger got busted in Liverpool.'

'I heard he was . . . taken.'

'The VAT man, I spose.'

'You don't need to pretend with me, Mr Scully.'

'What?'

'We don't want any trouble here. I mean we're all good Catholics here, but . . .'

Scully looked at him. The man was pale.

'We just want to leave all that behind us. We don't want the Guards crawlin all over the countryside, unmarked cars, questions at all hours.'

The postman's huge ears were red now and a sweat had formed on his brow.

'Pete –'

'We just want to live our lives. I'm sorry to give the wrong impression.'

'There's something here I'm just not getting.'

'I have two hundred pounds here in cash, and I'm a man who can keep his mouth shut. I should have known, oh God. You turnin up like that out of the blue and wantin this house in the middle of nowhere. It was the accent, I spose. I didn't think . . . yeah, with Mylie inside you'd be recruitin lads.'

'What lads?'

'*The* lads,' said Pete, tilting his head a moment to look directly at Scully for the first time. 'What d'ye mean, what lads? Are ye playin with me?'

Scully stood up carefully. 'What the hell are you talking about?'

Pete licked his bloodless lips. 'You mean you don't . . . before the Mother of God you'd swear you don't know?'

'Know what? Tell me what it is I'm supposed to know!' Now that his blood was up and his eye wandering somewhat, Scully looked threatening to the uninitiated.

'You swear it?'

'Alright, I swear!'

'You're a Catholic, then?'

'No, I'm nothing.'

'So the name's false.'

'No, my name's Scully, I was christened C of E.'

'You mean it might be honestly possible that you don't know? Oh, Jaysus, Peter, you fookin eejit of a man, what a fright you've given yourself! Mr Scully, it wasn't the VAT man who got Mylie Doolin at Liverpool, it was the Special Branch. You're fookin luckier than you think. What a sweet, innocent child of God you must be! Mylie is with the Provos.'

Scully put down his glass. 'You mean . . . you mean the IRA?'

'The very same.'

'Fuck a duck, you're jokin!'

'Do I look like a man enjoyin himself here?'

'Shit. It can't be.'

'Ah, drink up now and don't worry yourself,' said Pete, wiping the sweat from his face and finding his grin again.

'Are you sure?'

'Life is mysterious, Mr Scully, but *that* I know for sure.'

'I never even . . . you think he had anything to do with the Remembrance Day thing? All those bloody kids.'

Pete-the-Post emptied his glass and shrugged. A wind was moaning outside now. 'He went in before. Weeks ago. Still, it was all such a fook-up, who could tell. You never know anybody properly, not the whole of em. A man barely knows himself, wouldn't you say?'

Scully stared into the fire. Pete chuckled to himself a moment and hauled himself to his feet.

'I'll be by at one again. Don't you worry about Mylie Doolin, that booger. By God, I nearly had mud in me trousers tonight! Goodnight, then.'

'Yeah, righto. Watch out for snakes.'

ALONE, WITH THE FIRE WILD IN THE CHIMNEY, Scully drank and thought of that year of high-jinks with Mylie's lads. He'd known they were hard men. Once, when some blazer-and-cravatted old bastard pleaded sudden poverty at the end of a job, knowing the Irishmen had no recourse to the law, Mylie opened up the fifth floor window and began calmly to hurl TV, microwave and stereo into the street until the cash appeared magically on the table. Another time, at the end of a horrible three-week lightning renovation at Hampstead, they discovered that the landlord had bolted to Mallorca and they would never be paid, so Mylie put instant concrete down all the toilets and sinks. A little Jetset here, a little Jetset there. You could almost hear it turn to stone. Three floors of plumbing utterly stuffed. It wasn't the same as money in their pockets, but it gave them a bit of a glow in the pub afterwards. Mad Irish boys, he thought they were, but extortionists and bombers? Terrorists and thieves?

All evening he sat there, forgetting to eat, going through those London months again, wondering and not quite disbelieving, until near midnight he dragged his sleeping bag onto the old door and climbed in.

## *Seven*

SCULLY WORKED ON, THAT NOVEMBER WEEK, pausing only to eat and sleep, or to now and again find himself staring out across the valley to the Slieve Blooms and their changing light. He heard his own sounds in the cottage, his breathing, his footfalls and scrapings and hammerings, and knew that this was as alone as he'd been in all his life. So busy was he, so driven with getting the place habitable, that he had not even met his neighbours yet, though he knew them by name because of Pete-the-Post who came daily with mail, a newspaper, building materials and more often than not, a few pints of milk, a loaf of soda bread and a packet of bacon for the rough fryups they had on dark afternoons with the rain driving outside and the smell of burning peat in their faces. Pete gave him company most afternoons, made him laugh, and sped up the work enormously. Scully bragged shamelessly about his feisty daughter and all the barefaced things she said to people, how fearlessly she corrected teachers and shopkeepers and policemen. The way she'd sit and read for hours and draw elaborate comic strips of their life in Fremantle, Paris, Greece. How she was their safe-passage through Europe, the one who softened-up officials, won the hearts of waiters, attacked languages like new puzzles to be solved. The things she said, how she wondered what a marlin thought the moment it saw the boat it was attached to, the faces staring down from the transom as it lay exhausted on its side, its eye on the dry world. Scully could see how the idea of her tickled Pete. He did impressions of her little voice for him and the streams of talk she was capable of. Pete listened with his head cocked and his ears aglow. Maybe he didn't believe him. Perhaps he thought it was just pride, just love. But Scully's excitement was infectious, he could see it himself. The postie chortled and whanged the trowel approvingly against the stones. Scully liked him better than any man he could remember. He had worked with men all his life, since his fishing days and on farm after farm, where he knew what it was to be ridden, paid out on ruthlessly or ignored on site. Especially the fishing days, they were the worst; seven days a week working deck for a Serb with an iron bar in the wheelhouse. That bastard Dimic paid out on him all the way out and all the way back in to port, and what could you do twenty miles out to sea alone and unsighted? He worked with subdued Italian men in market gardens whose soil stank of rust and chemicals, whose women were boisterous and sexy and dangerous. But the biggest pricks of all were the whitebread heroes at the university, men who'd murder you with words for the sheer pleasure of it. They put an end to his working-class fantasies about the gentleness of the professional life. It was the suits you had to fear. They were the real bastards. He didn't know what it was with Peter Keneally. It might just have been loneliness, but he was always glad as hell to see him.

The next Friday Pete brought another telegram with the pint of milk and parcel of chops.

Scully opened it carefully and stood by the window.

HOUSE SOLD. SETTLEMENT IN THREE WEEKS. ARRIVE SHANNON AE46, 13 DECEMBER. JENNIFER.

'Shit,' said Scully. 'I better open an account at the Allied Irish.'

'Good news?'

'We sold our house. They'll be here in three weeks.'

'You better get busy, then. You can't have em livin in a shitehole, so.'

Scully folded the telegram soberly. So that was that. Their house was gone. But the idea, the fact of it stuck in his head. The limestone rubble walls he'd pared back himself, the stripped jarrah floorboards, the big-hipped iron roof, the airy verandahs and the frangipani blooms. The morning throb of diesels from the marina. It was the whole idea he had of their life together. The weirdest feeling. A fortnight to sell a house? God knows people had gone stupid in the West in boom, but hadn't it all fallen over? Maybe they were buying real estate now – he didn't understand economics. But they were coming. That's all that counted. He had work to do. There was a house here. Wasn't that the idea to work to, to the future!

'Are you rich then?' Peter asked from the top of the ladder that afternoon.

'Rich?'

'I don't mean to pry,' he laughed. 'I just want to know if you've got a lot of fookin money.'

'Is that why you won't send me a bill, you crafty bastard.'

'Now you're gettin presumptuous,' said Peter, swinging a bucket of mortar at him.

'Look at these hands,' said Scully. 'Are they the hands of a rich man?'

Pete brushed a broken slate off into the air and they both watched it spear into the mud and disappear.

'Well, that's a disappointment to me,' said the big redhead. 'I thought you might be a drug baron or whatever they call em, cause you're too ugly to be a rock-and-roll star.'

'Have you been drinking that poteen again?'

'Well, you have to consider it from an ignorant Paddy's point of view. These two boogers come by one day in a Volkswagen, a *Volkswagen* from London Heathrow on the way to Perth Australia and say, aarrr, that's a noise hows, arrl boy it mate! Now I figure it's got to be three things: drugs, rock-and-roll, or fooking brain damage. Buyin this auld bit of shite in the Irish outback.'

'Here, pull that gutter off while you're up there.'

The postie dragged the rotten gutter down in a shower of rust and moss.

'I figure if it's rock-and-roll, it has to be your lovely wife who's the star and you carry the bags. I mean, where does a man get a tan like that?'

'Greece. We lived in Greece.'

'Thought you said you lived in London.'

'London first. Lived in Paris, too, most of last year.'

'Paris. My God.'

'Then Greece this year.'

'The three of yez? Wanderin like a bunch of tinkers. Tell me straight, cause I've got nephews. Is it drugs?'

Scully looked at him, grinning. 'Are you serious? Mate, I'm just a poor grafter like you. My wife's a public servant – well, *was* a public servant cause she quit at the end of her long service leave. I'm not rich and there's no drugs and precious little rock 'n' roll. And no terrorism either, you silly bugger.'

'Mind your head! Well, that's the whole gutter gone. I've got a good auld piece in Roscrea for ye.'

'Here comes the rain,' said Scully retreating down the ladder. It sloped in silently, ignored by the postman, while Scully took shelter in the lee of the barn.

'And what might you be doin, Scully?'

'Getting out of the bloody rain, what d'you think?'

'Afraid of a bit of soft weather, then?'

Scully shrugged.

'Get used to it, lad!'

'Bugger that,' said Scully. He gathered up his tools and went inside.

By the time Pete came in Scully was upstairs prizing out rotten floorboards and setting new ones in their place. The brassy taste of nails was in his mouth. For some reason it reminded him of the cowshed, that taste, the slanting jerrybuilt pile his father kept tacked together for twenty years. He went everywhere with nails in his mouth, the old man. The smell of fresh-sawn wood was sweet now, and the rain pattered against the windows. Scully looked at the attic slope of the upstairs walls. It felt like a cubby house up here. These would be snug cosy rooms, warmed by the chimney that divided them. He could see them waking now on mornings quiet and wet as this, their sleepy voices close in the angled space.

'Well come on, Scully,' said Pete, suddenly beside him. 'Don't just sit there lookin lovesick, tell me about her.'

'Jennifer?'

'Ye tell me nothin, Scully. I'm beginnin to believe you're English after all. A man works with you all day and ye don't say fook. Just stand there lookin dreamy.'

'Well.'

'Well my ass.'

Scully smiled.

'Oh, for God's sake, man, tell me about Jennifer. Make the day go by, boy, give me somethin to chew on. She's the workin type, you say?'

'That's right. Department of Immigration. Got to be a bit of a big-shot.'

'And now she's emigratin herself?'

'Yeah, she's quit. She hated it. Loved working, you know. She was never the type to stay in and look after the kids. That's more me.'

Pete clucked. 'And you claimin to be a workin man.'

'When Billie – our daughter – was smaller, I worked part-time so I could be with her.'

'Where did you work? What is it exactly that ye do, Scully?'

Scully laughed. 'Those days I worked in a tackle shop. Sold lures and things, fixed reels. You ever seen a Mackerel Mauler?'

'Oh, Jaysus I hate fish!'

'I left school at fifteen, went north to work the deck of a rock lobster boat. Great money. I spose I've done all kinds of things.'

'So where did you meet her?'

Scully wrenched a board up in a shower of dry rot. 'Geez, you want details, don't you?'

Pete poked in the recess with a chisel, searching out pulpy wood. 'Was it a dance, now?'

'Australians don't dance or sing, believe me. No, we met at university, can you believe. I was trying to do architecture. Went back, finished school and got in. We were in a class together. I forget what it was. Something in the English Department, some unit I thought I'd pick up so I could read a few books, you know? She was the bored pube getting *paid* to improve herself at night.

Black hair, pretty. I mean real pretty, and she didn't say a word. Well, neither did I. I mean, there's all these kids spouting books and people you never heard of, confident as you like. I just shut up and tried to keep me head down, and she was doing the same.'

Peter fiddled with the blade of the plane, adjusting it absent-mindedly. 'And, and?'

'She asked me if I wanted a beer one night.'

'She asked *you*.'

'Oh, mate.' Scully rolled his eyes thinking of it. She bailed him up against the window one night and came out with lines that had to be rehearsed. She'd been practising.

'What a friggin country it must be. Must be because it's so damn hot. No time for romance.'

Scully threw a handful of sawdust at him and went back to his sawing. 'We both quit university and got married,' he shouted. 'Eight years!'

'Well, what're ye doin *here*? She quit a good job to go lurkin through strange places and end up here on a hill with Brereton's cows?'

'Well, she was bored with her job, and restless, and I was game for a change. We rented our house and travelled, you know.'

'With a baby and all.'

'A five-year-old isn't a baby, Pete.' No, he thought. For a baby you needed somewhere still and snug and anchored. Somewhere like this.

'Whose idea was it?'

'Hers, I spose.'

'And you followed.'

'I was game for a change, yeah. I didn't exactly follow.'

'Used to be the women who followed.'

Scully laughed, but it stung somehow. Admit it, Scully, he

thought. You followed, you'd follow her anywhere. A few weeks ago you couldn't sleep for dreams of home, of hot white beaches and the wicked scent of coconut oil and the Fremantle Doctor blowing the curtains inward against the long table there in that house you sweated on all those years. You were a mad dog for it, mate, like a horse in the home paddock, bolting with your nose in the air, kissing Europe goodbye, letting it kiss your cakehole for all you cared, and then *wham!* you turned on a penny for her sake. On a queer feeling, a thing she couldn't explain, just to see her happy.

'Well, maybe it's our turn to follow anyway,' he said.

'Mebbe so. I don't know about women. These boards need sandin now. You need the power on, Scully. You can't do all this by hand.'

'It's the money, mate. I'm stuffed until the money comes through from home. I'm living on the change from my air ticket. I don't know if I can even pay what I owe you already.'

'What, you think I'm lyin awake at night waitin for to be paid? What a proddy you are. I'll have Con come by in the mornin and put a box in, I shoulda thought of it Monday. I'll be frigged if I'm comin by to do this shite by hand. And yev got holes in your chimney there, go make some mortar. Make it one part Portland, one of lime and six of good sand. If he don't show by eleven tomorrow, you must go in and get him. It's the Conor Keneally Electric in Birr. He'll be the poor big bastard looks like me.'

# *Eight*

BUT CONOR KENEALLY DIDN'T COME, not for days he didn't, and Scully thought it best to wait it out. He scraped mildew and dirt and pulpy mortar from the interior walls and caulked up holes and cracks, and then rendered the whole surface anew, filling the place with the heady stink of lime. He scraped paint from the low attic ceiling of the upstairs rooms and sugar-soaped it till his hands were raw. The house filled with shavings and sawdust and paint flakes and wall scum and began to look like the galley of a prawn trawler. Scully found himself squatting by the hearth at night, eating with his hands. In his sliver of mirror he looked feral. He worked on without electricity, driving himself, sleeping only on his oak door amid the drifts and draughts. He just couldn't bring himself to go into Birr and chase Conor Keneally up, not when the man's brother came by every day with a pair of cover-alls over his postal uniform and a trowel in his hand and a pint of Power's at the ready. The man came by with a gas bottle, for pity's sake, and a kitchen sink and beds brought piece by piece atop the mail of the Republic. The two of them would stand about at day's end silently observing the lack of electricity.

'You should get out now and then, Scully,' Pete-the-Post said. 'You're killin yeself here and meetin no one, not even your neighbours.'

'You keep bringing me my food. I can never think of an excuse to go in. You second guess me.'

'Well, I'm takin pity on ye, Scully.'

This caused Scully to laugh uncomfortably. Did he seem that pitiable? True, he was living rough, but it was a temporary thing.

'I'm getting there.'

'That you are, son. You work like a nigger.'

Scully winced but let it pass.

'I just wish you'd bill me.'

'Are you lookin for a job?'

'Come New Year I will be, yeah.'

'Well, when you get your job you'll get your bills.'

Scully didn't go looking for Conor Keneally out of respect. After a man said things like that, how could you go embarrassing him by pursuing his brother the way Scully felt like pursuing him, morning after morning when he failed to show? Scully's power tools lay downstairs in an ugly row and daily he went at things by hand, by candlelight, by firelight, funnelling his anxiety into work.

In two mad days Scully painted out the whole interior in lime wash, and the place suddenly seemed brighter, bigger, cleaner, and so strangely wholesome that it made him realize how foul it had been before, what scunge he'd really been dealing with day and night. Then he sealed the timber floor upstairs and buffed it by hand, and he lacquered the oak banister of the stair and the great beams that ran from lintel to lintel downstairs. From pine boards in the barn loft he made a cabinet for the kitchen sink that lacked only its ply cladding and the hinges for its doors. He shaved down spare boards for bookshelves and set them upstairs beside Billie's bed, and so pretty were they that he began to wonder whether electricity might spoil this life after all. Peter arrived with salvage ply and a box of panel pins and he finished the kitchen. The flags were dry and swept. It was a clean, simple place, his new house, a place he was glad to wake in now, but it was still without music, without voices and laughter for most of the day.

There were moments in Scully's day when he simply could not use a brush or plane or hammer for the thought of the summer he was about to miss at home: the colourless grass prostrate before the wind, the flat sea whitehot at its edge and the boats paralysed at their moorings with the heat and the smell of the desert descending upon them in the marinas and coves and riverbends. The great glossy weight of grapes hanging overhead and the smell of snapper grilling over charcoal. The seamless blue sky and the loose clothing on brown bodies. Lord, it gave him bad pangs, the thought of leaving all that behind, the idea of Jennifer and Billie packing that life into tea-chests and walking out of their old Fremantle house. Maybe they should have gone halfway on this, taken out a loan in case things didn't work out. The Fremantle house was worth ten times what they'd paid for this. They needn't have sold really. But then he thought of that dreamy, sweet look of happiness on her face that day last month, that look of resolution which made her seem unreservedly confident for the first time in years. It was worth following, it had to be worth the risk of trust.

Worse than the pangs of doubt and fear he felt alone at work, Scully had waking dreams of her here. They were so vivid he could feel her breath on him. He saw linen on his bed and the two of them glistening, gasping in the quiet, her black hair a shadow upon the sheet. Billie's sleeping form beside the gable window with the tarry sky behind her, and a cradle in the corner still swinging faintly in the clear, clear air.

Scully showered under the spray of a hose in the door arch of the barn at night, and so cold was the water that from out in the fields and down in the woods you could hear him bellow like a man truly suffering.

CONOR KENEALLY DIDN'T COME and didn't come, and one afternoon when Scully couldn't bear to be at it any longer, he threw down his tools and went out walking. The sky was low. The wind blew hard from the hills. He shoved his fists deep in his pockets and stumped between hawthorn hedges and fallen walls down the lanes into the valley. He heard a tractor slinging shed slurry onto a field somewhere and dogs barking. The smell of burning peat hung in the air. He skirted the castle and its farm and went on deep into the valley where the fields were dark and heavy and became bogs at the foot of the hills. A small church stood alone on the bend in the lane. Scully climbed the stile into the graveyard and walked among the granite tombs beneath the Celtic crosses and fossilized flowers. He loved those crosses with their topography of faces and plants and stories, so much more potent than the bare symbols of his Salvation Army upbringing. There was suffering there, life lived, and beauty. He touched their lichened veins and practised crossing himself a moment before walking on sheepishly.

In a quiet wood beyond he saw pheasants and a few fleeing rabbits. His own footprints were sinister in the leaf litter and his breath spouted out before him. The valley reminded him of the dairy farm of his childhood with its standing puddles and makeshift gates and diesel murmurs somewhere on the air. The buildings were stone here and had outlived whole family lines, pre-dated nations and accents and understandings, while the sheds and houses of Scully's childhood were all hewn from the forest around them, their flapping tin and sunsilvered wood ancient before their time. That was the life the banks had taken from his father. The suits came swooping and the farm slipped away. Scully only had the memory, the stirring now and then of that life before chest hair and girls and shopping malls. Maybe that's why I'm here, he thought, surprised. Maybe I'm buying back the farm in a way, buying back childhood. He thought of his broken father living out an adaptation in the suburbs, his mother dazedly behind him. The quick decline. The strokes. The suits alighting once again. Buying the farm, what a good way to describe oblivion.

Looking back he saw his tiny faded white house up on the hill against the sky. Between him and it were the sodden fields rising up to the huge bald oak before the shell of the castle and its outbuildings with all their black staring windows. He imagined six hundred years of peasants looking up from their work to see the severe Norman outline of that sentry at the head of the valley. It had as many eyes as God, that shadow up there. Little wonder they burnt it.

Scully stumped across the miry fields feeling the wind bright on his cheeks.

As he approached a stone wall looking for a stile, Scully heard dogs. He stopped and cocked his head and almost went backwards into the slurry as two rangy hounds came silently across the wall and over his head.

'Good day to ye!' yelled a farmer with one leg over and the butt of his broken shotgun following.

'G'day,' said Scully with the dogs about his legs.

The farmer eased down the wall to land steady on his feet in the mud. He was dressed for hunting.

'My name's Scully. We're neighbours now, I spose.'

'Ah, you're the Australian boy from Binchy's Bothy, then.'

'That's me. Pleased to meet you.'

Scully shook his little spotted hand. He was gaunt and gingery with crazy fat sideburns and bad teeth, and Scully liked the look of him.

'Jimmy Brereton, man of leisure. I don't mind tellin ye the first time I saw them candles in the window up there last week I nearly shit meself. I thought, it was auld Binchy back again, the lazy booger.'

'No, it's just me.'

'And the family comin, they tell me.'

'You been talking to Pete-the-Post.'

'Aw, Jaysus no,' the man laughed. 'Peter's been talkin to me!'

'He's a good bloke.'

'Ah, he's great gas is Peter. Follow Pete, they say, for wherever Pete is the crack is mighty.'

Scully laughed. 'Well they're right.'

'He says you're doin a fine job of it up there, workin like a nigger.'

'He's been a great help,' said Scully. 'I'll die when I get his bill, I spose.'

Jimmy Brereton kicked his dogs away apologetically and moved closer. 'Just between us, you know, Peter's the one keepin the show goin in there. He's as good as feedin his brother's family, God save him. Himself won't get out of bed most days now.'

'Conor?'

'I'd buy a whole big box of candles if I was waitin on power from Conor Keneally.'

Scully must have looked stricken because the other man laughed good naturedly then and swung his twelve gauge about.

'Ah, ye would'na been the first either, lad. Peter's doin all but the stuff you need a ticket to do, and even some of that, but there should be laws for good men and laws for eejit bastards. That's what I'd say if I was God.'

'How can you tell em apart?' said Scully with a smile. 'Good men and eejit bastards.'

'Well, if you were God and you couldn't tell you'd be out of a job, no? Us poor mortal friggers have to find out by experience. We have to be on the receivin end of good and evil in order to figure it out.'

Scully looked up at the big two-storey place near the road where smoke tore from four great hewn chimneys.

'That's your place there?'

'The auld coach house and stables. In the family, well God knows how long. By God, them horses had it good once.'

'So the castle's yours too?'

'Aye, since the Troubles, friggin thing. It'll fall on me one day, the bad-humoured heap of shite. The government won't let me knock it over.'

'Mind if I have a poke around it sometime?'

'Go by on your way home, but mind yourself. It's at your own risk, now. Bastard of a place. Should have done the job proper, those lads back then. Save everybody a lot of pain. Stop by one evenin, Mr Scully, and we'll have a pint.'

'Thanks, I'll do that.'

'Bring your gals with you when they come, hear? You see anythin movin down in them woods?'

'Coupla rabbits.'

'Come on, boys!'

Scully watched him go bandylegged down the slope toward the stands of ash and larch at the foot of the hills with the dogs streaking ahead into hedges and deadwood.

He heaved himself over the wall and walked up into the field below the castle whose foundation seemed to be a great granite tor buried in the brow of the hill. The closer he came and the deeper into its shadow he walked, the clearer its size became. He saw it plainly now. Scully had long thought that architecture was what you had instead of landscape, a signal of loss, of imitation. Europe had it in spades because the land was long gone, the wildness was no longer even a memory. But this . . . this was where architecture *became* landscape. It took scale and time, something strangely beyond the human. This wasn't in the textbooks.

It was not beautiful. The blunt Norman keep rose scarfaced between later gothic wings whose crenellations seemed afterthoughts and whose many tree-spouting windows ran on and on like a child's drawing. Scully stood beneath the oak tree which grew at the foot of the entry stairs and spread its bare fingers into the air beneath the first windows. The stones of the steps were in-worn and puddled with rain, bristling with moss. Grass and ivy and bramble sucked against the walls to smother the single gothic door. Scully whistled through his teeth and heard the cattle complaining from Brereton's sheds fifty yards away.

Scully pressed in through the vegetation and the half-open door into the rubble-strewn pit of the great hall whose floorboards lay in a charred and mossy pile in the cellar below. Everything had fallen through onto everything else. Great oak beams lay like fallen masts and rigging across cattle bones and tons of cellar bricks. Above it all, beyond the smoke-blackened gallery into whose powdery walls generations of local kids seemed to have cut their initials, loomed the vaulted ceiling, dark as a storm sky. He picked his way round a flagstone edge and heard the sickening burr of unseen wings high above. He came to the staircase built into the cavity of the keep wall. Walls twenty feet thick. A gust of wind angled through the place and stirred the scorched air. Scully got seven or eight steps up the spiral when he began to think of his warm kitchen and the iron kettle that would by now be hissing at its edge. Once around the first turn, the only light entering the staircase came from somewhere above. Grottos and torch niches became pits of shadow and his boots rang louder than he preferred. The light grew and a small chamber opened off to the side. Scully stepped up into its slot-like dimension and saw the huge bed of sticks and reeds left by the birds. The weapon slits let in planks of light and he looked down into the ash wood below his place. Birds wheeled down there, their cries rose plangently. He went on up the stairs, emboldened, and felt his way through the long damp curve until there was light again and a similar side chamber that he pushed on past to a long pillar of a door which yielded only slowly to his weight. Before him was a vaulted hall with long wide windows that let in blue light and illuminated the sea of twigs and marbled guano which stretched wall to wall. Rooks buffeted about, escaping as he came on, beating him to the glassless window where he stood looking out across the valley into the pass between castle and mountains where every puddle and window and flapping sheet of tin caught the light and rendered itself defenceless to the eye. The peaks of the Slieve Blooms ran with streaks of cloud and the ploughed fields fell away herringboned and naked. Scully crossed to the uphill window to look upon his little scab-roofed cottage beyond the wood. Its chimney ripped with smoke. Lanes and hedges and stands of timber and boggy boreens went out at all angles under his gaze as the wind tore his hair. From here it all seemed orderly enough, leading, as it did, to and from this very spot in every direction. It was a small, tooled, and crosshatched country, simple, so amazingly simple from above. Every field had a name, every path a stile. Everything imaginable had been done or tried out there. It wasn't the feeling you had looking out on his own land. In Australia you looked out and saw the possible, the spaces, the maybes. Here the wildness was pressed into something else, into what had already been. And out there beneath the birds, in the gibberish of strokes and lines and connections of the valley was his new life.

# *Nine*

AT DAWN NEXT DAY, when the ground was frozen thick and mist hung on him like a bedwetter's blanket, Scully knew that his days of coming out behind the barn with a spade and a roll of floral paper were at an end. Like reinforced concrete, the earth yielded only after the most concerted flogging with the sharp end of the mattock, and the hole he made was no bigger than a jam tin. It smoked evilly and caused him to moan aloud. It took the hope from his morning, that nasty little bore hole, and he felt utterly ridiculous crouched over it like some ice fisherman dangling his lure. His backside froze, his hands screamed pain. And only yesterday he'd hunkered down in the mist to have Jimmy Brereton come by in his tractor, waving gamely across the hawthorn hedge and doffing his cap ironically. Top of the mornin, indeed.

It wasn't even winter yet, and it could only get worse. Taking a dump was getting to be the most strenuous and cheerless occasion of the day, and for a languid outhouse merchant like Scully, who liked to plot and read and reminisce with his trousers down and the door ajar, the sacrifice had become too great.

As soon as his hands thawed and the pan was on the fire, he found pencil and paper and began to plan the septic system. What had Binchy and his family done all those years? Generations of them squatting out in the rain, the mud, the snow, in the barn itself, judging by the uneven sod floor. The trials of defecation alone might have driven the poor buggers to drink.

He was digging in the partly thawed field late in the morning when a black car drew by, hissing slow and quiet down the long hill with a train of other cars in its wake. He leaned on his shovel to watch the procession snake through the hedges, fifty cars and more making the turn to Birr with the sky the colour of dish-water above. Scully stood there, the minutes it took to pass, while the fields faded from their lustrous green, and when the last car was gone, the air was heavy, and the world suddenly becalmed.

PETE-THE-POST FOUND HIM waist-deep in the earth a little after midday. The ground was littered with the stones, bones and pieces of metal he'd heaved up past the mound of chocolate soil at the hole's rim. It was unpleasant in the ground which smelled too rich for a man grown up in sand. It was too soft, too spongy underfoot and he was relieved to see the postie come smirking across the field, mail flapping.

'Didn't you hear, they've dug all the gold out of Ireland, Scully.'

'I'm not withdrawing,' said Scully, heaving up a spadeful. 'I'm depositing. This is the septic. There will always be a corner of some foreign field that will be forever Scully.'

'Aw, you witty bastard. Depositin, now, is it.'

'How you been? Haven't seen you for days.'

'Bit of family business.'

Scully leaned against the wall of dirt and wiped his brow. The earth smelled burnt and rotten like the inside of that castle.

'Everythin alright?' he said.

'Grand, grand. Some mail for you.'

'Can you leave it inside? I'm filthy, Pete.'

Pete looked down into the hole and then along the pegs marking the trench uphill to the barn. The fall was good, the distance was good. 'Puttin the lavvy in the barn, are we?'

'No room in the house. Back home I'd stick it outside, but here no way. I don't wanna leave the skin of me bum on the toilet seat of a morning.'

Pete laughed and his ears glowed. 'I'll have you a pipe and a liner by four. You don't mind them pre-loved, as the Americans would say? I've even got a pan, pink and all.'

'Mate, pink is my colour and pre-loved is my destiny.'

'Rightso. Um, what about water, Scully?'

Scully looked up and gripped his shovel. 'Gawd! I forgot that.'

'Even if the pan is Teflon-coated I think you might have some problems without water.'

'Smartarse. Can we run it off the pump, you reckon? Hand pump the cistern full?'

'Jaysus, you're goin basic here, Scully. I presume you had it better at home.'

'A damn sight better,' Scully muttered.

'You need an electric pump off your well and full plumbin.'

'Well.'

'I know, I know. I'll see you at four. Sign this. Ah, you dirty booger. Wash your hands.'

SCULLY READ HIS MAIL BY THE FIRE with a mug of tea steaming beside him. There was a card from his mother with a hurt, distant tone to it. The picture showed the Swan River at dusk with the lights of Perth budding against a purple sky. A query from the Australian Taxation Office about why he had not filed for the past two years. This had been forwarded by Jennifer, it seemed, along with a card from the wife of a mate from his fishing days. Judging from the incoherent message she was drunk. The card showed a koala bear surfing. GREETINGS FROM GERALDTON. In a fat envelope was a news-stand poster from the *Daily News*, sent by a mate from the tackle shop. JOH GOES! Bjelke-Petersen, the doddery despot had finally quit politics. Thank God. In the registered envelope were all the documents relating to the sale of the Fremantle house ready for signing, and under separate cover, a cheque from Jennifer for two thousand dollars. The cheque was in her name from an account he didn't recognize, a bank neither of them had accounts with. There was no note. The writing and the signature were hers, the envelope postmarked Fremantle a few days ago. Why didn't she just transfer money into the account here with Allied Irish? It must be something specific. Maybe just enough to tide him over, clear the debt on the credit card. Money, it always made him nervous. He turned to the final item, a card from Billie. On the face of it was a photograph of the Round House, the old convict prison on the beach at Fremantle. Its octagonal limestone walls softened by sunset, rendered scandalously picturesque. It was somewhere they went often, him and her. Jennifer would be at work and the two of them would wander through town to the beach, talking about buildings, about what had been. He was grateful for those years, to have been the one who had her most days. She listened so carefully, you could see her hungry mind working. It was the reason he didn't have so many friends anymore, as if the kid was suddenly and unexpectedly enough for him.

> Today I went to Bathers Beach with Granma and now I am thinking about the convicts. They must of thought God forgot them. Like they fell off the world. When we went to London I was five. I felt like a convict, like it was too different for me. But I was only a kid. Granma says the tailer are good now. I can tie a blood knot, so there. Don't fall off the world, Scully. Do not forget about me, that is BILLIE ANN SCULLY.
>
> (all for one!)

And one for all, thought Scully. The house was quiet but for the mild expirations of the turf fire. Scully looked at the postmark and felt raw and unsettled. What a kid. She put the wind up him, sometimes.

He could see her now, the way she was the day they bought this place. Reading that old comic. She had all his old *Classics Illustrated* in a cracked gladstone bag from the farm. She had them all. *Moby Dick*, *Huckleberry Finn*, *The Count of Monte Cristo*. Yes, he saw her lolling back in that shitheap rented VW with her absolute favourite, *The Hunchback of Notre Dame*, with its gaudy pictures and forests of exclamation marks. Her lips moving as she snuffled at a bag of Tato chips, humming some Paul Simon song. Her hair bouncing, wide mouth rimmed with salt. The laces of her shoes undone.

On that strange day, when Jennifer got out and looked at the bothy, they exchanged looks, him and Billie, and he couldn't tell what it meant. Mutual doubt, perhaps. And even when he'd been won over by Jennifer's pleading, her infectious excitement and happiness, Billie remained doubtful. He remembered that now.

That and how resistant she was at the airport. Crying at the departure gate, tugged down the hall by her mother who looked simply serene. That was the only word for it – serene. Being pregnant maybe, or being decided. The afterglow. Black hair glossing out behind her. Arms swinging like a woman content and on course at last, relaxed the way she had never been before. Yes, her features serene but indistinct even now. And Billie like a sea anchor, dragging all the way to the plane.

BY THE END OF THE NEXT DAY, Scully had himself a connected, waterless toilet. On the barn wall beside it he had taped his poster: JOH GOES! He filled the cistern with a bucket and flushed it, hearing the water run away downhill. He laid planks on blocks between house and barn for a bridge across the mud. Pete stood by with a wry grin.

'Pumpin out the bilges, it'll be.'

'Come in and have a drink, you cheeky bastard.'

The north wind rattled the panes of the Donegal windows at their backs and the chimney snored beside them as they drank their pints of Harp. The room was warm and humid with simmering stew.

'You think your gals'll take to this place, Scully?'

'Well, I don't think Jennifer'll need convincing.'

'How old is that little one?'

'Billie? Seven, seven and a half.'

'A grand life for her here. You can bring her into Birr to play with Con's.'

The very mention of Conor Keneally caused Scully to go stiff with irritation.

'And there's a school bus by here to Coolderry. Nice little school.'

'She's not a Catholic you know.'

'Aw, they don't give a toss. And anyway, she might just become one. A little bit of civilization never hurt.'

Scully laughed. The thought of them trying to 'civilize' Billie! But they'd learn, and they'd like her. The Irish and her, they'd get on. They liked a bit of spirit, didn't they?

It was dark outside now and rain fell, light at first and then in roaring sheets. The fire hissed.

'You're a lucky man to have a child,' said Pete staring into the fire.

'Yes,' he said with his whole being. 'Yes. It's a surprise, you know, nothing prepares you for it. Nothing better ever happened to me. Funny, you know, but I'm so bloody grateful for it. To Jennifer, to God.' He laughed self consciously. 'You see, this stuff used to be automatic, you know, natural. Women aren't so keen to have them anymore, not where I come from, anyway. They've got other fish to fry, which is fair enough. But they don't realize, sometimes, what they're missing, or what they're withholding, you know? The power they have. I don't know if Billie was an accident or not. I thought she was. It's hard to tell, you see, with people. So I'm grateful, that's the truth of it.' Scully blushed. Yes. That was why he dressed her so meticulously when she was small, why he worried too much about seatbelts, why he infuriated the kid with lectures about tooth decay. It wasn't like him, but she wasn't to know. It was her, the fact of her. And when she fell from a bike or a tree she came running to him. It shamed him in front of Jennifer, the way Billie ran to him first. Did Jennifer feel what his own father must have felt, being the second parent? Maybe he just took it all too seriously. Perhaps other people didn't feel these things.

'You want some of your own, someday, then?'

'Oh, I could imagine it,' said Pete, refilling his glass and resting his boot on the hearth. 'There's just the little problem of matrimony, Scully. You know, if I wanted trouble, I'd move to Ulster. I like comin and goin as I fancy. And I have Con's own when the urge hits me.'

Pete watched as Scully got up and lit his three candles at the sill. Both of them stared at the twitching candle-flame and the reflection it threw along the panes.

'Did you ever come close?' Scully asked. 'To marriage.'

'Aw, once. But I was young. There's no point goin back on it. All the adventures are ahead of you, not behind. You got to go and find em. And I might say,' he said with a mischievous cast in his eyes, 'I believe in deliverin em now and then, too. You've been godly patient with my brother.'

'Pete, we don't –'

'No, no, I thank ye for your understandin on this.'

'Look –'

'Can you meet me in Birr tomorrow mornin early, say seven-thirty?'

'Sure. Why?'

'Power corrupts, you know, but without it, *you* can neither cook toast nor take a shit. Seven-thirty.'

THE STREETS OF BIRR WERE ALMOST LIGHT at seven-thirty next morning and its houses, shoulder to shoulder in the misty square, were grey and stirring with the shriek of kettles and the scuffle of dogs. Scully saw the van in the rain-slick high street and pulled in beside it as Pete climbed out grimly waving.

Pete led them to the little green doorway at the side of a shopfront. Pete knocked and blew on his hands.

A jaded and fearful woman let them in wordlessly.

'Mornin, Maeve.'

'He'll not be up for hours, Peter. Don't even bother yourself.'

'This is Fred Scully from out at the Leap.'

'Oh, yes, the Australian,' she smiled wanly.

'Pleased to meet you,' said Scully, smelling boiled cabbage, cigarette smoke, turf and bacon fat.

'Peter talks about you all day.'

'Oh. I hope it's not all bad,' he said limply.

'Ready, Scully?'

'Ready for what?' said Maeve Keneally.

Scully felt faint from the stuffiness and desperation of this house. It seemed no window had been opened here for generations.

'Just keep the front door open, Maeve.'

Scully followed the postman through the gloomy house and into a foetid bedroom where Conor Keneally slept in his boots, and they took him by those boots, and dragged him off the bed, down the corridor with its greenish pictures of the Pope and the saints and Charlie Haughey, through the front door and out into the drizzling street where, finally awake, he began to struggle.

'Watha fook! Geroffa me!'

'We've got a job for you to do, so you can get in the van, Con.' Pete hauled at his brother but the man slid back onto the lumpy pavement.

'I'm in the fookin wet street in me jammies, you bastard eejit!'

'Aw, Conor Keneally, you slept in your duds as ever. Get in your van.'

Conor struggled to his feet. He was bigger than his brother and redfisted. His sideburns were like flames down his cheeks as he braced himself against the Toyota van, copping a bit of PVC pipe in the back of the head as he staggered.

'No one tells me.'

'Shut up and get in the van,' said Pete trying to smile.

'Who's gonna make me, gobshite?' The big man straightened, smelling of the hop fields of the Republic. 'You, Mr Post?'

'No,' Pete said, pointing at Scully. 'Him.'

Conor struggled to focus on the scarred and wonk-eyed face of the Australian, who quite simply looked mealy enough to be up to it. It was no postman face.

'Now, Conor, this is one of Mylie Doolin's London boys and he needs a job done.'

The electrician slumped and held a great meaty hand to his head in horror.

'Aw! Awww, fook me now! Jaysus, what're you doin Peter Keneally, you eejit!'

'Don't be askin stupid questions. Get a meter box and all the guff.'

'There's one in there,' Conor said, sickly dipping his head to the van. 'I was after comin from Tullamore –'

'Let's go, then,' interrupted Pete gruffly. 'Our man will follow in the Transit.'

Conor covered his face with both hands now. 'Holy Mother, Peter. Mylie Doolin.'

'Aye,' said Peter winking over his brother's shoulder at Scully, 'Mylie himself.'

He watched them climb into the Toyota with a jug of sloe poteen. A dog barked. The rain fell.

SCULLY STAYED CLEAR OF THE BOTHY all morning, keeping to the draughty barn to sand down and varnish an old mahogany chair he found in the loft. Now and then he heard shouts from the house: anger, exasperation, hangover, fear. It was funny alright, but he felt sorry for poor Conor, labouring in there with an imaginary gun at his head and a very real hangover inside it. Scully worked away in the giddy fumes grateful to Mylie once more.

Just before noon when he could stand the cold no longer he went inside and heard a transistor playing fiddle music in the kitchen.

Conor was at the table shakily filling out some paperwork, and Pete was throwing turf on the fire.

'Power to the people, Scully.'

'Don't suck up, brother.'

Scully just grinned. Conor held out the sheets of paper to Scully who took them without speaking.

'Now that electric drill will work, Scully, me boy,' said Pete. 'Bit of kneecappin, no?'

Conor paled.

'C'mon, Pete,' said Scully, speaking in Conor's presence for the first time that day. 'Give the bloke a break.'

'This fooker's not Irish!'

'Australian,' said Scully.

'Desert Irish, you might say.'

The table crashed forward and Conor was reaching for his brother's throat when the noon Angelus suddenly sounded on the radio. Without hesitation, both Irishmen went slack, and adopted the prayerful hunch, snorting and trembling, as the church bell rang clear. Wind pressed against the panes. The fire sank on itself, and the bell tolled on and on into the false calm. Scully watched the fallen forelocks of the Keneallys and fought the fiendish giggle that rose in his neck. And then the last peal rang off into silence. The men crossed themselves and Conor Keneally noticed how upright Scully was, how his hands stayed in his pockets.

'Good Christ, he's not even Catholic, let alone Irish!'

'And that's not all,' said Peter, chuckling and preparing to be pummelled. 'He thought Mylie was in gaol for the VAT.'

Conor looked at Scully with a sudden mildness on his face – pity. 'Jaysus, man, where did *you* go to school?'

'Elsewhere, you might say.'

'You bastards.' Conor slapped his cloth cap against his knees. 'You fookers had me banjanxed. He's not with the Provos at all, is he.'

'I'm sorry,' said Scully.

Pete tipped his head back and laughed, and he didn't stop for a moment as Conor dragged him outside and rammed him into the door of the Toyota, and he kept it up as his roaring brother beat his head against the roof, holding his ginger forelock and slamming down once, twice until the big man let go and stood back and began to weep.

'Oh, God, my life.'

From the door of his house which poured music and the smell of burning soil, Scully watched as Pete grabbed his brother and held him fiercely in the wind. The big man sobbed and dripped tears and snot. His roadmap face glowed with shame and despair and a kind of impotence Scully had never seen before. Peter's hands were in his brother's ginger curls and he wept too, his eyes averted, his head high in the wind.

Scully went inside and stood by the fire, hung the kettle on the crane, threw on some more turf. The radio played a ballad, and a woman's mournful voice filled the cottage. He went back to the front door and offered the Keneallys a cup of tea. They straightened up, accepted with dignity and kicked the mud from their boots.

## *Ten*

ON THE ELEVENTH OF DECEMBER, a Friday with sunlight and sharp, clean air, Scully stood at a sink full of hot water and sang in his broken, growly voice, an old song he had heard Van Morrison bawling yesterday on the radio.

*But the sea is wide*
*And I can't swim over*
*And neither have*
*I wings to fly . . .*

The house smelled sweetly of turf and scrubbing. There was crockery on the pine dresser and a shelf beneath the stairs with old paperbacks on it already. There was a birch broom inside the door and a stack of larch kindling by the turfbox. An oilskin hung from a peg on the chimney wall above his wellington boots. Beside him, the little refrigerator hummed on the flagstones. There were cheap curtains on the windows, blue against the whitewash, and the sun spilled in across the stainless steel sink. Admit it, he told himself, you like it, you like the place now that it's full of things. Because you love things, always have.

Scully was like his father that way. No matter what the Salvos said, the old fella thought certain objects were godly. Briggs and Stratton motors, the McCulloch chainsaw, the ancient spirit level that lived in the workshed beside the dairy, the same bubbly level that caused Scully junior to have ideas of drawing and building. Ah, those *things*. The old girl thought it was idolatry, but she had a brass thimble she treasured more than her wedding ring.

It wasn't getting things and having them that Scully learnt; it was simply admiring them, getting a charge out of their strange presence.

Scully wiped the windowpane with his sweatered elbow and saw the rhinestone blaze of the frozen fields. Too good a day for working. He couldn't spend another day at it, not while the sun was out. Pete was right, he wasn't seeing anything, buried alive in work. He didn't even know where he was living.

On the kitchen table he began a letter home but he realized that it wouldn't reach them in time. He looked at the little aside he had written to Billie in the margin. *Even if I fall off the world, Billie Ann Scully, I will still love you from Space.*

He smiled. Yes.

THAT MORNING HE DROVE INTO BIRR and organised his banking. He had a cheque made out to Peter Keneally as part payment. He bought a leg of New Zealand lamb and a sprig of rosemary at insane cost. He found oranges from Spain, olives, anchovies, tomatoes, things with the sun still in them. Men and women greeted him as he humped a sack of spuds to the Transit in a light drizzle. He bought an *Irish Times* and read about the mad bastard in Melbourne killing eight in the Australia Post building. Jumped through a plate glass window on the tenth floor. Someone else in Miami, an estranged husband killed his whole family with a ball peen hammer and gassed himself so they could all be together again. Shit, was it just men?

Two kids in fluorescent baseball caps walked by singing. He started the van. Yes, at least they sing here, whatever else happens.

ALONG THE WINDING LANES HE DROVE, contained between hedges and walls, swinging into turns hard up against the brambles, skidding mildly on puddles hard as steel, until he came to a tree in the middle of the road, with rags in its stark branches. It stood on a little island of grass where the road had been diverted around it. Scully pulled up alongside and saw the shards of cloth tied here and there, some pale and rotten, others freshly attached. A sad little tree with a road grown around it. It looked quite comical and forlorn. He drove on.

AT COOLDERRY HE PULLED UP OUTSIDE THE VILLAGE SCHOOL. He got out into the light and stood by the hurling pitch as the bell clanged for lunch. The bleat of children made his heart soar.

A car idled down the hill.

'How are you, Scully?'

He turned and saw that it was Pete-the-Post with his arm out of the van.

'Me? A bit toey, I'd say.'

'Toey?'

'Anxious, impatient, nervous . . .'

'Antsy, then.'

'No, toey.'

Pete smiled and turned off the motor. 'Not long, son. Two days now, isn't it?'

'How's Conor?'

The postman pursed his lips and looked out across the muddy pitch where gangly boys began to mill and surge, their sticks twitching. 'Auld Conor's losing, moment by moment. The drink, as if you didn't know. It's the saddest sight to see, Scully, a man lettin his own life slip through his hands.'

Scully scuffed his boots in the gravel. 'Any reason for it?'

'Aw, too long a story to bother you with. Somethin terrible happened in the family, five or six year ago. Somethin . . . well, somethin terrible. Conor's the kind of man who'll not let it be. He never mentions it, of course, never utters a word. But he broods, you know. There's things that have no finish, Scully, no endin to speak of. There's no justice to it, but that's the God's truth. The only end some things have is the end you give em. Now listen to me goin on in your ear like a radio.'

Scully waved his apology aside. 'You're a good brother to him.'

'There's a grand singin pub over to Shinrone I'm goin to tomorrow night. Why don't ye come with me and we'll celebrate your last night as an Irish bachelor.'

Scully squinted, hesitating. He felt as reluctant as a hermit, and foolish for feeling so.

'Come on, Scully, be a divil!'

'Okay,' he smiled. 'Thanks.'

Scully stood in the blue cloud the AN POST van left behind and heard Pete go crashing gears through the village. He stamped his feet and heard girls squealing behind him. The little van suddenly braked on the hill, U-turned and came whinnying back. Pete pulled in again, blushing fiercely and shoved an arm out the window.

'Knew I stopped by for somethin. Telegram, Scully.'

He opened it while Pete drove off again.

SETTLEMENT THROUGH. CONFIRMED AE46 SHANNON SUNDAY MORNING. JENNIFER.

He stuffed it in his pocket and stood uncertainly there by the school, imagining them suddenly here with him. His hands shook. And then he realized – the bastard had read it. Peter knew before *he* did. Country life!

SATURDAY NIGHT SCULLY SHAVED and pulled on his best jeans, his roo-skin boots and a black pullover. From the tin trunk in the Transit he pulled the sleek black greatcoat bought one day in Place Monge in the desperate days of Paris. Four hundred francs secondhand. He shook his head even now at the thought. He'd worked hard for that coat. He brushed it down by the hearth and hung it up a while to air while he scrubbed his teeth with iron concentration. Scully, he thought, you look like a convict. You confirm every Englishman's deep and haughty suspicion. You can't help the face, but for goodness' sake get a haircut.

He stoked the fire and loaded it with turf, and then gathered up the house keys, big medieval things, that felt heavy as a revolver in his pocket.

He read the crumpled telegram again. CONFIRMED. SUNDAY. The paper lay pale and odd on the scrubbed pine table, casting shadows from the firelight across the wood.

He thought of the night they bought this place. When he woke in the wide musty room above Davy Finneran's pub to see Jennifer standing naked at the window, lit by the neon of the chipper across the street as the last drinkers rolled home down the street. Her body was dark from the Greek sun. The bed held the scent of their sex. Billie slept on a sofa by the door, her limbs every which way. Scully didn't move for a while. He lay in the hammocky bed, his mouth dry from celebrating. He just watched her over by the window as the church bells tolled. Her shoulders twitched; she sniffed. Scully loved her. He was not going home, he would never see his house and all his stuff again, but he loved her and she must know it. She wiped her eyes, wiped them and turned, startled to see him awake.

'A . . . a dream,' she whispered.

But she seemed not to have even been to sleep.

'You alright?'

She nodded.

'Come to bed.'

For a moment, her body suddenly graven, she hesitated before padding across to him. She was cold, almost clammy against him.

'I'm sorry,' she murmured.

'About a dream?'

Her breath was warm against his shoulder. He held her to him and slept.

Now Scully heard the Renault labour up the hill. He stoked the fire and switched out the light and went outside to meet Peter.

PETE-THE-POST DROVE THEM SLOWLY through the gathering rain to Shinrone, passing the half-pint of Bushmills to Scully now and then who sipped and watched the tunnel the headlights made between the hedges and stone walls.

'That's a grand coat.'

'Bought it in Paris.'

'Paris. Friggin Paris, eh?'

Scully laughed. 'Paris.'

'Is it like the movies?'

'Not so you'd notice.'

'I liked them Gene Kelly sorta fillums, you know with the dancin and the umbrellas and the kissin by the fountain.'

'Well, we did a lotta that, of course.'

'So what the frig *did* you do?'

Scully sighed. 'Worked me arse off, Pete. I painted and Jennifer wrote.'

'Painted? You didn't tell me you're the artist type.'

'I painted apartments, mate. Cash money. Worst job of my life, don't ask.'

'And the writin?'

Scully took a pull of the hot, peaty Bushmills. Paris really wasn't the kind of thing he had in mind on a fun night out. He wanted to forget the damn place once and for all. The long miserable days scraping the ceilings of tight-arsed Parisian skinflints. The desperate scuffle outside the school every morning with Billie, and those evenings of tears and rage when Jennifer's frustration was like an animal in the room with them. It was a kind of affliction for her. After the early buzz, the heady weeks of hope and excitement, the days she slugged it out in the tiny apartment alive with ideas, and new friends to try them on, she became this thwarted creature.

Some nights they stayed up and drank too much *pastis* while he tried to console her but she lashed out like something wild and cornered. It was his fault, she said. He was lazy, under-motivated – he had no ambition, no guts, which struck him as a bit rich, considering his circumstances. He did shit work all day so she could write. And gladly. God how he wanted her to break through into some kind of success, some new version of herself that made her happy.

But Paris was a black hole, somewhere where Jennifer came hard up against the wall of her limitations while all he could do was stand by and watch.

'Scully?'

'Hm?'

'Tell me about the writing. Are you asleep or drunk already?'

'Well, *I* liked it.'

'What did she write? For certain, she's the poetical type, takin the bothy the way she did.'

Scully smiled and passed back the bottle. 'Actually she's very businesslike, Pete. Likes things neat and sharp, you know. Comes from a very proper family. Escaped from them really. She's always thought her parents held her back from doing what she'd like to try. They pressured her into a career in the public service and stuff. She says they made her ordinary when she wasn't. Safe, dull, that kind of thing, which she isn't. I liked her because she was so . . . straight, I guess. But she hates that, being straight. Writing was one of those things she always thought of doing. You know, weird, risky things, the kind of things parents hate. All this travelling was her chance. She quit her job, had her heart set on Paris. Paris was poetry for her. And she wrote some nice poems, showed em to people and was kind of . . . crushed. Those bastards, her mates, they thought it was a bit of a joke. Well, fuck them. I thought the poems were good.'

'You liked them cause you love her.'

'No, I liked them cause I liked them.' Scully watched the

ragged hedges peel by. 'Anyway, it didn't work out.'

'So much for dancin by the fountains.'

'Yeah.'

Pete chugged on the whiskey bottle and gasped with pleasure. He steered with his knees a while and hummed theatrically.

'By God, Scully, you've seen the world!'

'On the cheap, mate, on the cheap.'

'And what did you do in Greece, lie in the bakin sun and drink them little drinks with hats on em?'

Scully laughed. 'No, I worked for a stonemason humping granite up a hill. Loved it. Great place. Greece is like Australia invaded by the Irish.'

'Good gravy, man!'

'It's true. Nothin works and no one gives a shit. Perfect.'

'And what did Jennifer do?'

'She painted.'

'Houses?'

'No, art painting. Well, you know, she had to have a try. She was okay, I thought. Trouble with Jennifer is she can turn her hand to anything. She's quite good at a lot of things, but she wants to be a genius at one thing. Maybe it'll happen. One day. She deserves a break.'

'You love the girl.'

'I do.'

They coasted into Shinrone, rain drifting oblique in the lights of the little town which seemed choked with parked cars.

'Arlo Guthrie was here last year, Scully. I came to see him myself. Remember that song:

*Comin into Los Angeles*
*Bringin in a coupla keys*
*Don't touch my bags*
*If you please, Mr Customs ma-aan!'*

'I remember. That's a drug song, Pete.'

'It never was!'

Scully took the bottle from him and laughed till it hurt.

'One of them U2 lads was down from Dublin to see the auld Arlo. I nearly knocked him over in the pisser. Where would we be without music, eh? It's not really a drugs song, is it?'

Scully only laughed, nodding.

'Fookin hell!'

IN THE HOT WILD FUG OF THE PUB that night, Scully lost the anxiety that had come upon him a couple of hours ago. The band tossed from jig to reel and the dust rose from the foul floors with the stomp of dancing and the flap of coats and scarves. The fiddle was manic and angular, the tin whistle demented, and the drum was like the forewarning of the headache to come. Someone came in with a set of pipes and an old man grabbed up the microphone and the fever of the place subsided as a ballad began. Scully couldn't recall a sweeter sound that the sad soughing of those pipes. This was no braying Scots pipe; this was a keening, a cry loaded with desire and remorse. The old man sang with his tie askew and his dentures slightly adrift, a song of the Slieve Blooms, of being left behind, abandoned in the hills with winter coming on. Scully listened, transfixed, until in the final chorus he put down his glass and shoved his way to the door.

Outside it was raining and there was no one in the street but a sullen black dog chained to a bicycle. Across the road the chipper was heating up his fat for closing time, his hard fluorescents falling like a block of ice into the street. Scully's face was numb in patches, and he stood with his cheeks in the rain, trying to account for his sudden moment of dread in there. That's what it was, dread. It's a song, Scully.

Pete stood in the doorway, peering out. 'You're not goin to puke, now are ye?'

'No, I'm fine.'

'You don't like the music?'

'The music's great. Grand, in fact.'

'By God, there's some rascally girls from Tullamore in there.'

'Go to it, son.'

'You alright, then?'

'I'll be in in a moment.'

Pete slipped back into the hot maw of the pub and Scully shook the rain from his face. The black dog whimpered. He went over and let him off the chain. It nipped him and bolted into the night.

AMID THE GREASY STEAM OF A PARCEL OF CHIPS the pair of them drove home singing.

*Keep your hands off red-haired Mary*
*Her and I are to be wed*
*We see a priest this very morn*
*And tonight we'll lie in a marriage bed . . .*

They came to the odd little tree in the middle of the road with its sad decoration of rags, and Scully asked about it.

'A wishing tree,' said Peter, stopping beside it and winding down the window to let in a blast of cold air. 'People tie a rag on and make a wish.'

'Does it work?'

Pete guffawed. 'Does it fookin look like it, son? Does the country seem so much like the island of Hawaii? Not many of us get our wish in Ireland, Scully.'

'Things aren't that tragic here, surely,' said Scully, feeling the mood slip from him.

'Jaysus,' yelled Pete. 'Can you imagine how fooked it'd be if we did!'

The postie's teeth were huge and hilarious in the gloom.

For a long way up the hill behind Binchy's Bothy, a hare ran doggedly before them at the roadside, his tail bobbing in the headlights as they slowed. On and on it ran, weaving now and then to seek an opening in the stone wall, skittering across glassy patches of mud, until finally, it veered left into a boreen and claimed the darkness of the field. Scully and Peter Keneally cheered him all the way to the crest of the hill.

At the cottage, Scully climbed out and stood a moment by the van.

'Cheer up, Scully. It's tomorrow already.'

'Tomorrow it is.'

'God bless you now.'

'Thanks for tonight. Thanks for everything.'

'Ye want me to drive ye down to Shannon after mass?'

'Thanks, but it's probably best on my own.'

'Well, see you Monday, then,' said Pete, setting off down the hill. His lights burned down the hedges and disappeared.

Scully opened the door. There was still some life in the fire. He heaped on some more turf and a few chunks of coal and stirred it back to brightness. Room by room he went through the place, trying to imagine them all in it, but he was too tired and drunk perhaps, for the images skidded away from him as he straightened a rug here, stood a chair there, then finally went to bed upstairs in sheets that smelled of factories and shops and sunnier places.

# *Eleven*

SCULLY WOKE SOMETIME IN THE NIGHT, his throat raw and dry. He heaved himself out of his bed into the cold and stumped downstairs for a glass of water. Cattle bellowed from Brereton's sheds down beyond the castle. At the sink he saw that the sky had cleared and there were stars out. A misshapen moon hung high and bright in the black. Down at the castle there were lights. He stood there naked and shivering by the window, watching them move through the trees. Kids, he guessed, local teenagers playing up on a Saturday night. He drank his water and placed the glass in the sink. He wondered if Jimmy Brereton knew. It couldn't hurt to take a look.

By the door he slipped on his greatcoat, walked into his gumboots and pulled a scarf about himself. The hard, icy air hit him flat in the face as he stepped outside into the night. The luminous dial on his watch said three in the morning.

Scully went cautiously down the field in the darkness. There was no wind, only a sharp mist rising from the ground. Down there through the trees – no, beyond the trees, right down in the valley – lights were moving. As he climbed the stile at the edge of his field, Scully saw how the lights snaked; they were a procession. He cocked his head for the sounds of revelry, but heard nothing except the sound of Jimmy Brereton's cows.

Scully crossed the road and climbed through the wall where the ash wood met the road. He picked his way over fallen branches, crunching through the frosty detritus with his own breath like a beacon before him. The great shadow of the castle reached out beyond the trees, silent, blank, still. With frozen grass snapping at his bare shins, he crossed the courtyard beside the ruins of the pumphouse, now just dark, reeling blocks at the corner of his vision, and came to the brow of the decline to see the romping melée of burning torches turn in across the fields and come circling beneath the bare oak beneath the castle steps. Torches. Yes, they were flames he saw travelling high off the ground. Now Scully heard the thud of feet, and as the lights passed beneath the old tree, he saw the glistening, steaming bodies of horses, he saw the bearded faces of men. Staffs. A lank standard. The breaking mud rose before them like a bow wave.

Ripping through blackberry and nettle, Scully bolted for the cover of a crumbling wall. The cold had reached his balls now, they felt brittle as Christmas baubles between his thighs. He pulled the coat harder about himself and peered through a gap in the stones. Down there, in the gently sloping field beneath the castle steps, the horsemen had assembled. There were about twenty of them in fancy dress. They were wildhaired, cloaked and highbooted. Two of them wore spattered grey chestplates and rags across their brows. Scully heard the horses snorting and heaving for wind. They shot out columns of steam and rattled metallic shudders. With firelight in the dark balls of their eyes, the riders looked up at the keep, and Scully tried to think, to find his way ahead of all this. He shook with cold. Out in the valley there were no more lights, no floods burning in the yards of local farms, no handy sign of life. He watched and waited, mesmerized. He saw weapons now, scars and blood, the restless twitching of reins. He saw the sheen of sweat along the horses' flanks and the united gaze of the horsemen. They looked a mercenary lot, fierce and stoic. In all his life he'd never seen men like these. From where he crouched he couldn't quite see the front of the castle keep, whether or not a light showed, if a door was ajar, or if someone was up there.

Around the ruined yard wall he crawled on his hands and knees till he could clamber across a mossy pile of rubble and make the cover of the blackthorn hedge hard up against the forecourt itself, but halfway to the hedge Scully put a foot down a hole and staggered and lost his balance completely. He tumbled and crashed and cursed down the slope, and when he came to a halt, smarting with pain and fright, he was out in the open, plain as midday. There was no use running. He figured it was just as well to stand and show himself in the weird light of the sputtering torches. He pulled himself upright, feeling the soft mud shift beneath the broken surface, but the riders sat unmoved from their fixed stations of expectation. Each of them was saddled, tense, eyes upcast to the keep where no light shone and no figure moved. Almost out of politeness he cleared his throat and kicked a couple of stones together to get their attention, but it felt as though he didn't exist.

With arms held high, he stumbled down onto the muddy grass into the strong smell of horses. Closer there was a sourer scent, the stink of unwashed men. At the sudden splash of piss from a horse in the rear, Scully grunted in fright but not a man stirred. Their torches crackled, flames rigid in the still air, giving off the reek of pitch. With his pulse like an animal trapped beneath his skin, Scully moved between the riders, all but touching the heaving, rancid flanks of their mounts. Some of the horses had black, congealed wounds on their chests, and they looked as tired and cold and dazed as their riders. Some were boys, their scrawny legs bare and stippled with gooseflesh. And how they craned their necks, these riders. It was as though any moment some great and terrible event would explode upon them, as if something, someone up there could set them in motion. The sky was a comfortless blanket on them. The ground was mired and trodden. Shit stood in vaporous cakes between hoofs. The castle keep rose as a cudgel before them. He felt himself craning, waiting, almost failing to breathe. A horse shook its mane and Scully felt the mist of sweat against his cheek. His feet took root in the ground as they continued to wait and he waited with them. It was true, he knew it, something was about to happen.

But the awful stillness went on.

'Is anybody there?' Scully cried out toward the keep, his voice breaking with the strain of it. He was gasping with cold now and feeling the earth suck at him, drawing him into the fecund mire. 'Is anyone here, then? Anyone at all?'

No head turned. Nothing stirred in the yawning dark of the keep and its broken wings. The ivy feeding off the ancient stones glittered with firelight. The crooked hewn steps of the castle approach stood bare of everything except rabbit pellets but the riders waited on undeterred. Scully's skin hurt now. His eyes felt blistered. The air in his lungs scorched him and the buttons of his greatcoat burned all down his body. His legs stiffened and he was suddenly afraid of being swallowed up by the earth. It would kill him to stay any longer, but he stood transfixed, unable to imagine a cold worse than this, unable to convince himself to move. You'll die, he told himself, you'll die if you don't go. He heard his heart creaking in his chest. Like a man outside himself he saw his body move. He was a man trying to fly and the earth and the cold tore like a curtain as he pulled the coat about himself and ran.

AT THE TOP OF THE HILL, quaking at his own door and sobbing with cold and fright, he turned again and saw the lights that burned patient as nature itself, burning as stars through the trees.

## *Twelve*

ALL DOWN THE LONG, stinky tube of the jumbo jet, the lights come on and people stretch like cats. Billie looks up from her comic book about the poor, ugly hunchback to see her mother yawn and uncoil on the seat beside her. Her hair is black. It shines like a crow's wing, like something that can fly at a moment's notice. She looks over at the picture of the bellringer and wrinkles her little nose at Billie.

'That old thing.'

Billie shrugs. It's still her favourite, even though the pages are ratty. Used to be Scully's when he was a boy. She has all his old comics and his Biggles books (which are plain stupid, really) and *The Magic Pudding*. In a tea-chest somewhere now, she has a whole snake-skin, a stick for finding water, and an old bag with books and papers in it. It's hard to think of your father as a kid. Milking cows. With no TV. Before space rockets, even. Living like Tom Sawyer, that's how Billie thinks of it. She feels sorry for kids with ordinary fathers. They only made one Scully. He isn't handsome, but he's special. He taught her how to swim and ride a bike. Before school he taught her how to read and write. Billie doesn't forget things like that. He knows things and he doesn't have secrets. What you see is what you get, like he says.

Once, in Paris, a lady fell down in the street right next to them and started wriggling all over the cobbles. It was a fit. She went bubbly at the mouth and the whole works. Everyone started steering away, saying 'Oh-la-la!' But Scully made Billie stand there while he got down next to the lady and stuck his newspaper between her teeth to stop her from biting her tongue off. The lady bucked and jumped but he talked to her the way she imagined he talked to cows when he was a boy. Probably, like a cow, she couldn't understand a word anyway because he talked in English, soft and friendly, while all the people around them gasped. He brushed her hair with his hand and Billie wanted to sick up right there. But she was glad he made her stay. He was crying, she saw him cry while the French lady bit on his newspaper and jiggled on the road. She knew it then, that they only made one Scully.

She jiggles her legs, careful not to kick the seat in front and get the old bloke with the hair growing out his ears all mad again.

Her mum grabs her handbag and slips on her shoes. Pretty feet with red nails. Pretty feet.

'Just going to have a wash,' she murmurs.

'Okay,' says Billie.

Billie goes back to her story. She likes the hunchback. He's ugly and sad but his heart is good. He sees a long way out across the city. Paris. She lived there once and knows there should be an Eiffel Tower somewhere in this book, something the guy drawing the pictures forgot. Old Quasimodo can see forever. He's got the free birds up there and the sky and the music of the bells that wrecked his ears, he loves them so much. Up there on big, scary Notre Dame with the statues stuck into doorways and the pigeons and donkeys out the front. When she closes her eyes she can see the bellringer darting around up there – she doesn't need the comic anymore to do that. His hump weighing him down, bending him over like Jesus under the dragging cross. No one loves him, specially not the beautiful gypsy girl. She just sees his poor face and his hump. No one loves him the way Billie does because she knows there's good in his heart.

People in the plane pull up the dinky little window sliders to let in some light. The plane is so high up it's nearly in space. That nervous feeling comes back. She's going to live in a little stone house with square windows and a chimney. Her dad will be there. She shouldn't be afraid. But it's hard to stay calm when you're nearly in space, when you don't know what's coming.

# *Thirteen*

SCULLY WOKE TO THE HARANGUE of a fresh norther in the slates, and at the thought of the cold outside the eiderdown his body stiffened. His face felt tender and his throat itched with the promise of a headcold. His hands tingled with nettle stings and one of his knees throbbed. He closed his eyes again in the still dim house on a hill in a strange country, and then with a slow burning in his limbs, he softened. This was it. Today was the day. He scrabbled at his watch. Man, he was late; it was after eight already and the flight got into Shannon at ten.

He whipped back the eiderdown and roared with the shock of the cold, and it was while he was wrestling with his jeans that he saw the mud on his legs. It was caked between his fingers, too, and there in the sheets. He remembered the cold and the riders distantly, as though recalling a dream. This afternoon he'd go down and have a look around, just to satisfy himself. Maybe talk to Brereton. But now he was late. Now the sun was up.

He stripped the linen and took it downstairs where the hearth drew breath and the windowpanes chattered. He should have been up two hours ago. With this day hanging before him so long, how could he have slept in?

In water cold and hard as brass, he washed himself standing in a tin tub. He shaved badly and ran upstairs with clean sheets. Then he found his Levi's, his boots and pullover and pulled himself into shape.

Eight thirty-five. Now he was frantic, frantic enough to heave the tub of grey water against the closed kitchen window which sent it right back at him. He sat down, soaked and sober, moaning in frustration. He looked around, saw the dishes in the sink, the dirty sheets and mud-scuffs, the pool at his feet. He'd worked his guts out to get the place near perfect and now it looked like a student dive. Still, they'd see the change, they'd know how his heart had gone into it. He got up, lit the fire, stacked it with coal, and went out into the wind in his wet clothes.

ON THE TWISTING HEDGE ROAD into Roscrea, Scully drove hard and close, sending up curtains of mud everywhere he passed, with the walls and blackthorn against the streaming windows. Rain smeared his glimpses of fields and open places. There was no sky.

The town was jammed with cars parked wildly for Mass, and bells rang along the close grey rows of houses and shops. Out on the open road, Scully pushed the Transit to the limit, jiggling now, sweating with anticipation. The hills spewed cloud and water and the Tipperary fields opened up to the rain, sprouting here and there the ruined backbone of a tower, a gatehouse, a manor of old. He saw cottages collapsing under the weight of thatch wild with grass. All down the highway, across the country, there were solitary chimneys, great lonely walls, fallen churches with lichened crosses tilted like levers in the earth. Much rarer was the sight of a stand of timber, a wood, a forest remnant before more chocolate soil and squat, stucco farmhouses with grey gravel forecourts and Spanish arches. Every town said *Failte*, Welcome to Moneygall, Toomyvara, Nenagh, and each was jammed with the cars of Mass and the umbrellas of the walking faithful and the toll of bells, while the roads were quiet and blessedly free of trucks. Three cheers for a God-fearing nation, Scully thought, and for truckers on bended knee.

In the slate sprawl of Limerick he caught the time in a chipper's window as 9.55. He crossed the bridge and saw the choppy surge of the Shannon beating seaward, and somehow his tension broke for a moment into wellbeing: he'd make it now, he'd be there soon.

The rain backed off. The road was clear.

ON THE LONG, flat dismal approach to the airport, Scully was grinning so hugely that other drivers veered away and kept their distance. A Pan-Am jumbo heaved itself into the air and passed over with its shadow trailing like a dragged anchor. Bon voyage, he thought; enjoy New York, have a happy life, all you people. The world is good and the aeroplane a gift of evolution.

INSIDE THE TERMINAL BUILDING the air was thick with cigarette smoke, the smell of wet serge and the shouts of people leaving and meeting. Here and there were the checkerboard slacks of Americans making their way to the Avis counter and the Dan Dooley Rent A Car. There were Irishmen in terrible jackets and thick-soled boots heading upstairs for a pint, and women with briefcases awaiting the shuttle back to London.

Scully sat a moment beside a coin-operated fire engine and saw a man cross himself – spectacles, testicles, wallet and keys – on his way up the escalator to Departures. Go well, old fella, he thought.

The flickering monitor said the Aer Lingus flight from London would land in a minute or two. What timing! They'd be tired after the twenty Qantas hours from Perth and the wait at Heathrow. He'd cook them lunch, stoke the fire and put them to bed with the wind rattling outside. Hell, he'd climb in with them, sleep or no sleep. He wondered if he could find a decent bottle of wine somewhere in this country before dark. Not on a Sunday. Now he needed a leak. He was like a kid, jiggling and fidgeting.

Down the hall he found the Men's. At the mirror he stared at himself a moment. His curls were ragged and upstanding, and his dodgy eye and flushed complexion gave him a desperate look. He was lucky the Gardai at the terminal entrance hadn't pulled him aside to search him for a Semtex suppository. He grinned slackly, straightened himself up best he could, pushed his hair down with the sweat of his palms and went out to meet them.

The monitor flashed LANDED. A wall of people curved around the electric doors of the customs exit. Scully wormed his way in and with a bit of foul play he found himself at the front rail itself.

The briefcase jobs appeared first, snapping their trenchcoats about them, hardly looking up at the press of other people's relatives at the chrome barrier. Then came the trolleys with their teetering stacks of suitcases pushed by the bleary and the weeping. Shouts of recognition commenced. Families grappled and sobbed at the rail. Babies were passed head-high to the front. Scully could barely stand the guffaws and shrieks of other people's happiness. He was crushed sideways and shunted from behind and he began hopping from foot to foot, straining to catch some familiar feature in the oncoming stream of faces.

And then, waist high, he saw the blonde curls.

'Billie!'

She disappeared behind someone else's trolley.

'Billeee!'

When she emerged he saw the small tartan suitcase in her hand, the fluorescent green backpack on her shoulders and the female flight attendant beside her. Billie's eyes found him and blinked recognition. The poor kid looked pale and tired, completely wrung out. Scully looked for the trolley behind, that Jennifer must be pushing. He couldn't imagine the excess baggage they must have forked out for. But the trolleys behind were all pushed by men. Scully saw the green sticker on Billie's jacket. Saw her small hand holding the hand of the woman in uniform. Saw the clipboard and the brittle, cosmetic smile. He leapt the rail.

'Billie, you should have waited for Mum.'

He grabbed her up, case and all, and felt her clinch him like a boxer. My God, but it felt good. She smelled of raspberry and of Jennifer. Through the haze of Billie's hair he saw the trolleys coming on in small batches, then petering out altogether.

'Mr Scully?'

He turned. The Aer Lingus woman smiled.

'I'm afraid we need some identification, sir. The regulations, you know. She's such a quiet girl.'

'I'm sorry, I don't think I . . . she's got her passport, hasn't she?'

'Oh, yes, I have it here.'

Billie pressed into his neck so that he felt his blood beating against her forehead.

'Well, what identification? Have they lost the bags?'

'No, sir, this is all there was.'

'It's okay, we'll wait,' he said, smelling Billie's hair; he was delirious.

'Just a driver's licence, Mr Scully, and a signature. All unaccompanied child passengers need –'

'What did you say?'

He lifted Billie and saw the Junior Flyer badge. He put the child down and took the proffered clipboard as though it was a bloodied weapon. Unaccompanied Child Passenger B. Scully, female, seven years old. Scully held the little pen in his hand and let it shake above the paper and then looked back at the Aer Lingus woman.

'Right there where it's marked, sir.'

Scully signed, and his name was barely recognizable. The arrival doors closed now. There was no one else coming. He looked back at the form. London Heathrow–Shannon, December 13. Jennifer's signature.

'The ID, sir?' The woman's smile had begun to fade.

Scully looked down at his daughter. She was white, stiff as a monument.

'What's happening? Weren't there enough seats? Is she bringing the bags on the next flight, then? You probably left the note in your pocket, eh, Bill?'

Billie stared at him with the gaze of a sleepwalker. Christ, he suddenly needed to shit.

'Mr Scully, please –'

He dug in his back pocket for the thin wallet, flicked it open without even looking at her. His International Driver's Licence, the American Express card, an old photograph of the three of them on the beach. The woman scribbled down details and snapped her clipboard shut.

'Goodbye, Billie,' she murmured, and left.

Billie looked at people passing.

'What the hell's going on, love? Why isn't she here? Where's all our stuff? She shouldn't have made you come ahead on your own.'

He stooped and went through the many pockets of Billie's denim jacket. Wrappers, a packet of raspberry gum, a plastic Darth Vader, ten English pounds, but no note from Jennifer. Right there on the floor he unzipped her little tartan case, and to the great amusement of the next shift of meeters and greeters, he went through it with unmistakeable desperation. Gay coloured clothes, an ancient comic book, toiletries, a folder full of documents, for Godsake, and some photographs. Toys, more clothes. His mouth went gluey. His bowels turned. He glanced up at the monitor. The next flight from London was a British Airways in twenty minutes, and there was another Aer Lingus at noon, a Ryanair in the middle of the afternoon and nothing much else till six.

'Come sit over here a minute, mate,' he said shakily, 'I have to go to the toilet.'

He got her to a vinyl bench, put her suitcase beside her.

'Now don't move, okay? Don't talk to anyone, just stay there. And while I'm gone,' he said, trying to get his voice down from panic pitch, 'think hard so you can tell me what happened at London, orright?'

Billie blinked. He just couldn't stay.

In the bright, horrid cubicle he shook. He was shitting battery acid. His toes curled in his boots. What? What? What? She's too responsible to break a plan. She's too solid, too bloody Public

Service to deviate without a hell of a reason. His mind boiled. Qantas to Heathrow, Lingus to Shannon. Any delay and she'd telegram and wait, keep everything together. Sunday, Scully, no telegrams. Okay, but she's a bureaucrat, for Godsake, she knows about order and the evils of surprise. She'd think of something. She'd send a message with Billie. No, something's happened. Call the cops, Scully. Which bloody cops? No, no, just slow down, you're panicking. Just settle down and get it clear and straight. Clear and straight – Jesus.

SCULLY PUT THE BUCKET OF CHIPS and the orange juice in front of his daughter and tried to think calmly. She'd said not a word since arriving and it compounded his anxiety. They sat across the white laminex table from one another, and to strangers they looked equally pasty and stunned. Billie ate her chips without expression.

'Can you tell me?'

Billie looked at the buffet bar, the procession of travellers with red plastic trays in hand.

'Billie, I've got a big problem. I don't know what's happening. I expected two people and only one came.'

Billie chewed, her eyes meeting his for a moment before she looked down at her juice.

'Did Mum get hurt or sick or something at the airport in London?'

Billie chewed.

'Was there a problem with the bags?'

Shit, he thought, maybe it was Customs ... but she didn't

carry anything silly, unless there was some mistake, some mix-up. And would she go through Customs in London, or would she just have been in transit there? Scully held his head.

'Was she on the plane with you from Perth? She must have been. She had to be. Billie, you gotta help me. Can you help me?'

Scully looked at her and knew that whatever it was, it wasn't small, not when you saw the terrible stillness of her face. She was a chatterbox, you couldn't shut her up usually, and she could handle a small hitch, ride out a bit of a complication with some showy bravery, but *this*.

'Tell me when you can, eh?'

Billie's eyes glazed a moment, as though she might cry, but she did not cry. He held her hand, touched her hair, saw his hands shaking.

AT THE BRITISH AIRWAYS COUNTER, Scully tried to cajole Jennifer's name from the passenger list, but the suits were having none of it.

'I'm afraid it contravenes security regulations, sir.'

'I'm her husband, and this is her daughter. What security?'

'I don't make the rules, sir. It lands in a moment. Then you'll see for yourself.'

'Thanks for shit.'

Scully dragged Billie over to the Aer Lingus counter where he moved into lower gear and hoisted the child onto his hip.

'I know it's agin the rules and all, mate,' he said to a soft-faced fellow with sad eyes, 'but we've been waiting for our mum, haven't we, love, and she wasn't on the flight a while ago from London and . . .'

'Aw, sir, it's awful for you, I know, but they's the rules.'

'Well, I'm just thinking should I wait here all day, or what d'you think? The little girl's just put in twenty hours from Australia and you can see how tired she is. I just drove all the way in from County Offaly, and if I go back and my wife arrives . . . and the little girl's so keen to see her mother . . . I mean, what harm could it do to know if she's coming or not?'

Scully saw the genuine apology in the first reluctant shake of the head and pounced.

'Listen, why don't I give you her name? If she's not there you just turn away. Any sign of Mrs J. Scully on a BA flight to Ireland today, orright?'

The Aer Lingus man sighed. Oh, thank God for the hearts of the Irish, Scully thought. The keys on the console rattled. Scully clung to Billie, sweating again.

'No.'

'You don't even have to say anything, just nod or shake your head.'

'No, I mean she's not listed, today, yesterday or tomorrow. I'm sorry sir.'

Scully felt it go down like a swallowed ice cube, shrivelling his guts. 'Thanks anyway, mate. Is there a Qantas office in Ireland?'

'Doubt it, sir. They don't fly here.'

'Of course.'

'Goodbye now, sir.'

SCULLY WAITED TILL THE LAST EXHAUSTED BUGGER staggered off the British flight and the last trolley heaved into the hall before gathering Billie's case and leading her towards the exit. That was it.

'D'you want to go to the toilet first, love?'

Billie let go his hand and veered for the Ladies'. Scully stood there as the door swung shut. He held the tartan case and faced the wall. He could smell Jennifer on the bag and even on his neck, and how it hurt to smell it. One of his legs began to shake independently of the rest of his body. He stood alone in the milling crowd, staring at the door that said *Ladies*, until the panic crept on him like a spasm of nausea. His little girl was in there alone, in an airport in a foreign country. Her mother was lost and he was standing out here trustingly like an eejit. He all but knocked down the shrieking women as he barged through the door and went madly among the cubicles calling her name.

## *Fourteen*

ALL THE WAY BACK UP THE DUBLIN ROAD, though the rain had stopped and the wind had eased, the land looked flattened and every human monument grey as bathwater. It was a litany of ditches and slurry-smears, wracks and failures. The men he saw in the streets of grimy towns were coarse-faced idiots and the sky above them a smothering blanket about to fall. Scully clawed the wheel. He tried to think of things he could say, reassuring things, but it was all he could do not to break out screaming and plough them both deep into the fields of the Republic. The small girl sat with her feet not touching the floor, saying nothing for miles, until, mercifully, she went to sleep.

SCULLY POURED COAL INTO THE GRATE and heard it tumble and hiss. The bothy was warm and momentarily heartening. He went out into the afternoon chill to bring Billie in from the Transit. She was tilted back awkwardly, mouth agape, and she merely stirred when he murmured in her ear and touched her, so he unbuckled her belt, took her in his arms and carried her upstairs to her new room. It was cool up there, but the stones of the chimney kept it from being cold. As she lay on her bed he unlaced her boots and slipped them off. He eased her from her jacket and slid her in under the covers, where, on the pillow, she seemed to find new ease and the faintest beginning of a smile came briefly to her face.

At the end of the bed, he unzipped her case and pulled out the small bald and one-legged koala that was her lasting vice. He held it to his face and smelled the life that he knew. He tucked it in beside her and went downstairs.

He set the iron kettle over the fire and sat at the table with his hands flat before him. My wife has sent my child on alone. No message, no note, no warning. Yet. It's Sunday, so no telegrams. There'll be a message tomorrow. It's no use panicking or getting bloody self-righteous about it. You're worried, you're disappointed, but just show a bit of grit here, Scully. Tomorrow Pete'll bring a telegram and we'll all laugh like mad bastards about this.

THE SUN WAS GONE BEFORE FOUR O'CLOCK. Scully found himself out behind the barn in a strange cold stillness looking at the great pile of refuse he'd hauled out there on his first day. The rain had battered all Binchy's chattels down into a slag heap, a formless blotch here at his feet. In the spring, he decided, he'd dig up this bit of ground and plant leeks and cabbage, and make something of it. Oh, there were things to be done, alright. He just had to get through tonight and the rest of his life would proceed.

The light from his kitchen window ribboned out onto the field. Scully's nose ran and his chest ached. He told himself it was just the cold, only the cold. A cow bawled down the hill in some miry shed somewhere, and Scully watched, marvelled, really, as his breath rose white and free on the calm evening air.

THAT NIGHT SCULLY KEPT A VIGIL OF SORTS. It was doubly lonely sitting in the bothy knowing Billie slept upstairs remote from him in whatever dream it was that had hold of her. Poor little bastard, what must she be feeling?

He unpacked all her clothes and folded them carefully. Her little dresser smelled of the Baltic, of the wax of aunts and calm living. Downstairs he looked through her things, her Peter Pan colouring book, her labelled pencils, the Roald Dahl paperbacks. He put aside her tiny R.M. Williams boots and brushed some nugget into them. In the kitchen the sound of the polishing brush had the comfortless rhythm of a farm bore. On the table he opened her folder of documentation. Birth Certificate, 8 July 1980, Fremantle Hospital. Yes, the wee hours. He went home that morning with the sound of off-season diesels thrumming in the marina. Yellow vaccination folder. School reports, one in French, the other in Greek. A single swimming certificate. Three spare passport shots – the perky smile, the mad Scully curls. Taken in the chemist's on Market Street. A creased snapshot of her standing at the mouth of the whalers' tunnel at Bathers Beach with some kid whose name escaped him.

Scully went upstairs to watch her sleep. It was warmer up there now under the roof. It was late. His eyes burned but there was no question of sleeping, no chance. Not till this was over, till he knew Jennifer was alright. Carefully he lay beside Billie and held her outside the eiderdown, felt her hair and breath against his face. In the band of moonlight that grew on the far wall he saw the flaws of his hurried limewash. The long, relentless unpeeling of the night went on.

Just before dawn, in the milled steel air, he filled buckets with coal in the barn by the light of the torch. The land was silent, the mud frozen. At the front door he paused a moment to look down at the castle but saw no lights. The stars were fading, the moon gone. He went in and built up the fire. For a moment he thought about their baby, whether this house would be warm and dry enough. And then he caught himself. God Almighty, where was she?

The day came slowly with the parsimonious light of the north, and Billie slept on. Scully resolved to list out all the possibilities on a sheet of paper, but all he got was her name three times like a cheesy mantra. He re-read all his mail, looked at each of the smudged telegrams. Nothing. It was only a month – what could happen in a month, or in an hour at Heathrow?

Late in the morning he put the leg of lamb into the oven. The smell filled the house but Billie slept on and the roast cooled on the bench, juices congealing beneath it. Scully ate a cold spud, made himself a cup of Earl Grey.

The mail van slewed along the lane sometime past noon. He heard it bumbling round in the valley and he went outside nearly falling in his haste, but it never came back his way. No mail. No telegram. Out on the thawed mud, Scully puked his cup of tea and his roast potato, and when he straightened to look back at his smoke-pouring house, wiping the acid from his chin, he saw Billie at the open door rumpled with sleep.

'Rip van Winkle,' he said brightly, scuffing the soiled mud with his wellingtons.

Billie shivered, her legs squeezed together.

'Need a pee?'

She nodded solemnly.

'I'll show you. It's out in the barn.'

She gave him a doubtful look but let him carry her across the mud on the duckboard bridge to the barn, where, at the back the old Telefon booth stood in the corner. She looked at the JOH GOES! poster.

'Great, eh?'

He put her down on the rotting straw and she pulled open the door dubiously, and then turned, waiting for him to leave.

'Great dunny, what d'you reckon?' he said, retreating outside. The sun's shining, Scully, he thought; show a bit of steel, for Godsake and brighten up. She doesn't want you to hang over her on the bog.

He looked down the valley and saw the birds wrapping the castle keep and the low clouds motionless on the mountains. Light broke in sharp moments all across the fields. The trees stood bare and maplike with their knots of nests plain to see. It was a rare day.

He heard the flush.

'What a toilet, eh?' he said as she emerged, blinking at the miry ground. She looked out at the empty fields, at the hedges and fences and sagging gates. For a long moment, she stared down at the castle keep.

'No animals, huh? First thing I noticed,' he said. 'They keep them indoors because of the cold. Imagine that. Every couple of days you see tractors hauling these big trailers that hurl poop all over the paddocks. What a scream. Come on, I'll get you something to eat. What d'you think of the house? Did I do a good job? Haven't painted it yet.'

Billie held his hand and walked with curling toes across the duckboards. It frightened him, this silence. They were so close, the two of them, such mates. Nothing innocent, no small thing could close her up like this.

She drank Ovaltine by the fire and ate her bread. Scully warmed some fresh clothes on a chair by the hearth and poured hot water into the steel tub.

'You can wash yourself while I make your bed. New Levi's, I see. A present from Gran?'

Billie chewed and looked at the coals.

'I'll be upstairs.'

Wait, he told himself. Think and wait. The telegram will turn up. Hours left in the day yet. Upstairs he leaned against the warm patched chimney and prayed the Lord's Prayer like a good Salvo, the words piling up like his thoughts in the snug cap of the roof.

No telegram came.

Billie slept again. Scully napped and sweated. He prowled the stairs, listening for the sound of a car, the arrival of an end to this scary shit. But nothing came. In the wee hours he was mapping things out, thinking of London, of his friends there, of a simple explanation. Jesus, why didn't he get the phone on?

The night reeled on, lurching from hour to hour, from impasse to foggy hole with the world silent beyond.

NEXT MORNING, SCULLY DROVE INTO ROSCREA with Billie, bubbling away cheerlessly like a jolly dad on the first day of the holidays. He could see it didn't wash for a minute because Billie stared mutely out at the countryside, bleak as the breaking sky. Not a thing. Not a word. Well, the waiting was over. He had to do something before it killed him.

He drew a blank at the Post Office. Pete was out on his

round. No telegram anyway. He cashed a bagful of change and made for a Telefon down the high street.

'I JUST NEED TO CHECK whether she was on QF8 from Perth via Singapore the day before yesterday,' he said as evenly as he could manage to the voice in London. 'This is the fifth ... No, no there isn't a problem, really.' The phone booth fogged up with their breath. 'I just wanted to make sure, you know – twelve thousand miles is a long way. I know what can happen with schedules ... Yes, I understand.'

Billie passed him up some more coins from her squatting position in the booth.

'Ah, terrific, so she was aboard then ... out at Heathrow, great. And did she have an onward transfer from there?'

A truck from the meatworks heaved itself up the hill, shaking the glass beside his face. MAURA SUCKS NIGGERS, someone had written on the wall in felt pen. Absently, Scully began to scrape it out with the edge of a 20p coin. He noticed the beauty of the design on the coin. A horse, like a da Vinci study. Only the Irish. The voice turned nasty in London.

'Yeah, but, I know, but I'm her husband, you see. Yes, but be reasonable about this ... No, I don't think I have to ... oh, listen, I'm asking you a ... well, fuck you!'

He whacked the receiver down and coins spilled free. Billie sniffed blankly.

'Scuse my French. Sorry.'

Scully looked down the narrow, grey street and went back to scraping. So, she arrived in Heathrow, sent the kid on alone. Either she's in London, or, or she's gone on somewhere else. But why? Oh, never mind bloody why, Scully, *where* is the issue first up. Think, you dumb prick. Start at the least likely and work your way back. What are the possibilities? The house deal falling through? Some stock market economic glitch, some problem with the papers? Maybe she's gone back to sort it out, save you worrying.

He dialled the house in Fremantle. Evening in Australia. Summer. The Telecom message chirped – disconnected. Automatically he dialled his mother but hung up before it could ring. No.

London. It made all the sense. She'd be at Alan and Annie's. She was having a bleed. God, it was trouble with the baby and she was stuck in . . . but Alan and Annie, they were saints. They'd be looking after her. Yes, pain at the airport, a cab to Crouch End.

He rang them, his fingers tangling in the stupid dial.

'Alan?'

'Sorry, he's out with Ann.'

'Who's this?'

'Well might I ask.' Who was this snot with the Oxbridge lisp?

'When will they be back?'

'Who *is* this?'

'Scully,' he said. 'A friend.'

'The Australian.'

'Listen, when will they be back?'

'Don't know.'

Scully hung up. It was Tuesday for Godsake. They worked at home – they never went anywhere on a Tuesday. He called back.

'Listen, it's me again. Have they had visitors this weekend?'

The kid at the other end paused a moment. 'Well, I'm not sure I like the way this conversation is going.'

'Bloody hell. Son, listen to me. I want to know if a woman called Jennifer –'

The kid hung up. Shit a brick. Who else could he call? They had friends all over Europe, but in London they had all their eggs in one basket. There was no one who knew them as well as Alan and Annie. The house was always full of waifs and strays. In London it was the *only* place she'd go. What could he do – call the embassy? Everyone else he knew from London was probably IRA. Sod that.

He waited. He scraped. He dialled Fremantle again. Nothing. He dragged the little address book from his pocket and called the number Pete once gave him. Nothing. Twists of paint dropped into Billie's hair. He began to shuffle on the spot. He made a fist, pressed it against the glass. She was losing the baby and he was in some frigging Irish abbatoir town, helpless.

He dialled Alan's again.

'Scully?'

'Alan, thank God!'

Alan sounded startled, a little sharp even. Maybe he'd got an earful from young Jeremy Irons or whoever.

'How's Ireland?'

'Ireland?'

'We're dying to come out and see the place. Maybe we can pretend to be Aussies. You know, improve our standing.'

'Alan, listen, did Jennifer drop by yet?'

'Jennifer? Are they back from Australia yet?' Scully's mind rolled again. He couldn't pull it back. But Alan sounded odd.

'Course she's very welcome, they both are. Great about the house, eh?'

'How, how d'you know about the house?'

'Got a card. Is everything alright, Scully?'

'Yeah. Yeah, it's fine.' Tell him, he thought. Tell him.

'Should I expect them, you think? We can make up a bed.'

'You wouldn't hide anything from me, would you, mate? I mean, she's your friend as well.'

'What's happening, Scully?'

Why can't you tell him? What kind of stupid suspicious pride is it that –

'Scully, are you alright?'

Scully listened to the hiss of the Irish Sea in the wires.

'I thought it might be the baby,' he murmured.

'What baby? No one told us about a baby. Annie! Annie, get the desk phone will –'

Scully hung up. He couldn't do it anymore. His mind was twisting. They were the only people in the world he could trust. It wasn't London. Friggin hell, it wasn't London.

Coins jangled out onto the floor. Billie looked up at him knowingly. She knew. He could see it, but what could he do, beat it out of her?

'Listen sweetheart,' he said to Billie, dropping to her level, wedging himself like a cork at the bottom of the booth. He grabbed her by the hands and looked imploringly into her shut-down face. 'You gotta help your dad. Please, please, you gotta help me. If you *can't* talk I understand, but don't . . . don't not talk because you're angry, don't do it to get back at me. I'm worried too. I'm so worried . . . I'm . . . Tell me, was Mum sick or anything on the plane, at the airport? Did she seem sort of strange, different somehow? Did she say anything to you, when she'd be coming, where she was going to, did she tell you to say something to me?'

Billie's forehead creased. She clamped her eyes shut. Scully put his fingers gently on her eyelids. So tired, so frail and shell-shocked. This was a terrible thing, too terrible. He wanted to ask other things, worse things. Was there anyone else on the plane, in the airport? Had there been anyone else around these last weeks in Australia? But there were things that, once uttered, couldn't be reigned back. He had the fear that saying more might bring some worse calamity down on his head. Once you stopped thinking of innocent possibilities, the poison seeped in, the way it was already leaching into him, the ghastly spectrum of foul maybes that got to him like the cold in the glass around him. Old Scully, who according to Jennifer, hadn't the imagination to think the worst. Something she said once, as though neurosis was an artform. Said without bitterness, accepted with a shrug.

Scully felt himself levelling off again, going back to the likely alternatives. Did she just have cold feet? Okay, she made a mistake, it wasn't too late to change their minds about Ireland. Maybe the sight again of their old house in Fremantle after two years had brought all their plans down around her ears. Hell, it was a whimsical idea in the first place, and plainly hers. She was embarrassed, that's all. It could be that simple. But why this? Why the silence? Being pregnant hadn't made her strange before. Maybe more timid than usual. Could be that. But women didn't suddenly lose their brains with a baby on board. Could be she was biding time for a while, trying to work up courage to tell him she couldn't go through with Ireland. All this was manageable, they could ride it out. Only it just didn't feel right to him, none of this did. He was dangling, just hanging, dammit! What was it? Was she trying to send a message about the marriage, expressing some dissatisfaction? She wouldn't be that cruel, surely. And then he thought of those ugly Paris nights, the rage she had when cornered. His gut churned. She could have some surprise lined up. No. Today's mail would tell. By one o'clock Pete-the-Post would be by. And there was still time for a telegram to arrive. Do the right thing and wait. Think of Billie.

But if it wasn't London and there was no telegram? The glass was cold against his cheek. A ragged convoy of Travellers' vans ground slowly past with horses and donkeys in tow. He watched them all the way up the hill.

'Let's go to the travel agent, Bill. We'll get you some nice brochures you can cut the pictures from.'

He crashed the booth door open, free of the cupboard air, and felt some kind of resolution settling on him. Yes, he had to *do* something.

THE TRAVEL AGENCY DOWN BY THE RIVER was a modest affair. It catered mostly to locals' trips to London and Lourdes and Rome, or packages to the Costa del Sol. Scully went in fired up with smiling charm, but the agent, a small woman with flaming pink cheeks, was nervous all the same.

'I'm just looking for flight connections, you know, good connections from London.'

'Er, when would that be for, sir?' the woman said, smiling gratefully when someone else walked into the little shop.

Scully was flushed and fidgety, his eye roving alarmingly in his woolly head.

'Hm, today, yesterday, ah, about this time of year,' he mumbled. 'Listen, why don't you serve this lady and toss me the book and I'll flick through.'

Billie sat in a cane chair looking at her feet. The travel agent looked at Scully uncertainly, and passed him the thick schedule book, transferring her attention to a tall tweedy woman with a fedora and a horsey Anglo accent.

Scully sat back with Billie and lurched around the book. He found yesterday and his heart sank at the mass of information. He thought of Billie's flight and arrival into Shannon. Okay, about an hour's flying time, say a nine-thirty flight out of London. The Qantas flight in was a six a.m. arrival. Now . . . Did she put Billie on the Irish flight herself? He simply had to believe that a mother would do that, whatever her state. Then she was still at Heathrow till . . . there it is, Aer Lingus 46 . . . till 9.35. Now, where did she go from there? A cab into London, maybe, but if not?

Scully found a list of flights out of London close to 9.35.

Karachi, 9.40.

Kuala Lumpur, no.

Moscow – in December?

Miami.

New York.

Rome.

Paris. Maybe, yes, maybe. But why would she go back to the scene of her failure?

Barcelona.

Athens, 10.25. Yes. A Qantas flight, too. She was paranoid about air safety. Yes. Greece made sense. She knew it and loved it. The island would be a kind of sanctuary. Somewhere to sort herself out. If it hadn't been for the pregnancy she'd have stayed on indefinitely, he knew. He felt more or less the same. If the shit hit the fan, where in Europe would *he* go to hole up? Greece. Yes. Yes.

Scully looked back at the Paris flight. British Airways – she hated them and she wouldn't fly with them or anyone American. Hmm, they were quite the world travellers now, weren't they.

No, it was only Qantas, Singapore, Thai or KLM. The Athens flight, then, it had to be. How bloody easy it was, plonking down the magical, scary credit card and moving from place to place. As long as the card didn't melt and the magic didn't evaporate. A trickle of poison seeped into his chest. Had she told no one? Not even Alan and Annie? Didn't she know Scully would call them first? He had to believe they didn't know. Leaving no message – it seemed crazy, but wasn't leaving no message a signal in itself? Hell, he needed some sleep. But didn't she know he would figure this out, that if it wasn't London it had to be Greece? He knew how her mind worked. It was private, a thing between them, like the baby. God, it *was* a message. She needed to talk, to meet, but somewhere safe, somewhere good, familiar. Like the island, where things had been best.

For a moment, it seemed, the fog of hurt and tiredness left him. He made a map in his head, a schedule. He did a bit of mental arithmetic and took out his American Express card. Even now he held it like a working-class man, as though it might go off in his hands at any second. He double-checked his figures. Yes, he had some credit left, maybe half a card's worth. Enough anyway. He held his breath and placed the card carefully, almost reverently, on the counter. It was a relief, like a suddenly open window, the feeling of doing something, of making decisions and acting. Yes, it was a start.

SCULLY TRACKED PETER KENEALLY DOWN on the road from Roscrea. It had just finished raining and water stood in bronze sheets by the lane. He saw the little green van through a stand of bare ash and pulled over as far as he dared onto the soft shoulder until he saw the van reverse out onto the road.

'He's a friend of mine,' said Scully, shaky with resolution. 'See, he never looks in his mirrors, he'll get skittled one day.'

The postie pulled out and swivelled his head. His eyes widened in surprise.

'Well, I'll be damned to hell if it isn't the Desert Irish himself!' said Pete as Scully pulled up beside him. Pete's cheeks were aglow, his uniform askew and his hat was capsized on the seat beside him. In his lap was a sorry nest of envelopes.

'G'day, Pete.'

'Well, go on, man, tell me how it all went. Aw, Jaysus, I see someone up there beside you. I wonder who this could be now? Good day to ye! She's a grand lass, Scully.'

'Billie, this is Peter.'

Billie lowered her eyelids bleakly.

'Aw, she's shy, now. Look at that suntan on ye, looks like ye just came from Africa.'

Scully saw her observing Pete's ears. They were like baler shells – he'd become used to them.

'We'll be gone a few days, Pete. Would you mind keeping an eye on the place? I'll leave a key in the booth in the barn.'

Pete's grin softened and disappeared. 'Is everything alright?'

'Just some business to sort out.'

Pete's mouth failed to complete several movements. You could see him straining good naturedly to mind his own business. Scully thought: I hope to God he doesn't think I'm doing a runner and leaving him with the bill.

'Couple of days, Pete. Listen, gimme your home number again, just in case.'

Puzzled, Pete recited the number. Scully wrote it on the strap of Billie's backpack, more as a show of stability than anything else. 'Any mail for me?' he said, feeling a last bubble of hope in the back of his throat. 'A telegram?'

'Not a thing.'

Scully closed his eyes a moment.

'You want help?'

The postie licked his chapped lips, anxious now.

'I'm fine, mate.'

'You look shot and killed.'

'See you in a coupla days.'

Scully put the Transit in gear and lurched away.

IN THE COOLING BOTHY, Scully made lamb sandwiches and sat down with Billie to eat dutifully, mechanically, the way he ate those too-early fishermen's breakfasts hours before dawn in another life, chewing for his own abstract good and without pleasure. From the china jug he poured glasses of milk. At the mantelpiece he took down the photo Dominique had taken and he cut it down to fit inside his wallet. The sound of the scissors was surgical. Three faces, a tilted Breton headstone.

He laid their documents on the table, checked their visas, the state of their crowded passports. Map. Swiss army knife. Some aspirin. Cash. Into Billie's tartan case he packed a change of clothes for each of them. He placed their documents in her fluorescent backpack with the Walkman, her Midnight Oil tapes, her comic and her colouring gear. She pulled the Darth Vader out and put it on the mantel.

'Are you alright, love?'

She sat down and drank. The milk left a moony glow on her upper lip. She shrugged.

Scully found a brush on the sill and gently straightened her hair. It was so like his own. In a few years it would be exactly his, completely beyond redemption, the kind of clot you run your fingers through and shrug at.

'I like this house,' he murmured, packing a few toilet things. 'Everything'll be alright in this house, Bill. I promise you. Here, I polished your boots. You need a horse with boots like that. An Irish hunter. Yeah.'

He stood, feeling the stillness of the place, the look in her eyes.

A car heaved up the hill in low gear. Scully waited for it to pass, but it pulled in and he recognized it.

'Scully,' said Peter at the door.

'Hi, Pete.'

'You're off then.'

'To the train station, yeah.'

'Dublin?'

'Yep.'

'Let me drive you.' Pete pressed his hands together and leant from boot to boot, averting his eyes.

'You needn't worry, mate. We've got a flight to Athens in the morning.'

'Athens, Greece? If you leave that van there at the station the friggin tinkers'll have it up on blocks before dark. Let me take you.'

Scully stood there with his hand in Billie's hair watching the postie think.

'Fair enough. Thanks.'

'Athens. Can we have a drink?'

'It's just two days, Pete. Don't look so worried.'

'Oh, it's not worry, son, it's just fresh out today.'

Smiling, Scully took the bottle of Bushmills off the mantel. 'Here. *Slainte.*'

'*Slainte.*'

Then Scully took the bottle back and took a good hard slug, felt it bore down cruelly into his roiling gut. 'You're right,' he said, laughing emptily. 'It's cold out.'

A LITTLE WAY DOWN THE ROAD in the tiny green van, Pete slowed down and pulled up beside the frail tree in the middle of the road.

'Can I have a loan of your handkerchief, Scully?' he said, opening the door and stamping his feet on the glistening road.

Scully dragged out his disgraceful face rag, expecting to see the postman lean over and throw up into the muddy grass. But Pete strode across to the wizened little tree and tied the handkerchief to a branch. He crossed himself twice and came gravely back to the van.

'Don't say a word, Scully. Not a blessed word.'

THE TRAIN PULLED INTO ROSCREA STATION, easing up onto the deep granite cutting to stop right before the three of them. Pete opened a carriage door and helped Billie up the step, doffing his cap comically like a doorman.

'Don't do anythin clumsy, Scully, ye hear me?'

'I'll try.'

'Just be back for Christmas.'

'Are you kiddin? This is two days, Pete.'

'I tell you, I don't understand women or God.'

Or men, thought Scully, who could think of nothing dignified or honest to answer him with, short of telling him everything, breaking down on the platform here and blurting out all his fears. He was a friend, wasn't he, a frigging patron, even. He deserved to know, but some iron impulse told Scully to shut up and get on with it, to stop feeling and start acting. Doors slammed along the line. Scully hesitated, stepped up.

'Look after that girl, Scully.'

'You look after my house.'

The train moved away.

# II

*I saw the danger,*
*Yet I walked along the enchanted way*
*And I said let grief be a falling leaf*
*At the dawning of the day . . .*

'Raglan Road'

## *Fifteen*

Arthur Lipp pushes open his doors and steps out onto the wind-ripped balcony with his head near bursting with pain. The flannel gown flaps on him. His sparse hair is ruffled and instantly his eyes water in the wind. It surprises him after thirty years to quite suddenly hate the onset of winter. Certainly, the confounded tourists are gone with their tee-shirt slogans and sunburn, and prices have come back to normal in the tavernas. The dust has been sluiced off the alley walls and the donkeyshit from the dizzy steps by the first rains, and the mainland peninsula stands pink and clear across the gulf, the air sweetened by the change. He should be ecstatic as an Englishman seeing the first snow – the Englishman he once was.

But the outlook is loathsome, he has to admit it. For the first time, he dreads the long, cosy quiet of winter, and now, the very year he wants to escape it, fly up to Norwich to see his mother, to Chamonix to visit his old chums, the Bluster Boys from Cardiff, or to bloody outback Australia where everybody talks through their big, healthy teeth, he hasn't a ghost of a chance. The Crash he thought he'd escaped has come for him after all. A few unsound portfolio moves. A series of bluffs that came undone. And then a humiliatingly gauche spending spree on that Danish undergraduate in the autumn. Suddenly he hasn't enough for a civilized fortnight at the Grand Bretagne in Athens. The honest word is stranded. At least for a few months he's in the same league as poor pathetic Alex, and at the very thought he whimpers with rage and dashes at the tears with the back of his hand.

Boats sway and tip in the harbour between the deserted moles and the great houses of the buccaneers of history. He turns his back on them and goes inside, forces the doors shut and confronts the ponderous and intolerable sound of the clock on the bureau. Beside the clock lies the little crayon drawing of the island with its spidery inscription, *To Mister Arthur from Billie S.*

Lipp places his hand on the rosewood desk and sees his body-heat fog the varnish. Well, he thinks, they escaped in good time. This island's gone to the pack. There's something rotten at its core, something we're all making day by day.

With only the clock and his hangover to give him company he spends the hour before his first drink thinking of them, those strange Australians. The woman with the legs and the fierce hunger to be noticed. The sponge-haired child with the wild accent. And the big friendly shambles of a man who followed them like an ugly hound, loyal and indestructible in his optimism, in his antipodean determination to see the best in things. Such a family. The original innocents abroad. He wonders if he's ever encountered a man as strange as young Scully. For the past thirty years men his age have all come as angry young lads, but Scully was so easygoing as to appear lazy. Arthur saw him work, though. Like a black, he worked, for Fotis the stonemason. He was just unnaturally sanguine, and goodnatured to the point of irritation. Seemed to like nothing better than to dive like a hairy seal all around the island and when your contempt for him rose to the back of your throat, he'd drop by with an octopus or a few fish for soup, as if to shame you. Salvation Army. It explained a few things.

Scully and the daughter, like two peas in a pod, smirking at each other across the taverna table all the time like retards. Thick as thieves, they were. Talked a language all their own. He envied him that, the closeness, the companionship. And she was a clever child. Picked figs for him out of his own tree. Asked him about Victor Hugo and let him ponce on for hours.

A family of primitives. He can't honestly say he doesn't miss them slightly.

The sight of those luscious brown legs. The easy smile of the lad. The polite way he failed to kowtow to his betters. Simply the freshness of them.

Well, stay home on your own big island, he thinks, and do yourself a favour and never leave. Never grow old. Never chase the hard buttocks of Scandinavians. Do not stand for winter, by God. And never leave your teeth in a glass of Newcastle Brown Ale at night, lest ye become a sad, sick travesty like someone we all know but do not quite care for.

Gravely, and with a great horrible smile cut into his round face, he unscrews the Stolichnaya and pours a breakfast inch without catastrophe.

## *Sixteen*

QUITE SUDDENLY, AND WITHOUT A CHANGE in direction, the jet lumbered out of the cloud and into the world again. Scully who had not slept or rested his mind a moment, could instantly see past his sleeping daughter's head, the harrowed stones, the great gullies, the expressionless mountain faces of the country below. It was late in the day and the land crawled with shadows. Only weeks ago he left Greece sad enough to feel he was leaving his homeland all over again, but now when he saw it he felt nothing, not even dread.

Stewards came down the aisles smiling grimly. Billie woke, saw the sea looming beneath them as the plane banked. She looked at him with an expression he couldn't read.

'Greece again,' he said.

She put her hands in her lap and looked down on the brassy sea. He put his fingers in her hair and she shook him off gently.

IN THE MAULING TRAFFIC, Scully knew they'd miss the day's last hydrofoil to the islands. The light was going and the taxi got deeper and deeper into chaos, so he resigned himself to a night in Piraeus. He could smell the difference winter had brought to Athens. The stinking *nephos* was largely blown away by sea winds, and the place was only as foul as a regular city. The ubiquitous raw concrete was freshened with rain and Athens seemed subdued, humbled by the onset of winter.

Near the Zea marina they got out and walked under the streetlights to a little hotel he knew. The wind put the hair in their eyes, but it was an easy walk uphill.

'It's just tonight,' he said. 'The first boat goes early. Hungry?'

Billie nodded.

Behind them the masts of the harbour jounced in the weather, and the rain came on through them, chasing Scully and Billie to the hotel door.

'WE'LL SLEEP TOGETHER, WHAT D'YOU THINK?' said Scully, pulling back the curtains to look down into the street.

Billie sat on the double bed and looked at the fan of drachma notes beside her on the coverlet.

'Stops us being too lonely, eh?'

Silently she began to weep, and Scully sat beside her, held her gently, and felt that first shaft of hatred return to him like heartburn. How could you do this, Jennifer? What's happened to you that you could do this to us? He felt his teeth meet hard and shake his jaw, but the feeling receded. He looked about this cold bare little room.

'You can tell me, love.'

Rain sprayed against the long unshuttered windows and Billie said nothing.

NEXT DAY THE SUN WAS OUT and the sea beyond the marina was choppy but madly lit and blue. The sky was clear, the air fresh as they went aboard the hydrofoil which idled grotesquely against the wharf. A few off-season tourists had taken seats in the strange aeronautical interior, but most of the passengers were islanders heading home with shopping. Their crates and bags were piled in the aisles. A bearded man guarded a stereo, and a woman, an islander he didn't recognize, had a German Shepherd in a pine crate.

They sat astern and the craft backed out of the harbour past the forlorn yachts of the summer set and turned at the open water beyond the mole to rise up on its limbs like a great insect under the power of its diesels. Scully led Billie out onto the rear deck into the fresh air as the hydrofoil charged out into the Saronic Gulf. He saw Lykavitos and the Akropolis clear against the sky. He saw the fluorescent weal of the wake. He hooked his fingers in the strap of Billie's backpack. Greece. Just the colour of the water, the firm, plain outline of the stone and sky gave him memories. From the cabin came the solemn howl of a German Shepherd all at sea, and Scully managed a laugh.

After half an hour they cut past the undistinguished mound of Aegina and turned for Poros. The dog went on like a siren. The sun lit the deck.

At Poros the expatriate drunks and the Athenian rich were making the most of the sun on the terrace at the Seven Brothers and the sight of them caused Scully to think clearly of Jennifer for the first time that day. He hadn't planned anything beyond simply turning up. He didn't know what he would say, how he would proceed. Now he imagined her breakfasting at the Lyko or Pigadi, rolling up her khaki pants to get the sun on her legs. Or maybe the trousers wouldn't be fitting her now. A skirt. Yes.

A couple of tourists disembarked at Poros, and an American Scully knew from Hydra came aboard. Scully was grateful that the man, a party animal with a rich mother in Boston, sat up front and promptly fell asleep. It looked like he'd made a night of it.

The pastel frontages, the flags and tired mules on the waterfront fell behind as the hydrofoil surged seaward again. Scully looked through the small tartan case at his feet. An optimist's bag. A two-day trip bag. A Scully bag. And in the bottom, rolling about in lint and gum wrappers, three white candles.

SCULLY FELT THE FIRST CHANGE OF NOTE in the big diesels and knew that Hydra was looming. He was facing sternward and couldn't see it, but he sensed the shadow of it falling on the water. He took Billie inboard and arranged the backpack on her shoulders, straightened her up a bit and kissed her.

'This is it, Bill,' he murmured. 'Let's just take it as it comes. We'll get a room and go quietly.'

Other passengers stirred now, and the German Shepherd began to vomit. A horrid stink arose. Handkerchiefs came out. The dog sounded like an old man trying to clear his throat.

When the hydrofoil docked and the hatch fell open, there was an athletic scramble for fresh air, and the little crowd of onlookers parted in alarm as passengers bolted for the wharf.

Scully strode out onto the smooth flagstones with Billie's hand in his, and he saw the shuttered, wintry waterfront with its ragged pastel walls, empty balconies and idle mules. The water of the harbour was still, the moles bare but for a few men mending nets, and the yachts and cruise ships were gone. Up behind the harbour the island rose into the sky, its houses packed into the space between mountain peaks whose slopes showed patches of green he had never seen. The terracotta tiles of a thousand Venetian roofs blurred sweetly in the sun, and from the hills came a showering of goat bells falling on the breeze. A couple of tavernas were open by the water, but he was thankful it was still too early for the late breakfasters. He found the lane past the bakery where the smell of dough and heat and carraway seeds was overpowering. There was a line of mules outside Pan's Bar, and men were laying concrete on the corner, laughing with cigarettes in their mouths and ouzo on their breaths. Scully's heart jangled as he saw the familiar sidestreets and alleys, the bougainvillea, the little square with the lemon trees and their whitewashed trunks, the cats going through the garbage outside the pharmacy where even now old Vangelis stood coughing into his hands. Here and there a woman swept her steps or whitewashed her front wall, but there were few people in the streets and no tourists.

They went up the long steps toward the little hotel he had in mind, somewhere discreet and back from the water a way. He wondered if they'd been seen already, if Jennifer had been standing by a high window or on a sunny terrace when the boat came in. What was she thinking? Would she send a message, just appear, panic? She could be packing her bags this moment. He paused halfway to the hotel on a little terrace from where he could see a strip of sea, and the mountain breeze caught about his ankles. In the house above, a woman sang in a deep, stern voice. He knew the song, but had never been able to follow the Greek well enough to understand it. Billie stood passive beside him, scuffing her feet on the smooth granite flags whose centres were hollow with wear. Scully hummed a few bars and caught himself shaking there in the sunlight.

HE KNOCKED AT THE HEAVY COURTYARD DOOR and waited in the narrow lane. A small dark woman with an enormous bust under her black pinafore pulled the door back. With a broom in one hand, she regarded them.

'*Kyrios* Scully?'

Scully stuttered, unnerved to be known by someone he didn't recognize. Was she someone Jennifer knew? 'Er, *neh, Kyria, kalimera*, um, hello.'

The woman ran her hand through Billie's blonde curls and ushered them into the courtyard where sunlight piled in through the bare grapevines and lit her hanging gourds and her stone stairs.

'Uh, *Kyria*, do you have a room . . . *domatio*?'

'*Neh, neh, poli!*'

She led them to the stairs where cats lay indolent in the light, not moving as they stepped over them. At the head of the stairs she opened a door onto a large room with several beds and wide doors opening to a balcony.

'*Kala*,' Scully stammered. '*Kala, poli*. We'll take it. *Efkaristo*.'

'Is very good place, you come back.'

'Yes. Yes.'

'Cheap for you.'

'How about two thousand drachs?'

The woman pursed her lips doubtfully but shrugged in the affirmative. '*Endakse*.'

'Okay, good.'

She brought them towels and soap, opened the doors and left the room, beaming. Scully took the pack off Billie's shoulders and walked out onto the balcony. The fishhook of the harbour lay plainly below, and he looked out at the gulf and beyond it the mottled mass of the Peloponnese where the faraway smoke of charcoalers smudged the air above the peninsula.

He wondered where she would be. Unless she'd organized something from Australia, she wouldn't have a house yet. Maybe a hotel by the water or a spare room in one of the expats' houses. He tried to think. Where would *he* go after bolting in some kind of panic? God, the thought of her having a breakdown in some bare room twelve thousand miles from home. What else could make you act like that? Surely it couldn't be a way of making a point. You couldn't be right in the mind to do this to people you love.

Scully felt his fingernails in his palms and tried to shake it off. It was not time for macho bullshit. No breastbeating, no torrent of recriminations. Just be prepared to listen, he told himself; don't go shitting in your own nest.

He felt Billie's hand on the back of his leg. One of her shoelaces was undone, so he knelt and retied it and looked into her troubled face.

'We're gonna go down now and look, orright? It's a small place – we'll probably find her before lunch and she'll explain why it happened. Everything'll make sense somehow, and then I think we'll understand. I just want you to be brave and let us sort it out. Let her say what she has to say, okay? Sometimes people having a baby can be very nervous – flighty, you know, like a horse. Now are you sure there isn't anything you want to tell me first?'

Billie's eyes began to fill as she shook her head.

'It's alright. I'm gonna fix it up.'

On his way back down the jumbled steps to the harbour, feeling bilious and goosefleshed, Scully stumped through spokes of light that ran between the smooth white blocks of houses, and he only faintly sensed the brief heat of the sun's concentration. He was lighter without all the northern clothing he'd been wearing, and despite all this weirdness, he felt more himself because of it. Jeans, sneakers, cotton windcheater, the old Scully uniform.

At the waterfront with its summer marquees peeled back to let in the sun, there were a few tables set outside tavernas here and there. Fishermen, old sailors, and a few gold-toothed muleteers sat in the kafenion playing *tavla* and shooting the breeze. The gold merchants, the postcard stalls and claptrap tourist joints were shuttered up, and no speakers played 'Zorba' across the water. The bank was open and sleepy and the hardware-cum-liquor store had its doors wide to the water. The Up 'n' High was closed, the Pirate Bar looked forlorn without its summer Eurotrash. The place felt cleaner, happier for winter.

He ducked back off the waterfront and headed for the Three Brothers. In the lanes, islanders gave him troubled greetings, as though trying to place him, or even, he thought, trying not to place him, as if he was the last man they wanted to see this morning. He felt them turning, each of them, to watch him go. Living here the three of them had been distinctive, even among the *xeni*. No one forgot Billie and that rude awakening of blonde curls. She had been such a vivacious ambassador, easing their way every place they went, and here on Hydra she gave them respectability as well, the illusion of soundness, of family solidity.

Scully smelled pine and linseed oil as he passed a workshop whose saw fell silent. It was dark inside the double doors and he was blinded to its interior by the sunlight, but called a greeting and pulled Billie along when no answer came. It's as if they smell disaster, he thought, bad luck. Am I imagining it, or are they uneasy? They've seen her arrive and then me, put two and two together, and they smell trouble.

In the market square, the butcher hacked at a goat carcase, cigarette in his mouth. Scully did not speak as he passed.

In the lane outside the Three Brothers, a few tables stood in the sun, their plastic covers pulsing lightly in the breeze. Inside were a couple of old islander men with great smoke cured moustaches and waistcoats who greeted him dully, and in the corner was Max Whelp whose eyelids hung low as the ash that drooped from his cigarette.

'Max,' said Scully without sitting down.

Billie stood by while the old men pulled comical faces at her.

'Scully? You idiot, what are you doing back?'

'Where are they all?'

'The scum, you mean?'

'If you like.'

'Fuck em.'

'There's a kid here.'

'Fuck em twice. I'm banned. That fucking Alex!'

'You look terrible.'

'Strange, you know, but I feel better every day. 1963 I came here, Scully, and I'm feeling better every day.'

'Yeah, sure.'

Max pulled himself more or less erect and looked Scully up and down. 'Didn't you go back to the colonies?'

'Where you banned from, Max?'

'The Lyko. The smug bastards. Hm, that's a pretty girl.'

'It's my seven-year-old daughter, Max.'

'Lost-looking. Like her mother.'

'You've seen her, then.'

Max Whelp stubbed his fag out, looked hard at Scully and laughed. Scully hauled Billie out of there and headed back down to the water.

'When I was a boy on the farm,' said Scully to the child, 'my mum used to tell me to beware of worthless characters. I thought she was a bit hard on people, you know, being a farmer's wife and everything, but I found out otherwise when I came here. Max is a worthless character. Don't ever go near him.'

Billie held his hand and was jerked into a run to keep up with his long driving strides.

The Lyko, then. Okay, the Lyko. He didn't mind owning up to it: the expats had always intimidated him. In their presence he felt the complete farmboy, the toolslinger, the deckhand. He looked at them sometimes and felt his knuckles drag on the ground. They were world-sodden, tired, confident, and while you were learning Greek out of a two-buck Berlitz, they were unavoidable. Before Greece, Scully had never met people with hidden money, with independent means, and they fascinated and frightened him. They were Oxford graduates, poor aristocrats, American bohemians, artists and faded lower-order celebrities whose hopes had somehow fallen away. There was a mercenary from Adelaide who he quite liked, and a defrocked priest from Montana who came down from his hilltop eyrie now and then, but the ones who worried him were the ones you saw every day without fail, the ones who staggered down to the waterfront morning after morning and stayed till the wee hours, drinking, sniping, recalling better days. They lived for the youthful influx of summer when they could mingle with the fresh and the novel, when they could whine entertainingly and fall in love, strike poses, relieve each other of the burden of old gossip. They were bright, funny, lordly, talented for the most part, and almost completely idle. To Scully they were like bookish inventions. He learned not to bristle.

Jennifer found them engaging. She loved their backlog of stories, she envied the poets their old words, the sculptors their hands, idle or not, and the heirs their independence. She liked to swim with some of them in the afternoons, or meet them for dinner a few nights a week, and Scully went along, often as not for something to do. To Scully in private Jennifer told cynical jokes about the expats. The two of them rolled their eyes at the mention of oily Rory, the Canadian stud who wrote novels in his few daylight hours, or the two nice queers from Spain who carted a Steinway a thousand steps up to their house with a donkey and two old men. Scully knew why she liked these people. They were not boys and girls who'd followed their parents' dreary instructions, gone to a sensible school, dated sensible boys, closed off all possibility of spontaneity and ended up as bureaucrats whose job bored them rigid and whose only act of defiance, late in their twenties, was to marry a little beneath themselves. Jennifer admired poor Alvin the gold dealer, who needed a bottle of vodka a day just to sign his own name. Alvin, she said, had class. He just refused to be browbeaten by commonsense, by the mean, the average, the sensible. She liked Lotte the destitute German princess who sublet her rooms in the summer and slept with every guest, male and female, and charged extra for services rendered. And there was Alex, who truly was a worthless bastard, who dined out on his friendship with Francis Bacon, his collaboration with Leonard Cohen, and his fling with Charmian Clift. Alex was a carbuncle, but Jennifer saw his painting talent as awesome, despite his not having squeezed more than a toothpaste tube since the early seventies.

Scully floundered among them all, at parties on terraces high above the harbour, or picnics they took in big rolling caiques to Dokos or Palamidas down the other end of the island, but he learned to survive and he saw what pleasure it gave Jennifer. He didn't need much to keep happy. He had the water, after all. He dived for octopus and walked the rugged hills with Billie. He had some space and plenty of sunlight, and a bit of work with Fotis the stonemason to keep his hands rough and the cupboard full. Maybe she was right, perhaps he was too easily contented.

On the mole at the edge of the harbour, an old man pounded an octopus, throwing it down at his feet over and over again. The water tanker tied up ready to pump its load into the town reservoir. Scully strode out along the arm of the wharf to where the little tables of the Lyko stood in the sun by the water, their plastic cloths flapping benignly. Scully hesitated a moment, took a breath. Was he imagining that sudden lull in conversations out on the terrace? He hauled Billie ahead and weaved through the door, into the smoky fug of fried feta, cigarettes, coffee and fresh bread. The furniture in here was simple and occupied. He saw the faces. In such a small place, the expats became a crowd, a nation unto themselves, and they faltered in their chatter as Scully fronted the bar.

'Good God!'

Arthur Lipp twisted hugely on his stool and butted out his Havana. Scully felt the field of upturned faces.

'G'day, Arthur.'

There was a long moment of discomfort and silence. Old Lotte shoved a white cat from her table and blushed gloriously. Bertie and Rory-the-Dick smiled thinly and Alvin raised his shaking hand in greeting.

'You look terrible, me little convict mate,' said Arthur.

Scully shrugged. Arthur rolled the dead cigar between thumb and forefinger, unnerved. A man Scully didn't know got up and went out. At the door he seemed to hesitate and look back. Arthur pursed his mouth. The man went.

'Do I look that terrible, Arthur?'

'How terrible do you need to look? Have you suddenly found ambitions?'

Scully pulled Billie up onto the stool and sat down himself with his chest against the bar.

'Honestly,' said Arthur, 'you look bereft.'

'Bereft.'

Scully was never able to figure out exactly what it was that Arthur did. He knew the old bugger had been here on the island thirty years, that he was a London Jew who drank screwdrivers for breakfast, that he always had some mysterious project on the go, that he took calls from London and New York but never quite disclosed what business he was in. In his sixties, he was bluff, beefy, loud, evasive and tended toward the pompous. A strange, lonely man with a kindly, magisterial streak. Scully had developed a grudging regard for him. He was a bit of a character and the unofficial king of the expats. Every summer, it seemed, the old goat fell for some luscious backpacker in a halter top who took his dough and gave him the bum's rush. He was a creature of habit. Beyond that he was unknowable.

'Bereft,' said Arthur. 'Quite.'

'Where is she?'

'She? She?'

Scully smiled, felt Billie pressing into his side.

'There's no she,' said Arthur. 'The little bitch took off back to Copenhagen the last day of summer. Left her bloody diaphragm in the bathroom cupboard.'

'That's not who I meant, Arthur. You know it.'

Everyone else went back to carefully talking at their tables.

Back in the kitchen, Sofia cursed and whanged pans about. Arthur looked at him and then at Billie. A little sheen of sweat appeared on his large brow.

'Come on, Arthur, let's not piss around.'

'Oh dear.'

'I'll give you a description, then. Tall, long black hair, serious suntan, long legs, as you once told me when you were smashed, Australian, practical, friendly, smart, married.'

'Can't help you.'

Billie looked at her knees. Her fists were clenched just above them on her jeans. Scully looked at her, saw Arthur glance down uncomfortably himself, and looked back out at the harbour through the smudged panes.

'I'm sorry, old boy.'

'About what?'

'That there should be trouble.'

'Are you expecting some trouble, Arthur?'

'I'm just offering my condolences, you ignoramus. Behave yourself.'

'You mean –'

'I don't mean anything, Scully. I liked you as a couple, that's all. Come up to my place for a drink later. How long are you staying?'

'Everyone looks a bit shellshocked,' said Scully loudly.

'Well you've only just left us tearfully on the wharf a few weeks ago. We thought you were in the colonies.'

'And Jennifer?'

'Jesus Christ.'

'It'd be easier if you just told me,' said Scully.

'Told you? Told you?' Arthur scowled and looked hard at him in a vexed and questioning way. He slapped his hand down on the bar. 'Does anyone want to *tell* him? Please, our Scully wants to be told!'

But only a few faces looked up. Someone smirked, someone else shrugged.

'Whatever it is, no one's telling you this morning, Scully.'

'I didn't think you'd be such a prick about it.'

'Could be your primitive manners,' said Arthur lighting up his cigar. 'Buy your child something to eat. She looks all in.'

'You're so fuckin sorry for us, *you* buy her something.'

'Be an adult, lad.'

'Where is she?'

'Your wife? You want me to tell you where your wife is?'

'I think I've had a breakthrough here, Billie.'

'She's *your* wife, boy. Have you mislaid her somewhere?'

'Mislaid!' giggled Rory.

Scully got off the stool.

'Rory,' said Arthur, 'you'd better go. Our friend has large calloused hands and your balls will be *fasolia* if he gets to them.'

'You got that bloody right,' said Scully between his teeth.

Rory got up and left, and then in twos and threes, so did everyone else but Sofia's deaf uncle Ioannis who smiled up gaily from his newspaper.

'Well, that *was* pleasant,' said Arthur. 'You seem to have everyone suitably on-side. I think I'll be off as well. I can't afford being biffed about at my age.'

It shocked Scully to see the fear come to people's faces, their instant expectation that he would do them harm. He felt stupid, misunderstood.

'Why don't you just tell me what's going on, Arthur?'

'Why don't you get off my sodding back and find out for yourself? Where did you come from?'

'Ireland.'

'To do this?' Arthur waved his cigar at the empty taverna. 'To make a fool of yourself?'

'I've always been a fool to you people.'

'It's only that you were such a terrible working-class puritan, Scully. It embarrasses you to see people having a good time and not paying for their sins.'

'Most of you can't seem to pay for your drinks, forget sins.'

'An insecure man is never a heartwarming sight. Less than sparkling company you might say.'

'Fuck you, Arthur.'

'Feed your child.'

Arthur stuck the Havana back in his mouth, gathered up his week-old copy of the *Sunday Times*, and left them there with Sofia studying father and child coolly from behind the counter.

# *Seventeen*

FATHER AND DAUGHTER SAT IN THE SUN on the terrace at the Lyko with plates of calamari, tzatziki and salad barely disturbed before them. Scully bought the food to placate Sofia after driving her custom away with his presence, and besides it was time they both ate, but his gut was tight and acidic and Billie merely picked at a piece of bread, legs dangling lank from her chair. Water flapped at the sea wall. Across the little harbour a donkey bawled itself hoarse.

'What d'you think, Billie? You think they know? Of course they know. See how they look at us – we're a bloody embarrassment.'

Billie's eyes passed over him a moment, and then she looked away past the mole where a man in a little wooden boat was jigging for squid.

What the hell is the woman doing? he thought. I'm here, I came, and every bastard on the island is watching me squirm. What else does she want? What have I done? What can I do? Give me a clue, something to go on.

Just after one o'clock, Scully ordered a half jug of *kokkineli* and a Milko for Billie. They sipped without speaking as curious islanders sauntered by, shaking their heads. The resinated rosé soothed him a moment.

Wait it out, he told himself. Calm down. Give her time. Just being here is enough for now. Sit tight.

At two, Billie shucked back her chair and went inside to the toilet. Christ, why wouldn't she speak to him? He hurled his glass out into the harbour and sat back. He ate some squid, sponged up a little of the yoghurty dip with the bread, and thought back on his life here with Jennifer to find a wrinkle in things, something that might have brought this on. He'd been patient here. It was easy to be patient in a place you loved, but he honestly believed that he'd acted well here. It wasn't like Paris where he was being ground to a pulp by the city itself, but even in Paris he'd made no waves for her sake. London was the same. Hell, it was always the same; he was always ready to give way for her sake. He loved her. That was all it came down to. In Greece it was easy to love her, easy to wait for her to find whatever it was that might let her relax at last and be herself.

Hadn't they been happy, the three of them?

Look at this place! A world without cars, without paperwork, without a calendar half the time, amongst good simple people who were content to live and let live. Old Fotis the stonemason was a gentle taskmaster and the work was satisfying and inconstant. There were long days on the pebble beach for just the three of them, the mountain walks, mosquito coil evenings out on the terrace with muscat grapes heavy overhead and the rats riffling through like relatives. Long letters home, endless meals, collaborations on the Mickey Mouse colouring book and readings from Jules Verne. There was the golden colour of their always bare skin. Songs. Silly moments. There was the day Billie learnt to swim, like a Sunday School miracle. In the afternoons he would come down from the mountain where that great house was taking shape in the side of the cliff, to the cool terrace of their place by the shore where a few cold bottles of Amstel waited and Jennifer and Alex wound up the day's lesson. Billie coming in from the Up School on the horse with the neighbours' boys. Oh, yeah, they'd been happy or he was worse than stupid.

He was even more or less happy about Alex and the daily painting lesson which kept the old fart in drinking money. Alex Moore. Worthless, as Scully's mother would have said, but likeable enough. His paintings hung in some good American collections, but all Scully could go on were the canvasses from the sixties that he saw in some of the bigger expat houses on the island. They were better than good, as far as anyone who had finished high school in his twenties and bombed out of university could tell. Alex had pissed it all away and had done nothing but cadge and bludge and weasle and whine since men first went to the moon.

Having the smoke-cured old blight there every day and for half their meals took some taking, it was true, but Jennifer felt she was getting somewhere. She was so infectiously excited that Scully simply wore it. The house at the edge of the sea soothed him. She came to bed at night with the sweet musk of ouzo on her breath and the creamy moonlight on the sheets and they made love like in the old days.

Looking back, Scully saw nothing to strike a real note of warning. True, he occasionally argued with Arthur or one of the expats' summer friends, and he was cranky when the *meltemi* blew its guts out in August, but then everyone was shitty with chalk in their eyes and the sea too dangerous to swim in, and the heat sucking the sweat from you.

Billie returned from the toilet. She had splashed her face with water and her cotton sweater was blotched with it. She moved her sneakers in small circles on the smooth flags.

Scully sat with the taste of resin in his mouth and tried to think. He hated to drink wine during the day. It did exactly this, it stopped your brain.

Just then, Arthur came wheezing back along the wharf, his white ducks sweaty and soup stained.

'Sofia's trying to shut up shop, Scully.'

'Hmm?'

'It's afternoon. She wants a rest. You're sitting out here like yesterday's milk.'

'I fed my child.'

Arthur sat down. 'What the sodding hell has happened to you?'

Scully smiled and ran his fingers through a puddle of *kokkineli* on the pine tabletop. 'That's what I'm here to find out, Arthur.'

'Get back on the hydrofoil, save yourself a horrible scene.'

'Now why did Rory leave in such a hurry this morning, you think?'

'Because he's vain. He was terrified you'd mar his great asset.'

'Mar, now there's a word.'

'There's a hydrofoil at six.'

'I wouldn't have thought Rory, though.'

'Rory is a dung beetle.'

'You're quite right, no change. I don't suppose she's up at Lotte's?'

Arthur closed his eyes against him.

'You're not going to tell, then.'

'Oh, for Christ's sake, there's nothing I can tell you but get off this island for everybody's sake.'

Scully's head pounded. Some shadow flickered at the back of his mind, something trying to get his attention, but it just wouldn't come. He kept seeing Alex's yellow face, his long smoky forelock.

'Tell me, where's Alex these days? It's not like him to mar a gathering by his absence.'

Arthur's teeth met beneath his moustache in a click audible enough to startle Billie. A raw nerve there, to say the least.

'He's not keeping company, just at the moment.'

'You're kidding. Has the world gone mad?'

'He's up the mountain.'

'Now you're just winging it, Arthur.'

'Shut up, Scully.'

'It's just that it's a long way from a taverna, isn't it.'

'That's the point.'

'He's quit drinking?'

'Well, it remains to be seen. He's looking after the place you and Fotis built for Bertie's Athenian chum.'

'Up at Episkopi.'

'Don't go up there.'

Arthur put a hand on Billie's head with a look of real pity. His skin was smooth and deeply tanned, and with his down-turned moustache he was like a great seal shining there in the sun.

'Arthur, what do you mean, don't go up there?'

'I mean, don't go up there! Have the Irish turned you stupid already?'

'Is he alone?'

'Sofia wants you to go.'

Scully slapped some money down and stood up. Billie got up mechanically beside him.

'Go home, boy.'

Scully mouthed that word. Home. He wasn't sure where it was just at the present.

'How long have you been here, Arthur?'

'Thirty years. You know that.'

'Did you stay too long, you think?'

'That remains to be seen.'

'You remain to be seen.'

'I do at that. That's my achievement.'

'Not everybody remains to be seen, Arthur. Like my wife. She did not remain and neither is she seen. By me, anyway. Every other bastard seems to have a secret, though.'

'You're drunk.'

'No, but I'm unsteady. C'mon, Billie.'

'Where are you going?'

'Oh, probably back to the hotel. Siesta, you know.'

'Six o'clock, the boat goes.'

'I won't be on it.'

'For Christ's sake, don't go up there!'

SCULLY LED BILLIE UP DONKEYSHIT LANE into the maze of houses, steps and alleys built vertically into the hill. They were like teeth in the jaw of the mountain, these houses whose white-washed walls and bright-painted doors hid lush courtyards and shadowy cellars, whose glossy blue shutters lay ajar for the quiet rest of afternoon. On a small terrace before a taverna that bore no name, they came upon a chained dog that broke Billie from her trancelike gait.

She veered to where it stood beneath a bare fig tree. The dog watched her a moment, ears up, but sank back onto its haunches as she came close. It was the poor dog from the hydrofoil. Scully recognised the Shepherd and its owner who came out sweeping expressionlessly onto the terrace.

'*Kalimera!*' said Scully.

The woman stopped, inclined her head toward him and went on sweeping. The taverna was closed. Its geraniums stood naked in olive oil tins on the terrace.

Billie patted the dog on the snout and the two of them walked on up the hill, climbing toward the street of the Sweet Wells and the great houses from the buccaneering days of the last century. At Kala Pigadia they found level ground awhile and saw the harbour and its terracotta roofs far below. They walked on past the sound of hens laying behind rubble walls, past a tethered horse and three scrofulous cats eating from the same upturned bin. House shutters were closed and no people were about as they moved along the spine of the mountain and the ridge of ruined mansions that had begun to fall, piece by piece, into the long scree gully that twisted down to the village and marina of Kamini. The air was cooler up here, the Saronic Gulf a mere strip of sea below. Classroom chants floated across the wall of the Up School. Billie pressed her hand against the rubble parapet and listened. He could only wonder what she was thinking. He let her stay till she'd had enough. He said nothing. What could you say? Soon they came to the old people's home with the soughing eucalyptus outside the gate, and then the walls became farm walls, cemetery walls as the land above and below the smooth stone road became orchard and field and the steps began to fall away before them.

Scully just followed his feet. The fields, steep and riven between the trackless bluffs of the mountains, had gone green and were tufted with wildflowers. There were stone sheep folds with thornbrush gates like pictures from a kid's Bible. Shepherds' huts lay tucked into hollows. A breeze cooled the sweat off their brows as Scully and Billie followed the path down through the rugged gorge country where the breeze became a wind in their faces, funnelled between haggard cliffs and balding bluffs, gulched and rock-strewn all the way down to the tiny village of Vlikos where a dozen whitewashed houses found the water's edge. Scully felt it press into his cheeks, that wind, as he followed Billie beneath the familiar ruin of the stone bridge to the bottom of the scree gully where a donkey stood tethered to a lone pine and boats lay upturned like steeping turtles on the stony beach.

The emotions came like a fresh gust. He was thankful for the closed shutters of the siesta, to be able to pass through unseen and unjudged on the clay track between the houses of his old neighbours. But he paused a moment outside the place with the dark green shutters, knowing Billie would anyway.

The rocky yard fell away to the water in a maze of apricot, almond and plum trees. The figs were finished, the grapes and olives also. Four rivergums sprawled ironically in the ravine beside the house where they once hurled coffee grounds and olive seeds from the terrace of an evening. Sultry nights when bouzouki music trailed across the water from fishing boats and the mauve mass of the Peloponnese glowed on after sunset with the fires of the charcoalers. Just on dark he would climb from the water, his spear catching whatever lights were on, with a bag of octopus or a groper-like *rofos* with its gills still heaving. The air sharp with smoking grills and laughter from other houses.

Scully picked his way alone down the little ravine. Billie stayed up on the path, biting her lips, watching him creep across the dry, crackling ground beside the old house, up to the green shutters, up against the window itself. He crept in under the trellis of the bare grapevine, his heart mad in his neck. The granite terrace, the cubic substance of the whole house and its mirror shadow. A conspiratorial shush from the shorebreak below, the tumble of pebbles. Hadn't they been happy here? After all the bedsits and borrowed apartments and shitty pensiones, hadn't this been the dream place? So like home, and yet fresh, clear, new.

But the looks on the faces of those worthless mongrels in the Lyko this morning – the downcast eyes, the suppressed giggles, the shuffling embarrassment out in the street. Arthur's horror at the mention of Alex Moore. It made you wonder. Had he lived in some Pollyanna blur all this time? Was he missing something? Was she miserable and bored? And worse?

He peered in through the half-open shutter of his old place and saw a man and a woman asleep there. Middle aged. Arms cast about like kelp from the stones of their bodies. Strangers. In his bed. Queer, but the sight of them brought back a memory. That one thing. That old embarrassing thing. He stared in at the twisted sheet and the overturned shoes and thought of the day he came down the mountain from work to the empty house. The strange feeling he had. Billie playing with Elektra's kids next door, her mile wide accent echoing up the dirt lane. The easel and some daub on the stretched canvas. Alex's bloody fag ends all over the terrace. And the bed all torn up like a dog had been in it. It took the longest, longest time for the dread to seep into him, that unfamiliar poison hitting him as he casually straightened the sheets and then ricked them back like a lunatic, scrabbling all over for some sign, some nasty wet mark that wasn't there. Nothing. And somehow there was no comfort in finding nothing. The blind infant rage of jealousy. God, how pathetic. Was there anything more pitiful than a howling man rifling his own bed for someone else's sperm? She came in on him like that, dripping from the sea and cheerful and he wanted to die from shame. Homesickness, he said, don't worry. He cried in her arms. She pushed him down on the bed, salty and slick, fierce with lust, and he never gave the business another thought.

Until today. Just now. Looking in on these strangers. Once you open the door you can't easily close it. You let your mind off on its leash and you have to go where it does. What did he expect, coming to the island? A rescue mission? A meeting? A quiet reckoning? Certainly not to be standing outside his old house entertaining the kind of thing he was thinking of now. Of that nicotine-stained old wreck slipping it to his wife. Of the afternoons they had, the bottles of wine and shady grottoes they might have found, of all the stupid brainless things he was letting himself think now, and thinking them with a kind of cold pleasure. Thinking about that baby now, of the marvellous heart-warming fact that it might not be his, and that Jennifer had set him up in some simple Irish decoy and gone home to cash in her chips and fuck off back to the great man. What a shitheaded moron he was! What a blind fuckwit! What an understanding little dickhead.

He bolted up the ravine and onto the path to where Billie stood mesmerized.

'Someone else lives there now,' he said, hearing the quaver in his voice.

She took his hand a moment and he sensed an opening in her, a pressure of tenderness. She tugged him in the direction of the harbour and for a few paces he let himself be led. But then he dug in.

'Episkopi,' he said. 'This way.'

Billie flung his hand away. He reached for her but she fell down in the dirt with her head between her knees. So she knew. God help him, his kid knew. She was told at the airport.

'C'mon,' he croaked, 'I'll piggyback you.'

He stood there as the wind plied between them. Crickets hissed around. He heard her get up and dust herself off, and when he opened his eyes he saw her setting off along the road to Episkopi.

AT PALAMIDAS, the little oil-streaked bay beneath the island mountain, Scully took Billie on his back and slugged up the winding track through the gnarled olive groves, feeling the child's breath against his neck, her body relaxing against his as she slipped into sleep. He felt the smoothness of her ankles beneath his callouses. He just didn't know how something like this could be abandoned. What was there after a child, what could you want more?

He didn't know what to expect up at Episkopi, how he would act. Why was it easier to hope that she'd gone crazy? After all, her mother had 'episodes'. At sixty she'd been found running naked through the streets of Perth. Madness was its own excuse, it was everybody's absolution. What a shit to think that way, what a coward.

Sweating and panting Scully came to the pine country and the final doglegs of the track as it found its way to the summit. What a joke it was to think of Alex and her living in the very house he'd been building while they were at it out on the terrace this year. Think of the irony. Such a civilized business, thinking of irony. What a master of self-control he was. Think of the irony, Scully. Don't go in like a thug. Think of the kid, for Godsake.

At the brow of the incline in a small clearing stood a chapel white as a star there above the sea. There was fresh dung outside and he stopped a moment and sniffed. His stomach tightened strangely. Horse dung, a magical smell. He stood a few moments, looking at the dung and the chapel, blowing a little after the long climb. He stumped over to the door and touched it, pushed it gingerly back on its hinges. Behind him, a stand of quail flushed unseen and caused him to flinch.

A musty breeze circled out of the dimness of the place. Scully stepped inside. It was cool. The narrow windows let in rods of light ahead, and against the gable was a simple sanctuary and altar. An ikon, a sad Christ face all gold and burgundy, was animated by the three candles that burned there in the silence. Scully's mouth went dry and his arms ached. He had a horrible weak urge to kneel here on the concrete floor, but with the child on his back he was spared the exercise. He pursed his lips to speak, but the silence of the chapel was overpowering, so he turned for the door and saw, framed in the light, a woman. He flinched and grunted. She had a black dress and shawl.

'*Yassou*, *Kyria*,' he said in greeting.

Her eyes were black and on her feet were wide, men's shoes. She held a twig broom in her hands and inclined her head towards him and stood aside to let him pass.

'*Efkharisto*,' he whispered. 'Thank you.'

She pointed her broom across the flat ridge where the road continued on across the spine of the island to Episkopi.

She knows, too, he thought. The wind lapped around her shawl and she did not move. She kept pointing along the road and her face was expressionless. As he came by her through the door, he saw the gob of spit hit the gravel before him and heard it again behind. He turned and saw her calmly making the sign of the cross against her flat chest.

He stumped off up the road, too angry to pause and drink at

the cistern beside the track. The child was a sack on his back. All around him the pines sounded like an inhaling choir. He went on, determined now to get it over with and get on the hydrofoil at six as Arthur suggested. He might just make it. Say his piece, whatever it was he had left to say when it came down to it, and piss off back into the smoking ruins of his life.

UP FROM THE FINAL STONY GULLY, he came into the ragged conglomeration of huts, hunting lodges and houses that was Episkopi. A few mules were tethered outside a pillarbox lodge that echoed with snores. Scully felt drool running down his neck. He hiked the kid up on his back a little and walked on through to the big fresh whitewashed house at the cliff where the island fell away to the open sea on the other side.

The house was broad and plain and seemed to have settled into the topsoil of this bony edge of the mountain. The solitary fig stood before it, casting a black rag of shadow at its feet. The grey shutters were ajar and as Scully came up closer, he heard the sound of a tin whistle fidgeting from inside. He was footsore, perspiring, thirsty, and all his rage had left him. He looked up at the house he'd cut and carried the blocks for with nothing more than sadness.

'Alex?'

The tin whistle faltered and stopped. A low voice. Or voices.

'You there, Alex?'

A scuffling sound, a chair kicked across a stone floor. Scully slipped Billie from his back and let her stand groggy beside him. He wiped the sweat from his eyes and then his hands, and braced himself at the door. He was way past irony, further past violence.

In his rumpled cardigan and bifocals, as he tipped the heavy door back, Alex Moore didn't look anything but guilty. His hand went to his mouth. He stepped back, looked across his shoulder a moment and then back at them.

'Oh. My stars. Billie girl!'

'Hello, Alex,' said Scully.

'Scully!'

'Ask us in, Alex.'

# *Eighteen*

ALEX STOOD IN HIS DOORWAY A MOMENT, swaying, scratching his head, and Scully thought maybe he should thump him one after all, just to get things rolling, but the old man suddenly backed away indoors and Scully took Billie's hand and followed.

The interior was a raving shambles. There were bottles underfoot and saucers brimming with fag ends, cheese rind, olive pips. Every surface was covered with old pages of the *Observer*. The place stank of retsina, of smoke and bad food. On the big pine table lay a block of creamy paper, a bucket of tubes, a jar of pencils and nibs, and a small raw canvas on a stretcher, all lying there ceremonially untouched.

'You heard, then,' said Alex, pushing open the doors onto the terrace.

Scully followed him out into the clean air.

'No bastard told me anything.'

'Well, you must have known something.'

'Guess I had my suspicions.'

'Well. Here it is. Here I am.'

Scully looked at the defeated curve of the little man's back and then glanced again around the house. It's a sign, he thought. She's lost her mind. The little shit's using her while she's not in a fit state. No one would come and live like this without having fallen off the edge of the world somehow. This isn't bohemian, it's Third World.

'Didn't last long,' murmured Alex. 'I'm a living wreck. It always starts well, doesn't it, a resolution, a new thing.'

'So she's gone?'

'Hmm?'

'Oh, come on, Alex, don't shit me.'

'Well, you are the first to come gloating. If the others were capable of the walk, that's what they'd all do.'

'What'd you think I came all this way for, the smell of your dirty socks and the view from your terrace? I want my wife.'

'Your *wife*?'

Alex's Adam's apple twitched.

'Billie, go inside.'

'Scully, I –'

'I just want to take her home, get her some help, Alex. It's alright, I'm not gonna *do* anything.'

'Jennifer.' Alex leaned against the cool wall and looked down the blackened slope to the sea. Billie stood by the door expressionless and unmoving. A cat slid between her feet, leapt up to the parapet and stood before Alex expectantly.

'Where is she, Alex?'

Alex smiled and looked at him with moist eyes. 'You're looking for her here, with *me*? My dear boy, are you well?'

'I'll go up myself. Billie, stay here.'

Room by squalid room, Scully went through the place, his disgust and fear mounting as he opened cupboards and poked under beds. The main room upstairs had its share of bottles and crusts and stubs, and the four-poster bed was tormented with grey linen and blankets which he prodded fearfully in the gloom. He sat on the bed a moment, staring at the assembly of pill bottles on the table beside it, and knew finally that she wasn't here, that she'd probably never been there at all. There would have been some relief at least to have seen and known the worst. And that was it – he saw how much crueller it was to know nothing at all.

When he came back down onto the terrace, Billie sat with her back to the house wall and Alex had his head in his hands. A breeze lifted up from the sea, bringing with it the carbon smell of burnt country. He knew that smell from his own continent. The afternoon sun lay across the water and a yellow haze crept up on the horizon to seal out the distance.

'Alex, I'm sorry.'

The old man wiped his eyes on the sleeve of his cardigan and smiled hopelessly.

'You know, it's very flattering, really. I haven't had a scene like this for ten years.'

Scully opened his hands and closed them.

'You see it has an ugly irony, this scene, even without a child present,' he murmured with his neck bent meekly. 'Because you see, Scully . . . well, it's just plain bloody funny, really.' Alex laid his almost transparent hand along the parapet. His nails were yellow, he smiled his saurian kiss-arse smile. 'Because I'm, I'm not up to it, any more. I'm fucking *impotent*. Hah, now there's a phrase!'

'Alex –'

'Why don't you stay for dinner?' the old man said, clapping his hands together feebly.

Scully laughed. 'Oh, my God!'

Alex laughed a long time with him but his guffaws grew into sobs that bent him in half, and Scully stood there a while, watching the poor wretched bastard cry, before going across and putting a hand on his back.

'It's alright, mate.'

Alex straightened and clutched at him.

Scully felt the other man's head against his chest, his breath hot on him. He glanced at Billie who had already looked away. The afternoon died around him, the six o'clock hydrofoil came and went and night came on quickly.

AFTER SCULLY GOT THE FIRE GOING with olive twigs and chunks of almond wood, he went through Alex's sorry kitchen and found sheep's yoghurt, garlic, a cucumber and a few things in cans that he went to work on while Alex played the tin whistle to Billie. On the table stood a bottle of rosé from Patras and a litre of Cretan red. Billie stroked the cat and smiled weakly now and then during Alex's shaky rendition of 'The Wild Colonial Boy'. With all the lamps lit, and some tired old pasta boiling on the stove, Scully cleaned the place up a bit.

'You're spoiling me,' said Alex.

'Well.' Scully smiled, couldn't help himself. 'You're used to it, aren't you? Let's face it, Alex, you've been pampered all your life.'

The old man assented grandly with a flutter of eyelids.

'How long has she been gone?'

'Two days,' said Scully. 'I went to the airport to collect them and only Billie got off the plane. Hasn't said a word since.'

'What about the police?'

'Maybe after I've tried everything else.'

'My God, we're both in the wars,' said Alex pouring himself a glass of rosé and emptying it in one gulp.

'Things are bad for you too, then,' Scully said, looking at his own empty glass.

'I came up here to work. Dear Arthur suggested it. Trying to save my life and talent, he fancies.'

'Not working.'

'No, I'm lost, my boy. You know they used once to take their old people up to the cliffs in baskets, on this island. When they had become a burden. In harsher times. Used to throw them off, you know. Gives a new twist to the old fogey's sport of basket-weaving, don't you think? Or being a basket case.'

Scully watched him drain another glass, and finally just poured himself one.

'I used to be a painter, Scully, and then something of a cocks-man and a scoundrel, excuse me, dear, and nowadays I'm lucky if I qualify as a scoundrel.'

'Oh, you'd scrape in,' said Scully, watching the old bugger hammering the wine again.

'You think so?' said Alex brightening.

Scully brought tzatziki to the table with some wrinkled olives, three boiled eggs and some fettucine in garlic and kalamata oil.

'Poor man's fare tonight,' he said sitting down. 'Billie, come and eat something, mate.'

The three of them sat with the fire snapping peaceably behind them. Outside the wind pressed about in the silence. Scully watched Alex chewing tentatively, as though his teeth were sore. He sucked down more rosé. He looked like a greedy little boy.

'Don't waste your life, Scully. Or hers,' he said, motioning with his head at Billie.

'I don't plan to.'

'She's a nice girl, Jennifer.'

'Yeah. I always thought so.'

'But no artistic instincts whatsoever.'

'What?'

'Well, besides sensibly deserting domestic bliss.'

Scully poured himself the last of the rosé to ease his discomfort. 'She wants to be something creative,' he murmured.

'It's not something to want. It's something you have. It's a curse. One she doesn't have.'

'You weren't saying that to either of us when we were paying you to teach her. Sitting out on the terrace with the easels up and all that.'

'My dear boy, I needed the money and it was no ordeal. She has the most delectable pair of legs.'

'You *are* a bloody scoundrel,' said Scully just managing a friendly tone.

'Well, all is not lost.'

Billie finished picking at her food and slid off her chair to return to the cat. Scully thought he'd better finish up and go.

'I think Jennifer missed something she wants to get back, that's all,' said Alex with grease down his chin. 'She's something of a snob, a dilettante. She wants recognition. She wants to be more *interesting*.'

'Yes.'

'And she has wonderful legs.'

'Is she on the island?'

'I've been here for weeks and see no one but old Athena who looks out for me down there at the chapel. I couldn't say.'

'You've got no idea? No one you think she might . . . be with.'

'The expats? No.'

'Rory?'

'Good God, no, give her some credit. Rory's a reptile.'

'I think he's modelled himself on you.'

'Badly, badly.'

'No one?'

'One of the islanders? No, they couldn't keep a secret longer than a nanosecond, though plenty would have had hopes, I dare say. A summer fling that stuck, perhaps?'

'Hadn't thought of that,' said Scully. 'A tourist, you mean?'

Alex shrugged. Scully thought of it. It meant she probably hadn't come back here at all necessarily. And the baby? Oh, why did there have to be the baby? But he still knew nothing. There might have been no fling, no other man. She might have arrived in Ireland by now, having expected Billie to pass on some message. God, his head was fit to burst.

'I'm sorry for all the money,' said Alex without much conviction.

'She'll slit your throat in your sleep when she finds out.'

'I'd have thought she'd be rather flattered. Tell her about the legs part.'

'Alex, she's serious. I don't think it's a fad. She really wants to be something more.'

'You're too soft on people, my boy. You think the best of them. She just wants to be noticed.'

'What happened to you, Alex?'

'Me? Oh, the opposite. I became too interesting. To myself and others. I became a sodding entertainment. I stayed too long.'

'Why don't you just leave, get off the island?'

The old man laughed. 'In a basket perhaps. I don't know how to live in the world anymore. Thirty years is a long time.'

Alex sighed, opened the litre of Cretan red and poured himself a glass, leaving Scully's empty again.

Scully reached for the wine and poured a long glass. It tasted as dark as it looked.

'I suppose you'll go back to town and tell them I'm up here with nothing to show for the great retreat. I can see the gloating tradesman's look on your face even now.'

'Have an olive, Alex.'

The old man pressed his fingers into his eyes and sighed. 'I'm sorry, Scully. I'm a pig.'

'Scoundrel is the polite term, I believe.'

Alex laughed, his eyes tearing up again.

'You can't paint?'

'Your wife and I have that in common now. So, what will you do? Now that you're a deserted husband.'

Scully drank off his wine, poured himself another, and looked at his scarred hands. 'I don't know.'

'Don't follow them, it's undignified.'

'I don't care about dignified. I'll follow. Anyway, I have to think about it a bit. What about you?'

'I'm going to put myself out of my misery. Cheers!' Alex gulped at his wine and closed his eyes with pleasure.

'I've gotta go.'

'Yes, there's a child to consider. You could stay here,' he said hopefully.

'Thanks, but we'll hoof it.'

'Wait, I've got something for you.'

Alex scurried upstairs while Scully straightened Billie's pullover and retied her shoes. There were bluish shadows beneath her eyes and she reacted irritably to his touch.

'Here it is.'

Scully stood and helped Alex with a battered folio which he laid over the table, across the food and unwashed dishes. From it the old man drew a yellowed sheet of paper which Scully accepted silently. It was a pen-and-ink drawing of a Parisian street scene, richly detailed and quite beautiful.

'Rue de Seine,' said Alex. 'Nineteen-sixty.'

'I was three years old in nineteen-sixty.'

'Just promise me you won't show it on this island. Those vipers have had their last laugh on me. Bacon liked that one.'

Scully felt giddy with wine and fatigue. It was a real piece of work, even he could see it.

'Thank you, Alex.'

'Here, roll it up. Say hello to that girl when she turns up. Tell her to go back to bureaucracy. As a form of parasitism it's far more efficient. Speaking of which, you wouldn't have a few spare drachs, would you?'

Scully dug in his pocket, laughing.

THE NIGHT WAS CLEAR AND SHARP. There was no moon and the gravel track unwound dimly. The island was silent as Scully carried his daughter across its spine and down through the piney groves in the shadow of the mountains. It was late when he found the wide flat path above Kamini and came by the cemetery with all its lit candles and shrines. He stopped by the wall feeling Billie asleep against his sweating neck, and watched the flickering at the heads of tombs where cats slunk about fattened with shadows and bristling at the rattle of plastic flowers. Sweat turned cold on him, and looking at that little lake of candles, he was afraid without knowing why. He went on, almost at a trot, until he began the descent into the harbour of the place he had once loved.

He came finally and sleepily to the hotel whose courtyard door was still ajar, and he took Billie upstairs, fumbled noisily with the key as she slid down his back, and got her in to lay her on the bed. He undressed her and slipped her beneath the blanket. Starlight sloped in faintly through the balcony doors and the fishhook of the harbour shimmered below. He needed to sleep, needed to think, but the water reminded him hopelessly of other nights, and he left Billie sleeping, crossed the courtyard and slipped out through the gate.

## *Nineteen*

ALEX MOORE SHUFFLES BACK from the donkeymen's hut with the bootleg ouzo clutched coldly to his chest. The stars hang down through the sighing pines in the most irritating and painterly fashion. The earth is uneven, so bloody terrestrial ahead of him.

The big white house yawns before him, empty, virginal – yes, face it, virginal in every imaginable sense – and he goes stooped and bagtrousered up the steps to the heavy door and the waiting silence.

Out on the terrace he pours himself two fingers of ouzo and doesn't bother with the water. Damnation, what he's done with two good fingers in his time. He laughs aloud and hears the nasty little crone sound of it. Here's to you, Scully, this one's yours, you poor creeping jesus.

Alex feels the papery smoothness of his palms brushing together. Out in the distance the late slice of moon tracks across the water in a showy effect that's quite risible in anyone's terms. The whole dreamfield of the Aegean warps off into blackness. He lights a cigarette and watches the prissy little glow of it out here in the waning night. Look at that moon. God making a mockery of good taste, a final petty insult.

He finds himself thinking of those heavenly caramel legs, stretched before him on the terrace down at Vlikos. If he'd been up to it, would he have? She was such an eager beaver, and thwarted ambition is so sexy. After all, isn't that what they went for in me all these years, my heroic and erogenous failure, the glory of my tremendously fucked-up life? I should know.

Alex tries to think of who did, but no one springs to mind. He tips the glass off the parapet and drinks straight from the bottle. What a prize she'd have made. Poor simple Scully. She was a bomb waiting to go off on him. And such a nice boy, cooking and cleaning and buying a man in extremis a bottle. Something terribly provincial in that kind of niceness. The patience of Job and the face of the Cyclops. A strange lack of pride. Women want monsters, doesn't he know?

He lurches up and opens his fly, pulls his poor dead dick, the old John Thomas, his faithful Ioannis Tomassis, out into the moonlight. A real man should take it out into a field and shoot it the way he would a lame horse. He pours ouzo over the beaten little bugger and feels it sting righteously. Like a lump of jade in his gut, green and ragged and heavy, he feels his envy for that poor little shit, Scully. Hatred. A stone in him of real hatred for what he has despite it all. The also-rans will inherit the earth, the whelps, the meek and the fucking nice, and that's what he can no longer stand.

Alex throws his head back and lets the ouzo trickle down his neck, first rate to the bitter end. *Voilà!*

# *Twenty*

THE ALLEYS WERE EMPTY and the whole town smelt of exhausted geraniums and chalky whitewash as Scully wound his way down the labyrinth of steps to the harbour. Along the waterfront the lights still shone but the last taverna was closing. He bought an ouzo from a sleepy man and his wall-eyed son who swept around him and stacked chairs against the wall. Scully sat half in the light and sipped, listening to the sea chop outside the mole. Caiques and smaller boats tossed lightly and turned at their moorings. Across the smooth flagstones cats went stalking. Scully's back ached from hauling Billie and his feet were sore, but inside now there was a curious deadening, a rising blank. He had a second ouzo which he drank quickly so as not to keep the men awake any longer. A little tipsy, he bade them goodnight and walked out by the water, where tiny mullet flickered under the lights.

He was dead inside now, but it didn't stop him remembering. Quiet nights like this back over in the village at Vlikos. Breathless nights with heat still radiating from the stones of the island, when the house was heady with the smoke of mosquito coils and the drapes hung lifeless against the walls, and the little cluster of houses lay in darkness. The only sound the tinkling of goat bells up the mountain. Those nights, under cover of darkness, the two of them left Billie asleep and slipped down naked and giggling to the pebble beach. The water was cool and black. They stroked out between moored boats, stirring up trails of phosphorescence that clung to their bodies like strings of tiny pearls. Old Sotiris, soaking his feet below the local taverna, would puff on his cigarette at the end of his long day and not see them out in the darkness. Some nights he played his battered guitar and sang mournfully, unaware of their presence.

In September, the night she came back from Piraeus with the pregnancy confirmed, they made love down there on a smooth ledge where his back pressed into the rock and the water surged through her slick legs as they clamped about him and her breasts glistened in his face. He held her buttocks in his hands as she rose on him. On the cliff above, mules clattered along the track. She pressed him hard into the rock, hard into herself, the flat of her hand across his face until she cried out like a bird, a surprised, plaintive sound that travelled across the water, across his skin as a sudden burn. Scully was never so happy. He had the life he wanted, the people he loved.

Scully walked up by the old cannons at the head of the harbour and looked down at the roof of the grotto. The sea was fairly placid but a change was upon it. He stepped down over the smooth rocks and found the swimmer's platform the town fathers had built for the tourists. For a moment, he sat, looking down at the faint light on the water. The sweat of the day, the shock, the worry, the fear and disappointment were rancid on him. There was dust in his hair and grit in his shoes. There was no one about

– stuff it, a swim was better than a bath, and he needed something, some good clear sensation to sponge off such a bastard day.

He stripped and hit the water in an ugly flat dive that stung his belly and rang his balls like bells, so it took him ten seconds or more to realise just how cold the water was, and to know suddenly how much booze he had on board. Submarine light, a phosphorescent glow struck the ceiling of the grotto and lit the submerged rocks with a ghostly ice blue that pulsed and surged like the garish pool of a five-star hotel, a blue that slipped further from him the longer he watched.

'Ugh!' His shock was audible. He struck out in a frenzied crawl, the hurried stroke of the dam swimmer, the creek scrambler, the Pommie tourist, the pissed and careless idiot. He punched the water. It burned pale in his eyes, and when he rested to check his progress and calm himself, he saw that he'd made no ground at all, and the grotto was slipping to the right. He went at it again, measured and hard, kicking straight and postponing every second breath, stretching himself, making cups of his hands as he raked downward, till lights spattered his vision and the taste of ouzo rose in his sinuses. His breath was gone. He couldn't do it. God, he couldn't do it. The grotto slipped further round. He went into a hopeless, panting breaststroke and saw the grotto disappear altogether, swallowed by the black featureless bluff that reared like the face of God. Scully stopped swimming. He hung there, hyperventilating. He turned on his back. That blackness was too much to behold. His nuts felt like snapper sinkers.

Geez, Scully, he thought, you've really made a day of it. A class act. Making an arse of yourself in a thousand ways, and now this. Live stupid, die young.

He felt the first twinge of cramp in his toes, up his calves.

Scully, you're a loser.

That vast field of black towered above him.

Spineless, that's what. A stumblebum. Of course she left you – there's nothing *to* you.

Cold eddies tweaked at his limbs. He could feel his body closing down and he began to shake. There were no stars in the sky anymore and his ears roared with a cruel lapping sound. He guessed this was the moment when you were allowed to feel sorry for yourself. The blow to his head shook him right through and suddenly it was more than he could stand for. He rolled angrily on his belly to face down this last humiliation and saw the otherworldly mass of the harbour mole sliding past an arm's length away. The flashing light of the navigational beacon blurted in his face, and a small wave picked him up and dumped him splayed and spluttering on the cold glossy rocks where he lay too sick and sorry to be either grateful or amused. He held on and thought glumly of his clothes right around the other side of the harbour and the long naked walk under lights that awaited him.

# *Twenty-one*

FROM A DREAMLESS PIT OF SLEEP, Scully came to himself alone in bed with the shutters shuddering and his head a stone on the end of his neck.

'Billie?'

He lurched upright. 'Billie?'

He saw his grazes and bruises as he dragged on his clothes. He lurched out into the corridor and down to the bathroom, but the communal door was ajar and the smelly room empty. Three at a time he went down the stairs into the courtyard where rain speared in and cats congregated in tiny patches of shelter in the corners of walls where withered grapevines and dripping painted gourds rattled in the wind.

'*Kyria? Kyria?*' he called, his voice breaking.

The heavy oak door to the kitchen opened.

'*Neb?*'

The little woman wiped her hands on her apron and narrowed her eyes at him contemptuously. Scully stood in the rain and saw behind her, sitting by the range with a bowl of soup in her lap, his daughter who looked up curiously at him.

'Oh, oh, good-oh.'

Right there in the rain, across the kalamata tins of battered geraniums and the wall of bougainvillea, he stood aside and puked until the door closed on him.

IT WAS AFTERNOON when Scully woke again. He showered gingerly, packed their things and went down to collect Billie. The rain had not let up and the wind bullied across the courtyard where his mess was long gone. He knocked at the door and the woman looked him up and down, stepped aside to let him in.

'*Signomi, Kyria. Ema arostos*. Sick. I am very sorry. Um, we'll go now. Thank you for looking after my child. How much? Um, *poso kani*?'

Scully put some bills on the table and the woman shrugged.

'C'mon, Bill.'

Billie stood up, hair freshly brushed, her mouth and cheeks raw with the spreading rash, and came to him. *Kyria* Dina stooped and kissed her thick curls, and then Billie put her hand in his and they went out into the rain, across the courtyard, and into the alley where water ran ankle deep in a torrent gathering from the mountain, the high town, the Kala Pigadia. They made their way down, hopping from step to dry step without conversation.

THE WATERFRONT WAS DESERTED and awash with storm water that spilled across the wharf and into the harbour. Boats lunged against their moorings. The sky was black above the sea and the swell ponderous against the moles.

At the flying dolphin office, the clerk informed them that there would be no hydrofoils and no ferries today. The harbour was closed, and no vessel was allowed to venture out. Scully looked out at the heaving sea. Even the Peloponnese was just a smudge. Things could change, he knew, and a boat from Spetsai or Ermione might come by if the swell dropped. But it would be quick turnover at the water's edge, so the only way to be sure of a passage was to wait the day out close by. He gathered himself giddily and headed for the Lyko. There was no choice – it was the closest to where the boats pulled in, and besides, nothing else was open. And, God help him, he had to make sure.

The taverna was smoky and full, but aside from the rain thrumming against the fogged panes and the crackling of the charcoal grill, it was quiet. The pale ovals of faces turned momentarily, then obscured themselves. Scully hefted his case between chairs and tables and led Billy to where Arthur Lipp folded his newspaper and cleared space for them at his table beside the bar.

'You might as well sit.'

'Hello, Arthur.'

'You look terrible.'

'I feel terrible.'

'Not terrible enough, I fear.' Arthur pulled at his moustache and regarded him carefully.

'Gee, thanks.'

'You went up to Episkopi.'

'Yeah, I did.'

'You can't be told, can you?'

'What, am I in school? I thought my wife was there, Arthur. I went to see.'

'Your bloody wife!' Arthur tossed his paper aside. 'For God's sake, man, she's left you, so why don't you just take it on the chin and go home!'

'Why don't you mind your own business, you pompous little shit?'

'Because it's your business and our business now!' yelled Rory from a table across the way.

Scully stood up. 'Look at you fuckers sitting around day after day like some soap opera! What business of yours could possibly interest me?'

Arthur Lipp sighed. 'The final business of Alex Moore.'

Scully looked down at Arthur whose tan had gone yellow and his eyes quite pink.

'I didn't interrupt any work, if that's what you mean. He hasn't done a thing, poor bugger.'

'Poor bugger indeed.' Arthur looked away. 'What on earth did you say to him?'

'I had dinner with him – hell, I *cooked* dinner for him. Stayed a while and walked back. What d'you think I'd do to him, beat him up? He's an old man. I apologised for busting in, cleaned up his kitchen . . . anyway, he said you could all get stuffed.'

'Stavros Kolokouris the donkeyman found his body at the bottom of the cliff this morning.'

Scully looked at Billie. She shouldn't he hearing this, none of this today, or yesterday or the day before. This wasn't right.

'The police have set out to recover the body. It'll take them a good few hours without boats.'

'He . . . he gave me . . .'

'They'll want to know if he was pushed.'

'There wasn't a note?'

'Why, write one, did you?' yelled Rory.

'I –'

'Save your story,' said Arthur, not unkindly.

'You mean the cops want to see me?'

'Well, they know you were up there.'

'Shit, thanks for putting in a good word.'

'You were seen,' said Arthur.

He caught Rory's glance, grabbed his case and Billie's back-pack and hoisted her along with him, through faces and talk and smoke into the wild clean air of the harbour. In blasting rain he dragged child and luggage along the waterfront. Sponge-crowded windows ran with the blur of water. He came to a lane that led to the Three Brothers. Lying miserably on its leash in the rain, was a big dog so saturated as to barely look like a dog anymore. Scully and Billie swept by it and ran to the door and the smell of frying calamari.

Fishermen, muleteers, old men and loungers drank coffee and ouzo and played *tavla*. Scully saw a table by the wall and claimed it.

'Eh, Afstralia!'

It was Kufos – the Deaf One – rising from his chair.

'*Yassou*,' said Scully, dripping onto the plastic tablecloth.

Kufos strode over, gold teeth glinting, his keg chest expanding as he came.

'Leetle Afstralia!' he said, digging Billie in the back of the neck with his thumbs. '*Ti kanis?*'

Scully motioned for him to sit down and the old caique captain flicked up the wicker-bottom chair and sat.

'No happy today, ah?'

Billie shook her head.

'You come back to Hydra?' he said to Scully. 'So fast.'

'Only for today,' said Scully with a shrug. 'For Piraeus, no boats today.'

'Ah, too much this!' said the skipper, making waves with his hands.

'Yeah.'

Scully always liked Kufos. He was a proud and arrogant old bugger who liked to curse the tourists and take their money. He had been a merchant seaman and he told Scully garbled stories of Sydney and Melvorno and the girls he'd left weeping behind. Nowadays he ferried *xeni* around the island and fished a little for octopus, but he preferred to sit out under the waterfront marquees and watch the tourist women in their bikinis. He was a fine sailor, and given credit on the island for being the last man to call it quits when it came to a big sea. Scully ordered him an ouzo.

'Sick, this girl?'

'Sad.'

'*Kyria* in Afstralia?'

Scully smiled noncomittally.

'We need to go to Piraeus.'

'Is too much. Finis, today. No dolphin, no boat.'

'Yeah, I know. But would *you* go?' Scully said, leaning into the man whose grey whiskers were as stiff as a deckbrush.

Kufos looked doubtful.

'For maybe three thousand drachmae, Captain?'

Scully wrote the number in the plastic with his fingernail and the old man pursed his lips.

'Four thousand?' Scully murmured.

Kufos scratched his chin.

'Okay, five, then.'

Plates clashed in the kitchen and men laughed and argued around them. The drinks came and the waiter, unasked, laid a bowl of soup before Billie. She looked at it a moment, its steam rose in her face and she took up the spoon.

'Five thousand,' said Scully. 'It's fifty dollars. Not even to Piraeus, just to Ermione across the channel.'

Kufos sipped his ouzo and sat back a while, watched Billie eat her soup. She paused after a few moments and the old man wiped her face with a paper napkin.

'This is good girl. You like my boat?'

Billie nodded. She seemed to have rallied somewhat. She was a little more responsive. He knew he had the old man close to a deal. It was time to go. He didn't know where to go, but it was definitely time to get off this island. He felt certain Jennifer wasn't here. She might never have been here. She might have caught the six o'clock hydrofoil yesterday while he was at Episkopi. She had plenty of warning, if she hadn't wanted to see him. And now with this Alex business he was panicky, feeling trapped. At the very best, if the cops were relaxed about it, it would take time and the trail would cool. What bloody trail – he just had to get off the island.

Outside the rain had stopped and the dog caught his eye, rising to its feet to shake itself. Water blurred from it and Billie slipped off her chair.

'Don't go far, love.'

Billie passed by the crowded tables and headed for the door. Scully saw now; it was the dog from the hydrofoil again.

'Ermione is too much.'

'Fifteen, twenty kilometres.'

'Too much this,' Kufos said with the wave motion again.

'How about Hydra beach just across there. That's less than ten.'

'*Signomi, Kyrios* Afstralia. My boat she is too much slow for this. You take taxi Niko.'

'Nick Meatballs?'

'*Neb*. Is fast. Volvo Penta.'

Scully sat back. Meatballs was the biggest macho on the island. His taxi was the envy of every man and boy. Seventeen feet. 165 horsepower sterndrive and a sliding perspex canopy like an old Spitfire fighter plane. Forty knots on a smooth sea, no sweat. Joan Collins and Leonard Cohen had been among his passengers last summer. Meatballs was a living legend.

'*Pou ine?* Where is he?'

Kufos shrugged, seeing the money elude him.

Scully ordered a bottle of Metaxa for the old man and offered his thanks. Then there was a growl and a scream from outside, and the whole taverna was in uproar.

## *Twenty-two*

SCULLY RAN ACROSS TABLES to get outside where Billie sat bellowing inside her mask of blood. Her eyes were blank and wide as coins. Scully held her rigid in his arms and spoke quietly to her in the moments before the terrace was overrun with shouting men and women. With his fingers he probed her face for the wounds and found punctures in her cheek, her forehead, an eyebrow. With his handkerchief he wiped the gore away for a moment and saw that there was a gash in front of her ear and a hole in her scalp that showed a flap of fatty tissue. He tried to soothe her, calm her before anything else, but it was impossible with all the yelling and the many hands that reached for her in sympathy. He hoisted her on his hip in time to see old Kufos beating the dog to death with his unopened bottle of Metaxa, and he ran for the hospital.

Along the cobbled alleys slippery as creekbeds, Scully slid and lurched, leaving a bright trail on the stones. He saw the open eyes and mouths of people at their doors as he plunged across the square and through the ghostly trunks of the whitewashed lemon trees to the clinic steps.

He found a dim corridor, an empty room, then a roomful of bored people with their backs to the walls. They rose, startled, fearful, shouting, and then the mob came behind to surge in with their roars and bellows and great indecipherable swathes of language. He wanted to shout, to demand, but his breath was gone and he could not think of enough words in Greek.

Two women in white stiff-armed their way through the crowd and their eyes widened and their businesslike boredom evaporated. The child's face was so disfigured by lumpy, dark blood, and her clothes so spattered and gluey with it, that it was hard to know what she was, let alone what the problem might be. They grabbed her, but Billie clung to him. Her nails pierced his clothes and found his skin. Men shouted across him to the staff who dragged them both into another room where a male doctor waited with a cigarette and a stethoscope.

The doctor motioned kindly, almost jovially as the nurses continued to pry Billie from Scully's chest. At the big stainless steel sink they held her arms and head and swabbed her face. Her eyes were mad. Cattle eyes. Killing yard eyes. Her screams felt as though they could shave paint from the walls. The staff squinched up their faces. They lost any composure they might have planned on displaying when she bared her teeth and lunged at all those dark, hairy forearms locked about her.

*'Ochi, ochi!'*

The doctor howled as Billie latched onto his wrist, gnashing and growling. The others let go in an instant and Billie crashed back against her father's chest.

'That's it! That's enough. She's fucking hysterical, she's scared out of her mind, for Godsake!'

'Scully?' someone called behind him.

He wheeled and saw Arthur with Kufos who had blood and brains all down his tunic.

'Tell them to give me some stuff and I'll fix her up myself! She's shitscared.'

'What are you going to do, sew her up on your own?' cried Arthur.

'Just tell em.'

'What about the scars?'

'Oh, Jesus Christ, help me!'

Screaming, screaming. Circus. Nightmare. Slow-motion pantomime. Scully's sinews sprang in him like wires. His spine creaked with fear and hatred. He was drowning in noise, flapping hopelessly between words he couldn't recognize. He tried to soothe Billie, almost sobbing his pleas to her, while Arthur and Kufos argued with the staff who shook their heads and waved their hands in outrage. Back and forward, the words, the scowls, the pleading, the slapping of fists and hands, and then when Scully realized he wasn't breathing anymore, he turned with Billie in his arms and bolted from the room with the crowd parting fearfully before him. Down the long antiseptic corridor, the anterooms with their lordly portraits, and out onto the rain fresh steps beneath the sky where he roared until he felt her hands on his bursting throat and her voice in his ear.

'Stop. Stop, it hurts!'

## *Twenty-three*

ARTHUR BROUGHT ANOTHER BOWL OF HOT WATER and Scully gritted his teeth and cut the patch of matted hair with the nail scissors. Billie closed her eyes and sucked in a breath as his fingertip pressed the flap of scalp down and took up the disposable razor. Arthur averted his eyes. Scully felt his arse tighten as he applied the blade to the wound and shaved the ragged skin. He saw the tears run from her tight-shut eyes and kept at it until the wound was clean and bleeding freshly again. The scalp lifted enough to sicken him.

'You can't sew that, Scully.'

'Gimme those strip things, will you? We'll press it flat and get it together again.'

'The hospital wants you to sign a form.'

'Just wash those scissors again, will you?'

Billie began to whimper as he squeezed antiseptic into this last gash.

'You're a brave girl,' he murmured with a quaver in his voice. 'Nearly finished.'

'Kufos came for me,' said Arthur.

'Yes,' Scully said, wiping the bald patch dry.

'He said you wanted Nikos Keftedes.'

'Arthur, the strips, okay? She's in pain here.'

'The sea's treacherous out there,' Arthur said, wrestling a pack of steri-strips open.

'Here, hold the flaps down with your thumbs.'

'Oh, dear. You should have –'

'Just put your thumbs . . . right, I'll bind it closed. Hold tight, love.'

Billie cried out as the men's fingers pressed at her. Her feet rose into their bellies and her back arched from the sofa. She was sweating and the strips wouldn't stick.

'More strips.'

No light came in through the unshuttered windows now, and the wind harried the glass. Scully smelled the tobacco closeness of the Englishman as they worked on grimly with the child squirming and crying out. He whispered and crooned, hating the bluntness of his fingers.

'That's got it.'

'Thank Christ.'

Scully took Billie in his arms to steady himself. Her face was livid with wounds, swollen and plastered in spots, her hairline ragged above one eye.

'Thank you, Arthur. Can you sell me a blanket?'

Arthur stopped fussing with the bowl and implements. 'Sell you?'

Scully reached down and grabbed the small suitcase and the child's backpack in one hand and hefted Billie onto his hip.

'The cops'll be back about now.'

'You're not saying you really did it?'

'I'm saying I want to go.'

'They might chase you, you know.'

'Maybe.'

'What the dickens happened to you?'

Scully laughed sourly. 'You could say I'm having a bit of a rough trot just now.' He felt his mouth losing shape as he said it, and the Englishman put the bowl down, went to the window and lit a cigar.

'I just have to know.'

'Why should you be the only one getting answers?'

'He was a friend.'

'He talked about how they threw old people off the cliff in baskets. I didn't think anything of it. I was preoccupied, I guess. I'm really sorry, Arthur. It's horrible.'

Arthur puffed on his cigar, trembling a little. 'Of course he was making that little bit of folklore up. Vain little prat.'

The house was cold and quiet. Its seaman's furniture gleamed darkly. The Persian rug across the marble floor looked thick and deep enough to sleep in. On the wall across Arthur's shoulder was a small canvas that both of them lit on at the same moment.

'One of his,' murmured Arthur unsteadily.

'I know.'

The painting was a luminous landscape, quite simple. Bare, pale rock. Sleep-blue sky. Perched on a granite cliff over the water was a small, white chapel.

'You know the chapel?'

'Just before Molos.'

'Yes. The wine chapel. A sea captain with a load of wine from Crete was caught in the worst storm of his life, just in sight of this island. He prayed to the Virgin to deliver him and he promised that if he lived he'd build a chapel in her honour. That's what happened. He mixed the mortar with his cargo in payment.

Cement and wine. The wine chapel. Alex's favourite. Not hard to see why. At least that piece of folklore is real.'

He left Scully and Billie alone in the living room. Scully looked at the painting and thought of the afternoons he'd swum below the place spearing octopus and *rofos* with the sun on his back and the water moving across his body like a breeze. In the water there was always a stillness denied the rest of the world, a calm hard to recall standing here shitscared and shellshocked. Underwater there was just temperature, no time, no words, no gravity. It was the kind of thing monks disciplined themselves for, junkies destroyed themselves chasing. Is it what dolphins and birds had now and then, a still point in the centre of things? Murderers? Marathon runners? Artists? Is that what Jennifer was after, this total focus? It was something worth feeling, he had to admit.

Arthur came back in with blankets, painkillers and some food.

'Ten minutes from now, outside the Pirate Bar. Fifteen thousand up front.'

'Thank you.'

'I'll help you down there.'

'I thought Kufos might come by.'

'He's as pissed as a rat, I'm afraid.'

'You mean he didn't break the bottle?'

'The Metaxa? No. He's a big hero tonight.'

'Poor bloody dog.'

'Well, it's a quicker death than the traditional mothball in the minced beef.'

'The owner should be shot.'

'The owner is Kufos' wife. The Albanian.' Arthur waved aside his open mouth. 'Don't ask. Let's go, shall we?'

## *Twenty-four*

ALONG THE DARK SHUTTERED WATERFRONT in the storm, Scully held the shivering child to him and saw Arthur ahead holding grimly to the luggage that bucked and swung in the wind. The sky was starless and whining. Masts lurched amid the shriek of rigging and the seance groan of hawsers. Scully felt himself gone from here. He was almost faint with relief. His eyes ran in the wind and his hair ripped back from his head till it ached at the roots.

Beneath the statue of the hero, its head lit wildly by an upstairs window, the shadow of a man came forth. Arthur met him and Scully heard their hissing. He waited, feeling light, careless, away.

Arthur came back.

'Forget it, Scully. He wants twenty thousand.'

'Give it to him,' said Scully, holding out the flapping wad.

'The price is too high and the sea is too bloody rough.'

'Tell him we go now.'

'For God's sake!'

'Give it to him, Arthur.'

'You're not thinking!' said the Englishman, the pale palms of his hands flashing. 'You're overwrought, Scully!'

'Let's go.'

Scully felt his body unwinding, the heat leaving his temples and feet, and he knew that if the boat didn't leave he'd simply spring from the wharf and hit the water swimming. He saw the flash of Meatballs' teeth, the twinkle of his fingernails as he took the money. The Greek led them down between fishing boats to where his taxi laboured in the swell.

'Was she here, Arthur?' Scully asked as Meatballs slid the canopy back.

Arthur scowled. 'I can't get a straight answer out of anybody. Rory and his chums say things, but can you believe them? Seems certain she's not here now.'

'Fair enough. Thank you.'

'Well, what a pleasant visit.'

'I'll miss the funeral.'

Arthur grunted, shrugged and walked back down the mole.

Scully watched him a moment before stepping down into the taxi. The big Volvo started and purred. Meatballs cast off fore and aft and the boat eased out among the pens. Billie lifted her head to see the lights of the town rising above them like Christmas.

Meatballs throttled down hard.

'You sit! Sit!'

Scully went back to the upholstered bench as the canopy slid shut above them. The Volvo began to bawl. The lights of the Maritime School blurred by above. The boat rose to the plane and then the water beneath them began to harden up as they left the harbour wall.

The first wave crashed across the bow as the navigation lights went on. Water streamed down the windows. Meatballs wore a green halo from the glow of his dashboard. With the harbour police and the moles out of sight already, they rode down into the trough and broke the back of the next swell with a crash that jarred Billie and Scully to the deck. Shaken, the two of them clawed back up and looked for ways to brace themselves. The luggage raced about at their feet. Meatballs shoved a cassette into the tape deck so that bouzouki music screeched through the little cabin. Scully held himself in position and watched Billie's face as they ploughed on into the darkness.

The sea came at them from every point. The boat pitched, rolled, plunged and fluttered. The prop screamed free of the water and hit again. The fibreglass hull shuddered – Scully felt the impact in his teeth. Already he was withdrawing into the deck-hand's stupor, the blankness that kept him sane all those years ago. When it got too awful out there in those days, you simply shut down inside and carried on in autopilot. The deck lurching and heaving, the chop breaking in cold sheets across the wheel-house and the stinking bait washing through the scuppers. Dreamy, that's how he was, with that animal Ivan Dimic at the wheel and the ropes fidgeting from their coils to race over the side. The stinking pots clashing up onto the tipper full of lobsters and sharks and writhing octopus. Yes, Ivan Dimic, last of the fleet to leave and first to return. He fished all day at full throttle, hungover and vicious. From the flying bridge, shrieking down on your dripping head. His was the kind of bestial voice the mad heard, only the man was as real as the torment. Buy first, pay last, and always get your punch in before the other poor cunt sees you coming, that was Ivan's philosophy. Scully stayed with him for the money of course, outrageous in those boom years, and because he believed that things could only get better, that he was capable of getting on top of it. But he didn't come from the same stock as Ivan and the crews he knew in his fishing days. Scully simply wasn't a fighter and the only way to win Ivan over was by force. The deckhand's revenge. Oops. Over the side twenty miles out. It happened. But not for young Scully. All those February mornings hacking back into the easterly, Scully imagined himself elsewhere. But tonight there was only so far out of himself he could go.

Billie began to vomit. There was no way to direct it anywhere; he couldn't hang on and help her as well, so he took the steaming little gouts against his jacket as he hugged her to him. It slicked the seat and filled the cabin with a bitter stink. The poor little bugger. He felt her hands at the back of his neck and hated himself for his stupidity and clumsiness, for letting this happen to her, for being in this insane situation. What else could possibly happen to her? She was so strong, so resilient, but how much could a kid take? He thought maybe he should have stayed, but what use was he to her in jail on a Greek island? There was no telling what could happen with the business of Alex, how things might turn out. He might have gone to a pharmacy, got the doctor out to Arthur's, but the cops were too close and he simply couldn't risk it. And the sight of her mad with fear amongst all those screaming people, the nurses wrestling her down like an animal. No, he couldn't do it to her. He had to pray that she understood, that she knew him well enough to see that this was not normal, that this wasn't what he would ever do unless he had to. But it wasn't right, it shouldn't be like this, she shouldn't have to endure it and the enormity of it cut him to the blood. Some father, Scully, some father.

Meatballs turned, scowling.

'Ermione no good! Hydra Beach we go! Hydra Beach!'

The boat rose out of a trough and hung bawling in the air so long Scully could feel it moving laterally in the wind. When it hit water again, Billie's tartan suitcase burst open and flung underpants, razors, paper all over. He let it go and hung on.

'There's nothing *at* Hydra Beach this time of year! I gave you two hundred bucks!'

'Hydra Beach. Only this.'

Water sluiced back across the canopy and the bow buried momentarily. It was claustrophobic underwater. Strings of pearly bubbles pressed against the screen. The boat shuddered and ground up into the air again. They were an hour out already and Scully knew it could take a lot longer to get down the coast to Ermione. It might take half the night at this rate.

Billie stiffened. The wound in her scalp had begun to bleed again and she was too weak to even cling to him anymore. The deck slopped, and at his feet, half curled and blotted, lay Alex's sketch of the Rue de Seine, its buildings solid and angular, its pavements thick with people, dogs, cars, its high window perspective stupidly reassuring. He found himself staring at it, looking out through its window at the solid earth below.

'Hydra Beach, Afstralia!'

Scully looked up at Nick Meatballs and saw him scared and greenfaced, all the macho bullshit gone. His lips were creamy with spit. Scully looked about for signs of lifejackets – none – and just then the bouzouki clamour fell silent, and the shouting voice of a man on the radio receiver was audible between clashes of static.

Imagine a breakdown in this shit, he thought. All those granite islets. The cliffs of Dokos.

They rolled heavily and crashed sideways into the water that pressed black against the glass.

Alex would be lying on a slab in Hydra harbour by now. The

cops ringing around. The wake being planned. Arthur passing the hat. Buried as an infidel, no doubt. No matter how long you stayed you were always a foreigner in or out of church, alive or dead. Was it me, Alex, because of me?

'Afstralia?'

'Okay, Hydra Beach.'

'You smart boy!'

'Tell me about it.'

He looked down at the smudging Rue de Seine and saw women on the pavement, their hips high with walking. He wanted to go there, to be inside that picture with its smells of Chanel and coffee and cake, to be inside the life of it, in its steady, perfect composition and lightness of touch, but the real world, the twisted nightmare around him had hold too tight. The sea sucked and grabbed and hissed and snatched and Billie's sweat glistened greenly. There was no going into the neatness of the imagination. He could only pray for her to forgive him, to take what was left of him, to strike him dead, to save him.

## *Twenty-five*

DEEP IN SOME BIG, MAD STORY, a Jonah story, a Sinbad story, a Jesus and the fishermen story, the kind that's too true to be strange, too dreamy to be made up, Billie hung onto Scully's jacket and heard the sea growl and saw the sky go underground with her. Sorry sorry sorry sorry sorry sorry sorry sorry he was saying, like a ship's engine driving her along, pushing her across the waves of sickness and pain and pictures that wrenched her. In her head, too, she heard the song from the Up School floating across the wall.

*Something, something, parakalo,*
*Something, something, parakalo . . .*

Her head was too crowded, she was forgetting Greek. What was it they were asking for? For everything to be still? For everything to go back to the way it was? For it all to stop?

Billie saw the poor wet dog. The way its eye moved slowly. The big, pink inside of its mouth and the meaty smell of its breath. And all the people. Yelling at her. The gold in their teeth, the blood stinging her eyes like Pears shampoo. All of them pushing and trying to take her away, twisting her arms, their hairy soft hands all over her. And Scully holding on, his face like a pumpkin, fat and bulgy with fright. She saw the newspaper in the lady's teeth, his hand on her hair, brushing her like a dog, saying words too soft for language. His big heart there in his shirt, the love in his neck. He didn't let go, he didn't let them. The fat cigar, the stink of Mister Arthur's cigar. Gentle fingers on her face. Every shot of pain the chime of an aeroplane toilet sign – ting, ting, ting. A white face in the cloud. Somewhere, too, a tin whistle pweeting. Another surge of people and glass doors peeling back like the sea for Moses and Scully's busted face on the other shore beneath the chiming, tolling, swinging bells. Him not letting go, their fingers making bloodknots and bimini twists and not slipping, tied properly, not giving an inch. The dog had no one now and she had Scully. She was the lucky one.

*Something, something, parakalo,*
*Efkaristo poli . . .*

Yes. She had Scully's heart whamming in her ear like a bell, like God singing.

## *Twenty-six*

SCULLY FELT THE VOLVO BACKING DOWN and knew suddenly that he'd been asleep. The sea was different, the swells long and even. The canopy slid back and a burst of air rushed in. He stood and saw lights, the shapes of houses, a beacon, a mole. They hissed into lee water, throttling down and Scully saw it was Ermione after all.

Billie sat stunned and pale while he got down and shoved their things together. He snapped the case shut, and fitted the little backpack to Billie.

'You know people here?' he said to Meatballs, unsure of whether the bloke had changed his mind or found the port by accident.

'*Neh*, some people,' Meatballs said as they slid in among moored boats.

'Get me a taxi, then, a car. To Athens.'

They swung in against the slimy black fenders of the wharf and Meatballs killed the motor and leapt up to secure them. When Scully hoisted Billie to the dock, the Greek was gone.

The wind was cold and it had recently rained here too so the air was bright and liquid as they stood between clunking boats. Scully brushed the girl's hair, careful to avoid her wounds. He dipped his handkerchief in the sea and wiped their clothes as best he could.

'You okay?'

'Yes.'

She looked terrible under the wharf lights.

She closed her eyes and her heavy curls bustled in the wind. 'It hurts.'

Scully dug out some paracetamol. Was she too young for paracetamol? He found a tap and cupped her some water in his hands. She shuddered at the taste of the pills and held the crusty bowl of his hands. Drinking like a dog.

Out to sea the lights of Hydra showed faintly now and then.

'Afstralia!'

Scully turned and saw the boatman's face in the flare of a cigarette lighter.

'Taxi.'

'Good.'

'For Napflion.'

'I want Athens.'

Meatballs shrugged.

'Okay, what the hell.'

A battered Fiat stood at the end of the mole. A rotund little man got out buttoning a lumber jacket and opened the boot. Scully shook his head at the open boot and climbed in.

The car smelled of cigars and garlic. It was sweet and homely after the boat, it's motion smooth and straightforward. Never before had he thought of cars as such luxurious conveyances. Down sleepy streets they went, a numbness coming over him.

'Napflion, *neh*?'

'*Ochi*,' said Scully, 'Athini.'

'Athini?'

The driver pulled over beside a dim taverna and twisted around in his seat.

'*Neh*,' said Scully, 'Athini.'

The driver put on the interior light and looked carefully at them. Clearly, he didn't like the look of things. There was blood all down Scully's denim jacket, and he was unshaven and looked like a crim. Billie's face was swollen and showing the first bruises. Her hairline was savaged and little pieces of sticking plaster hung off her. She reeked and looked stolen at worst, neglected at best.

'Dog,' said Scully, showing him the wounds, making a set of jaws out of his hands. 'Dog, dog, it bit her, see?'

'Hydra?'

'*Ochi*, Spetsai. Happened on Spetsai, we came from there just now.'

Scully pulled out twenty thousand drachs and laid the fold across the seat between them.

'Athini, *endakse*?'

The man pursed his lips and sighed. Scully smiled raggedly and took out their passports, showed him the pictures.

'*Papa?*' the driver said to Billie, pointing at Scully.

'*Neh*,' said Billie, nodding wearily.

'*Postulena?*'

'Billie Ann Scully.'

He smiled at her and handed back the passports. But it was with a lingering look of concern that he took the money and turned out the light. They were well into the mountains before Scully felt sleep coming at him like a faint wind across water.

On a slick pale sea with the rising sun behind him, Scully watches the rope in the winch and sees the cane pot break the surface of the water, bristling with feelers. It crashes onto the cradle at the gunwhale, smelling of salt and rotten bait and cabbage weed, alive with the cicada click of rock lobsters. The boat surges ahead and a mad school of silver trevally chases leftovers in the clear reef water. Two dolphins break ahead and the world is good, the sea lives, the sky goes blue forever.

Billie woke in the dry mountain air and saw nothing beyond the curving road. With his head back and his mouth open, Scully slept on. She watched him in the dark as the man in front sang quietly to himself, and the night throbbed on out there beyond her hurting face. She thought about that castle, the tower down the hill from Scully's little house. There were birds around it like a cloud. The whole world still except for birds. She wondered if you could love someone too much. If you could it wasn't fair. People didn't have a chance. Love was all you had in the end. It was like sleep, like clean water. When you fell off the world there was still love because love made the world. That's what she believed. That's how it was.

Scully woke in the parked taxi. He saw the empty driver's seat, the keys gone from the ignition, his daughter sleeping beside him, their belongings scattered in the dark at their feet. He saw the dimness of the park across the street, and with a spasm of dread, he registered the police station right beside him. Police. For several seconds he listened to the cooling tick of the motor, then he gathered up their things and shook Billie.

'Let's go, let's go.'

The child came to quickly and got out beside him. Together they crossed the deserted street and slipped into the darkness of the park. The air was cool and damp and Scully's mind skittered. He led her to a clump of bushes that smelled like thyme and gave them some cover. Behind was the bus station. He painstakingly read the sign. Korinthos. Corinth. No sign of life there either. Scully squatted down to think. Was the driver in there reporting them as suspicious characters, a couple of strange looking *xeni*? A child looking battered and stolen, a man with desperado written all over him.

'Scully?'

'Shh.'

Scully saw the driver emerge from the police station with something in his hand. A piece of paper. He put his hand to the door of the Fiat and stopped. He hunched down to the back window and stood up to look around.

'*Kyrios?*' he called faintly. 'Mister?'

The town was so still his voice carried plainly across to them, little more than a whisper.

'Scully?' Billie tugged at his sleeve.

Scully watched him carefully. He thought of the long wait till dawn and the first bus or train out of here.

'Scully?' the kid murmured insistently.

The taxi driver pocketed the sheet of paper and walked around the car once, looking up and down the street. Scully thought of the cops on Hydra. They've sent out a warning to the mainland. Do they know in there? Then why did the driver come out alone, and what's on that piece of paper? He's stalling for time. They're waiting inside, for more men, for a call from Hydra to confirm. And where can you go, a couple of conspicuous foreigners in the offseason before dawn in Corinth when the trains aren't running yet and the streets are bare?

Billie was halfway across the park before Scully could take it in. She walked forthrightly, as if determined, or angry, and she didn't look back. He gasped and stood up. The driver swivelled and grunted in delight. He threw up his hands and laughed. Scully saw him open the door, chattering and still looking about, and that's when Scully gave up, grabbed the gear, and stepped out into the open.

When the taxi pulled away with the driver still telling him how be became lost in the wide, squat city with the *xeni* asleep in the back and how he stopped by the police station for directions, Scully had already decided not to go to Athens at all. Athens was the airport and the airport meant deciding where to go immediately, and he just didn't know where to head for right now. For the past ten hours or so he'd just been moving, going blindly. Hydra was becoming a series of migraine flashes. But he knew Athens was wrong and he had to rest and think, decide with all his mind, not just the white hot bit that ran when everything else shut down.

He was working up the Greek words in his mind to break it to the chattering driver, when he noticed that they'd slipped onto the new expressway heading west instead of east. He saw the sign for Patras and heard the driver gasp.

'Patra!'

'Patra is okay,' said Scully, 'Patra *endakse*.'

'Patra?'

'Yes, keep going.'

A blaring semi blasted past and the driver snatched his worry beads from the rearview mirror. They drove on as the great barren scape of the expressway unfolded. The air smelled of monoxide and pine resin. Billie slept again and Scully held his hands between his knees for the hour it took for the port city to come into view in the wan light before dawn.

## *Twenty-seven*

SCULLY WOKE IN THE CHALKY LIGHT OF AFTERNOON. He lay still. On the bed beside him, with her back to the scabrous wall, Billie scratched in pencil on a sheet of Olympic Airways paper. Her face was taut with concentration, so like the beleaguered intensity she was born with – that expression which implied that only willpower and doggedness had gotten her out into the noise and light of the world. But now her brow was grey and green with contusions. He wanted to touch her but he daren't. He listened to her shallow breathing, the scrape of her pencil, and after a minute or two she looked down. Her mouth moved hesitantly. She went back to her sheet of paper.

'Drawing?' he murmured.

She held it up. A house. A tree. A bird. The bird's nest was huge as a sun in the branches of the tree.

'Ireland?'

'Heaven,' she breathed.

He saw that her tee-shirt was on backwards. The Ripcurl tag flapped beneath her throat. He hadn't noticed, not last night, nor all yesterday. Today it was the pharmacy – first thing. There was no excuse today.

Billie picked up another sheet of paper, the ruin of Alex's pen-and-ink of the Rue de Seine.

'When is a dream . . . kind of not a dream?'

Scully turned on his hip. He savoured the husky tone of her voice. 'When it's real, I guess.'

She nodded.

'I'm sorry about all this,' he said. 'I had to do it. Go looking for her.'

Her face closed over like a moving sky. She went back to her sketch and he lay there flattened against his pillow.

After a long time he got up and ran her a bath. It had cost an extra ten thousand drachs not to have to share the shower down the hall. He was low on cash, but there was no question of not having a bath, not the way his mind was working at dawn. He emptied the case and found some spare dressings and some swabs. Billie ignored him. The water bored into the big enamel tub. He unbuckled his heavy diver's watch and took it over to her.

'Here, you can wear this in the bath.'

Billie held her arm out and he strapped it on. It ran round her wrist like a hoop. The last hole on the strap might have fitted her ankle. She twirled the dive dial. A ratcheting sound from another life.

In the bath she let him swab her wounds. She clung to the lip of the tub. Scully felt the floor cold on his knees. Her puckered gouges seemed clean, if firm. Maybe he could get an antiseptic ointment here in Patras. He had to keep the wounds closed to minimize scarring, but clean, always clean. He needed more gear. And what about tetanus? She had shots at five. He took her himself. He recalled how damned stoical she was about it. How long did a tetanus shot last? Ten years? Five? Five, surely five. And the dog. He couldn't help worrying about the bloody dog's papers. Were they fake? Kufos swore black and blue. Arthur said they were for real. Geez, the idea of a series of rabies shots. That would be the end of her. No, she was safe there.

He held her head cradled in his hand the way you bath a baby. She let him tilt her back into the water, her eyes trusting. He couldn't help but think of his mother bathing his head like this the day he hitched back to the city delirious with his face smashed and bloated, the poison purple in him, the way she held his head and dabbed at his holes.

Billie lay back with the water over her ears, her hair waving like seaweed. He didn't know why she trusted him. Maybe she knew him better than he could have imagined. Maybe she didn't trust him at all. He washed her hair gingerly and let her soak till the water went cold. He tidied up their things and soaked stains from their clothes. He scrubbed them with soap, rinsed them several times and rolled them in towels to speed their drying.

'We'll get you a hat today,' he said brightly. 'Till your hair grows out at the front. A Greek captain's hat, what d'you think?'

She lay on the bed, head tilted back, mouthing the words of a song he didn't know. He hung their clothes in the open window and stood watching her a long time.

THE SUN WAS FIRMLY ON THEIR BACKS as they climbed the wide steps to the *kastro* above the town, Billie with her new hat covering the worst patches, Scully impassive behind his sunglasses. The walls of the old town were heavy and worn, reverberating with the sound of mopeds as young people darted through the narrow streets.

They sat and ate *tsipoures* at a small place with the sun on their legs and the sea below. Neither said much. The fish was good and Scully had a half-bottle of the same brand of rosé he'd drunk with Alex. The taverna terrace was all but empty.

A woman alone at the next table smiled at Billie and made a face. Billie looked at her plate for a moment, but looked up again and poked her tongue out. Scully put down his glass.

'What happened to your face, darling?' the woman asked in English.

Billie pulled the hat lower. Scully looked at the stranger a moment and saw a straw hat, mirror glasses, black bobbed hair and a sleeveless dress the colour of watermelon. There was an ouzo on her table, a jug of water and a manila envelope.

'I got bit by a dog,' said Billie.

'Oh my God, you poor lamb.'

Scully smiled perfunctorily and went back to his fish. A tiny germ of pique lit up in him.

'Let me see,' said the woman.

Billie tilted back her hat and exposed the swellings, the shaved patches and blue-yellow bruises.

The woman clucked and lit a cigarette. Her skin was white and Scully saw immediately the bruising on her upper arm and wrist. She smiled as if in acknowledgement, in collusion somehow. It made him want to leave.

'And what became of the dog?'

'Beg your pardon?'

'What happened to the dog, darling?'

'It got killed.'

'Very good.'

'Beaten to death with a bottle of brandy,' said Scully without warmth.

'Bravo.'

'Poor dog,' said Billie.

'Oh, no, your father did well.'

'Her father didn't do it,' said Scully.

'You are not the father?'

'I didn't kill the dog.'

Scully saw himself – mouth open – in her sunglasses. It wasn't a happy sight. Pale. Hostile. Guilty. Blinking. Below his reflection was her too-wide mouth, a smear of lipstick on her teeth and a cigarette.

'Eat up, Billie,' he said, turning to his meal.

There were ships leaving the harbour now, blowing columns on the breeze. The Adriatic was the colour of chrome.

'I'm sorry,' said the woman. 'I've forgotten my manners since the church this morning. They have Saint Andrew's head there. It disturbed me. He was the one who first signed an X for a kiss, did you know? At the bottom of letters. How many times I have done that. They crucified him on an X. Especially. It upset me.'

'Well, X marks the spot,' said Scully.

'The boat for Brindisi doesn't leave till ten tonight.'

'Must be hard for you,' said Scully, motioning to a waiter and forking out some drachs. The big-handed Greek took his money gruffly and bade them goodbye. Billie looked back at the woman as they left, but Scully went ahead as though she had never been there.

FOR AN HOUR AFTER THE PANTOMIME at the pharmacy, Scully sat on the long harbour mole watching boats come and go: trawlers, caiques, ferries, the occasional liner, all peeling rust and pouring diesel smoke, their horns bleating, decks smelling of fruit, fish, flowers, wine, cigarette smoke. The wharf was scattered with mangy backpackers and the well-dressed middle class of Patras promenading with their black-eyed children, their Mercedes keys a-swing. The briney stink of the sea washed over Billie and Scully as they shared a bag of pistachios, wincing as their thumbnails became sore. They spat the shells into their laps and swung their legs.

'Everywhere,' he murmured, 'all over the world people are going places. Ever think of that?'

Billie looked at him guardedly.

'Every single day.'

She nodded.

'To be a real traveller you've got to not care much, just enjoy the trip, you know. The going. That's why I'm not much of a traveller. I just want to get there. Like "Star Trek". Zap – that's how I wanna get there.'

Billie nodded again, and smiled. But it felt like charity. He watched her as she got up in a tinkling shower of nutshells and walked over to the water's edge where gulls hung like bunches of scrap paper in the updraught on the mole. There she was, all his life amounted to, apart from a couple of good buildings and some memories. Wasn't she enough? The sea butted its head against the wall and he watched, wondering.

IN THE HOTEL STAIRWELL, Scully shoved stupid amounts of coin into the phone to get an international connection. Billie sat on the stairs with her backpack on and the tartan case at her feet. Pete's phone rang out. He'd be down the pub, no doubt. The coins cascaded out and he went through the performance again, dialling Alan and Annie.

'Hello?' A crackly, subterranean line.

'Alan?'

'Scully!'

'The very same.'

'What's happening? You put the wind up me the other day.'

'Tell me straight – have you seen her?'

'Jennifer? Where are you, Scully?'

'Can I trust you?'

'Scully, it's *me* for Godsake.'

'Swear to God.'

'Swear what?'

'That you haven't seen her.'

'I swear it. Where's Billie. Scully, where's Billie?'

'With me.'

'Where are you? Lemme come and get you. Where?'

Scully pressed the tips of his boots against the wall. It was tempting, no joke. Let Alan come, let friends come. Let someone come and fix this whole business. But he couldn't wait that long. Just the thought of Jennifer out there somewhere. Sick. Confused. Injured somehow. Or sweating on some disaster with the mail – waiting somewhere obvious without any way to contact him. Such a jumble of prospects and counter-thoughts. For a moment here he thought he might have chucked it in for the taste of the quiet moment, like this hour on the wharf without anxiety – the sound of the sea and birds and the sight of Billie – but the cold gnawing of not knowing was like a rip dragging on him. Not London. Not Hydra. He couldn't stay here like this.

'Scully? Please, where are you?'

'Mate,' he said. 'I'm all over the place, believe me.'

He hung up and caught his change. Billie got resignedly to her feet.

# III

*On Grafton Street in November*
*We tripped lightly along the ledge*
*Of a deep ravine where can be seen*
*The world of passions pledged*
*The Queen of Hearts still baking tarts*
*And I not making hay . . .*

'Raglan Road'

## *Twenty-eight*

THE JADED LIGHTS OF PATRAS silvered the water a long way behind them now, and a train of phosphorescence dragged along in the chunky night water of their wake. The decks of the Adriatica ferry were littered with rucksacks and suitcases, skis and tennis racquets, sleeping bags and drunken Finns. The breeze was fresh and the swell was long and steady before them, more comforting than unsettling. Billie lay back on the bench, her head in Scully's lap, and they looked out at the stars that hung like lint on a black sheet. She thought about those olden days, when it was all for one and one for all. Just the three of them in it together, like Scully said.

Maybe to him it seemed good and that's why he didn't like now. He wanted then, but when she remembered then she saw how hard he tried to be happy, specially in Paris where no one liked them and the sun would never go down at night. She remembered the fights with him outside that rotten school. That school where words came out of people's mouths like noise from machines, right at the beginning when she didn't know about languages. Lady teachers with cold smiles and their hair pulled back like elastic. Their shining foreheads. Every morning they waited for her and nearly every morning there was a fight. She saw Scully cry once, he was so mad. The two of them in the cobbled museum street grabbing and pushing like wrestlers. Scully pleading. Sometimes, when she won the fight over school, she went to work with him and saw how he bent up at the top of his ladder, scraping ceilings, how bits stuck in his hair like snow. The apartments were big and full of things she wasn't allowed to touch. She sat in a corner and played trucks or looked at picture books. Those days she could write names but she couldn't read. It was him who taught her to read. Afternoons in the café near Notre Dame with books about Spot the Dog. Baby stuff. Reading was like swimming. You can't do it, you just can't do it and then one day, like magic, you can. No, in Paris he wasn't happy. He walked her through the streets and told her about buildings, things she forgot straightaway except the way he said them. He liked buildings. He drew them on envelopes. He was an excellent drawer. But he didn't remember so great. All for one and one for all. It wasn't something they said for fun, it was to stop one of them crying, usually Billie. The three of us in it together. It wasn't such a great idea, it just meant they were all lonely. In Greece it wasn't so bad; you didn't get so lonely with the water, and anyway the people were nice. The island people. The kids hurt animals, but they were okay really. But Paris, no, all three of them in Paris were just scared.

Billie listened to Scully's stomach. It was like a factory in there. She thought about Paris. The apartment they borrowed all that time while Scully fixed it up. Nights at Marianne's or Dominique's. The ten times they saw 'Peter Pan' in French. The way the French called him Peter Pong. That cracked her up.

Rubbish trucks in the street. Sirens. Black men sweeping dog poop off the cobbles.

'Does this go to Paris?' she murmured.

'Brindisi,' he said. 'Italy.'

But Billie had seen him staring at Alex's picture. He was thinking of Paris for sure. Poor Alex. His eyebrows always looked like they were slipping off his face. There was a cloud in Billie's head – she would think along so far and there it would be, cutting her off, blocking her way. Right at the very thought of . . . well, Her.

'Gran Scully says you're not teaching me about Jesus.'

'Oh?'

She thought of the picture of him on Gran's mantelpiece. His old face, before the bung eye.

'Tell me about Australia,' he said, a bit excited. 'How does it look now? Tell me about the Indian Ocean. Could you see Rottnest? Was it hot? Did you hear the sound of people's voices? Did you forget much? Tell me about Gran.'

She knew the story about his eye. How the skipper Ivan Dimic made him kill every octopus that came aboard because they ate lobsters and cost him money. How they sucked the guts out of lobsters and left the shells. Even octopuses big as your thumbnail he had to kill and he hated it. Scully pretended to kill them. He whacked the deck and slipped them back over the side alive, but the skipper saw it. One day, out over the Shelf, Ivan Dimic came down off the flying bridge with an iron bar big as a horse's dick. Got him across the arm. There was a fight, just like TV. Sharks in the water. All this time the winch was going, pulling a pot up from the very deep. It was deep as the Eiffel Tower out there. The deck going up and down. The rope winding and tangling with no one to coil it. Ivan Dimic cracked him one across the face with the bar, right across the eye. Nearly popped it out of his head. Imagine. And right then the pot comes up, hits the tipper, and Dimic is right in the way. Steel and wood, heavy as a man. Knocked him flat. Scully brought the boat in himself. His last day fishing. It was before she was born. Billie missed all the good stuff. Look at this eye, he used to say. For an octopus? So look at this face, she thought, feeling the shrinking tightness of her own skin. For a dog?

'Billie?'

He was like the Hunchback, Scully. Not very pretty. Sometimes he wasn't very smart. But his heart was good. She pressed against him, hearing that pure heart lunking along like a ship's engine, and felt sleep coming again.

The deck vibrated beneath them. The lights of Greece faded to pinpricks and then oblivion. In sleeping bags all around, the murmurs trailed off into silence. Scully nursed his disappointment and hugged Billie to him as she slept. He thought of the woman she might make if this whole business didn't bugger her up forever. She would be strong, funny, confident, wry, and yes, smart as all get-out. Just as she was now. People would be forced to take notice of her the way they always had. Now that he thought of it she was probably everything her mother dreamt of being. Was that it, then? Would that cause you to bolt? Jealousy, discouragement, some meanness of spirit? 'People like you,' she used to tell him. 'You don't get it, do you? You like your life just fine, you take whatever comes with a sick kind of gratitude. That's where we're different.' He had to agree. He just *didn't* get it.

It was plain cold out now, and Scully began to shudder. Without blankets it was hopeless out here. Time to find some corner below. He threaded the pack onto Billie as she slept, and he hefted her and the suitcase to pick his way across to the companionway. It was precarious going, but he came down into a coffee-smelling lounge where Germans and Italians chattered and smoked blearily. It was bright here, too bright for sleeping, so he looked for a nook somewhere along the maze of corridors, but down there it was only toilets and first-class cabins. He returned to the lounge and found an upholstered booth back by the stairs where a bit of fresh air blew in but where it was still warm. He was about to lay Billie down when he saw the watermelon dress.

'There's nowhere for her to sleep?'

Scully cursed to himself, smiled and shook his head. The woman from the *kastro*. She wore a denim jacket over her thin dress and held a bottle of Heineken in one hand.

'Too cold up on deck,' he said.

'I knew you would be on this boat.'

Scully moved to lay the child across the seat, but the woman put a hand on his arm. He flinched and felt his face burn.

'Please. I have a cabin. Let her sleep in there.'

'Thanks a lot, but –'

'Really, she's tired and it's so awful out here. It's no trouble.'

'She'll sleep anywhere. She's a robust kid.'

The woman in the watermelon dress looked at Billie and he followed her gaze. The child didn't look so robust tonight. Her face was swollen and creased where her cheek had pressed into his jacket. Sleeping children, they have a hold on you.

'Please.' The woman was anxious, earnest. Her eyes were sad, pleading. She was somehow alarming to him, but it was true, the kid was stuffed.

'Alright, thanks. That'd be great for her.'

'Beautiful, beautiful. Here, this way. Let me take your case. You don't bring much.'

Scully followed her down the first-class corridor. At her door he smelt smoke on her and some scent. She opened the door and cleared the bottom bunk of bra and panties and a crumpled *Herald Tribune*.

'Here.'

Scully hesitated a moment before edging inside and laying Billie along the bunk. She opened her eyes a moment and looked at him wordlessly, and he simply smiled and she went back to sleep. Reaching for a blanket, the woman brushed hips with him, and he flinched again at the closeness of another body. She tucked the blanket around Billie and smiled. The air was cool in here and the ship's movement reassuring.

'Can I use your toilet a moment?' he whispered.

'Of course.'

He stood inside the neat little cubicle that smelled of antiseptic and corrosion. He took a leak and looked at himself in the mirror. Wild Man of Borneo. What was it he saw there – fatigue, disappointment, desperation? His face was harder than he remembered, more set, like those farmers he knew as a boy, the ones on a long losing streak, whose jaws never deviated into a smile. Men past caring, immovable, expecting the worst, ready to endure. No, he didn't like that look.

The door opened.

'Are you seasick?'

Scully shook his head.

'Let's get coffee.'

OUT IN THE LOUNGE a few of the Germans were drunk, some asleep, the Italians murmuring in a cluster and crackling Hallwag maps. Scully sat at the bar with a Turkish coffee and a shot of Metaxa.

'It's very nice of you,' he said to the woman on the stool beside him.

'It's good to be nice sometimes.'

'Where you headed?'

'Oh, home. Berlin.'

'I can't place your accent.'

'Liverpool.'

'You must have been in Berlin a good while then.'

'No. Five years. I studied for an accent.'

'Well. Ringo meets Sergeant Schultz.'

'I didn't like how I sounded before.'

Scully shrugged. 'You been on holiday?'

'Oh, it began as one.'

'Why come this way? You could have gone right up through northern Greece, Austria.'

'Yugoslavia. I hate it. I'd rather go the long way.'

'It is a bit like going through a sheep dip, isn't it?'

'You're Australian.'

'Yeah.'

'And where is home?'

Scully shrugged. 'Ireland, maybe.'

'Australians are sentimental about Ireland.'

'Not this one.'

'You're married.'

'Yes,' he said after an unpleasant pause. The ring flashed on his hand. 'My wife's . . . gone on ahead.'

'Yes.'

He looked at the woman and saw her smile. There was something knowing in it, not quite a smirk.

The barman, a heavy Greek with a birthmark down his arm like an acid burn, called for last drinks before the bar closed, and Scully ordered another brandy.

'What about you?'

'I'm organized already,' she said.

'If she wakes in the night I'll be out here with all the barfing Germans. Just send her out here.'

'You're welcome to sleep with her. There's still room on that bunk.'

'Thanks, but I'll leave you alone. It's cramped in there already with all our stuff. I'll just slip in there in a minute, take her shoes off.'

'She's a nice kid.'

'Yes. She is.'

'My name's Irma.'

'Irma.'

'It's Billie and . . .?'

'Scully. Everyone just calls me Scully. I'll be back in a moment.'

'Scully?'

'Yeah?'

'The key.'

He took the key and went back to check on Billie. She slept with her head back and her mouth open. He bent over her in the dimness and eased off her shoes, smelling the bready scent of her breath.

'Sleep with her.'

It was Irma, standing behind him in the doorway. He could smell her. The ship's engines stroked away beneath them.

'I have a bottle of Jack Daniels.'

'Listen, I –'

'Have a drink and go to sleep. She'll be afraid if she wakes and you're gone. She doesn't know me.'

Scully straightened. She was right. He'd already frightened the kid once, and he'd promised never again. He wanted to be alone, to avoid complication, conversation, to just organize himself tonight and make a plan. He hated sharing space with strangers, but it was safer this way. He just didn't like this woman. The memory of her bruises and that proud smile back in the *kastro* made his bowels contract.

'Okay,' he murmured. 'Thanks.'

'I'll be back in a couple of minutes.'

'Sure.'

Scully adjusted the porthole a little for some air and saw the black ellipse of sea and night. He pulled off his shoes and shucked his jeans and climbed in beside Billie, pulling the blanket up to his chest. Should have forked out the extra for a cabin, he thought; the money I've been blowing, it wouldn't have been so dumb. I'll offer her some money. Should have thought. Should have.

SCULLY WOKE SOMETIME IN THE NIGHT and saw Irma crouched on the floor in the yellow light of the toilet. She had his case open and was holding a bent candle and his wallet. He saw the whiteness of her panties, the tongue concentrated in the corner of her mouth, and the half-empty bottle of bourbon on the floor beside her.

'Don't tell me,' he murmured, 'you've lost a contact lens.'

She started, but then smiled. 'Lost more than that in my time.'

'There's nothing worth stealing.'

'I can see that. You're broke, Scully, unless you've still got credit.'

'What time is it?'

'Two.'

'What've you been doing?'

'Drinking. Watching you two snuggled up there like two bugs.'

'You're easy to entertain.'

'People say that.' Irma held the wallet open. 'This is her, then.'

Scully felt pins and needles rush to his right arm as he shifted his weight.

'Beautiful black hair. Nice face. Good legs. They say good legs mean a good fuck.'

He grimaced. 'Who says?'

'Not true, huh? Well, someone must believe it. How long's she been gone?'

Scully held his hand out for the wallet.

'You're abandoned, Scully, I can see it. You're a sad sight, the two of you. And she wasn't even good in bed. Must be love.'

'Gimme the bloody wallet.'

'And what are these?' She held up a lint-furred candle.

'The wallet.'

'Three of them.'

'Please.'

'Show more guts, Scully. Less pride and a bit more guts.'

Scully slid off the bunk and Irma gasped, cowering almost.

'We're just gonna go. Pass me those jeans.'

'No.'

'Look, I just wanna get dressed. I'm not gonna hurt you or report this.'

'Don't go.'

'It was nice of you to offer us a bed, but I'm not used to strangers going through my stuff.'

'I'm not a stranger.'

'Look, you've had a lot to drink and –'

'Don't wake her up, let her sleep.'

'She'll sleep out in the lounge.'

'You've got another thirteen hours, Scully. I'm sorry about your things. I wasn't stealing, I was curious. Truth is, I need the company. Stay for me.'

'I want to sleep.'

'Sleep then. We're in the same boat, you know.'

'You don't say.'

'I mean our situation. I'm abandoned too.'

'I need to sleep.'

'We'll talk about it later. Get back into bed. Here, your wallet.'

Scully took it and slipped back in beside Billie. He watched Irma pack things neatly back into his case and stow it under the bunk beneath him. For a moment, shoving it under with both arms, she lifted her head and met his gaze, her face so close he could smell the Jack Daniels on her breath.

'Sleep, Scully.'

He lay back as she climbed the bunk. He saw that watermelon dress floating, saw insect bites or cigarette burns on her legs. Her toenails were silver blue, her heels dirty. The ship moved languorously, as if asleep itself, and he felt Billie's breath against his neck and slipped back into the long blank of sleep, knowing even as he did that he'd regret this, that he was too tired and weak to change his mind.

## *Twenty-nine*

When Scully woke the pair of them were playing Uno in the light of the portal. There was a clanging somewhere below.

'Sleepyhead still in bed,' said Irma, smiling.

'You snored,' said Billie.

Scully lay still. Billie's hair was brushed and she wore a clean shirt. A pair of her knickers hung damp and wrung out from the knob of the toilet door.

'Morning,' he murmured uncertainly.

'Irma's a loser at Uno.'

'She's probably letting you win. Some people are like that.'

'No. I can tell.'

'She's like you, Scully.'

'No, she's her own girl.'

'You want to go to breakfast?'

'Gimme a minute.'

Scully nursed his morning hard-on till the card game reached a big enough peak of concentration to allow him to slip out of bed and crib across to the toilet.

'Morning glory, my favourite flower,' said Irma.

'Uno!' said Billie.

Irma winked and Billie saw how rosy and soft her lips were. She kind of liked Irma. She could reach her own nose with the tip of her tongue and do rolls with it and fifty funny faces. All the time Scully slept there all twisted on the bunk, Irma and her whispered and giggled. Billie remembered her from the taverna, remembered the dress and those mirror sunglasses. Without the sunnies she didn't look so grown up, and now that she thought of it, listening to Scully trying to pee quietly down the side of the toilet bowl in there, Irma wasn't really grown up at all. The way she played cards in her greedy way. She never gave you breaks like an old person. Her tongue stuck out and her giggle was a naughty girl's giggle. And she asked questions, so many questions – why, why, why – like a kid, so many you didn't bother to answer. She was fun, Billie could see, but you couldn't tell about her heart.

Billie asked some questions of her own, to see if Irma knew the planets of the solar system and the names of the main dinosaurs (just the basic ones) and who Bob Hawke was. She didn't have a clue, as if she never went to school or read books at all. She didn't know about convicts or fish or knots, and she laughed in an embarrassed way, as if she'd been caught out.

'I don't know much,' said Irma. 'I guess I feel things.'

Billie thought about this. 'Do you think someone can love too much?'

Irma just went back to her cards with a sad little smile and said nothing.

SCULLY FLUSHED THE TOILET, pulled the lid down and sat on it. Six hours till Brindisi. Out there he could hear them tittering.

Jennifer would never let herself get into a corner like this. She crossed all her T's and dotted all her I's. She was organized and he was a fool. Last night this woman had his wallet open and this morning she was dressing his kid. She's moving in on you, mate, and you're like a stunned mullet. What is she, a travelling hooker, a rich adventurer, a dipso nutcase? She murdered half a bottle of Jack Daniels last night and this morning she's giggling, for Chrissake. Still, you had to admit she's better sober. In the light of day she's human. But it ate at him, the sound of his daughter chirruping away all of a sudden. After all the sullen quiet. The ache of waiting. Gabbing to a fucking stranger. This Irma. Scully put his elbows on his knees and realized that he was afraid of her and didn't know why.

OUT ON THE DECK after their pre-digested breakfast, as Billie ran up and down between hungover Germans, Scully let Irma talk. The woman was bursting with a need to share information he didn't want to hear.

'He left me in Athens,' she said.

'No explaining people sometimes,' he said, his irritation not quite concealed. The sea fell by in the soft light and around them bleary backpackers sipped their industrial-blend Nescafé.

'You never really know them,' he added as one backpacker began to blurt and gasp foully at the rail. Scully turned his back to the puker and looked unhappily at Irma's bruises. She had them on her upper arms and around her neck and didn't mind his noticing them.

'I met him in Bangkok. He works there in some kind of security thing, I don't know. Used to be in the Green Berets. Had scars all over him. He's one of those vets who never came back from Asia. He's not quite crazy, but, well he is a Texan. Not beautiful, but hard, you know? I liked him. This was last year. I just walked into a bar and there he was, just like in the movies. The best fuck of my life, and free! We stayed together a week.'

Scully half listened to Irma and watched Billie skipping across the aft deck. Her face was blackening now with her own bruises. She looked like a kid with leukemia.

'So we arranged to meet in Amsterdam, last month. Had a wild time there, really, and then we sort of travelled, you know. Under the influence of various, well, substances as the Americans call them. Had a spree. My God, what a pair we were! Ended up in Athens. He left me at the Intercontinental. I was having a shit, can you believe. He packed his stuff and went. At least he paid the bill.'

'A gentleman,' said Scully, hearing the awful priggish note in his voice.

'That's where I saw her.'

'Who?'

'I got a shock when I saw your wallet. I mean, it was a surprise. Funny, isn't it, that we'd all been staying together without knowing it.'

Scully looked at her. She was flushed now and nervous. She wore a quilted vest and jeans. Her eyes were hidden by sunglasses and she fingered her bruised throat absently.

'Saw who? What are you talking about?'

'The woman in your photograph. Your wife.'

'You saw *her*?'

'At the Intercontinental.'

Scully ran a hand through his hair, looked about momentarily. 'My wife?'

'The one in your wallet.'

'You're sure?'

'I could be wrong.'

Scully licked his lips.

'Was she alone?'

Irma sank back a little, looking shaky now. 'I . . . I don't remember. It might have been a woman she was with.'

He looked at her and felt like spitting in her face. She's making this up. She's lonely, she wants a bit of mutual misery.

'So, you and your Green Beret, blasted out of your minds, bumped into them in the lift. And you remember it clearly.'

'In the reception, the lobby. I didn't see you. I would have remembered you.'

'I wasn't there. I've never stayed in an Intercontinental in my life.'

Irma smiled crookedly.

'You sound proud of it, Scully.'

'Could be I am.'

'The working-class hero.'

'How would you know what class I'm from?'

'Look at your hands, for God's sake, and that face. You're a brawler, Scully.'

He backed off a little, breaking into an angry sweat.

'A man could drive a truck down your nasty streak, Irma.'

'And back again, darling. Listen – we sound like the movies.'

Scully turned away and looked at the sea.

'You never saw her. She was never there, and you probably weren't either. Is this what you do, attach yourself to people? For a living?'

'You're frightened, Scully, thinking of all the possibilities.'

He knew now that he had to get free of her. She was like a foul wind, the whispering breath of nightmares.

'Billie and I are going for a walk.'

'Your things are in my cabin.'

'You want them out.'

'No. Just reminding you. You can't ignore me, Scully.'

'My friend Irma.'

She sighed. 'Jerry Lewis, I know. You're such a groundbreaker.'

He went over to where Billie shouted gaily down a ventilator and took her by the hand. He was shaking – he felt it show. The bloody woman was poison. She'd summed him up like a professional, hustling him. For what? Money? Company? A ticket home? She's sick. Jennifer never even went to Greece, he knew that for a fact. Well, an educated guess. As far as he could tell. Jesus.

BUT UP IN THE BOW where the air was freshest and the passengers weakest in their illness, Scully stood at the rail and thought of what it could mean if Irma was telling the truth. Jennifer in some flash hotel room with a mini bar and a big view of the Akropolis, a terry-cloth robe and people he didn't know about. Maybe old Pete-the-Post was right – you never really knew anybody, not even those you loved. People have shadows, secrets. Could be it's a jaunt with a mate, a few days blowing money and ordering up room service. She's just sold off a whole previous life back there in Fremantle, a scary thing to do, unnerving, upsetting. Maybe she just needs to blow it out of her system. Wasn't it the sort of thing men did all the time, going off on a spree and coming home sheepish and headsore? His own father would find a bottle of Stone's Green Ginger Wine and go off up Bluey's Knob for a night. Feelin black, he called it. He'd come down and fess up to Mum and they'd get the Bible out and have a howl and make up. That was as rugged as it got at the Scully place, a guilty suck on the Stone's Green Ginger and a contrite heart in the morning.

Alright. A jaunt then, say it's true and she has a spree. So who's the woman? He felt his fresh fortress of certainties crumbling again. A couple of days ago he was certain that Greece was a false start. And a couple before that he felt in his blood she was there. Now he didn't know what think.

'Scully?'

Billie tugged at him by the rail and he came back to the salt air, the sea forging and reaching beneath him.

'Yes, mate? You cold?'

'Irma wants to be my friend.'

'Yeah? How d'you know?'

'She said. She likes our hair. Yours and mine.'

'You tell her about your mum?' Scully's throat constricted as he uttered it. He could not stomach the idea that a stranger might have Billie's secret before *him* – he was churning at the thought.

'Nup.'

'Nothing at all?'

She shook her head. God, how he wished he could ask her again, know what had happened at Heathrow. But he couldn't push her now.

'You're a good girl.'

'What was here before the sea?'

He looked out over the Adriatic whose curved grey rim held the sky off and drew the eye beyond it.

'Nothing, love. There was nothing before the sea. Why?'

'I just thought of it. Irma said –'

'Bloody Irma.'

'She said nothing lasts forever. But I said the sea.'

'That fixed her. C'mon.'

IRMA HAD A HEINEKEN and a shot before her on the table when they found her in the lounge at noon. The sea was up a little and it was airless and mostly deserted down there. Most people were up on deck taking in a bit of mild sun, but Irma had settled in.

'What a pair you are,' said Irma.

'Billie, go get yourself a Pepsi.' Scully gave the kid some drachs and some lire and watched her saunter to the bar and tackle the stool.

'Tell me about the Intercontinental,' said Scully.

'Say please.'

'You're going to be ugly about it?'

'I am the good, the bad *and* the ugly.'

'You should stay off the piss for a while,' he said as kindly as he could. 'You'll hurt yourself.'

'Say please,' she said, tipping the bottle to her lips, eyes on him all the time.

'Please.'

She smiled around the bottle and he looked down at his meaty hands.

'You don't care for me, do you Scully?'

'Only known you twelve hours, and for most of that I was asleep.'

'Puritan, that's the word that comes to mind.'

'You wouldn't be the first whose mind it popped into. I was just asking about my wife. You claimed to have seen her.'

'Claim? You don't believe me, but you want more.'

Scully looked over at Billie who was using sign language with the big birthmarked barman. She had a Pepsi in front of her and he was showing his broken teeth in a smile.

'I thought you might tell me what you could.'

'I wonder.'

'What?'

Irma sat back, her chin up, neck stretched, some cleavage showing.

'How much you really want to know. What you'll do to get it.'

Scully stared at her. She flushed again and emptied the glass of bourbon with a grimace which became a smile. He wanted to grab that neck in both hands and wring it like a towel.

'You want money.'

'I prefer adventure.'

He pressed his fingernails together. 'This other woman she was with, what did she look like?'

'We haven't made a deal yet, Scully.'

'What deal, what do you want, for Godsake?'

'Come to the cabin.'

'Tell me here.'

'Come to the cabin.'

'What for? You can say it here.'

'I want to see if you have any guts.'

'Something must have happened to you once.'

'You look as though you just trod in shit.'

Got it in one, love, he thought.

'Let's go to the cabin.'

'Oh, goody.'

'Quick.'

He led her into the corridor and tried to think his way clear, but she came up so close behind him she literally trod on his heels.

'Scully, you –'

'Shut up. Where's the key?'

When the cabin door opened, Scully shoved her inside and she fell giggling to the floor. He grabbed his case and the back-pack and looked at Irma sprawled on the floor, legs apart, hair in her eyes.

'What a fucking disappointment you are,' she said.

He reached across to grab Billie's knickers from the toilet door but she beat him to it.

'Souvenir,' she breathed.

Scully felt his boot go back. His leg. Felt himself adjusting his balance to kick her, the way you might kick down a toadstool in a winter paddock, turning it into a noxious cloud of shit in a second, and then he saw the look of fear and exultant expectation on the woman's face and felt sick to his bladder. He staggered, bringing himself short, and almost fell on her.

'Gutless, gutless!' she hissed.

Scully reversed out of the cabin as though pressing back into a cold wind.

'She was beautiful!' Irma yelled. 'They spoke French. They were checking out, Scully. She was soooo beautiful. I can see why she made the choice. I saw them! I *saw* them!'

He bounced off the walls of the corridor, her voice chasing him from every direction, and up against the firehose in a rusty recess he listened to the shocking sound of his heart in his ears, shaming him with every beat.

In the lounge, Billie and the barman looked up in alarm and curiosity. Irma was screaming back there, hollow and faint. Scully swung the luggage into a booth, stood panting beside it and sat down sweating, nursing his fists like stones on the sticky table.

# *Thirty*

*THE SOLDIERS STAND MOTIONLESS . . . Quasimodo's one eye gleams wildly. They are held at bay for a moment . . . until one of the more adventurous men can stand it no longer . . .*

Out on the deck, in the fine cold, Billie read her comic and plugged her ears with her thumbs. Now that was a tantrum down there. The Hunchback bounded and raved, cried and shook and poured his bubbling lead down upon the mad masses of Paris. Sailors went bucketing downstairs to see what all the noise was, and Billie read on. It was even a bit funny. But Scully wasn't laughing. He looked shocking.

In the end it went quiet and birds landed on deck. She squeezed Scully's hand and tried not to feel the tight burning of her face. Boiling lead. The bells going mad. She knew this story like a song.

A while after Irma gave in and shut up, after passengers quit giving him the evil eye in his seat in the lee of the lifeboats, Scully felt Billie at his side nudging him out of his stupor. Out there, in the late afternoon gloom, the forts and rocks and lights

– the houses of Brindisi winking their languid green and gold – raised a cheer from travellers at the rail.

Scully gathered up their gear and bullocked a path toward the exit companionway. It took a cruel time for the engine vibrations to change pitch, a hard foetid wait wondering where Irma was in the shoving crowd but the great hatch finally did crack open and Scully and Billie were amongst the first on the dock. The sun was down beyond the drab blocks of the town's monuments and the quay was grey and close with the shunt and stink of travellers. Everywhere you looked there were people moving and waiting, watching, many of them without any obvious purpose or destination. They were faceless in the bad light, and sinister. Scully knew right off, clasping Billie's hand and surging ahead blindly, that he wouldn't stay in this town. He needed a shower and a sleep and they both wanted a quiet place to lie down but Scully knew they would have to keep travelling. Maybe his nerves were buggered and he was imagining a threat that didn't exist here, but he wanted the first train out of here. Somewhere behind was Irma, and she was enough excuse to keep going.

Up in the streets there were backpackers and vagrants dossing down for the night in cardboard and torn blankets and bright nylon sleeping bags. Monoxide hung between buildings. Garbage crackled underfoot. Scully kept a straight tack up the main drag, feeling her bounce and lag beside him. Everyone seemed to move in the same direction, from the wharf upward, so he kept on.

'What is this?' Billie asked.

'It's Hell,' said Scully.

'No, that's underground.'

'Well this is Hell's penthouse suite, Bill,' he murmured. 'Ah, see, STAZIONE, that's the stuff. Quick, this way.'

'Where's Irma?'

'Way back.'

'What a tantrum. I feel sorry for her.'

'Don't bother.'

'She's like Alex.'

Scully felt a stab at the thought of Alex. Maybe they'd buried him already, the great bearded priests singing dubiously over him, the cats prowling between the headstones behind them. How long had it been? Two days? Three?

He shrugged off touts and buskers as they came to the station, Billie pressed to his side. Scully hissed at anyone who came near. He felt a wild fervour, a queer joy as people made way, sensing that this madman would head-butt and bite his way clear if need be. People's skin was sallow, their teeth wayward. It was a lunatic asylum in here. Timetables rolled and clattered above their heads. Scully looked for any destination north, anything leaving soon, but there was only Rome at seven-thirty. A ninety-minute wait. It wasn't ideal but he changed some money and bought two tickets for Rome. At the kiosk he bought a week-old *Herald Tribune*. People swirled aimlessly about them, pressing, surging, crying out and spitting.

'I'm hungry,' said Billie.

'Okay, let's get some spaghetti,' said Scully hoisting her up out of the human current. 'God, let's just get out of here.'

BILLIE SAW SCULLY WINDING DOWN like that organ grinder's music out there in the street. All the wildness was gone now. He just tooled with some bread in a little puddle of wine and said nothing. He was awake but nearly switched off. She sucked up some spaghetti. It wasn't as good as he made. Anyway she could taste the antiseptic ointment on everything. It seemed a long time ago that she had spaghetti made by him. Out the window in the lights of the street the grinder's monkey scratched himself and tipped his head at her. The holes in her head throbbed like music.

'What country is this?'

'Italy,' said Scully.

'So they speak –?'

'Italian.'

'What town?'

'Brindisi.'

'Is it all like this?'

'Italy, I've only ever passed through. No, we stayed in Florence a couple of days, remember?'

Billie shook her head. There were too many places. Stations, airports, the flat heads of taxi drivers. She remembered Hydra and Paris and Alan's house, but other places were just like television, like they weren't for real. And that house, that little house Scully made was all in a fog, blurry, swirling, like the cloud that came down on her head when she thought of the plane. The steamy hot towels the stewards brought. The toilet light going off. *Her* coming, so beautiful down the aisle. Hair all stuck back like perfect. The white neck, so white . . . and the cloud coming down.

'All the statues have little dicks,' she said.

'I didn't notice. Wipe your face, you've got sauce all over your chin.'

'Why doesn't that monkey run away?'

He looked at the monkey in the funny suit on the grinder's box. 'Maybe he's too scared.'

'Doesn't look scared.'

'Maybe he needs the dough,' he said, trying to crack a smile.

Billie thought of all those people on the wharf and in the skinny streets. Like the ones you see in Paris, in the Metro and the hot air holes lying on boxes and sleeping bags.

'Are we going to be beggars?'

'No, love.'

'We haven't got much money anymore, have we.'

'I've got a card.' He got out his wallet, the one with the picture she didn't want to see. He held up the little plastic card. 'I can get money with it, see?'

'They should give them to beggars. Jesus would give em cards, right?'

'Spose. Yeah. I have to pay the money back later. It can be scary. People go crazy with them.'

'It wouldn't help Irma.'

He just looked out the window at that and didn't want to talk. He had a good heart, her dad, but maybe it wasn't big enough for Irma.

## *Thirty-one*

THE TRAIN PULLED OUT INTO THE DARKNESS. Billie tried to get comfortable. She bumped Scully's newspaper and he sighed. People murmured. Some had pillows and eyepatches. Lights, houses, roads began to fall by. Trains weren't so bad. You could see you were getting somewhere in a train, even at night like this, the darkness just a tunnel out there with you shooting through, roaring and clattering and bouncing through like a stone in a pipe, like the stone Billie felt in her heart now, trying to think of something good, something she could remember that wouldn't make her afraid to remember. Past the cloud. The white neck, she saw. So suddenly white as if the tan had been scrubbed out in the aeroplane toilet. Beautiful skin. The veins as she sits down. Skin blue with veins. Like marble. And talking now, mouth moving tightly. Cheeks stretched. Hair perfect. But the words lost in the roar, the huge stadium sound in Billie's ears as the cloud comes down, like smoke down the aisle, rolling across them, blotting the war memorial look of her mother in blinding quiet.

SCULLY HID BEHIND the *Herald Tribune* and tried to get a grip. But he was studying the reflections of the other passengers as though Irma might be among them. He was going mad, surely. He wasn't heading anywhere, he had no purpose – he was just going. Come to think of it he envied Irma her performance on the ferry. Kicking and screaming, head-butting the walls. Some total frigging indecorum, he could do with it. No, too tired. He didn't have a clue what he was up to. Funny, really, he was just going. Travelling. For the sake of it. It actually made him grin.

The paper fell in a crumple. Night warped by. It could have been anywhere out there. The mere movement of the train was soothing. Billie slept like a dog beside him. He saw himself in the glass smiling dumbly. A boy's face in a steel milk bucket. The face of a boy who likes cows, reflected in the still oval of milk – white, dreamsome, sleepy milk.

BILLIE WOKE FOR A WHILE IN THE NIGHT and watched the land and lights slipping by. It meant nothing to her, it had no name, no place that she could see. It was like the walls of a long tunnel just going by and by. She wondered about Granma Scully, if maybe she would come to live with them now in that little dolls' house. It was just country out there, more country. She thought of wide, eye-aching spaces of brown grass with wind running rashes through it and big puddles of sheep as big as the shadows of clouds creeping along toward lonely gum trees. That was a sight she could get hold of. Or the back step at Fremantle where the snails queued up to die by the tap. The sight of Rottnest Island hovering over the ocean like a UFO in the distance.

She went to sleep again, thinking of the island hovering there, like a piece of Australia too light to stay on the water.

COFFEE AND ROLLS CAME BY AT DAWN and Scully bought breakfast for them, but Billie slept on twitchy as a terrier. Towns were becoming suburbs out there in the dirty light. Time to freshen up, beat the queues. He clambered into the aisle. It was hard work picking his way through the outflung legs of sleepers. The whole car stank of bad breath and cheap coffee. He had his hand on the latch of the toilet door when he saw her through the glass partition between carriages. Second row, aisle seat. Totally out to it. Mouth open slackly, head back, leg twisted out into the traffic. Two grimy runs of mascara down her cheeks. Irma.

He stood there a moment in awe. Yes, she was something else, something else entirely. You could almost admire her doggedness – until you thought of her souveniring your daughter's underpants.

He went back down the aisle tripping on the ugly mounds of rancid backpacks and mattress rolls, stockinged feet, hiking boots, slip-ons. The train plunged and juddered. He snatched down their luggage and hoisted Billie to his shoulder. It took sea legs to move through the gut of that train, through doors and curtains of smoke, past suit bags and monogrammed luggage, around suitcases with wheels.

The toilet in first class was quiet and roomy. Scully sat on the closed lid of the seat with Billie still asleep on his lap and the genteel passengers of first class queuing patiently outside. In time the train slowed, but Scully's mind racketed on. Hit the ground running, he thought. Hit it running.

ROMA TERMINI WAS A VAST CHAMBER of shouts and echoes, metal shrieks and crashes of trolleys as Scully and Billie ran through the mob of beseechers and luggage grabbers toward the INFORMAZIONE office in the main hall. Scully felt smelly and gritty and wrinkled as he scanned the weird computer board that flashed messages in all languages.

'*Inglese?*' Called a thin dark woman from the counter behind them.

'*Oui*,' said Scully, panting. '*Si*, yes, English.'

He saw the destinations reeling off before him.

8.10 Berne
8.55 Lyon (Part-Dieu)
7.05 Munich
8.10 Nice
7.20 Vienna
7.20 Florence

He looked at his watch. It was 7.02. Too long to wait for Nice or Lyons. Irma was out there somewhere. Wheels yammered on the hard floor. Over the PA a man spoke tonelessly. Along the counter two backpackers argued, grey with fatigue. It had to be the first train north. He opened his wallet.

'Two tickets for Florence, one adult one child, second class. Please. No, make that first class.'

He slapped the American Express card down and the attendant smiled indulgently.

'The vacation is a big hurry, sir.'

'Yes, a helluva hurry. Which track, uh, which *binari* Firenze?'

'Train EC30. You will see it.'

'Thank you. *Grazie*.'

'*Prego*. Sir? Sir?'

'Yes?'

'You must write your name. Sign. I have your card.'

'Oh, yes, what a hurry. What a holiday this is!' Billie rolled her eyes. He suppressed a hysterical giggle. He was losing his marbles.

As the country softened into villages, muddy fields and bare trees, Scully and Billie stretched in their empty compartment with the sweat still drying on them. The upholstery of their long opposing benches was bum-shiny and cool. The air was tart as it rushed in the window. A giddy kind of relief came upon him as the train picked up speed. The sky was low and marbled, black, grey, white, pierced by poplars and the spires of little churches. The land was eked out between stone walls and graveyards, the squiggles of lanes. There was a softness out there, a picturebook safety in the landscape that soothed him. Like Ireland, Brittany. That time, the three of them and Dominique on the omnibus in the Breton farmlands. Scully had the same feeling looking out on it. Everything that there is to be done has been done here. This land will not eat me. It was land with the bridle on, the saddle cinched. In Brittany he found it sad, the loss of wildness, but today, looking out upon the soft swelling hills and symmetrical woodlands he felt his whole body unwinding with gratitude at the arrival of mere prettiness.

Billie squeezed his hand. He sprawled out on his seat, his first-class seat, and smiled.

'I was worried about you,' she said.

He raised her hand to his lips. 'Why, Miss, I do thank you.'

'Urk, boy bugs!'

'Get a doctor!'

And for a moment, for a longer moment than he believed

possible, they laughed together with their feet all over the upholstery. The feeling burned on warmly after they lapsed into silence. Billie took up her dogeared comic. He found his *Herald Tribune*. The train jogged and weaved, labouring into the hills.

FEELING THE TRAIN SLOW ON THE STEEP INCLINE, Billie looked up from Quasimodo and saw an amazing thing. A funny sound came out of her throat as she looked out of the rainstreaked window and saw two boys on horses galloping along the tracks, just behind. Boys, not men. Their hair streamed wet, dancing like the dark manes of the horses as they gained on the train. Trees blurred past. Their parkas bubbled and billowed, hoods bouncing on the back of their necks. Their feet were bare. Billie saw the horses without saddles. She pressed up against the glass as they drew alongside. Gypsy boys, for sure they were gypsies. Their white teeth flashed in smiles. The muscles in the horses' flanks pumped like machinery. It was beautiful – all of it was beautiful, and they saw her.

'Look! Look!'

Scully sat up, surfacing like a swimmer from his reverie, and the sight made him recoil in shock. The bulging glass eyes of horses. Mud rising in black beads against their bellies. The bare feet of boys. Their knees pinched high on their mounts, manes twisted expertly in their fingers. Scully saw the rain peeling off their faces, off the dun hoods of their rough coats, and their eyes upon him, black and knowing. Perilously close to the rails, they beckoned, each with a grimy hand outstretched, palm upward. Grinning. Madly grinning.

Scully wrenched the shutter down.

'No!'

Billie scrabbled at the handle until it ricked up again. The riders made a jump, a straining leap across a low wall, making arrows of themselves in the air and an eruption of mud on the other side. They gained again, drawing up beside Billie's window. Their hands were out bravely across the smear of the rails.

'Jesus Christ!' said Scully.

She saw him turn away, then back again.

Scully saw the blood along the horses' flanks where tree branches had left their mark. He was cold right through, slipping, sinking. Icy. He saw the insistence of the outstretched hands, the menace in the gaze. Even in the wicked bend of the crest they kept on, riding without fear, summoning, demanding, begging until he closed his eyes against them and felt the new momentum of the train in the downward run.

Billie waved as they fell back, her heart racing wonderfully. The gouged walls of an embankment filled the window and they were gone. She pressed her palm against the cold glass. Scully lay back licking his chapped lips. Billie felt lightheaded. Her head thumped. She touched him but he flinched.

'They were only boys,' she said. 'Just silly boys.' Peter Pan boys. Show offs. And they saw her.

## *Thirty-two*

OUT OF THE RUMOURS OF PLACES, of the red desert spaces where heat is born, a wind comes hard across the capstone country of juts and bluffs, pressing heathland flat in withering bursts. Only modest undulations are left here. Land is peeled back to bedrock, to ancient, stubborn remains that hold fast in the continental gusts. Pollen, locusts, flies, red sand travel on the heat, out across the plains and gullies and momentary outposts to the glistening mouth of the sea. And in sight of cities, towers, the bleak shifting monuments of dunes, the wind dies slowly meeting the cool offshore trough of air, stalls the carriage of so much cargo. The sea shivers and becomes varicose with change and in the gentle pause it clouds with the billion spinning, tiny displaced things which twitch and flay and sink a thousand miles from home. Fish rise as blown sparks from the deep itching with the change. Sand, leaves, twigs, seeds, insects and even exhausted birds rain down upon the fish who surge in schools and alone, their fins laid back with acceleration as they lunge and turn and break open the water's crust to gulp the richness of the sky, filling their bellies with land. And behind them others come, slick and pelagic to turn the water pink with death and draw birds from the invisible distance who crash the surface and spear meat and wheel in a new falling cloud upon the ocean. Out at the perimeter a lone fish, big as a man, twists out into the air, its eye black with terror as it cartwheels away from its own pursuer. There is no ceasing.

## *Thirty-three*

IN FLORENCE THEY FOUND A HOTEL near the Duomo with slick terrazzo floors and window shutters that peeled into the narrow street. The city air was fat with taxi horns and rain. Bells rang in towers and domes. The plumbing chimed in sympathy, and from below came the smells of espresso coffee, salami and baking bread.

Scully filled a bath and washed their clothes in shampoo. He scrubbed shirts and pounded jeans, rinsed rancid socks over and over and hung it all from shutters and radiators to drip dry. They climbed naked into their separate beds and listened to the plip of water on the floor. For a while they looked at one another, not speaking. Light fell in bands across the bed linen. Before long they slept, surrounded by the shades of their steaming clothes.

It was late in the day when they woke. Billie woke first. She felt shimmery. Her head felt bigger. She pulled a blanket around herself and sat flicking through their passports. She looked at their big, round, happy faces and all the stamps in weird languages. She was smaller in her photo. She liked how smiley they were in their old faces. Scully got up. She watched him brush his teeth till the toothpaste turned pink. He didn't look in the mirror. His bum wobbled and his nuts rattled stupidly. When Scully was in the nude he didn't care. It was because he wasn't beautiful. Only beautiful people cared.

OUTSIDE IT WASN'T RAINING but the city was wintry and dim. In a self-service place they ate pasta and bread. It was steamy and full of clatter. Chairs scraped on the floor. People shouted and laughed.

Afterwards they just walked. On a bridge there was something like a little town where African people, black people, sold shirts and watches laid out on the wet stones. Across the river they walked in pretty gardens and climbed to a fort that looked like the wrecked castle in Ireland. All across the roofs of the city were pigeons and the sound of bells.

Scully walked along with the kid feeling lightly stitched together, as though the slightest wind would send him cartwheeling. It was quiet between them. They merely pointed or tilted their heads at things, thinking their own thoughts. He wondered where the nearest airport was and whether there was credit left on the Amex card. He felt strangely peaceful. The muddy Arno rolled by. The Ponte Vecchio lighting up the dusk.

They walked in their case-wrinkled clothes past Italians who looked like magazine covers. Dagger heels, glistening tights, steel creases, coats you could lie down and sleep on. Their shoes were outrageous, their peachy arses, male and female, like works of art. Women ran their lacquered nails through Billie's hair and Scully stared at their glossy lips. *Buon Giorno.*

Billie saw him in the lights of shop windows. He looked dreamy but his blood was back.

'All for one,' she said.

'And one for all.'

BEFORE BED BILLIE CUT HER TOENAILS with the little scissors in Scully's pocket knife. He lay on his bed. Their washed clothes were half dry. All the edges of Billie's eyes, everything she saw had a shiny edge to it. While he lay there she clipped his toenails, too and marvelled at the glowingness of things.

UP IN THE FIG TREE with Marmi Watson from next door balancing beside her, Billie pointed down the street to the figure striding along, briefcase swinging, legs scissored, hair falling black from her neck. Afternoon light in her eyes.

'Look,' she murmured proudly. 'That's my mum. Just look at that.'

'ALL FOR ONE!' THEY SAID, the three of them on the bare floor of the Paris apartment. 'And one for all!' Laughing themselves silly in the mess, laughing, laughing.

IN THE WEAK HEATLESS LIGHT OF THE PIAZZA next day the kid didn't look so great. Scully didn't like the new pucker of her wounds. They seemed moist long after he bathed them. Billie refused to wear her hat but didn't complain of any pain. She seemed in fair spirits. He watched her feed crumbs to the pigeons. He tried not to bug her with conversation. But he resolved to get a list of English-speaking doctors at the American Express office when he went in to check the state of his account. He wondered if the damp had gotten back into the bothy. Winter solstice. How did the Slieve Blooms look today? He felt odd. Disconnected from himself. Yesterday and today. Without pain – almost without feeling. It was like having come through a tunnel, a roaring, blind, buffeting place and come out into the light unsure for a while, if all of you was intact. The disbelief of the survivor.

The bells of the Duomo tolled into the china bowl of the sky. He looked up at the gorgeous cupola. Look at that. It wasn't just love that flunked him out of architecture – it was visions like this, signs across the centuries that told him to give up and stop pretending. The world could do without his shopping malls, his passive solar bungalows. If it wasn't the gap of greatness, then nature would sap the remains of your pride. A drive out to the Olgas, to Ayer's Rock, to a terracotta polis of termite mounds, to the white marble plain of any two-cent salt lake would cure your illusions. Scully had no room left for illusions. What more could be beaten out of him?

DOWN BY THE PITTI PALACE, the Amex office smelt of flowers and paper and damp coats. They were hallowed, frightening places to Scully. Behind glass and wood and carpet, so much power. Queues of smooth, confident men in pinstripes. The well-oiled clack of briefcases. The casual shifting of currencies and information. The instantaneous nature of things. Like a pagan temple. Scully clutched his precious plastic card. Billie hooked a finger through his belt loop. Gently, conscious of the impression they were already making, he pressed the hat onto her head to cover the worst of her wounds. Cowed by the smell of aftershave, he found his Allied Irish chequebook, and brushed at the creases in his shirt. In five languages, all around, people bought insurance, travellers' cheques, guidebooks, package tours, collected mail, flaunted their mobility.

Cash the cheque, he thought. Pray it doesn't bounce. And the list of doctors.

Billie scuffed her RM's in the carpet. He would give up soon – she could feel his key winding down since yesterday. The money burred down on the counter at the level of her nose, she felt the wind of it against her hot cheeks. That little bed in the attic. A horse. A castle.

'And a telegram for you, Mr Scully.'

Billie felt his knee jump against her. She let go his belt loop and watched how carefully he opened the envelope. The money still there on the counter, and people in the queue behind them clucking with irritation.

'Billie?'

She grabbed the money and tugged at him. He smiled. It was a look you wanted to Ajax off his face with a wire brush. She pulled him back from the counter to the rear where old people argued over their maps and kicked their luggage.

'Just let me read it again,' he said vaguely, but she snatched it from him and pressed it flat on a low table.

SCULLY. MEET TUILERIES FOUNTAIN NOON DECEMBER 23. COME ALONE. WILL EXPLAIN. JENNIFER.

It was hard to breathe, looking at it. Not even the bit about him going alone. Just the idea, like a rock falling from the sky. The wickedness of it. It made Billie's chest hurt, as if she'd gulped onion soup so hot it was cooking her gizzards.

'She shouldn't be allowed,' she whispered.

The Tuileries. Paris. The part near the English bookshop. All the white gravel. Where she collected chestnuts and made a bag out of her scarf. Paris. It wasn't fair.

Her mother.

Questions hung like shadows behind Scully's head. His thoughts went everywhere and no place. Blasts, flickers, comets of thought. A miscarriage, a bleed contained. Missed calls and telegrams. Had she wired every Amex office in Europe to find him? Was she frightened and desperate, circumstances piling up, fear taking her whole body? Could she perhaps believe for a moment that he mightn't come? That he'd passed a point somehow. Oh God, was she feeling pain and panic like him, aching even in sleep for a break in the smothering static, simply not knowing? Chasing *them?* How little had they missed each other by? How would they find the distance to laugh about this later, at the comic weirdness of it, taking for granted the great terrifying leaps they'd come to so casually make from time zones and continents, seasons, languages, spaces. You forget so quickly the teetering bloody peril of movement, of travel. The lifting of your feet from the earth.

He flickered on in the wake of his own mind. A jilting, maybe. A thing, an attachment come unstuck. A mistake, a human fuck-up of the heart she'd suddenly seen. In ten days? Or some medical thing, like a blood test, an x-ray she couldn't bring herself to tell about until now. In Ireland he was so cut off, so bloody preoccupied with physical, urgent things, and his own sad-sack loneliness, for pity's sake. He wasn't paying enough attention. Should have called every second day, kept up with progress. Some terrible family thing maybe she'd kept from him all these years for his own sake. Or some . . . some development, some new coming to terms, some change of heart, some Road-to-Damascus experience, as the Salvos called it. Religion even. Or Art. Some blinding light, some stroke of luck or genius or force – who knows – even a simple, mawkish explanation would do him. A scalding blast of hatred. News of another man, a whole new life – he really felt he didn't care, that he could take it between the eyes. Because all he could hold in the spaces of his brain for longer than a second was her standing there in boots and a coat, her scarf like an animal round her neck. There on the arid geometry of the Tuileries. Bare trees, low sky. And only steaming breath between them.

He looked up to see Billie press out through the glass doors. He snatched up the telegram and surged out into the street after her.

'Billie!'

She was doll-like, her hands slack at her sides as she stumped along the cobbles, ankles tilting madly in her riding boots. The street was heady with coffee and cigar smoke.

He drew up beside her, laid a hand on her shoulder. She wrenched aside and kept walking.

'Billie.'

What if she wants me? Billie thought. You only get one mother.

'Billie, stop. What about the doctor?'

'I'll scream,' she said hoarsely. 'If you touch me, if you talk to me I'll scream and police'll get me. They'll take me off you.'

He stood there, stunned. Cars and cobbles shone in a drizzle he hadn't even noticed. She wiped her face on the dewy arm of her jacket and with a sobering visible force of will she straightened her back and pulled out the wad of lire he had left on the counter.

'Just don't talk,' she whispered.

And they said not a word between them all through the streets to the hotel and the station and the night train to Paris.

## *Thirty-four*

SCULLY PROPPED HIMSELF UP in his bunk to watch the lights of the Italian Riviera peel by. Boats were stranded stars out in the low darkness. Tunnels tipped him into roaring space and gave him gooseflesh. He couldn't see beaches but in the unlit gaps, in places no steel or concrete would fit, he sensed them out there. Palm-lined boulevards, stretches of sand. Breaking waves.

He recalled that weekend at St Malo in Brittany, the sight of a beach after so long landlocked in London and Paris. The wind off the channel was vile. The sand was ribbed by the outgone tide. It was so strand-like, so strange. In boots and coats the four of them belted up the shoreline, running in the wind, beneath the medieval ramparts of the old city. You could imagine Crusaders on this beach as easily as Nazi soldiers. Protected by a tidal spit, a fortress stood out in the sea as an advance guard. It wasn't much of a sea but it sharpened his homesickness all the same. Inside the rampart walls overlooking the channel, built into their very cavities, was a labyrinth of marine aquariums, a discovery that delighted him. While the other three charged on through, gasping and nudging on ahead with their girlish voices reverberating in the subterranean dankness, Scully lingered at every tank, studying fish he did not recognize.

It was a good weekend, a relief from Paris. Of all their Parisian friends Dominique was the one Scully came closest to relaxing with. There was no sexual brittleness between her and him, no vast cultural gap. She carried her Leica everywhere, that weekend. Along the waterfront, in the strange old cemetery, in cafés and wintry streets. In the deserted hotel they played pool downstairs and drank hot chocolate and calvados. The sound of the shutter clunking away. Pool balls socking into cushions. The channel wind outside. And sea.

Scully opened the train window and felt the frigid blast on his cheeks.

Paris. This time he'd get the best of the bloody place. This time he was free, just passing through. And he wasn't as green as he used to be. No pouting landlords to deal with, no scaly ringworm ceilings of the rich and tightarsed, no looks down the Gallic nose that he'd once had to take humbly, thinking of payday. The drudgery and anxiety of illegal work was gone – nights lying awake stinking of turps with fists like cracked bricks. This time he'd kiss no bums. No apologies for his hideous French or his hopeless clothes. No reason why he couldn't enjoy himself. This time he was taking no prisoners.

He slid the window back down and felt the pleasant numbness of his face. There was no fear tonight, just a wild anticipation. Anything was better than not knowing.

BILLIE WRUNG THE BLANKET AT HER CHEST as the black tunnel of night blasted by her head. Look at him tonight, like

Quasimodo up in the bells. That smiley shine on his face reflected in the glass. His knees up. Like the hunchback kicking the bells, right inside himself, setting bells going that he can't hear. She pulled the bedclothes up over her head and smelt the sourness of her breath. The train lurched and bucked. It felt like it wanted to leave the rails. Right there with the sheet between her teeth and the blanket like a fuggy tent above her head, Billie prayed for an angel, for a whirlwind, a fire, a giant crack in the world that might save them from tomorrow, from the other side of the cloud.

IN THE ZIRCON GLARE OF INDIAN OCEAN WATER – reef water, bombora water, shark water – Scully saw a furrow. He paused at the gunwhale stinking of mackerel blood and running sweat. He peered. A wake, a flat subsurface trail that made him think of dolphins. But this swimmer had limbs. He saw it now – the outline of legs, arms, a kelp fan of hair – and she surfaced beneath him in the clear shade of the boat, naked and slick, breasts engorged, belly huge. Jennifer. Laughing, calling, buoyant. He didn't even hesitate. He went over the side in his sea-boots and heavy apron, the gloves greedily sucking water at his elbows, and he sank like a ballasted pot, roaring down in a trail of bubbles to the hairy, livid base of the reef where Billie waited smiling, her face ragged from sharks, her body breaking up and the shadow of the swimmer on the surface passing over like the angel of death.

# *Thirty-five*

WITH THE HEATER BLOWING ITSELF into a useless fit and his hands stiff on the wheel, Peter Keneally pulls in off the icy road with the mail of the Republic sliding about behind him. He kills the motor in front of Binchy's Bothy, and heaves himself out. It's no damned colder out there. Jaysus, the sky is opaque as frozen ditchwater and the little house stands silent beneath it on the hill. Birds wheel and jockey down at that godawful pile of a castle and cloud spills down from the humpbacked mountains.

The postman unlocks the heavy green door and watches it heel back with a murmur. He's been wanting to do this for a week now, be in Scully's house alone. A smell of fresh mildew. Detergent. Paint and putty. The wee curtains all drawn, the womanly things here and there on sills and shelves. He sets a fire in the grate and lights it, goes prowling, hearing his big ugly boots on the boards and the stair.

The little bed, torn open and left. Some books. *Madeline*, *The Cat in the Hat*, *Where the Wild Things Are*, *Tin-tin*, a big Bible with pictures. The fresh paint on the walls. A whiff of smoke from a chimney crack somewhere. And the big bed all rumpled and strewn with toiletries and clothes dragged out in a hurry. There are books here too. *The World According to Garp*, for Godsake. *Slaughterhouse Five*, *Monkey Grip*. Newspapers, hardware catalogues.

Peter sits on the bed and uncaps his pint of John Jameson. The whiskey goes down like a pound of rusty nails. His heartbeat is up, being in this house. It has the strange fresh feeling of the new. It doesn't look Irish anymore. The nicely made bookshelf beside the bed, the sanded chairs, the bright rug thrown across the floor. The house of a man who knows a few things, good with his hands and thoughtful. A careful man, and thorough, able to cook and do all these womanly things. A fella with books by his bed and stories of Paris and the red desert and huge blinking fish. A man with a child, no less. Yes, he envies old Scully, no way round it. All that coming and going. Even this little house now – he envies him for what he saw in it.

The postman gets up and opens a few drawers. He touches shirts and pencils, picks up a photograph of a girl with coal black hair and a ghost's still face. The sky is blue behind her. His mind goes blank just looking at her, and he returns the photo to the drawer and sits back on the bed to look at his boots.

Conor. That's who Scully reminds him of. The old Conor. Could be why he likes the man for no good reason, could be why he doesn't move in here and squat, take possession in lieu of payment for all those bills unpaid. Scully's fierce about life, like old Con. Life's a fight to the friggin death, it is.

The fire chortles in the chimney and the postman lies back, takes another belt of Jameson and finds himself thinking the Our Father, just thinking it like a man afraid for himself, while the mail of the Republic lies crumpled down there, going nowhere.

# IV

*Well I loved too much*
*And by such and such*
*Is happiness thrown away . . .*

'Raglan Road'

## *Thirty-six*

IN THE SOUPY LIGHT OF DAWN, as the train tocked and clacked languidly into the glass and steel maw of the Gare de Lyon, Scully brushed the child's hair tenderly and straightened her clothes. With his handkerchief he buffed her little tan boots before repacking their meagre things. Porters and tiny luggage tractors swerved across the platform. Pigeons rose in waves. His joints, his scalp, his very teeth tingled with anticipation. He felt invincible this morning, unstoppable. Today was the day. The Tuileries at noon. Look out, Paris.

'This morning,' he said, 'after we find a hotel, I'll take you somewhere, anywhere you want to go. You choose. Anywhere at all, okay. You just name it.'

Billie looked up, feverish with prayer and worry. 'Anywhere?'

He'll know, she thought. He won't have to ask. He'll know where I want to go.

She felt the train stopping. The world swung on its anchor a moment. Everything rested. Nothing moved inside or out of her.

It was like a sigh. Billie held on to the moment while the edges of things shimmered.

WITH HIS FACE IN THE FRIGID SKY and the sweat of the climb turning to glass on him, Scully tilted his head back and laughed. The wind rooted through his hair, billowed his hopelessly underweight jacket and tugged his cheeks. He laid his bare hands on the stone barrier and looked out across the whole city whose gold and green and grey rooftops lay almost vulnerable beneath him. Yes, Paris was beautiful still, but not crushingly beautiful. Up here it had a domestic look – all its intimidatory gloss, all its marvels of hauteur and hubris failed to carry this far. To the north the wedding cake of Sacre Coeur, to the west the rusty suppository of the Eiffel Tower. Even the monochrome turns of the Seine seemed quaint between spires, mansards, quais and balding regiments of trees. It was just a place, a town whose traffic noise and street fumes reached him at a faint remove.

He swept along the parapet, the tour guide barking behind him. The wind made tears in his eyes, blurring his vision of the sculpted rectangle of the Tuileries across the river. Within a spit of the bell tower. Just beneath him. Here, at kilometre zero.

Billie watched him scuttle out along the walkway, bent over in the freezing wind with pigeons scattering before him. He had his arms outstretched like a conqueror, like a kite, but the wind made a rag of him beneath the overhanging twists of carved stone, the laughing goblins and gargoyles. He wouldn't jump – she knew he wouldn't – but he was airborne anyway with his face bent by gusts of cold.

The others in the tour were turning already, heading back for the protection of the spiral stairs and the creeping dark of the stone walls, but Billie stayed out with him to see the dull glow of the city, marvelling at the way it stood up. The whole underneath of Paris was an ant nest, Metro tunnels, sewer shafts, catacombs, mines, cemeteries. She'd been down in the city of bones where skulls and femurs rose in yellowing walls. Right down there, in the square before them, through a dinky little entrance, were the Roman ruins like a honeycomb. The trains went under the river. There were tunnels people had forgotten about. It was a wonder Paris stood up at all. The bit you saw was only half of it. Her skin burned, thinking of it. The Hunchback knew. Up here in the tower of Notre Dame he saw how it was. Now and then, with the bells rattling his bones, he saw it like God saw it – inside, outside, above and under – just for a moment. The rest of the time he went back to hurting and waiting like Scully out there crying in the wind.

The tour lady yelled from the archway.

Yes, you could see clearly up here. Sanctuary, sanctuary, sanctuary.

She never wanted to leave.

THE HOTEL ON THE ILE ST LOUIS was more than he could afford but Scully figured that for one night it was worth it. All that time in Paris he'd passed it, staring in at its cosy, plush interior, on his way to a painting job with his back aching in anticipation. Hotels like this, their lobbies glowed with warmth and fat furniture, their stars hung over their doorways like gold medals. Hell, you deserved it once, and there'd never be a better day.

In the tiny bathroom he shaved carefully and did the best he could with his clothes. He picked the lint from his pullover, poured a bit of Old Spice inside his denim jacket and helped Billie into her stall-bought scarf and mittens. She shook a little under his hands.

'Nervous?'

She nodded.

'Tonight we'll be all together. Look, two beds.'

'We could go home now,' she murmured.

'In the morning. Be home for Christmas.'

Billie's face mottled with emotion. Wounds stood out lumpy and purple on her forehead. She ground her heels together.

'We don't have to,' she said.

'I do.'

She pushed away from him. 'You go.'

'I can't leave you here.'

'You left me before.'

'Oh, Billie.'

'You'll choose her! She'll make you choose! She said come on your own! I can read, you know! Do you think I'm a slow learner? I can read.'

She didn't want to be there. She didn't want to see, but deep down she heard the tiny voice tell her – you only have one mother, you only have one. She felt his hands on her baking face and knew she would go.

THEY LEFT THE TINY RIVER ISLAND and crossed the Seine at Pont Marie. At the little playground past the quai, Billie stopped to peer through the wrought-iron fence at the kids who yelled and blew steam, skidding in the gravel. She looked at their faces but didn't know any of them. Granmas stomped their feet. A ball floated red in the air. Scully pulled her and she went stiff-kneed along the street into their old neighbourhood.

Scully steered them past the Rue Charlemagne without a word. There wasn't time to think of the sandstone, the courtyard, the smells of cooking, the piano students plunking away into the morning air. They walked up into the Marais where the alleys choked with mopeds and fruit shops, delicatessens, boutiques and kosher butchers. The air was thick with smells: cardboard, pine resin, meat, flowers, lacquer, wine, monoxide. At the fishmongers Scully resisted the urge to touch. Cod, sole and prawns lay in a white Christmas of shaved ice. The streets bristled with people. It was a vision – he felt giddy with it.

Billie yanked on his arm. 'I need to go.'

'To the toilet? Didn't you go back at the hotel?'

'No.'

'Jesus.'

'Don't say that. Gran says you've forgotten the true meaning of Christmas.'

'I'll parcel you up and post you to Gran if you don't –'

'I'm bustin. D'you wanna argue with my vagina?'

'Keep your voice down, will you?' He looked up and down the street, saw a café. 'C'mon.'

He hoisted her into the smoky little joint and found the toilet under the stairs.

'In there,' he murmured, nodding to the patrons propped against the bar.

'*Messieurs.*'

The proprietor, a fat man with earrings and peroxided curls raised his eyebrows.

'*Et pour monsieur?*'

Scully took a moment to get it. No such thing as a free piss.

He ordered an *espress* and sat looking at the bleary men with their English rock-star complexions. They all had moustaches, it seemed, and had taken the night's revelry into the morning. They looked spent.

His coffee came and Billie emerged from the stairwell.

'I looked for *Femmes*.'

'Yeah?'

'But they were all Homos.'

'*Hommes*.'

'No, it was Homos on both doors. There was a man in one.'

Scully paused, coffee halfway to his mouth. 'Oh?'

'He was asleep on the floor. Too tired to pull his pants up, I spose. He had a flower sticking out his bum.'

The coffee cup clacked back into its saucer.

'Come on.'

Scully left some francs on the table and hoiked her out into the street.

'Let's stick to the automatic toilets from now on, huh?' The further he got from the little café the sillier he felt.

'The ones you put money in? The money dunny?'

'That's the one.'

'They have music so no one hears you fart. And they wash themselves, you know. But the music's the best.' She looked at him, smiling suddenly. 'I reckon someone stuck it in for a joke.'

'What's that?'

'The flower.'

'Oh gawd.'

'Still,' she smiled shrewdly, 'it could have grown there. If he didn't wash.'

All the way up the Rue de Rivoli, bumping against each other like drunks, they screamed and giggled.

IT WAS COLD AND STILL IN THE TUILERIES. The long arid promenades of white gravel crackled underfoot. Bare chestnuts and planes stood without shadows. From the Louvre entrance they walked nervously, eyes narrowed with alertness. Now and then, in their path, lay a horse chestnut left over from the time of sunlight and leaves. Only a few people were about. Children in hoods and mittens chased by au pairs. Old men playing boules. Up at the Concorde end the fountain stood in the air straight as a flagpole.

Scully scanned the terraces toward the Orangeries museum. Twenty minutes to spare. His jaw ached with the tension. Billie scuffed in the gravel beside him, hat low on her brow. He dug out five francs for the swings and watched her tip and soar for a while. Bit by bit his sense of triumph was ebbing. What would he say? How could he control himself? He mustn't frighten her off with the intensity of his feeling. He felt like a ticking bomb. No outburst of questions, no hint of recrimination. No bawling and breastbeating. Just try to be dignified for once in your life.

Scully gave Billie sixteen francs for the carousel. The coins rattled damply in his hands. Billie climbed up onto a white horse with a flaring tail. He sat beside two teenage girls who chattered and admired one another's cowboy boots. The lights and bright paint of the carousel made a livid whirl in the dull midday. Scully shifted from buttock to buttock in the cold, swivelling now and then to scrutinize the trees behind him. He felt watched. Or paranoid. Or something. The girls beside him grew uneasy and moved off.

Five to twelve. He stood and prowled about the carousel, handed the operator more money, and waved sickly to Billie. Her horse's teeth were bared, as if striving to bite the tail of the horse in front. They were all the same, each horse bearing down upon the next. The gay antique music set his nerves on edge.

Shit – would she show up? Okay, he'd brought Billie, despite the strict instruction of the telegram, but what alternative did he have? How could she hold it against him? He was without a clue. He had searched himself, as the Salvos said, he had examined his heart and come back to complete incomprehension. After all his guesses, all his agonies, he couldn't know why she hadn't shown at Shannon and now he didn't know why she was turning up here. Faith. He was running on the scrag end of faith. In ten days Jennifer had become a ghost to him, an idea, a mystery. But her telegram crackled against his chest. A sign. It was all he had to go on.

She'd get off at the Concorde Metro and come in by the Jeu de Paume entrance, outlined by the blank expanse of the fountain pool. Their old route from St Paul when they'd come to buy Billie books at W.H. Smith across the road. Yes, that's the way she'd come. No ghost. His wife. He knew her too well.

Tonight he'd take them out somewhere flash and traditional. Brass, leather, lace curtains. Waiters with their thumb up their arse. Snails, tails and quails – the full Gallic gallop. A good Bordeaux. A stroll on the quais. A return to civilization.

'I don't feel good,' said Billie climbing down.

Noon. The ground felt spongy beneath him.

'Sit down for a minute. You're dizzy.'

Billie sat in the spinning shining world. Her skin was bursting and the blood inside her boiled. A chime went off inside her head. She saw sculptures up behind the fountain. They danced in the woozy glow. The seat shook like the floor of a jet. The marbled veins in that white, white face. Billie reaching out, scared to touch, scared not to. Her fingers outstretched to feel the white skin before it sets and goes hard. The smile tight as cement. The skin cold. Right before her, Billie sees it, as the cloud of silence comes down in the air of the plane. Bit by bit, her mother is turning into a statue. Something stopped. Something the rain hits and runs off, something whose eyes pale over. With an open mouth, saying nothing.

Scully saw the hooded figure appear on the terrace and felt a rash of gooseflesh. The figure froze, then turned in a whirl of dark coat as Scully straightened. He watched it stride toward the Orangeries, walking too fast for a stroll in the park. A white flash of face, a quick look and suddenly the figure tipped into a run.

Scully grabbed Billie's arm and broke for the terrace steps. The fountain hissed. The gravel squinched and cracked like ice underfoot. He felt Billie wheeling and stumbling beside him, her legs too short to keep balance at such speed. She cried out, wrenched away and went skidding on all fours but he didn't stop. The terrace steps were blows in the spine, the handrail burning cold, and at the moment he made the last step, he saw the shoulders and hood ducking down the street entrance to Place de la Concorde, so he wheeled right, knowing the Metro entrance was out on the corner and he had an even chance of coming down ahead of her. The gravel slurred, gave perilously beneath him. He hit the stairs and went down five at a time, barely in control, and heeled around the corner to the Metro entrance where there were more stairs and steel doors that swung to as he hit them. He burst through into the stink of piss and electricity and the sound of the train doors closing below. Empty stairs, drifts of butts and yellow *billets*. Four ways she could have gone and a train pulling out. The gritty air hung on him as he stood gasping and impotent against the tile wall.

'You're killing us!' he screamed. 'Fucking killing us!'

Two kids in a French parody of surfwear came up the steps nudging each other at the sight of him. The doors opened behind him to let in a shock of fresh air that stung his eyeballs and pressed him flat to the wall like the shadow he was.

UP IN THE COLD CHOKING FOG Billie screamed and saw it all about her. Whirling all around were statues and birds and her own frightened voice, and pee ran down her legs hot as molten lead, burning her up, just burning her up.

## *Thirty-seven*

SCULLY CARRIED THE CHILD tightly wrapped in his denim jacket down the Rue de Rivoli. In the steadily rising wind, the Christmas crowd avoided contact, made way, registering the desperate look of them in a second. Billie did not talk. Her face was swollen with weeping and something worse. The wind battered the canopies of oyster stalls and the upturned collars of holly sellers. Wreaths and wrapping paper skidded out into fogged gloss of a thousand gridlocked cars. Outside the glass doors of the BHV department store Scully submitted to the body search with a kind of hopeless rage. The guards smelled the piss on Billie's jeans and recoiled. Scully hurled the wet jacket into the street and greeted the warm rush of air as the doors opened before him.

BILLIE TRIED TO PULL THE NEW JEANS UP over her knees but the floor was sagging everywhere and her skin was cooking. She looked in the mirror and saw a crybaby, a sook, a beggar with scraped knees and no knickers, glowing like a bushfire.

With an armful of elastic-backed jeans, as Christmas muzak

rained on him and women bustled by with chirping kids, Scully stood outside the changing booth and tried to complete a thought – any thought. Knickers, jacket, credit card. Words, things petered out in his mind.

'Scully?'

Billie's voice was quavery.

'You alright?'

He slid the curtain aside a little and saw the kid pressed against the fogging mirror, pants around her shins.

'Can't you get them up?'

She turned slowly as a tightrope walker and he saw the glassy sheen of her eyes. 'I'm . . . I'm hot.'

Scully fell to his knees and touched her bare skin. She had a fever. God, she was burning. Her wounds pouted nastily beneath their moist plaster strips.

'Okay,' he murmured. 'Let me help you. We'll get undies on the way out.'

He had the little jeans almost up when he felt the shadow of someone behind the curtain and heard the sharp intake of breath. He swivelled and saw a woman with a hand to her mouth. A livid flush came to her cheeks as he pulled the jeans up and snapped the press-stud without looking down. He tried to shrug casually and smile in a comradely parental way, but the woman turned on her heel. Scully set his teeth and finished up grimly. He gathered Billie in his arms and headed for the register.

## *Thirty-eight*

INTO THE WINDTUNNEL OF THE RUE DE RIVOLI they come, bent as a single tree, clothes and shopping demented with flapping. She slips back into the bleak doorway to let them pass blindly by without feeling the heat of her love. She knows where they are going. She knows everything there is to know about them the way the dead see the living. The wind pricks her nipples and knees, the tip of her nose, and she watches her life limp by in the weird light of afternoon while she decides how far to follow, wondering when enough is enough, asking herself why it hurts to need so badly.

# *Thirty-nine*

A TELEPHONE, THAT WAS THE FIRST THING. Somewhere out of this wind, a phone. Dominique would be in town. She'd have a GP. She could translate for him. God, Scully how could you let this happen?

The streets were icing up now, the cobbles slick with it. Clochards hauled themselves out of doorways and headed for the shelter of the Metro. Billie's mittened hand fluttered against his cheek. Car horns bleated in the narrow alleys of the Marais. He knew a place, a good place.

He swung into the fuzzy doorway of Le Petit Gavroche where the goldfish still swam in its glass orb atop the beer tap. The barman greeted him noncommitally, trying to place him. Faces came and went here. Scully slipped past the bashed zinc counter into the blue bank of cigarette smoke and found a table by the payphone. He sat Billie down, unwrapped her a little, and stowed the shopping bags beneath her.

The place was full of the usual crowd, mostly site workers on their lunchbreak. Scotsmen, Paddies, Luxembourgers. The cash work crew, hard men without papers, dodgy truck drivers, some local students, a few old hookers with big smiles and eyelashes like dead crows. It was Scully's place. He'd heard a lot of stories here. The food wasn't much but the beer was cheap and there was always someone lonely or drunk enough to talk to you.

Scully ordered hot chocolates and sat down to remember Dominique's number. He cancelled Billie's chocolate and made it lemonade. The kid sat there dreamily, trying to pull her mittens off. No, he was a blank. He dragged the butchered phone book out of its slot and looked it up. Yes. What was wrong with him? A simple thing to remember. God, his mind was going.

He stood up, stuck some francs into the phone and dialled. It rang and rang without an answer. The drinks came. Billie drank greedily. He got up and dialled again but no one picked up. Bugger it – that meant he had to ring Marianne. There just wasn't anyone else. He dialled.

'*Allo, oui?*' The familiar deep voice. She had the timbre of a forties movie star. He paused a second, hesitating.

'Marianne, it's Scully.'

'Scully?' The mellifluous tone wavered. 'My Gahd, Scully, where are you?'

'Just around the corner, as it happens.'

'*Comment?* Scully, what did you say?'

'The Marais. I'm in the Marais.'

There was a considerable lag at the other end, as if Marianne were reaching over to turn something off – coffee pot, word processor, stereo. Scully saw Billie picking at the crust around the lid of the mustard pot.

'What . . . what a surprise,' breathed Marianne.

'Listen, I'm sorry to call out of the blue but I was wondering if I could drop by for a second.'

'N-no, it's not possible,' she murmured. 'You understand, I have my work –'

'Yes, of course, but listen –'

The line went dead. He rang back. Engaged. He flopped back into his seat. Shit – what was all that about? He was not exactly Marianne's cup of tea, he knew, but they'd always been civil. She was flustered, really put out. And hostile.

He gulped at his coffee.

'You don't look good,' said Billie.

'Speak for yourself – Jesus.'

'Don't say that!'

A coat flapping down the stairs. A hooded coat. A blur, but not a ghost, someone real. I showed up and *someone* saw me. Jennifer, or someone else. Someone acting for her, maybe. To make sure I would come, to see that I was in town. Dominique? No, she was too decent. She would have talked to us. And she never struck me as that tall, that light on the loafers. But Marianne. Marianne doesn't fancy me. She wouldn't have qualms about giving me some stick. In fact, she'd probably enjoy it. Was everyone in on this? Why send a message and not show? Were they playing with him?

Billie licked sweat from her upper lip.

All those people you read about. The bloke who goes out for a packet of fags never to be seen again. Families whose kids go missing. People who live in limbo for years, always expecting the phone to ring, a door to open, a face to appear in a television crowd. Every mail bringing an absurd hope. And all the time really waiting, begging for the *coup de grâce*, the last swing of the axe to put them out of their misery. Horribly grateful to have the mangled, molested bodies of their loved ones finally uncovered in some vacant lot so that they can give up the poisonous hoping and be free.

Was that how it would be? A life of waiting by the phone? No. He didn't care what it took. He'd find out for himself. He wouldn't sit back and go quietly. Bollocks to that. In his soul he'd stepped beyond some mark he didn't understand. Here, quietly, in a crappy café with a lukewarm chocolate in front of him. No, he was too tired, too scared and pissed off to go quietly.

# *Forty*

SCULLY LEANT INTO THE IRON WIND on the Rue Mahler and felt it ride up under his eyelids and whistle in his molars. He skated with Billie across the cobbles and shouldered his way past the sumptuous grey door into the frozen calm of Marianne's courtyard.

Lights burned up on the third floor. Scully's heart beat painfully. He felt the metal of the wind in him.

'Take no prisoners,' he muttered.

Billie quaked and said nothing.

In the entry hall which smelled of mail and polish he jabbed the intercom button hard enough to feel bone through the numbness. His twenty-five-franc mittens were stiff and damp.

'*Oui, allo?*'

'Me again.'

Nothing. Just static. A blizzard from that little speaker box. He looked at his boots, felt the chill of the wind still in his spine, saw Billie's feverish eyes and livid cheeks.

'It's cold down here, Marianne. And I've brought Billie.'

It was a long ugly few seconds before the access door clicked open. He took Billie's mittened hand and they went up silently in the elevator. It was familiar, that little red box. He remembered coming down in it with Jennifer a couple of times, both of them four sheets to the wind and giggling like kids.

Up on her floor Marianne had the door open. Her thick auburn hair was free and she wore little lace-up shoes and a black woollen suit. She fixed him with a firm smile.

'Scully, you look –'

'Terrible, I know.'

She presented her cheeks to him in the ritual manner and touched Billie's head gravely and then the three of them stood awkwardly in the hallway.

'We're house-trained, Marianne. It's safe enough to let us in.'

She hesitated a moment and turned on her heel. Scully followed across the lustrous timber floor into the kingdom of steam heat and hired help. Marianne's two fat Persians loped away to hide. The apartment smelled of polish and of the oil of the puce abstracts that hung huge on the white walls. Scully couldn't help but run his hand across the painted surface of the plaster as he went. His first job in Paris, this place. It was perfect. He worked like a pig on it and took a pittance, setting the tone for the rest of his time here. Still, they were friends, Jennifer's new friends, and he was eager to please.

But sometimes he wondered if the cheapness of his bill hadn't caused its own problems. Marianne had been more friendly to him first up – effusive, even. But after the paint job she cooled off. For a few weeks he tried to think of anything he could have done wrong. The job was excellent, but had he spilt primer on something, scratched the floor somehow, pissed on the toilet seat? There was nothing – not even a *Rainbow Warrior* joke. It was the size of his bill. She wasn't insulted – Scully always let her know that he knew she and Jean-Louis were loaded – but it was as though she felt he expected something in return. A fresh guardedness lay across the top of her Parisian diffidence. She saw him as a loser, he thought. Not just a tradesman but a cut-rate one at that. Europe – it was hair raising.

'I'll have coffee and Billie'll take a hot chocolate,' he said brightly. 'She's a bit sick. You remember Marianne don't you, Billie.'

Billie nodded. Marianne stood beneath the big casement windows, mouth contracting on its smile. She was all diagonals – nose, hips, breast, lips – and not at all like Jean-Louis who was more the fulsome type with the lines of a nineteen-forties automobile. Jean-Louis was easier to like, softer in nature as well as in shape.

Not that he'd instantly disliked Marianne. She was smart and funny and seemed genuinely interested in Jennifer, even read her work and showed it around. She worked for a chic magazine and knew people. Her friends were amusing yuppies, handsome, curious and unlike people they'd known before. It felt like a lark to Scully, knowing these people. Jean-Louis had a romantic European fascination for wild places and people. He defended France's right to test nuclear bombs in the Pacific and yet turned purple at the thought of roo-tail soup. Scully liked to shock him and his friends with redneck stories told against himself and his country. Chlamydia in koalas, the glories of the cane toad. The wonders of the aluminium roo-bar. For a while he felt almost exotic at Marianne's parties, but it wore off in the end, playing the part of the Ignoble Savage. He kept up a kind of affable relationship with Jean-Louis, without any intimacy, and a diplomatic air of deferral to Marianne for Jennifer's sake. The parties became a bore. Scully loitered at the bookshelves picking through art books, most of the time, and they left him to it. When Dominique came he relaxed a little more and joined in. And the wine was a consolation. He wouldn't be drinking that stuff back in the borrowed apartment.

'I'll put the kettle on, will I?'

'Scully, I am busy.'

'Too busy for a cup of coffee?'

She sighed and went ahead into the white kitchen and he noticed her limp.

'Hurt your leg?'

'It's nothing. I was sitting on it. It will give me bad veins.'

'Nearly broke my own leg today.'

'Things are not going well for you. You look wild, Scully.'

'Oh, I am wild.'

'Have you done this to Billie?' she said filling the kettle. Her hands trembled. She was fumbling.

'You mean her face? Marianne, she was bitten by a dog. That's what I wanted –'

'In Paris?'

'In . . .' he caught himself. 'Doesn't matter where.'

'She looks like . . . *un fantome*, like a ghost.'

Marianne leaned against the blinding brightness of the bench, sizing him up. Billie came in, her eyes following the cats.

'I have to pee,' Billie murmured.

'Down the hall,' said Scully. 'You remember.' He watched her go.

'I can't help you, Scully. You know I never liked you. Such a woman with . . . *un balourd* like you.'

'I won't even pretend to know what that means.'

'No, you never did pretend. Such a simple man's virtue.'

'Tell me about the park today.'

Marianne's hoarse laugh was a tiny sound in that bleached space. 'Scully, you are losing your mind.'

'Yeah, I'm tired and mean and desperate.'

'I can call the police. You are a foreigner, remember.'

'Oh, I remember.'

Marianne reached for a pack of Gauloises and lit up shakily. She smiled.

'Share the joke, Marianne.'

'Oh, Scully, you are the joke.' She dragged hard on the cigarette and blew smoke over him. 'So you are all alone.'

'You know, then.'

'Scully you are the picture of a drowning man. I do not have to *know*.'

'Where is she?'

'If I knew do you really believe I would tell you? My Gahd!'

The kettle began to stir.

'You're enjoying this, aren't you?'

'Oh, yes.'

Scully's skin crawled. A cold anger percolated through him.

'I figured you were a little nasty, Marianne, but I thought deep down you were probably human.'

She laughed.

'Listen to me. Try to listen to me,' he breathed. 'Forget about me. Forget about Jennifer and the baby and what I'm going through. I have a sick –'

'Baby?' Marianne's glossy lips parted. 'She's pregnant?'

'She didn't tell you, then.'

Marianne waved her fag non-commitally. 'It's 'er body, Scully.'

'Of course it's her fucking body. You think I need a night-school course on sexual politics? Do I need permission to be worried out of my bloody mind? I didn't call the cops, no private detective, I go softly, softly and play the game but I'm sick of playing the game, you hear me?'

He kicked a stool across the floor and watched it cartwheel into the wall, jolting shiny implements from their hooks in a horrible clatter. He saw the whiteness of his own fists and the way Marianne had edged into the corner and he thought of Mylie Doolin and the men who did this all the time. She was afraid and he felt the power. He remembered Irma and the ferry. Oh yes, he was capable of anything – he was no different.

'I always believed you beat her, Scully,' she said feebly and then with more defiance. 'The working man out of his depth . . . the charming woman with 'opes for something better. Did you beat her much, Scully? Were you rough in bed, were you 'ard on her, Scully?'

Scully forced his hands into his pockets. The kettle began to boil and he felt the sinews locking up in his arms as he listened to her warming to it, sucking on her fag, getting into her stride.

'You are a basher, aren't you, Scully? Tell me about your face, your very sad eye. It makes me think of beasts, you know.'

He heard the toilet flush and thanked God Billie hadn't heard all this. Christ, at least he'd spared her that

'This is just entertainment for you, isn't it?' he said, choking. 'Like . . . that's all it's ever been. An amusement. The quaint girl from Australia, the one with the clear skin and sun-bleached clothes with all her dreams and optimism and the way she looked at you like you're a queen or something. Your little salon with your wonderful accents and all that fucking confidence. You played with her. You took her under your wing for fun, to see what would happen.'

'You were like a stone on 'er, Scully, an anchor on 'er neck, and now you blame me –'

'I wouldn't blame you for anything except not caring enough to tell her the truth. I heard you, Marianne. You beefed her up to her face, got her excited, told her she was a genius and laughed behind her back. She was just the other primitive. Only she didn't see it. Not even afterwards. She was so keen, so impressed. You kicked the shit out of her and she thanked you for it.'

Marianne sighed. 'Why did you come to Europe, Scully?'

'For her,' he said. 'Both times.'

'It's very touching,' she said doubtfully.

No, he thought, it's fucking pitiful.

Both of them flinched when the phone rang. Marianne clutched the benchtop, nails shining, and let it ring until the answering machine kicked in. Scully knew the voice.

'Why don't you answer it?' he murmured.

'I have visitors,' she hissed.

The message was breathy and urgent, the French way too fast for him.

Dominique. He reached for the phone but Marianne kicked the socket out of the wall.

'She does not need to talk to you.'

Scully took a step back from her, his fists hanging off his arms. He saw a pulse in Marianne's throat. Then Billie came in behind him. She pressed against him, held him round the waist and he felt the heat of her through his clothing, across the flush of his fury.

'Marianne, I need a doctor. I'm here because Billie's got a fever. Will you please, *please* give me a number. Someone who has English, someone close.'

For a while Marianne stood there, arms folded as though to

keep herself together. Scully felt the lightheadedness of real hatred. He was almost disappointed when she reached over to the Rolodex and flicked through it with trembling hands.

'I will call,' she murmured. 'It will be faster for you.'

'Thank you,' he said, unable to refrain.

# *Forty-one*

'YOU SAW THE PAPERWORK ON THE DOG?'

The doctor already had a syringe out. Billie lay on the table, face averted. Scully stood by her, his hand on the radiant nape of her neck.

'Yes.'

'You read Greek?'

'I had a Greek reader with me.'

'This is Flucloxacillin,' said the doctor tapping the syringe, his silver specs glinting under the lights. His accent was American but his body language was European. He even pouted like a Frenchman. 'This should get it, this and the course of tabs. When was her last tetanus shot?'

'At five. I have the certificate.'

Billie inhaled sharply and squeezed his hand. Scully felt sweat settle in his hair.

'There you go, Billie. Not so bad, huh? Here, Dad'll help you with your jeans.'

Billie rolled carefully onto her back, blinking back tears.

'She's brave,' said Scully, for her benefit.

'You're South African?'

'No.'

Scully kissed her hand, let her lie there a moment while the doctor disposed of his tray.

'Five days, you say.'

'Yes. I had to use steri-strips.'

'Well, you could have done worse, I guess. Lucky the big one's above the hairline.'

'Yes.'

'Gimme your address again,' he said, hovering at his desk.

Scully gave him the old St Paul address, suddenly suspicious.

'You see out of that eye?'

'Most of the time.'

'How'd it happen?'

The doctor came back with some fresh dressings. Billie squirmed as he sponged away the clear seepage of her puckered wounds.

'Industrial accident,' said Scully. 'On a boat.'

'Uh-huh.' The quack wasn't buying it. 'How do you make your living, Mr Scully?'

'I'm a builder.'

'You have a *carte du sejour*, then.'

Scully smiled. The doctor washed his hands and peeled off his specs, tilting his head gravely.

'How about seeing me again tomorrow?'

'Thought you'd be all booked up, Christmas Eve.'

'No, tomorrow's good.'

'No problem,' said Scully, helping Billie down from the table.

The doctor proffered the prescription. His smooth hands were neatly manicured. Scully took the papers, seeing it in the other man's face. Tomorrow was something else altogether. He thinks you did it, Scully. The wounds, the grazed knees. He thinks you're scum, that you're not fit to be a father. And how wrong is he? Really, how wrong?

'There's a pharmacy on the corner. Then straight to bed for you, my girl. Plenty of fluids. Nurse will set your appointment.'

'Tomorrow,' said Scully.

'*Au revoir*, Billie.'

'*Au revoir*,' she whispered, leaning on Scully's hip.

At the front desk, Scully presented his credit card and the starched Frenchwoman with the grey chignon made a call to verify its status. He hoisted Billie to his shoulder and stirred at the narrowing of the woman's eyes. She put the phone down, opened a draw and took out a pair of scissors.

'This card is cancelled "Mister Scully".'

'No, no, it's valid till next November.'

She snipped it in two. The pieces clicked to the desk.

'What the hell are you doing?' He lurched against the desk, grabbing the two halves of his card.

'Reported stolen,' she said backing off with the scissors held before her.

'It can't be. Only I can do that. Shit a brick!'

'Of course you have papers of identification?'

'A passport, yes. Here, I have it . . .'

Scully had it almost into the woman's hands before he saw the surge of satisfaction come to her features and he suddenly knew how irredeemably stupid he was. He reeled back, stumbling against a row of waiting patients and stiff-armed his way to the door.

AT THE END OF HIS TRIUMPHANT DAY IN PARIS, Scully lit three deformed candles in the ashtray on the bedside table and watched his child shivering like a small dog under the blanket. Her hair was flat from the shower and her skin waxy in the yellow light. Her trunk was burning, but her hands and feet were cold, and all her nails blue. It terrified him, seeing her like this.

'Christ, what've I done to you.'

She opened her eyes. 'Nothing,' she said. 'And don't say Christ.'

Steam hissed in the walls, burbled in the radiator. Billie closed her eyes again and went to sleep.

Scully ate some bread and cheese and opened a bottle of screwtop red that tasted like deckwash. A pile of crumpled francs and lire and drachmae lay on the eiderdown before him, enough to feed them in couscous joints and *friteries* for a couple of days. He had half a *carnet* of Metro tickets, an Irish cheque book and some dirty clothes. He stank of sweat and fear and frustration and his bad eye was wild in his head. Sooner or later the hotel would twig to his extinct credit card. He was buggered.

He thought of going back to Marianne and begging for help. No aggro, just butt-kissing humility. Or simply robbing the bitch, just busting in and knocking off stuff he could flog in the flea-markets. But he'd never get past the damn security. Besides, he'd never stolen anything in his life and was bound to stuff it up somehow.

He'd try the Amex office. Sort it out. He'd see Dominique. The way Marianne was acting, not letting him talk to her, it could be that Jennifer was over there at Dominique's. Well, no one was answering, even now. Maybe Marianne was just pissing him off, prolonging the nasty moment with that pulled-out phone plug. They'd sort it out. Something. Bloody something.

He took a long swig of his eight-franc wine and gasped. He could be back in Ireland tomorrow night. The mournful wind, the turf fire, the valley unrolling out the window. Pete-the-Post dropping by for a pint and a bit of crack.

Dominique would help him. He gulped down more wine. She had plenty of money, some kind of trust fund that let her pursue photography. And she had a heart. 'Softness', Marianne called it with distaste. He remembered Dominique's show on the Ile de la Cité. Scully turned up ancient with paint specks and people made room for him as though he was another kind of painter altogether. Dominique's photographs were moody tableaux of women in bare rooms into which chutes of light fell. Her subjects' gazes were outward and self-possessed and they reminded Scully of his mother. Marianne hissed out the side of her mouth that the images were *soft*, as though that were a sign of feeble-mindedness, but Scully liked them and Jennifer thought they were works of genius.

She said that a lot in the next year or so. Other people were geniuses. They were gifted, remarkable, ahead of their time, special. Scully began to wonder why people couldn't just be good at things. It went beyond seeing the best in people. All this genius, it was like a blow to her, every stroke a bright light on her failure, her ordinariness. And his too. In Paris she had a way of blinking at him sometimes, as if trying to see something more than steady old Scully. It made him nervous, that blinking stare. It wasn't the cool look she shot him across the tutorial room back in the beginning. It caused him to put his hands in his pockets and raise his eyebrows, appealing hopelessly, for a flicker of recognition. But she simply blinked and stared, as if he was a tree in her window, something she was looking through to a more brilliant world beyond.

He even mentioned it to Dominique, that look. 'She is excited,' she said. 'Only excited.'

'Yes,' he agreed. Maybe that's all it was.

Dominique responded to Jennifer's enthusiasm right from the start. He watched them become friends in the jerky ritualized way the French and English had. He felt welcome at the huge apartment on the Rue Jacob and he saw Dominique's effort to cut some slack for Billie whose feral energy seemed to startle her. Billie was not the ornamental child these people were accustomed to. Billie was, she said, very direct.

Scully saw photos of her place on the Isle of Man, the houseboat in Amsterdam, horses, women he didn't know. It was a calm place, that apartment. He'd go there tomorrow, first thing. He belted the rest of the cheap plonk down and heard a bedhead somewhere butting the wall. A woman was moaning. He finished the bottle and listened to her cry out greedily, and for a moment Billie's eyes opened and fixed on him fiercely and then closed in sleep.

BILLIE COULD SEE HIM UP THERE NOW, swaying in the blistering cold, dangling there with firelight in his huge eyes, snagged by the hair in the huge bare tree. Scully. Crying, he was, calling out, begging for help and no one down there in the deep mud moving at all. Just the baying of dogs and him calling, the hair tight at the sides of his face and his arms flapping. There was no way back from that final bough, nowhere for someone that size to go anywhere but down and Billie just prayed for an angel, prayed and prayed until she burned like a log and horses shook and suddenly someone else was up there, someone small and quick and crying. Billie saw it now, it was her up there, Billie

Ann Scully in her pyjamas with something in her mouth like a pirate. A silver flash. She saw it, the little glowing hand reaching out with the scissors open like the mouth of a dog, and Scully screaming yes and yes and yes, and the sound of his hair cutting like torn paper, Billie cutting his hair free so that he fell, calm and still, falling a long time from that skeleton tree with his eyes open until he hit the mud a long way down and was swallowed up and gone beneath the feet of strangers. Billie saw herself up there, the crying girl with wings, slumped in the tree like a bird.

## *Forty-two*

In sleep Scully felt like a flying fish, a pelagic leaper diving and rising through temperatures, gliding on air as in water. He heard the great oceanic static. He felt seamless. Weightless, free.

He woke suddenly with Billie's face close to his, her eyes studying him, her breath yeasty with antibiotic. She ran the heel of her palm across the stubble of his cheek. Her skin was cool, her eyes clear. The surf of traffic surged below.

'I'm hungry,' she said. 'I feel ordinary again.'

He lay there, muscles fluttering, like a fish on a deck, feeling the dry weight of gravity, the hard surprise of everything he already knew.

Mist lay across the soupy swirl of the Seine. It hung in the skeleton trees and billowed against the weeping stonework of the quais. The river ran fat with whorls and boils, lumpy with the hocks of sawn trees and spats of cardboard. He felt it sucking at him, waiting, rolling opaque along the iced and slimy embankment. It made him shudder. He held Billie's hand too firmly.

'This isn't the way to Dominique's,' she murmured.

'Yes it is. More or less.'

In every piss-stinking cavity the mad and lost cowered in sodden cardboard and blotched sleeping bags. Out of the rain and out of sight of the cops they lay beneath bridges and monuments, their eyes bloodshot, their faces creased with dirt and fatigue. Was it some consolation to imagine that Jennifer might be here among them? Did the idea let him off, somehow, take the shame and rage away? These faces, they were generic. Could you recognize a person reduced to this state? Maybe he'd walk past her and see some poor dazed creature whose features had disappeared in hopeless fright. Would she recognize him, for that matter? Was his face like that already?

Beneath the Pont Neuf he stepped among these people and whispered her name. The stoned and sore and crazy rolled away from him. Billie tugged at his hand but he stared into their eyes, ignoring their growls of outrage until a big gap-toothed woman reared and spat in his face. Billie dragged him out into the faint light of day. She sat him down in the square at the tip of the island, and pressed the gob away from his face with his own soiled hanky. He let out a bitter little laugh. She hated to see the way he trembled. She hated all of this.

Scully looked back toward the bridge. Something in the water caught his eye. Something, someone out in the churning current. He shrugged off the child and went to the edge of the embankment to peer upstream. Dear God. He saw plump, pink limbs, tiny feet, a bobbing head. He wrenched his coat off. Please God, no.

'Sit down, Billie, and don't move! You hear me? Don't move from this spot!'

He edged down the slick embankment, grabbing at weeds and holes in the cobbles. The current was solid. He looked about for a stick, a pole, but there was only dogshit and crushed Kronenberg cans. Close to the water he found a ringbolt and he hung out precariously from it, tilted over the water, reaching with one arm as the tiny pink feet came bounding his way. The steel was cold in his anchored hand. His face stung. His heart shrank in his chest. He saw ten perfect toes. Creases of baby fat. Dimpled knees. He poised himself, seeing his chance, and in one sweeping arc he reached out – and missed. Oh God! His fingers sculled hopelessly on the water. And then he saw it clearly as it floated gamely by – cherry mouth pert and cheeky, plastic lashes flapping as it pitched, cupped hands steering it through the soupy convergence at the end of the island.

'I'm not really into dolls,' called Billie, standing precariously close to the edge. 'But I'm glad you tried.'

Scully hung there panting, the sweat cold on him already. He hated this town.

THE RUE JACOB WAS SLUSHY WITH THAWING ICE. Scully struggled in through the courtyard door to the quiet world of Dominique's garden. Cypresses, sunning benches. Banks of tall elegant windows and Romeo and Juliet balconies. At the foyer he buzzed her floor and got nothing. It was early still. He buzzed again, waited a few moments without result. Then he leant on the button half a minute or so, feeling his hopes ebbing. All day yesterday she hadn't answered. Last night again. But that call at

Marianne's. Where was she? Wherever she was, Marianne would have called her. Told her God knows what.

In her mail slot there were bills and a plastic-wrapped copy of *Photo-Life*. He looked at Billie who avoided his gaze. Her nose was rosy, her cap askew. He peered at the postmarks. Yesterday, the day before. She wasn't in Paris at all.

He stabbed the button for the apartment next to hers.

'*Allo. Oui?*'

'Er,' he stammered. '*Excuse moi, Madame, je . . . chercher Mlle Latour.*'

In the long pause Scully felt his accent, his foreignness sinking in upstairs, and he knew he was probably buggered.

'*Qui? Qui es la?*'

'*Je m'appelle Fred Scully, un ami. Je suis Australien.*'

'*Australie?*'

Then the woman spoke quickly, too quick for him to understand, and all he really heard was '*le train*' and then she signed off sharply and he could get nothing more from her. He hammered the button till his fingertip throbbed. The train? That definitely didn't mean the Metro. Where would she go by train? What did it matter anyway. She wasn't here. No help. He still needed money. He couldn't go back to Marianne. Maybe Jean-Louis, but he'd be at work now, and besides who knows what Marianne had told him. Fat chance there. In a whole city, somewhere he'd lived the better part of a year there was nobody. Not a soul. It was hard to believe. He was water off a duck's back.

That left American Express. Or the embassy. Way to go.

Out in the street a lonely Japanese tourist beckoned for him to take a photo in front of some statue, but Scully waved the camera aside and dragged Billie toward the nearest Metro.

Underground the city was surging, pressing, breaking into a jumbled run, thick with mittens, caps, greatcoats, mufflers and a foetid steam of damp and overheated wool. The tunnels were sweet and septic, echoing with shouts and the march of feet. A saxophone mooned around some corner. Stalls of flowers, their colours crazy and shocking down here in the monochrome blur, erupted at intersections where masses of bodies merged like forks of thc khaki river above.

Scully stepped over men with scrawled cardboard placards, around women with swaddled babies and rattling cups. In a corner by the paper shop the *Flics* bailed up an Arab and snatched at his papers. Scully steered Billie down to the platform as a train came gushing out of the darkness on a blast of dry, stale air.

AS THE CARRIAGE HURTLED THROUGH THE DARK, a gypsy child made her way through the crowd with a small leather purse held open, her voice chirruping gaily down the aisle. When she came to Scully he closed his eyes against her and smiled faintly. She moved to Billie who stared uncertainly at her and then down into the purse. The gypsy child knelt daintily, her black eyes upturned, and Billie reached out and touched her hair. Scully shook his head, still smiling. The train braked hard and wheezed into the next station and the girl stood up, shrugged, smiled brightly at them, and made for the doors.

'I liked her,' said Billie as they careered off again.

Scully nodded, preoccupied.

'Was that begging?'

'I guess.'

'She didn't look poor.'

Not as poor and raggedy as us, he thought, and that's for bloody certain.

'I could do that,' she murmured. 'If I had to. To get us home.'

They bumped snugly on, legs pressed to one another, their wiry curls bobbing enough to catch the eyes of other passengers who exchanged small smiles at the sight.

The *train*, thought Scully. Dominique caught the train. She had a house on the Isle of Man, houseboat in Amsterdam. You didn't catch a train to the Isle of Man. Well, good luck to her.

UP IN THE STREETS AROUND THE OPERA the air was still and a faint sun caught in brass door trims, on the panels of turning buses. It lit the flowing breaths of shoppers as they strode four deep along the pavement; it caught coffee cups, boot heels, earrings; it wrought glory and fire amidst the gilt statuary above the Opera itself and forced a beauty upon the crowded streets lined with oyster stalls and the outlandishly decorative carcasses of pigs and half-plucked poultry. Scully navigated the crush past wine cellars, brasseries, airline offices. He held Billie in against his hip and found the building.

At the Amex entrance he felt the hot gust of conditioned air and smelled perfume, leather, money. The armed guards frisked him gently and patted Billie down in jovial Christmas spirit. A poster of Karl Malden's beaming benevolent face looked down on them. That turnip nose – Scully recognized a brother there.

Inside was a calm civilization. Floors of it. There were slick counters and windows, glossy rails, armchairs. People queued thoughtfully or sat with folders and umbrellas in their laps as though they'd come inside simply for refuge. Midwesterners in checkerboard slacks, and chinos. Golfing shoes, pork pie hats, customized baseball caps. Women in nylon slacks and virginal Nikes, their hair hard with spray, quilted jackets thrown across their knees. Camcorders swung at hip level.

He'd come here before to change money, and collect rent wired from Fremantle every month. Each time he wondered if the miracle would fail, whether the money would somehow evaporate in the wires, and the hieroglyphs on his plastic card lose their power. He envied these cologned businessmen browsing in the merchandising department, signing cheques and releases with their Mont Blanc pens. They had faith. They were certain of their rating, their status, their on-bookings and connections. They spoke in the plangent tones of the righteous and unselfconscious. There was nothing apologetic about their English or their requests.

Scully went down the spiral staircase, avoiding the sight of himself in the field of mirrors, and sloped across to the customer service desk.

The clerk was cool and sympathetic, his English precise, his tailoring exquisite. Scully tried not to think of the figure he himself cut. The man was doing his utmost professional best not to look suspicious or disdainful, but Scully could see his resistance to the story. He repeated it all calmly.

'Before anything else,' he said, 'I'd like to know who reported it stolen.'

'Of course you have some identification, sir.'

Scully laid his passport on the counter. The blue seriousness of it, the emu and kangaroo of the coat of arms were not reassuring.

'Hmm.' The clerk fingered it and clacked on his keyboard. 'You have another signatory to this account, sir, do you not?'

'Yes, my wife. J. E. Scully. We share it in my name. Not very modern, I guess.'

'According to records, sir, it was you who reported this card stolen.'

Scully hopped from foot to foot. 'Well. Well, as you can see, it's right here in my hand.'

'In two pieces, *monsieur*.'

Scully swallowed. 'Yes.'

'Well. I believe we can fix this problem. Hmm.' The clerk clacked a little further, narrowed his eyes unpleasantly.

'Are you in Paris long?'

Scully retrieved his passport as casually as he could. 'I don't know. No.'

'Will you be making a payment on this account soon?'

'I have credit still, don't I?'

'Yes, *monsieur*, you still have twenty-eight American dollars.'

'What?'

Heads turned. Billie pressed against him.

'The computer says twenty-eight –'

'That's nearly four thousand dollars. I haven't spent that much!'

'The account is before me, *monsieur*.'

Scully thought about it. With what he had rattling in his pockets he'd never pay off the hotel or even get out of the country.

'Can I see that account?' he croaked.

'I can read the details off, sir. It would be quicker. If you would prefer –'

'No, read it out.'

Scully looked at the clear sweatprint of his hand on the counter. There were old scabs on his knuckles. He saw dirt in his nails. It simply wasn't possible that he'd blown his credit, unless Jennifer had spent up in Australia. Or since.

'Just the places for the moment.'

The clerk sighed and recited tonelessly.

'In December: Perth. Perth. Birr. Roscrea. London/Heathrow. Dublin. Athens. Rome. Florence. Paris. Paris. Amsterdam. Amsterdam.'

Scully set his nails against the counter and breathed. 'Yes. Of course.'

Amsterdam.

'Sir, here is the form for the reporting of –'

'Can you give me the details on Amsterdam?'

'A restaurant, sir. Three hundred dollars. And a fine art gallery. One thousand two hundred and seventy-five dollars.'

'No hotel?'

'In Amsterdam? No, sir.'

Scully could see pity in the clerk's face. A softening somehow.

'The form, sir.'

'No. Don't bother.'

'*Monsieur*?'

Scully turned away, pivoting his whole body as though he was encased in plaster. There was no use waiting for a replacement card. It would be worthless. They'd cut it in two before the day was out. Amsterdam.

Faces, arms, umbrellas slurred by. He ascended the staircase like an old man, the child holding his elbow. Billie piloted him for the doors.

'Look!' she cried.

Scully straightened. He stared at the entrance Billie was

heading for. There, accepting the pats and poking of the guards with great pleasure, was Irma. He could not believe it and yet he was hardly surprised. She saw him and her face lit up like a grill and something turned inside him so that he saw clearly, with the logic of a shithouse rat, his ticket out of Paris and the cold sweat of this day. He began to laugh.

## *Forty-three*

BILLIE FELT THE SWEET STICKINESS of Irma's lipstick against her cheek. She smelled of flowers and chocolates and smoke and she was so small compared to Scully. Billie hugged her, surprised that her arms could go all the way around.

'Europe is so small,' she murmured. 'And you, Billie, you're so big.'

'Well, fancy this,' said Scully.

They all stood there a moment. Irma's eyes were bright. She wore black tights under a little denim skirt with pointy boots. Over her saggy jumper was a cracked leather jacket. Her ears jangled with rings and studs.

'I was thinking about a walk,' she said.

'Don't you have business in here?' said Scully.

'Oh, it can wait.'

Scully smiled. It was a surprise to see it. 'Sure,' he said.

They went out into the river of people on the street and just went with the current. Billie walked between the two of them, holding their hands. The town looked polished, all the way down the big streets toward the river. A woman with two dogs came their way and Billie leaned away from them, turning her face.

'Christmas Eve!' said Irma. 'Can you believe it?'

'No,' said Scully and Billie at the same time. He blushed.

They walked on a long way until her legs got tired. Irma led them into a café. She ordered apple juice for Billie and Pernod for them.

Irma pulled off her jacket and rolled up her sleeve.

'Look.'

She had a tattoo of a knife on her white arm. The knife had flowers around it.

'Did it hurt?' asked Billie.

Irma laughed. She pulled a flat packet out of her pocket.

'They're stick-on, silly.'

Billie tipped them out on the table. One was an anchor. There was a snake. One said MOTHER but the next one was a shark.

'Can I?' Billie said to Scully.

He shrugged. The café was full. He looked busy again, in his head.

Scully watched Irma lick the kid's arm wet. She looked up as she did it, deliberately engaging his gaze. Billie pressed the shark tattoo to her arm triumphantly.

'Australian,' said Irma gulping her *pastis*. 'She chooses the shark.'

Billie held her arm up to the long mirror behind them. 'It's cool.'

Scully nodded. 'Yeah. It's clever.'

Irma raised her eyebrows innocently. He thought about Amsterdam. Irma had been in Amsterdam lately herself.

'I have to go,' said Billie.

'It's just there,' said Scully pointing to the WC door beneath the stairs. 'I'll come with you.'

'No,' said Irma. 'I'll go.'

'I'll go myself,' said Billie. 'So embarrassing!'

'Lock the door,' said Scully.

'What a pair you are.'

'What's the story, Irma?' he said when Billie was out of earshot.

'What story?' She gulped the rest of her *pastis* and called for another.

'This remarkable coincidence.' The moment he opened his mouth, he started seeing it clearer. 'Our meeting at Amex the very day I have to go in and see about my stolen card. The card somebody reported stolen. I'm thinking of the ferry, Irma. Your adventure into my luggage. You got the number then, didn't you? What is it you want from me? I've got no home, no money, no wife. Are you some kind of hustler, a travelling whore?'

'Not professionally, no.'

'Is there an amateur league for whores?'

Irma smiled. Her cheeks flushed. Around the glass tumbler, her nails were uneven, some bitten, some long and glossy with varnish.

'You've been with us since Greece, Irma. That's a long time.'

'Okay, I followed you.'

'*And* the rest.'

'That's all.'

'The Amex card. Who cancelled it, then?'

'Alright, the card, then.'

'And the note. You were in Florence.'

'No, there was no note from me.'

Scully rolled his eyes.

'What note?' She drank greedily and licked her lips.

'And the so-called sighting in Athens. You never saw my wife at the Intercontinental, did you?'

'Yes, I did.'

'Geez, you don't even know when you're lying, do you?'

'Why would I lie, Scully?'

'Why? Why? Why would you get my credit card stopped? Do people like you have reasons?'

Irma smiled bashfully and licked a crimson smear from her teeth. 'People like me? You think I'm mad and just do one thing and then the next thing and then something else, don't you? But that's exactly what *you* do, Scully. It's what you're doing this very minute, it's what you've been at all day, all this week. You follow whatever moves. We're not that badly matched.'

Scully's mind reeled. Was he crazy? Had he lost it so completely?

'Are you a friend of Jennifer's?'

'You might ask yourself the same question, Scully.'

'You are, aren't you?'

'I've never met her,' she said, raising her glass at the waiter and smiling coquettishly at him.

'Never met her? Not even at the Intercontinental?'

'Don't be clever. I told you, I just *saw* her. You're clinging to me like . . . like a Greek to a wooden horse. I saw her. I'm sorry I ever told you. Honestly, can you image Jennifer and me together?'

'What exactly do you mean by that?' said Scully hotly.

'Well, she's like *that*,' she said squinching her index finger into a circle so that a pinhole of light showed through at the centre.

Scully held the table by the legs. 'And you're, you're *what*?'

'Me? I'm interesting. She's just trying to be.'

'Still, you've never met her?'

'I'm like you, Scully. I like being who I am.'

'Irma, just what you are is not real clear.'

'I said *who*, not what. What a sadly *male* thought. I'm like you, Scully. A little rough around the edges. I can take it as well as dish it out. I already forgave you for bolting on me. The ferry. Remember?'

'I'm surprised *you* remember.'

'Okay, I was blasted. Listen, I like you. I like Billie. I just think I deserve another chance. I know you do.'

Scully shook his head and bit back the stream of abuse that bubbled in his throat. But he smiled despite himself. She was a phenomenon alright. And he needed her if he wanted to get to Amsterdam. Time to suck eggs.

'You look wild, Scully, but you're soft.' She laughed and accepted the new *pastis* from the waiter.

'Oh?' That word again. He felt a ridiculous pang of shame at this. 'Really?'

'I meant tender, Scully.'

Irma put her hand on his and for an instant he liked her. She was mad, a liar, a bad dream from hell but she was flesh and blood. Just the touch of a hand, a human touch. God, he missed being wanted. The café smelled warm and friendly with its scents of onions and coffee and tobacco. He felt himself loosen a little.

'Is it that you're lonely, Irma? This business?'

'I'm not lonely,' she hissed. 'Don't feel sorry for me.'

Scully looked at her, the way her neck stretched back and her eyes narrowed like a snake about to strike. It cleared his head immediately.

'Okay, Irma,' he said, meaning it. 'I won't.'

'You don't understand simple attraction.'

Scully made a smile. 'Well, maths was never my thing.'

Billie came back, trying not to smile as she climbed onto her chair.

'What?' said Scully.

'The toilet,' she burst out, scandalized. 'It was just a hole in the ground!'

He looked at Irma. 'My daughter has toilet adventures everywhere she goes. Travel with Billie – see the toilets of the world. It's a squat, Billie. You've seen them all –'

'No,' she said. 'No, no, that bit's gone. Like someone's stolen it. It really is just a hole in the ground.'

'So what took you so long?'

'I was trying to find the button.'

'Here,' he laughed. 'Take your tablet.'

'Let's go shopping,' said Irma. 'It's sad, the two of you on the road at Christmas.'

'Jesus was on the road at Christmas,' said Billie.

'Yes,' said Irma, flummoxed at last. 'Yes.'

## *Forty-four*

AFTER LUNCH IN THE CAFE it was a long noisy afternoon in the shops with Irma. She took them to Fnac and bought tapes. Ry Cooder for Scully. Hoodoo Gurus for her. At Les Halles she bought herself Ysatis and splashed it on. In a taxi she took them to Galeries Lafayette where she found the same perfume cheaper and didn't care. She bought Scully a silk shirt there and little red dancing shoes for Billie. In another taxi they went down to the big street market past Bastille and bought lychees and bananas and oranges. There were so many people and smells you couldn't move. Irma found a saddle in the fleamarket but Scully said no, they couldn't carry it. It was disappointing but she knew he was right. Then in a big street of ritzy furniture shops they saw a man with a wallaby in a dog-collar. It was a bad moment, but Irma didn't notice.

And then, so quickly, it got dark.

ALL DAY SCULLY LET HER DRINK and buy while a strange cold calm settled on him. He saw it all pass by as though he weren't quite in it himself. The feeling intensified in the little brasserie off the Rue Faubourg St Antoine. Amid the platters of Breton oysters, the bottles of champagne, the flash of cutlery and linen, the hiss of butter, the caramelizing scent of roasted garlic, time slipped by almost without him. He knew what he was doing, but he couldn't actually believe it was happening.

He thought it was the terrible, necessary thing he was about to do, but it could have been the fact that he drank along with Irma. By nine he was cold, calculating and shitfaced.

Irma and Billie laughed at some half-arsed joke and jostled one another. He saw Irma's even white teeth and the bleary brightness of her eyes. Pressed against his, her leg was warm and comforting, hardly the shock it might have been this morning. There was something complete about her tonight. She looked strangely content, magnanimous, and not all of it was the champagne. Maybe this is her, he thought. Maybe this is the person she must have been once – warm, funny, generous. Tonight her mouth was sensual and without a trace of cruelty. What horrible thing had happened to her between Liverpool and Berlin, between the big stops in her life? Those bruises, they meant other bruises, damage he couldn't even guess at.

'Are you dreaming, Scully?'

'Hm? Yes, a bit.'

'Billie was telling me about when she was born.'

Billie giggled in embarrassment.

'Well . . . she was born fugly, you see.'

'Fugly?'

'Like extra-double ugly with cheese. It's when ugly goes off the scale. She looked like an angry handbag.'

Billie squawked in delight. 'Tell the truth!'

'That is the truth. Scout's honour, I asked for my money back.'

'Stop!' said Billie giggling out of control.

'Here, take another pill.'

Irma's eyes glistened. She ordered more champagne and held both their hands. She seemed about to cry. She leaned into Scully and he felt her breath on his ear.

'I hate her for leaving you,' she whispered.

Scully set his teeth. 'We don't know she did,' he said carefully, awkward in front of the child.

'Even if she didn't I'd still feel the same.'

'Well,' he chuckled mirthlessly, 'you're just hard to get along with.'

'Try me.'

LATER THEY STUMBLED UP toward the old neighbourhood. The sound of bells roosted on the wind.

'Hear the bells?' cried Billie, exhausted and jumpy. 'Hear the bells?'

In the Little Horseshoe, where labourers, junkies, transvestites and students gathered to see in Christmas, Irma began to drink Calvados and Scully backed off onto beer. Now that she'd stopped moving, Billie wilted quickly and Scully saw that it was ten o'clock. He tried to steady himself. Not a bad place to say goodbye to Paris. This was it, his last drink. Irma was blasted. This was surely it. He dragged them out into the street.

Beneath the bare chestnuts, her breath billowing back from her, Billie ran ahead on a final burst of energy while Scully helped Irma along the pavement.

'Did you enjoy the day?'

'Yes,' he said. 'Thank you.'

'I hoped you might forgive me.'

'Of course I forgive you,' he lied.

'Christ, look at that.'

Up ahead, outside the Prefecture of Police and the armoured booth at the doorway, Billie danced with two cops, a man and a woman. Round and round they went, the three of them holding hands. Submachine guns clanked at their hips. Their quiet laughter carried on the cold, sulphuric air, rooting Scully to the spot.

THERE WAS A MERCIFUL CROWD in the tiny hotel lobby, a warehouse of piled luggage and language that Scully weaved through unchallenged with Irma and Billie, grateful he'd kept the room key on him all day. The mob noise echoed up the curving stairwell as Scully urged Irma along. Billie went ahead with the key.

'Nice place you have here,' Irma said, slumping against the banister. 'Is this a spiral staircase or am I just pissed?'

'Both,' said Scully looking up at her firm backside and giving her a shove onwards that caused her to shriek and giggle. He was drunk himself but he could still see the whole night ahead.

'How many more floors?'

'Next one.'

Irma tipped on her little boots and rested against the wallpaper. Hair fell into her eyes and she tilted her head back to clear it, exposing her long neck, white and marked.

'Help me, Scully.'

'Come on, you can make it another flight.'

'Help me.'

Scully joined her on the step and she opened her eyes but did not look at him. She grabbed his lapel.

'Can't you help me, Scully?'

'You want me to carry you.'

She pulled him to her and looked into his face. She kissed him with her eyes open while her tongue travelled across his teeth, his lips, his chin. Scully felt her pelvis rock into his and he reached behind with one hand and pulled her tighter, feeling her butt clench.

'It's what you want,' she said. 'To help me.'

Scully picked her up and staggered on with her sucking his neck and pulling at his sweater. Up the stairwell from the ground floor came the screech of brakes and a roaring cheer as somebody's bus arrived. Scully saw the open door and steadied.

'And I'll help you, Scully.'

He couldn't bring himself to answer, but he knew she was right.

BILLIE FELL ASLEEP WITH HER SHOES on and her backpack still hanging from one arm. Scully lowered Irma into a chair and knelt down to make the kid comfortable. He pulled off her boots, unhooked the pack and her jacket, and rolled her under the covers. He turned out the light and left the bathroom door ajar. The drapes lay open to the soft sandstone light of the city. He leaned his head against the window to get his breath back. Behind him, Irma fished in her bag for a bottle and sighed.

'Where are you staying?' he murmured. 'Where's your stuff?'

'Here.'

He turned and saw her holding the bottle out to him. He shook his head. He walked past her and locked the door. He felt the bottle pressed into the small of his back and he turned to where she sat smiling blearily up at him. Irma placed a heel on his thigh. It bit into his skin. He looked down her leg and then back at the sleeping child. Irma tilted the bottle and drank deeply. He watched her, saw her pale neck moving in the dimness.

He took hold of her ankle and she planted the other boot on his free thigh. He moved his hands down her legs. Her tights crackled with static and he was surprised at the softness of her flesh as he held her calves. He held tight to keep his hands from shaking. Weeks of pent-up frustration smoked in him. He watched her pull down her tights and pants, still drinking from the bottle.

'Billie,' he whispered hoarsely.

'Billie's no longer the point.'

Her skin was ivory in the dark. The bottle fell and Scully lost his clear, hard sight of the night and yanked her to the floor where she grabbed at his belt and ricked up her skirt till her boots ground at the back of his legs. He slid into her with her breasts in his hands and his knees burning on the carpet. Her breath was volatile. It filled his mouth.

'You need me, don't you,' she gasped.

'Shh.'

He covered her mouth with his hand and felt her tongue between his fingers and then her teeth in his palm and her nails in his buttocks. She was soft to touch, too soft, like something overripe, but he clung to her knowing she was right. He needed her in more ways than he could make plain to anyone. He felt his desperation winding into hers, his lies into hers, his gratitude, his shame, the shocking current that surged down his spine.

## *Forty-five*

NEAR MIDNIGHT SCULLY STOOD dressed in the stark bathroom and emptied Irma's shoulder bag into the sink. Her snores carried from behind the closed door as he shuffled through dental floss, crumpled tissues, lipsticks, a notebook in scrawled German, old boarding passes, mints, tampons, a condom, a receipt from the Grand Bretagne in Athens, some fibrous strings of dope that lay like pubes against the white enamel, a spectacle case and finally a python-skin wallet.

Inside the wallet was a lock of snowy hair, an EC passport in the name of Irma Blum with a photo of an auburn-haired Irma with a wicked smile on her face, a sheaf of carelessly signed travellers' cheques in American dollars, a Polaroid snap of a fat baby, and eight hundred francs in crisp new notes.

Scully stuffed the money into his pocket and picked up Billie's backpack from where he'd put it on the toilet cistern. His mouth tasted of cigarette ash and his head hammered. He looked at the brassy tube of lipstick a moment, hesitated and picked it up. He pulled the cap off, wound the little crimson nub out experimentally. Then he signed the mirror. XXX. Before the idea of it sank in he dropped the tube and turned out the light.

The city glow chiselled in through the open drapes and showed Billie and Irma in deep sleep, their limbs cast about the bed before him as he crept across the room. In sleep they could have been mother and child. He crept closer. Irma's mouth was open. The room stank of booze and dirty socks. Her arm lay across the counterpane, white and still shocking. Billie bunched up at an angle to her, fist against her own lips.

He picked up Billie's boots and coat, stuffed them into the backpack looped over his arm, then peeled back the bedclothes a way and gathered her up. Irma snored on like a surgical patient. He held the child to him and looked down a moment upon this strange woman. He felt a twinge of tenderness and a momentary impulse to wake her, but he was heading for the creaky door even before it passed.

Out in the sudden light of the landing he laid Billie on the carpet and pulled the door to without daring to breathe. He put his ear to the door. Nothing but snores.

As he struggled to get her boots on, Billie stirred and muttered.

'What? What?'

'Don't talk – shh.'

Then she opened her eyes; they widened awfully a moment and settled on him. He put a finger to his lips in warning and went back to booting her up. She sat up to receive the coat, her hair upright, her scabs livid.

'Hop up, love. You'll have to walk, at least till we get down to the street.'

She began to whimper. 'I'm tired!'

'Me too,' he said, clamping his hand over her mouth. 'Now shut up.'

WITHOUT LUGGAGE and with him grotesquely whistling Christmas carols with barely enough breath to get a note, Scully took Billie through the tiny lobby without arousing suspicion from the dozing concierge. Out in the street it was all Scully could do not to break into a mad run. He drank in the frigid air and saw his breath ghosting before him. That's it, that's all it took to desert someone, to leave a woman behind with his bag of dirty clothes, his candles, his sodden picture by poor dead Alex, the strewn presents of the drunken day and his strapping hotel bill. This was how it felt to be an empty cupboard, to know you were capable of the shittiest things.

He hoisted Billie onto his back to cross the Pont St Louis as a great barge churned below. The bells of Notre Dame began to toll midnight, plangent and mournful. They rang in the cellar of his belly. Around them the cafés roared, echoing along the shadowy buttresses of the cathedral, setting his teeth on edge.

'Where's Irma?' murmured Billie, twisting her fingers in his hair.

'Listen to the bells.'

Scully felt the child's breath against his neck and knew he needed to eat, but he was afraid to miss the Metro at Cité by the flowermarket before the system closed down for the night.

'Where'd she go?'

'Don't talk for a minute.'

'I'm falling, look out!'

Scully tottered and found the perpendicular again but Billie scrambled down off him.

'You'll drop me!'

He'd drunk more than he thought. Now that he was in the open he was all but reeling.

'I'm cold,' he said, pulling himself up on the arrowheads of the fence. 'I'm so cold.'

Billie took the backpack from his arm and shrugged into it. 'It's the middle of the night,' she murmured.

'I have to get inside for a minute. A café, anywhere.'

'Here,' she said, pointing to the great cathedral which fattened with music and the voices of the dead and the living and the tolling of bells in the sky above them.

Scully looked up at its dripping gargoyles and the mist of light that hung over it, spilling faintly down its buttresses like rain. His drunkenness settled heavily on him, his throat burned and his vision was speckled with stars and blips of all kinds. He felt like a man who'd walked through a sheepdip, his skin was so clammy. Oh God, not tonight, not when his hands smelled of Irma and his heart was a clump of oozing peat.

Billie tugged and worried at him. He batted her off. Their shoes chafed on the cobbles.

'It's Christmas,' she said. 'This is where we should be.'

No, he thought, feeling himself steered like a big stupid animal, no, it's much worse than that, much worse than Christmas. He was too dizzy to resist her, though. The entrance with its kingdom of faces and upraised fingers and sceptres and staffs rose above him like the opening of a tunnel where he joined a river of figures. They smelled of wine and burnt butter and onions, these people, the slow-moving and dreamy, half-hearted and freezing. Their coats were buttoned and their scarves tight, their midnight mass faces shining in the gloom. Sounds of feet on the smooth stones until the roar of the organ pipes as they made the vast vaulted cave of the cathedral itself with its haze of incense and candle-smoke, the perfumes of a thousand women, the feel of sweat-oiled timber and cool sepulchral air of an underground city.

Scully felt himself a man on sea legs. He sensed people making space for him as though they smelt sex and failure and theft on him. They edged politely but firmly from the sight of his weeping rogue eye, and they saw into him. They *knew* and it made his teeth chatter. You're no better, their compressed lips said. No use feeling outraged anymore – you bastard. You know how easy it is to bolt and leave them sleeping.

The bodies of saints flickered all around.

The great kite of the crucified Christ loomed and caused the crowd to vibrate. Like a pyre before him the bank of burning candles waited. The hot pure smell of burning. A woman's fan of blonde hair in front of him scented like roses as he walked. Billie beside him, her face glowing with hurt and understanding. He lit a candle and held it up before him. God, how his head soared and pitched, how rod-like his blood went in his veins. A candle for the birth of Christ, for the squirming of Job in his own shit, of Jonah running like a mad bastard from the monster he knew he was. A candle for Jennifer, just for the sake of it, for his poor deserted mother, for Alex, and Pete and Irma, poor Irma who was making him cry and laugh right in the middle of things here in the cathedral of Our Lady of Paris. Our friggin lady who let him cry and stumble into that rose-smelling hair with the writhing flame of his candle suddenly spitting and cracking and bursting hilariously into true fire right before him and the others whose mouths were open as if in adoration at the weirdness of miracles. Tongues of living fire as he went falling, falling into the yielding squelch of people, God bless them.

# V

*On a quiet street where old ghosts meet*
*I see her walk away from me*
*So hurriedly my reason must allow*
*That I have wooed not as I should*
*A creature made of clay . . .*

'Raglan Road'

# *Forty-six*

WITH HIS HEAD BACK and his mouth open like a clown you put balls into, Scully snored and sprawled across the seats stinking of train stations and fire and cement and the long, horrible night. There'd been so many rotten nights for Billie, it was all rotten almost as far back as she could remember, but last night was the worst. Last night he really was the Hunchback, no pretending about it. Like a hurt animal, he was, frightened and scary, almost setting fire to that lady's hair and falling over in church with the priest like an angry king up there in his robes. She got him out of there real fast, before people could do anything to him. It was terrible to see, him falling all over like a killed bull trying to lie down and die. He was so heavy and crying and awful that it hurt in her heart and she knew even then that only she could save him.

She swallowed her pill without water. It wormed down her neck as if it was alive. Her hands felt gritty and she needed a glass of milk or a little bottle of *jus du pommes*, the kind with hips that reminded her of Granma Scully. Her face didn't hurt but her eyes were sore from staying awake and keeping watch.

There weren't too many people in the carriage. Some men, some women, no families. Most of them looked like her Scully, as if they'd slept in a train station on Christmas Eve. She could tell they had no roast lunch to go home to, no presents waiting to be opened, no dollar coins hiding in the pudding, no afternoon at the beach, no party hats, no box of macadamia nuts to scoff on till they got crook. Billie didn't care about all that, herself. She was a bit shocked not to care, but she had a job now. Looking around the train she bet half these people got on this morning just for something to do, somewhere to be that wasn't Paris.

She looked at the knees of her new jeans and thought about Irma. She felt bad about her. Irma wasn't a real grown up. She was little inside, but her heart was big. One day Scully would see that. Irma wasn't a statue. And she would come looking again, she'd find them. She was just like Scully. Maybe that's why Billie liked her. Yes, she'd find them and Billie wouldn't mind at all. All anyone needed was a good heart.

Billie's head ached. She rested it on the seat in front where some doodlehead had burned two holes with a cigarette. The sound of bells still went around in her head. That and him shouting and crying in the Metro tunnels. Paris exploding with bells. Even underground you could hear the bells in all the churches. Him lying across plastic chairs and on the floor in the Gare de l'Est while all those crazy people ran in the tunnels and crashed trolleys and busted bottles. And the old men sleeping in hot puddles and the sleeping bags rolled against the tile walls. Like under the bridges, it was. Paris was pretty on top and hollow underneath. Underground everyone was dirty and tired and lost. They weren't going anywhere. They were just waiting for the Eiffel Tower and Notre Dame, the whole town, to fall in on them.

She picked up the last piece of her baguette and munched on

it. No one in the carriage said anything. It rocked quietly, thumping on the rails. Rain streaked the windows. She needed to go to the toilet, so she put the tablet bottle back in her pack and took it up the aisle to the hissing glass doors.

In the toilet she listened to the roar of the tracks and felt the cold air spanking at her bum. A hopeless flap of light came in the little window and made her think of her bedroom in Fremantle. The big, big window that looked out on the boats. All the straight trees, the Norfolk pines, like arrows by the water. And the sun on the wall of her room, the block of sun with all the tiny flying things in it. When she was little she thought they were the souls of dead insects, still buzzing in the light. The wooden wall. The bare floor with little trucks parked on it and bears asleep in rows. No use thinking of it. It was all gone. There was a room in that little dolls' house Scully had made in Ireland. And out the window a castle. And a paddock for a horse. It was all in a fog – that whole day was in a fog and she was glad, but fog always rises, she knew that. One day it would be clear, even the parts she didn't want to see. Even the airport. Even that.

In the toilet mirror she looked dirty, like a gypsy but not so pretty.

She soaped up and cleaned her hands and face and clawed her hair back with her fingers. She was still glad she looked like Scully. He wasn't pretty either, but pretty people weren't the kind you need. Pretty people saw themselves in the mirror and were either too happy or too sad. People like Billie just shrugged and didn't care. She didn't want to turn into anyone pretty. Anyway, she had scars now, you only had to look.

Billie wet a paper towel and went back down the carriage with it. Scully had four seats now; his boots and legs were across the aisle on hers. His baggy jeans were stained and smelly, and stuff rode up in his pockets.

She stood there poised a moment, the puddles of land slipping by, before she reached into his pocket and eased out the fold of money. She left the coins right down against his leg. This was more money than they had before, much more. She slipped it into her jacket thoughtfully and took up the wet paper towel to scrub him down. He moaned and turned his head, but didn't wake, not even when she got to his hands. When she finished there were little balls of paper on him here and there but he looked better. Billie stuffed the grey pulp into the ashtray and sat across the aisle from him with the pack on the seat beside her as she looked through their passports, at their old faces, their big watermelon smiles. She counted the money again – five one-hundred francs – and stowed it in her jacket and fell quickly to sleep as Belgium trolled by and by and by without her.

THROUGH THE STRANGE, neat ornamental suburbs of Amsterdam Scully rested his head against the shuddering glass and felt Billie patting at him like a mother at a schoolboy. The headache had gone ballistic this past half-hour, so frightful that the beating glass made it no worse. His throat, raw with puking, felt like a PVC pipe lately introduced into his body and he smelled like a public toilet. The other poor bastards in the carriage looked ready to climb onto the return train the moment they pulled in. The deadly power of Christmas.

He felt in his pockets for something to chew and came up with change in four currencies.

'I took the money,' said Billie across the aisle before it really registered.

'You? Why?'

She shrugged. 'I'm scared.'

'Of me?'

Billie looked at her boots.

'You'll need to change it into guilders, then. Dutch money. This is Holland.'

'Holland.'

'You know, the boy with his finger in the dike.'

She nodded gravely.

'Beats having your head down the dike, I guess,' he murmured against himself.

'Why are we here?'

'I have to see Dominique. She's got a houseboat here.'

She sighed and looked out the window. Scully gathered his limbs brittlely to him and nursed his nausea. Call me Rasputin, he thought. Poison me, chain me up, kick the hell out of me, but I'll get up and keep coming. A crooked grin came to his lips. Come to think of it I can do it all to myself and still keep coming, so don't underestimate me, Christmas Day. But deep down he knew he had nothing left. Last night was a dark cloud at the back of his head. His teeth ached, his chest was hollow. Anywhere he walked today, he knew, would just be walking to keep from sinking. The whole earth slurped and waited. It was no use pretending. He had nothing left. Jennifer would be here. He'd find her, he knew it now, but he'd be an empty vessel. She'd get her way in the end.

CENTRAAL STATION was empty of passengers, its kiosks and shops shuttered, but it was crowded with people who looked as though they lived there. Ghetto blasters and guitars reverberated in every corner. Junkies and drunks lay nodding in hallways. Dreadlocked touts hustled limply by the deserted escalators, disheartened by the holiday. A madman in fluorescent tights shrieked at his own reflection in the windows of the closed-up Bureau de Change. Hippies of seventeen and eighteen who looked German to Scully swilled Amstel and laughed theatrically amongst themselves. Scully snarled at them and pushed by. The air was warm and foul with body odour, smoke and urine so that the street air was a sweet blast to be savoured a second or two. It revived him long enough to sling the pack over one shoulder, raise his eyebrows doubtfully at Billie and stump out dazedly into the feeble light and the unravelling plait of tramlines in the square before them.

A canal, hundreds of uptilted bicycles, a stretch of pretty buildings encrusted and disfigured by neon. A fish sky low enough to make Scully hunch a few moments until he got into some kind of stride that never graduated beyond a victim's shuffle, a lunatic's scoot, the derro walk. He was a mess. He was ratshit.

The city was beautiful, you had to notice it. Beautiful but subdued to the point of spookiness. There was almost no one on the streets. Now and then bells rang uncertainly and a pretty cyclist, male or female, whirred past dressed to the gills and intent on being somewhere.

They went down the wide boulevard of closed-up cafés and cheap hotels, change joints, souvenir pits until they came to a big square. Beneath the monument in the square a few dark-skinned men smoked handrolled cigarettes and a sharp young Arab offered cocaine in a hoarse whisper.

'Piss off,' said Scully, feeling the spastic twinge of the newcomer, the fear of being in a city he didn't know. He was surprised to feel anything at all, but there it was, the bowel-clenching sensation he remembered from London the first time, Paris the first time, Athens. An emotion, by God. It was worse without crowds, without currents he could simply slip into, hide in and follow while he got his bearings. Every door was closed to the street. Their footfalls rang clear on the sharp air. Scully had to stand there and look like a rube without a shred of cover. Why should he care? Screw them all. The hell with Amsterdam and Christmas Day.

In time they came to a Turkish joint where they flopped into plastic chairs and ate ancient hommus and tabouleh. They drank coffee and chocolate while young women swept and wiped around them. Scully stared out at bell gables and wrought-iron and immense paned windows. He tried to produce a lasting thought.

'Where's the houseboat?' said Billie, cleaning her teeth with a paper napkin.

'Dunno,' he murmured, watching her eyes widen in disbelief.

'You haven't got the address?'

'Nope.'

'This is a city!'

'Nice work, Einstein.'

'Don't make a joke of me!' She looked at him with such fury that he shifted in his chair.

'I'm sorry.'

'I could leave you,' she murmured. 'I've got the money.'

'Don't.'

'Don't make me a joke.'

She got up and went to pay their bill. He watched as she carefully unpeeled a hundred-franc note and was amazed that the Turkish girls decided to accept it. They thought she was a scream, you could see. How doggedly she waited for her change. His kid. Billie turned over the bright guilder notes in her hands and thanked them politely before returning to the table.

'Scully?'

'Hm?'

'Let's go home?'

Scully shook his head.

'I want to stop looking.'

He shook his head again and felt the pulse jerk in his temples.

'You don't even know where to look.'

He smiled. 'How hard can it be to find a houseboat?'

Billie whumped a fist onto the table and walked out into the eerie street in disgust. For a while he watched her blowing steam out there and kicking the cobbles. Pigeons kept back from her, pumping their necks cautiously. He smiled at her through the glass. She scowled back.

## *Forty-seven*

EVENTUALLY THE KNOCKING GOES AWAY and she lifts herself onto one shaky elbow. A sick noon light lies across the twisted bedclothes. The room is strewn. Pretty red shoes. Black tights. A tartan suitcase pillaged and open. Shopping bags, gift wrap in drifts. The bathroom door is closed. Christmas Day. Of course, the little darlings, they'll be in church. God, she needs a cigarette, but where is her bag in all this mess?

Slowly, with infinite care, she inches to her feet. Like a rolling boulder, she feels the headache coming. She kicks through the junk – no bag. She knocks on the bathroom door. Opens it slowly. All over the vanity, in the basin even, her stuff. She finds the light switch, hisses at the sudden fluorescence and sees her wallet on the floor. In her hands it still smells of Morocco. Travellers' cheques, all signed, still there. But no cash.

Her passport, tampons, ticket stubs right there on the vanity. And on the mirror, right in her face, three X's. Kiss, kiss, kiss.

Irma snatches up the Gauloises, finds the lighter and lights up. She takes a deep scouring drag with her head tilted back and the pain gathering at the base of her skull. XXX. You bastard. You asshole.

She begins to laugh.

## *Forty-eight*

ALONG THE SILVERY CANALS they wandered as the weather fell, Billie and her dad, moving up streets called Prinsengracht, Herengracht, Keizersgracht, words that sounded like talking with cake in your mouth. Drizzle wept from bridges and drowned bikes meshed together beneath the clinching overhang of bald trees. Along the brick banks of the canals, dinghies, runabouts and rubber duckies were tied up beside every kind of houseboat you could dream of. They weren't yachts, caiques and crayboats like in Greece and Australia, but big heavy things that hardly moved. With their pots and pots of yellow flowers, the houseboats lay low in the water, creamy with paint and varnish, their rudders strapped alongside like wooden shields. They were fat and wide with rounded backsides and windows full of green plants and frilly curtains. From their chimneys rose smoke and gas heat and the smells of cooking. Dog bowls stood out on deck catching the rain and chained bikes and garden chairs and party lights dripped. To Billie they looked made up by kids, painted like dolls' houses. The whole town looked that way – every skinny house was a cubbyhole and hideout. The little streets and canals were so small you could imagine having built them yourself.

But soon the streets just turned into streets, and the boats just more boats as the rain gave the water goosebumps and she stumped along with Scully coming alone behind like a lame horse. Billie's collar filled with drizzle and her jeans were wet from brushing the fenders of parked cars, and she began to wonder if saving him was too much for her. The long skinny houses started to look like racks of burnt toast. The sky was misty with rain, a sky that could never hold sun or moon or stars.

Now and then someone emerged from a hatch to pull in washing or hoik a bucket of dirty water over the side or just puff a cigar with a Christmas drink in their hand, and Billie ran toward them with the photo from Scully's wallet. The black-and-white, cut down and crooked. It was the three of them but she couldn't look. She just held it out to them as Scully hung back in shame. It burnt her hand, that photo, but she stopped caring. Today was Jesus' birthday and she had his hands; she felt holes burning there but couldn't look for fear of seeing Her in the picture. If Billie laid eyes on that face with its smooth chin and black wing of hair and beautiful faraway eyes, she knew all her love, all her strength would break. Pee would run down her legs and her hands catch fire and she would turn to stone herself and be a statue by the water. So she ignored the acid sting in her hands and held up the photo to people with pink cheeks and Christmas smiles.

The houseboat people looked at the photo and then at Billie and her father in their rumpled clothes and busted faces and shook their heads sadly. Sometimes they brought out soup or pressed money into Billie's hand, but no one knew the face and Billie felt bad about her relief each time.

On and on it went through streets and canals with the hugest names while the drizzle fell and her lips cracked and her hands burned up. All the time she waited for him to give up, praying for him to give up, telling him inside her head to wear down and quit at last, but when she looked back he shooed her on without hardly looking up at her and Billie kept going to gangplanks, stepping over ropes and tapping on windows. Every shake of the head, every flat expression was a relief. No, not here, no, no, no, she wasn't here. Billie was afraid that if they kept at it long enough someone's face would brighten horribly and recognize the face. That'd be it. That would kill her. She just didn't know what she would do.

On a corner, surrounded by green posts with rolls on the end like men's dicks, she saw the closed-up shop with the posters of Greece and Hawaii and big jumbo jets in it. On the wall was a blackboard with long words and prices. A travel place. She felt the money against her leg and walked on like she'd never seen it. Next door was a SNACKBAR with a menu on the window. *Sate-saus*, *Knoflook-saus*, *Oorlog*, *Koffie*, *Thee*, *Melk*. It was closed as well. Everything was closed.

Church clocks bonged and rattled and Billie went on, just going and going while the light slowly went out of the sky and the air went so cold it felt like Coke going down your neck. And then suddenly it was dark and they were standing out on a little bridge looking at the still water and the moons the streetlights made in it.

'Nothing,' said Scully.

'No,' she said.

People had begun to come back out into the streets. Their bikes whirred past, their bells tinkled, they called and laughed and sang.

'Scully, it's cold.'

'Yeah.'

'Let's . . . let's go somewhere.'

'Yeah.'

He just stood there looking into the water, his mittens on the green rail of the bridge, until she took him by the sleeve and steered him into a narrow street where the windows were lit and cosy-looking. The first place she came to, she pushed him in and followed, smelling food and smoke and beer. There was sand on the floor and music and hissing radiators on the walls.

Billie followed her father to the big wooden bar and climbed up on a stool beside him.

'He'll have a beer, I spose,' she murmured at the barman. 'And one hot chocolate. *Chocolat chaud?*'

The barman straightened. His eyes were enormous. His glasses were thick as ashtrays. Up on the bar he put a balloony glass of beer with Duvel written on the side and plenty of fluff hanging off the top. Billie put her chin in her hands and watched Scully looking at himself in the bar mirror.

'You have a bad day, huh?' said the barman.

Billie nodded.

'He is okay?' he said, inclining his head toward Scully.

Billie shrugged. Scully gulped down his beer and pushed his glass forward again.

'You be careful for that stuff, man,' said the barman kindly. 'They don't call him the Devil for nothing. You watch him, kid.'

Billie nodded grimly and looked at the blackboard. 'You have sausages and potatoes?'

'Baby, this is Holland. It's all sausage and potato here,' he laughed. 'For two?'

Billie nodded. She pulled out money.

'Hoh, you are the boss for sure.'

She liked him. People in Amsterdam weren't so bad. They weren't afraid of kids like they were in Paris and London. They had sing-song voices and cheeks like apples, and she wondered if Dominique felt the same way. Dominique was sad like Alex. Her pictures were lonely and dark and sad. She was like a bird, Dominique. A big sad bird. Maybe she came here to cheer up, to see rosy people and do happier pictures.

In the corner a man with pencils through his earlobes was chattering on the phone. He looked ridiculous and should have been ashamed of himself. He sounded like a budgie talking away in his language, whatever they talked here. There were too many languages, too many countries. She was sick and tired of it. She climbed off her stool and crossed the sandy floor to where the phone book hung against the wall on a string. She picked up that book and opened it flat against the wood of the wall. But it was hopeless. She didn't know how to spell Dominique and she forgot her last name.

She should know these things, she knew. She should be in school reading books and writing in pads and playing softball. She should be *at* someplace, somewhere they knew her name and what she was like. Somewhere she didn't have to save people.

The phone book fell to the wall with a thump that startled everyone in the bar.

'How do you spell Dominique?' she asked Scully.

But he looked at himself in the mirror with his eyes half open. Their food came.

'Your father need some help, maybe,' said the barman kindly.

'Yes,' said Billie. 'I'm helping.'

The smell of food was dreamy. It made her feel strong again.

THE LONGER SCULLY sat there the thirstier he got. The Trappist beer was rich and lovely. It seemed as though pain was behind him. He could calmly think all his worst thoughts, every nightmare flash across the brain-pan, without pain. He was close to her now. It wasn't just in his mind anymore, no delusion, no desperate wishful thinking. She was here in Amsterdam and it was only a matter of time. A good night's sleep, an early start, a clear mind, a bit of system.

No pain. Not even thinking about Dominique. There couldn't be any doubt that she was with Dominique, though in what way she was with her was more of a lottery. Was their friend giving Jennifer sanctuary against her own better judgement? Was she in two minds, at least, her loyalties just a little divided? Or did the two of them share the same – what else could it be? – hatred for him? What else did they share? A bed? The very idea was supposed to make men wild, wasn't it? It was supposed to be the ultimate humiliation, being left for a woman, but it didn't seem any worse or any better just now. Whatever it was, however it was, Scully was stuck with a kind of precious disappointment with Dominique. What did it matter *how* it was? Dominique had held out on him.

No, no pain. Just a thirst.

Shit, for all he knew they could have been at it in Paris right from the beginning, with him so bloody glad she had someone to be with. Marianne, Jean-Louis, they probably knew all along. Their disdain, it was contempt for his blind trust, his weakness. And the baby, the baby was a hoax, just a vicious bloody decoy to free herself with. Setting him loose on the tumbledown bothy, buying time. He'd never laid eyes on an ultrasound image, a doctor's bill, a test result in Athens, trusting prick he was. He had no other child, then. That still got close to pain. A couple of days ago, knowing that might have broken him. But he'd gone past something. He'd crossed a line. No baby. No wife. No marriage, nothing he could look back on with certainty, nothing that didn't look like quicksand. And who knows, maybe she'd bolted with all the money as well. In the name of what – love? Personal development? The bohemian life?

It meant he'd done all this to himself, to poor Billie, to Irma, just so he could see a corpse. Across Europe and back to obligingly identify a body. With dignity. Yes, it meant, in the warm light of this bar, feeling no pain, that he had nothing. Not a hole in the ground, not even the dying echo of an idea of his life. In fact, sweet fuck-all.

And that just made him thirsty.

## *Forty-nine*

SCULLY HIT THE HARD CHRISTMAS AIR of the street at God knows what hour of the night. The kid was pink-eyed and sluggish but he was floating, hovering above the glassy cobbles, four sheets to the wind and free.

The streets were streaming with walkers and riders and scooting cars. The mothwing whirr of bicycles fanned by his ear. Bells tinkled tiny on the road and gross in the air where pigeons rose from church towers and clouds lay low across the city. Clots of people weaved through traffic bollards and tossed their scarves with gusts of perfume. The tramlines shone, the great paned sashes of glass held figures and furniture and music and the jaunty gables rendered the Calvinistic brickwork severe and silly. It was shaking, this city, shuddering at its moorings as Scully swept down alleys past thickets of voluptuous wrought-iron with the sweet anaesthesia of Trappist beer coming to his cheeks like true belief. God, how pretty everyone was here, how young and apple-arsed on their bikes. The café windows were pats of butter melting at his feet, the air was bright-clear and etching cold.

In the Spuistraat a ramshackle warehouse festooned with gilt chains and aerosol banners in Dutch raged with upstairs light and music. Across its walls was a wild dream of graffiti. They sounded like birds up there, like German birds about to burst into English any second now – as soon as they cleared their throats properly. Look at that, even their squatters were house-proud – what a people.

He elbowed his way into a warm darkwood café, suddenly surprised to find himself inside, and ordered more Duvel and some of that evil clear stuff they were downing all along the bar. The sweet crunch of sand on the boards underfoot buoyed him now against the haggard glare of the kid at his elbow. Shit a brick, look at those students, the belts cinched gorgeously over their navels, the peek of white flesh through carefully ripped Levi's, the broad bright bands in their hair, the way their foreheads shone, the curve of their calves against the denim.

He threw back the clear shot and chased it with beer and thought for a moment of the mad, glowing ears of Peter Keneally. His own ears were gone now and his eyebrows were melting. His chin was off with the pixies but his mouth held good. The barman's apron snapped like a spinnaker, the brass taps were winch handles. No sweat, he had the sea legs of an octopus now. Eight legs and six of them Irma's.

'To Irma!' he blurted.

The kid fingered the guts of the wallet and found guilders.

'To Irma's Christmas on the Ile St Louis.'

The barman took the money and smiled indulgently at his sober, saving daughter.

'To the six wraparound-suck-me-dry legs of Irma the squirmer.'

He felt the toes of her little boots against his shin and busted out laughing. She pummelled him with fists the size of apricots and her hair was a blur before him. The girls along the bar shifted in their creaking leather jackets and smiled. Scully felt himself leaving backwards, falling across the room, dragged by the belt and waving at those fruit-arsed honeys as the cold and fragrant night air rattled down his neck. He was losing transmission now and then. The kid stood there like a bollard but he was moving. He held out his hand and surged on.

The streets became pink and thumping. Trash clacked underfoot and the alleys were gamy. He couldn't tell if he was suddenly tired or if maybe everyone was older here.

A chrome-headed little runt stiff-armed him at a sluggish turn in the pedestrian surge, whispering foully at him in a language he couldn't stay with. Scully shrugged him away and ricocheted into a clownfaced lunatic with a half-inch chain around his neck. There were syringes underfoot and aquarium windows full of whores.

'Over here!' someone screamed from a throat-like doorway. 'See real life focking! Real focking!'

He stumbled through a fresh map of vomit and landed against the hot plane of a plate-glass window which shook with resistance. He pulled himself up to see a field of photographs. It hurt to focus; it puzzled him, that world of images. People, it looked like, well, it might have been people or the inside of an abattoir. Pink, pink flesh and shocked, hurt faces with bared teeth. He found his ears with his hands and held his head there before it, struggling to understand. Yes, that was a woman. Part of a woman. And razor blades. Oh, God help me. There it was, the Auschwitz of the mind, the place you'd never dreamt of going, the hell they said wasn't real. His face came back to him like a nightmare, the fingers in his jacket held like snared fish. He saw Billie crying, and behind her a rush of black hair in the passing crowd, the blind swoop of his whole life that set him running like a man in flames.

Billie skidded on a half-sucked lemon in the pink piggy light of the doorway and stumbled to her knees. There was a farmyard smell to the street and a look in people's faces that made animals of them. Low aquarium windows loomed with ladies swimming in purple light, their eyes foxy and shining. Music bashed up out of doors in the ground and hot air gushed in her face pricking her scars with sudden heat. Into the tunnel of hips and legs and voices they veered, her grip slipping as Scully tipped away. Horse manure and food steamed on the uneven cobbles. Away into the tunnel he was falling, against a wall of pink bodies under glass like a graveyard, his hair streaked out against the tangle of fingers and legs and teeth, snarled and hanging. She saw the bottle in the girl's vagina, the safety pin in the face beside it, the harness, the shocked cattle look of the eyes in the pictures hardened with glass as her father slid down watching someone pass. He was falling, falling, too heavy for her to hold. And then he yelled out *that name*, his voice hoarse and breaking.

'Jennifer!'

Billie felt her nails break as he fought clear. She saw his back, his hair sinking in the moving squelch of bodies and he was gone. She could chase him, she knew. She was small enough to worm her way through and catch up to him, but the name froze her where she stood. Did she really see that glossy tail of black hair that moment in the corner of her eye?

Billie stood there, breathing but not moving with the light flickering on her and the canal shimmering like the entrance to the centre of the earth.

Piggy-looking people herded by her, snuffling and clacking

and bristling up against the windows. The trough of the canal flattened off under the bridge.

A man in a baseball hat put his hand on her head, talking something she didn't know and then stopped. 'You talk Inglis?'

Billie twitched.

'Ten guilder I be you daddy, uh?'

She stared at him. He had a face like a dog someone had beat up every day, sad and saggy, but with teeth still, and leery like he might snap if you turned your back.

'I got my own,' she said, backing up, but the bollard stopped her.

'You nice little girl.'

She pressed against the bollard and felt it cold against the small of her back.

'Very nice.'

Billie smelt antiseptic and sick in the street and this man's sweat through his black coat. His yellow teeth parted his lips. She felt his hand cold on hers, pulling it toward him, right where his coat opened and his belt buckle hung like a falling moon. She punched him right there hard as her fist would go and burrowed into the crowd. She clawed and kicked her way through, going forward, getting clear enough to run and then she saw Scully near the bridge angling like a sailor across the pavement.

SCULLY ELBOWED THROUGH CONFERENCES of negotiating boys and drooping junkies, outside the Hard Rock Café and saw her make the bridge beneath the tolling church. In the light of the bridge lamps the tan flash of legs. He broke into a run, bouncing against all corners, all handrails, all sudden, surprising gusts of pain. Across the canal he found the corner but the alley was glutted, the heads and shoulders and slit thighs tidal. Steam rose as a cloud before him and the grinding monotony of rap music blasted in his face.

He caught a glimpse of raven hair enamelled by the light of a doorway. He scrambled ahead, his heart truly hurting him now, goading him to keep up. His bad eye closed out on him, bending, twitching the night before him. She hovered in the doorway, a shimmering curtain of hair, and went in. Scully slowed to smooth himself down a little. He tilted against a bollard and ground the fur off his teeth with the collar of his pullover. He ran fingers through his greasy hair and patted himself down hopelessly. This wasn't what he expected. He wasn't ready. He shook like a schoolboy, wondering if maybe he should just walk away, show a bit of pride. But he'd come too far for bloody pride. He made for the door.

Stepping down into the clinical fluorescents, Scully hesitated. It was a kind of sex supermarket, slick-shelved and lit, laid out for tourists and lonely hearts straight off the bus. Everything was wrapped in cellophane and ordered according to genre, like a music store, and it seemed suddenly hilarious. Shit a brick. He didn't know her at all. Had she lit out for stuff like this? He felt a moron smile split his face and saw her moving between shelves.

'Of all the sex joints in all the world,' he blurted, louder than he could have imagined, 'you'd have to walk into mine!'

The boy at the register, smooth-faced with a pearl earring and a sweater someone's mum must have knitted, smiled tiredly and looked away. Pink faces, apple cheek faces turned his way as he sailed down into the aisle. Exchanging their Chrissie presents, he thought. Let's hope they disinfected first.

The hair whirled up the back and his whole chest tightened.

To feel the proximity of her. He smelt perfume and heard the snick of heels as he closed the gap.

'Jennifer?'

The blur of a six o'clock shadow. Scully squinted as he lunged toward her, but already the wig was shifting beneath his hands and the startled bloke with the powdered face was falling off his heels and Scully was bellowing in fright. He staggered and shelves began to fall in sympathy. The fluorescent cavern echoed with screams and crashing. Scully wheeled with the outrage of the wig in his fist and caught the poor open-mouthed bastard in the yellow blazer right in the chops. People began to scramble across a drift of plastic penises. Scully held up his hands to placate them but the nice-looking kid from the register came armed with a circumcised cosh in a cellophane wrapper. Scully put his head down and went him. Just for the sweet feel of the blows on his face, for the quenching anaesthesia of a pain to fill the still darkness opening inside him.

BILLIE SAW HIM COME OUT HANDCUFFED and bellowing like the Hunchback on the Feast of Fools, blurred by her crying. The crowd shivered with excitement and made way. They didn't know him. They thought they did but they had no idea. The van flashed and someone touched her on the shoulder and she climbed in front to the smell of cigars and disinfectant. The doors slammed. The police talked their bird language. In the back, behind the glass, he was laughing. Someone, the driver, passed her a hanky.

'You know him?' someone asked.

Billie thought about it. She smelled the sweet soapy smell of the hanky and licked her lips. The narrow streets flashed by.

'Yes,' she said, without her voice breaking. 'He's my father.'

# *Fifty*

SCULLY WOKE WITH A HORRIBLE, head-shattering start and immediately felt the raw bitterness of his throat. His face was hot. The vinyl mattress squawked under him as he sat up in the bare cube of a room. A key gnawed like a rat in its hole and the big door swung open with its sliding window agape. Shee-it! He scrambled sluggishly to his knees, trying to catch up.

'Billie?'

A woman in a rumpled corduroy suit and a bowl of ash-blonde hair stepped cautiously in. Behind her hovered a bloke in uniform. His moustache was downy on his firm pink face. So where was Billie? Oh God, oh God!

'Hello?' said the woman. She was thin and handsome. In her forties, maybe. It seemed she had just climbed out of bed. Her eyes were red. 'You speak English, huh?'

Scully nodded gingerly, not liking this set-up at all. Billie!

'My name is Van Loon. I am a doctor.'

Scully nodded. He was still on his knees before her. The door closed a little way.

'Does your . . . head hurt?'

He put a hand to the side of his head and twitched.

'Dildo,' he murmured, remembering.

The quack wrote something in a notebook.

'They say you are upset,' she said. 'You are laughing.'

Scully looked at her questioningly.

'Two hours you are laughing.'

By the feel of his throat it didn't surprise him.

'What is your name, please?'

'Anne Frank,' he said looking around the cell. 'Have you got Billie?'

The doctor smiled. She pulled out some plastic gloves and put them on.

'Please take off your jacket. Will you do that for me?'

'Why?' he croaked.

'I want to see your skin. Your arms.'

'Arms?' But he peeled off, stiffly and showed her anyway.

'What drugs have you eaten today?'

'Booze,' he said. 'That's all.'

'This is why you fight?'

He looked at her hands in their plastic gloves and she shucked them off with a smile.

'Are you crazy?' she said kindly. 'I am here to see if you are crazy. To help you.'

Scully squirmed down off his knees. Two hours of laughing he couldn't recall. A bloody gaol cell and a shrink. Not good.

'Okay,' he murmured. 'I'm not Anne Frank.'

'Ah,' she found the notebook again and squatted before him.

'Listen, can you ask the cops about my little girl?'

'You are upset about her, yes?'

'Can you just ask them? Now? Please?'

Over her shoulder the doctor called in Dutch to the uniform in the corridor. It was a strange, comforting sound. Sweat began to germinate all over him. Scully held his head.

'They say she is upstairs yet.'

'Is she okay?'

'There is someone with her, yes.'

He didn't like the way it sounded.

'How old is your daughter?'

'Six. Seven, seven. In July. She's just a little girl.'

'You are British?'

'Australian,' he said.

'You have no papers, no money, no ID?'

He swallowed. 'Billie. Billie's got the bag, hasn't she?'

'What is your name?'

'Jesus!'

The policeman leant in and murmured in Dutch.

'He says there is a bag and passports.'

'I want to go now,' he croaked.

She backed away subtly.

'You are depressed, yes?'

'Oh yes,' he admitted. 'You could say that.' They'll take her away, he thought. These people will take her away if you don't straighten up. But he saw the quack's eyes on the straining veins in his arms, following them like a map of his hopeless travels. She was wondering if he would burst. He was interested himself. Was this when it would happen, when he'd burst like a watermelon under a car wheel, go off in a curtain of stale juice?

'I just want my daughter.'

'She is safe,' she crooned. 'She is safe.'

He got up, unfolded himself, licked his lips. She watched him cross the cell and come back.

'Can . . . can you tell me your name, please?'

'Yes,' he said. 'Yes.'

The floor was gritty and suddenly unbearable. The idea of Jennifer was simply a joke, just the notion of her. He was just a raw hole. There was nothing in him, he knew now, nothing to make an explosion, no mad fit of energy to bust him out of here. There just wasn't any juice left.

'You are from Australia.'

'Yes.'

She whistled. 'Such a long way.'

'Yes,' he murmured, feeling it.

'How . . . how long have you been in Holland?'

He tried to think, to find his way back through all those streets and lights and bars but he couldn't see where they began.

'I know,' he stammered. 'I know that.'

'You are restless.'

'Scared,' he breathed.

The uniform opened the door and spoke to the doctor. Scully stopped and watched.

'Coffee?'

'What time is it?'

'Two.'

'Please. Don't take her.'

'Be calm.'

'Yes,' he said. He began to weep and stopped.

'You can cry.'

'Today,' he said. 'We came to Amsterdam today.'

'Here,' she said. 'Lie down.' Her hands were warm and kind. He felt the plink of his eyelids against his face. She knelt beside him on the vinyl mattress, her downy upper lip quivering into a smile. She looked rag-arsed with fatigue.

'Tell me,' she said, 'about Australia. The animals with pockets. I want to know.'

## *Fifty-one*

AFTER ALL THE QUESTIONS, Billie sat with her mug of milky tea and ate the cake. It was dry and crumbly. People came and went. The police station smelt of disinfectant. The lights made her squint. She was tired. She thought about Dominique, everything she knew about her. Dominique was pretty. Kind of pretty. She had small hands and her apartment was full of sad photos. She was nice, Dominique, but she watched you. Carefully, like she didn't know what made you work, like she just didn't *get* kids. She looked at Scully sometimes. Billie saw her. He didn't know how she looked at him. Like he was a cake or something. Maybe she loved him. Billie didn't care. No one loved him like she did. That was a fact.

Dominique had a mole on her arm. Her shoes went kind of outwards when she walked. The floor of her apartment was all checked with wood. Sometimes, driving trucks across it Billie would look up and see the big poster on the living room wall. A dark face. White words. ATELIER CINQ. PHOTOGRAPHIES. And Dominique's name. LATOUR.

That was it. That was her name.

Billie put down the mug and the rest of the cake and went to the desk. The phone book was there like a brick. Two policemen told jokes by the window.

AMSTERDAM SCHIPOL

TELEFOONGIDS

PTT TELECOM

She opened it, saying the alphabet in her head. Telefoonnummers. Alarmnummers. Phones rang at desks everywhere. A siren wound up right outside. Dominique had bad breath, that was the other thing.

latour, d herengr. 6 627 9191

The page sounded like rain as it tore softly down the spine. She folded it neatly down into a parcel and put it into her pack.

'You want more cake, Billie?' called one of the cops, the one with all the questions before.

She shook her head. He turned away to finish his joke. Billie shifted the pack with the heel of her boot. On the strap was the number Scully had written that day on the road. The postman. Two numbers, she had. She lay down across the bench and went to sleep with sirens all around. In her dream she had wings, silver wings.

# *Fifty-two*

SCULLY WOKE and Van Loon was taking his pulse again. She had fresh clothes on and smelled of soap.

'All that boose,' she said.

'Yes,' he said. 'It was a lot.'

'You are strong.'

He shrugged, tried to muster some confidence. 'I feel better.'

'Good.'

'Am I crazy?'

'Not so much. Sad, maybe.'

'You look sad yourself,' he said, surprising himself.

'No,' she said with a chuckle. 'Crazy to have this job.'

'Is Billie still here?'

She nodded. 'She is like you?'

'What will the charges be?'

'No charges. Keep away from the dildos.'

'Yes,' he said meekly. 'You too.'

THEY LED HIM UP THROUGH THE TUNNELS into the fresher air. Amidst the snarls of desks and glass partitions he signed forms with his hands shaking. A meek daylight tinted the windows. He saw Billie standing by the glass. She waved minutely, face compressed. He felt a kind of remorse he had not felt before, a sense of humiliation that flattened even his relief. They could have taken her. He would have deserved it. He dropped his head a moment, unable to look. The cops seemed relieved to see the back of him. He watched her shaking their hands. A new shift straggled in. He stepped out to meet her.

## *Fifty-three*

FROM THE BIG HIPPED LINE of mountains a mist comes rolling and turning in the frozen light of morning, the sky grinding silent against the earth like the dead against the living. The stones of farm walls creak. Ice holds the grass stiff; the hoofprints of cattle are dead with it. At the head of the valley the lichened crosses lean into the sod and the lanes and boreens meander after their own shadow. In the sheds the slurry steams and the milk comes hot and ringing. Fields hummock and slant all the way to the bare and overreaching oak, it's a lake of frozen, stippled mud. Above it, the sunless monolith of the castle is ruled by the weft of birds. Rooks launch from the sills of a hundred slots and windows, across ash wood and lane. They settle on the smokeless chimney of the bothy on the ridge, cranking their heads warily. A sculpture of frozen tyremarks is set in the mud before the house. A vapour rises from it, from every surface, every thing. The day hesitates a moment. Nothing moves. Then, from the north, from someplace else, a wind springs up and day comes.

## *Fifty-four*

A SILKY DRIZZLE WAFTED DOWN through the shadows of busted empty warehouses and ships' masts in the morning light. Billie and Scully picked their way round ochre puddles and crippled bikes with the salty stink of the sea blowing in their numb faces. On the scabby embankment above the wharf were ragged deck chairs and rusted barbeque grills and weeds. Sticking up out of the dirt was a silver slipper. The whole dock looked like a war had been there. Piles of sodden clothes, mattresses, a clock, bent sunglasses, books lying open like fallen birds, a flat soccer ball with a pool of frozen rainwater melting in its cavity. From huge smashed windows hung twisted banners and stained bedclothes. A dog pressed against a wall, wary, and some scruffy boats lay on the water like more rubbish.

Neither of them spoke, they just walked. Billie listened to the snap and flick of her unravelling shoelace. They couldn't talk, she knew that. It was just too hard. They weren't really looking for anything, just walking. At first she had been following him, but now it was her leading. She steered him past the floating shed with the BAR sign hanging off the end of its slippery gangplank.

The seagulls sounded like TV seagulls. She held his hand. Money lumped in her pockets.

In a windswept square where pigeons bent their necks for shelter and newspapers eddied and wrapped themselves shamelessly about the legs of passersby, a young man with a sheet of livid hair and a windripped kilt played bagpipes. His gingery legs stepped a beat and his red hair was beautiful in its train behind him. The wheezing drone of the pipes wound through the puzzled crowd and hung in the air above them, a sound lonely here amongst the sober bricks.

They walked on.

AT THE END OF THE ALLEY was a sign and Billie heard a swell of old music, music from black-and-white movies and suits and ties, so she tugged him in out of the wind, beneath the street sign that he mumbled dully in passing.

'Gebed Zonder End.'

A great gush of warm air blew in their faces as they entered the café with its smells of coffee and cakes and perfume and denim.

Billie felt the sand underfoot and saw the warm wooden walls, the stools, the human faces, round and shiny-cheeked. She met a little table with battered edges and ran her hands along it and sat down. For a moment Scully stood there above her as if he'd forgotten how sitting down went, but he touched the table and slid onto a chair, blinking. Billie put money on the table and they ordered breakfast. Coffee, rolls, cheese, jam, cold cuts of meat.

'No more chasing,' he said. 'I promise.'

Billie put her fingers through holes in the cheese. 'They wanted to know things,' she said. 'All kinds of things.'

He pressed brown bread into the plate. She could see his prints in it when he pulled his hand away.

'Billie, I'm so ashamed.'

She nodded. 'I know.'

It was quiet again for a while. She watched him look for words. His big hands lay on the table. She would know them anywhere. Someone said your heart was the size of your fist. She unzipped her pack.

'Here,' she said, holding the bunch of paper out to him.

'What's this?'

It looked like a flower there in her palm. Billie hoped he didn't see how it shook.

# *Fifty-five*

BILLIE SAW IT STRAIGHTAWAY. Before they even crossed the narrow street, shuffling on the cobbles like old people in front of those cosy hotels and cafés, she saw it and stopped. She heard kids thumping a soccer ball in the square across the footbridge. A bird warbled in the bare tree above the parked cars on the canal embankment and somewhere a bike bell tinkled. Billie found a bollard and sat on it, feeling the dampness come through her jeans. Scully worked his way along the bank, his hair mad as a sun, his face uncertain, as though he didn't know whether to look or not. She watched him find the houseboat, the red one with the fat rotting mattress of autumn leaves on its roof, the one with the silly tilt like Granma's back verandah, and he straightened a moment, blinking.

'This one,' he said.

Billie looked away and saw ducks making vees in the black water. She thought of all the places she had seen that she had no names for, all the flats and hotels and houses in streets she couldn't say, towns she didn't know, where people spoke languages she didn't understand. All those people she just didn't know. All those stations and restaurants and airports and ferries that simply looked the same.

'We went past it yesterday,' he said quietly.

'Yes.'

'Looks deserted, huh.'

She shrugged. She was cold now and sad.

'Funny,' he murmured. 'I've sort of got the creeps.'

Billie looked at the pretty footbridge with its green paint and curly rails. She heard his boots on the deck and looked over to see him knocking at the door at the bottom of the little wooden steps. Maybe this is how it felt to be an angel, to be sad at helping, sad to finish. He cupped his hands to portholes and real windows, climbing up the deck.

'Come here, Bill.'

She thought about it a moment. That travel place was around here somewhere.

'Bill?'

She trusted him. If someone was home she had to believe he would understand her. She was not giving him back. He had promised. She trusted him. But her heart sped up anyway.

'Billie?'

She heard the glass break as she stepped carefully aboard and edged along the handrail to where Scully stood with an old chair-leg in his hand. Ducks rose from the water. Bicycles went past and out beyond the parked cars someone was laughing.

'You slip in, mate. You're smaller.'

'Are we stealing?' she asked, not really caring.

'No, just looking. Mind the edge – it's sharp.'

Billie heard her jacket tear as she wriggled in and fell suddenly headlong. She cried out, but the sofa was beneath her and musty with damp.

'You alright?'

'Yes.'

'Open the door.'

Billie looked about. It was like a big caravan in there. Curtains, cupboards, a desk and proper dinner table with chairs. And photos, Dominique's photos in frames on the walls.

'Billie!'

She slipped off the sofa obediently and felt the shock of cold water round her ankles. Her boots drank it up and her toes stung.

'It's sinking!'

'Open the door, love.'

She waded across to the outside door and fumbled with the handle.

'You got it?'

Her feet began to hurt and her knees knocked. The door came open with a little wave that crept higher up her shins and slapped quietly up against the other end. She climbed onto a chair as he came in wide-eyed, and she saw all the tightness go out of his face. No one had been here for a long time. He looked shocked and relieved and restless. His face changed like the sky. She watched him open the door beside the table. A kind of kitchen. The next door was a toilet. That was it. It was like the end of a tunnel down here.

Scully waded up forward to the brass bed against the bulkhead. In the centre of the quilt lay a single dirty sock and a pale blue pullover he recognized well enough. He picked it up carefully and pressed the cashmere to his face. It smelt of frangipani, of sunlight, of his whole lost life. He lay on the bed and hid his face. This was how it felt in the seconds of dying, the steer on the killing floor with the volts filling his head. Just falling. With the kid beside him, her fingers in his hair, her body pressing in from the living world outside.

'You're enough for me,' she said.

He heard it high above as he went on tipping into space.

## *Fifty-six*

ALL THE QUIET DAY, as rain slipped down the windows and plinked in through the smashed porthole, he lay there and she watched him. He hardly moved at all except to sigh or sniff or move his lips without making sounds. Sometimes tears squelched from his tight-shut eyes, but he never said a word. Billie thought of Quasimodo – she couldn't help it – his skeleton like a fence of bones on the gypsy girl's grave. You could die of a broken heart, she knew that.

She made a causeway of chairs from the bed to the table and pulled off her sloshy boots and socks. Her feet were grey and blotchy. She pulled open drawers and cupboards and found socks and pullovers high up that were still dry. She pulled so much stuff on she felt like the Michelin man but she was warm.

On shelves she found lipsticks, postcards, paintbrushes, Kodak boxes and some little china ducks. There was a wide flat carton full of Dominique's photos. She set it down on the table and went through them carefully. They were of people mostly, and some of streets that looked like Paris. There was one of Marianne in a white chair. Her mouth made a pencil line across her face. She found one of herself with her hair big as a hat and her face laughing. How smooth her face was then. She touched the picture with her fingertips and a little chirp came out of her throat that startled her in the lapping quiet.

Outside ducks pedalled by, laughing among themselves. Bike bells tinkled like goats in the mountains.

Billie kept flipping slowly through the photos. It was like seeing through Dominique's eyes. She was careful, the way she watched. You could see she looked at everything for a long time. These photos made you look like that, at the hips of the chair, at your own eyes big and warm, at your dad's paint-freckled face in the café with the coffee cup shining under his chin. Yes, his big funny smile. That was him. She wondered if everyone saw him the way she did, the way Dominique and the camera did.

There were photos of them all in a graveyard. She remembered the day. Scully had one in his wallet. Their faces were moony with laughing. The cross behind them had veins. It looked like a stone flower.

And then without warning, Billie came to the pictures of Her. It was sudden and scary. Billie's bum closed up and her scars went tight but her heart did not stop. For a moment she just panted and held on to the table. Then she counted them, seven photos. The first one, She was in the street at St Paul in a small dress. There was a tiny smile with those lips that pressed against your ear at bedtime. It was a face that moved, eyes following you across the table, worried for you, wondering how you were. There was blood under that skin. It was a face that loved you. It made your hands shake to see. But that was the only summer picture.

In the others, one by one, as she got more wintry and beautiful, you could see her turning to stone. Her chin setting, her dark eyes like marble, cheeks shining hard like something in the Tuileries.

In the last picture she was close, right up in your face and she had a finger pressed against her lips.

It had stopped raining outside and the ducks were gone. She looked at the shattered porthole and then reached up to feel the moisture round it. Then she stuffed those pictures out through it so that they skittered and skied across the deck to fall like lilies on the water.

A boat chugged past. The dark, smelly water beneath her rose in a scummy wave and slapped at the walls and cupboards, back and forth, until it tired itself out and the shag carpet went limp as seaweed.

Billie made little piles of money in all the colours and kinds. She found the address book and smoothed it out beside the money. Next to that she lay her Hunchback comic and then she emptied the rest of the pack into the water: apple cores, ticket stubs, fluff.

In the galley she opened a jar of olives and a stinky flat tin of sardines. She found a jar of hard red jam which she ate with a spoon. The olive seeds she spat against the wall until her lips ached. She tried to light the stove but couldn't make it work, so she gave up on trying to make him coffee and crawled across her bridge of chairs to the bed. Scully was still breathing, but his eyes were clamped shut. She laid out bits of food for him and shook him gently, but he only shivered. He didn't open his eyes, he didn't look at the food. Billie sat beside him and held his clammy hand as the air got colder and harder and her scars burned tightly. When his shivering got worse she foraged in high cupboards and found hairy coats and stretched jumpers that she piled across him till he was barely visible.

Now and then she tested the water on the floor with a broom handle. It was getting deeper. The air was dreamy with cold.

She looked at him. Inside his nest, under his skin he was still searching, still looking. Maybe somewhere in his mind he would always look. You couldn't blame him. Maybe it would happen to her too. Billie wondered whether she could ever be enough for him.

He opened his eyes a moment and looked about dazed, like someone pulled out of a car crash.

'Me,' she said.

He narrowed his eyes a moment and looked at her.

'You hear me?'

His eyelids fluttered and he was gone again.

LATE IN THE AFTERNOON, a mist came down upon the water to soak up the parked cars, the skeleton trees, the houses and steeples. Billie sat at the table with her teeth chittering and flicked through the grubby address book, saying the names to herself inside her head. The quiet was deep now and the mist moved on the water occasionally as if to let invisible things pass. Billie's breath became a fog in the dying light, and then it was dark. She sat there a while in the sinking night and then the phone on the wall burred like a cicada.

Billie picked it up. The earpiece burnt her face.

'Hullo?'

She listened to the fog quiet at the other end.

'Hullo?'

She heard the clomp of the receiver at the other end and then the peep of the dial tone. Her throat was raw with air. She felt her way across the chairs to the listing bed and climbed in beside her dad who sounded awake and alive and with her. It was strange how happy she felt, strange and sleepy and good.

# *Fifty-seven*

IT WAS COLD WHERE SCULLY WENT, and the great shifting weight of the earth pressed him from every angle, comforting in the dark. His limbs twisted into him, his tongue pressed against his palate and he felt the freezing weld of his eyelids against his face, the retraction of his balls, his nipples, his lungs. Feet, hands, stones, towns, trees leant on him in layers. The food in his gut turned to coal, while above him, outside, above the crust of everything, an insect rattled on and on in impossible summer. Just the sound of it, the dry, clacking sound of it gave the earth the Christly smell of frangipani and he felt his veins tighten like leather thongs. A single, living insect. Calling.

Afterwards, in the mounting silence, he woke to the dead night breathing. He heard the flinty ring of hoofs on the cobbles above. Billie slept beside him, her fingers hooked into the loose, ricked knit of his sweater as though she'd been trying to lift him, raise him. Her breath was tart and briny. He nested his cheek against hers and felt the life in her. His fingers felt tanned and brittle as he lay them in the blood knots of her hair. A horse snorted. Scully found her hand, settled his thumb into her palm.

Her pulse, or his, idled warmly. Above him he heard the deep, toneless murmurs of men and the leisurely gait of horses. Breath hung above his face. The cold was subterranean, sweet and lethal. Even awake he was drowsy with it. Hoof beats faded off into fresh silence. There wasn't even the sound of the canal against the hull, just his own living breath.

Then he stiffened. Out of the silence the footfalls of a walker. They were boots, hard-heeled boots, coming up the canalside cobbles, rapping up against the high walls of the Herengracht houses as his limbs went hard with recognition.

He unpicked Billie's fingers, slid out of the cocoon she had built for them and tamped it back around her in the watery inward light. Steady up the canalside came those footfalls as he slid off the bed into the shock of the forgotten bilge water. God Almighty, it was all he could do not to cry out, but his burst of breath rang like a thud in the sepulchral space all the same. The bloody boat was sinking. Against his shins he felt the scabs of forming ice, or maybe it was rubbish, as he waded blindly for the companionway past the line of chairs.

He cracked the hatch and tasted the colder air outside. His feet burnt away to an absence as he listened. Heels rang awkwardly now and then on the odd surfaces of the cobbles. His socks steamed beneath him. The footfalls stopped outside close by.

Up on deck the rotten leaves were treacherous. A mist buried the streetlamps and smothered the sky so that the only illumination was from muted yellow pillars of lamplight. They cast tidal pools here and there, between parked Opels and VWs, out on the stretch of cobbles where a steaming scone of horse dung revealed itself between the naked bodies of elms.

The air was soupy, maddening. Someone out there. Scully

stood there peering until he made out bricks. A fan of streetlight, a sense of the street corner, yes, the narrow alley there, he remembered. The blood beat in his neck. He made out a traffic bollard, some wrought-iron, the flat biscuity bricks of housewall. The mist shifted on itself, sulphuric in his nostrils. He saw it butting the buoyant rooftops of the city. He needed to see. See properly. He wasn't scared to feel watched like this, but he needed to know.

Scully hobbled numbly around the mulchy deck, keeping low as he could behind the cabin top. A single duck rose off the water, its wings whiffling like the school cane of memory. On the foredeck he crouched beside an ornamental coil of rope and rotten tackle and he saw the denim leg out there in the spill of corner light. The sharp-toed boot disembodied by mist and the angle. His breath quickened. He was calm but his body was loaded.

He measured the jump to the dock. It was close, furry with mist, but close. He figured four feet. It was twenty, twenty-five yards to the street corner. His calves locked up.

But he waited. Was he visible? It seemed unlikely. He saw a knee now. A fresh draught of recognition. He stayed put. Watched. He counted to twenty, forty, ninety. The creak of a heavy leather coat. What if she just crossed the cobbles to the gangplank, just pushed off that righteous Protestant wall and strode across and called out? What would happen, how would he act?

He heard the toes of his frozen socks slipping fractionally on the gritty slime of the foredeck. He gripped the searing metal rail, ready.

Then the boot turned and showed a Cuban heel, two. There was a worldly groan of leather and a shift on the cobbles. Out into the loop of strangled light blurred the hair and moonflash of skin as the figure turned unhurriedly up the sidestreet and was gone, leaving a wake of footfalls that set Scully off automatically. He sprang and lost ground, lifted and fell facedown in hemp and mire and leafy crap at the gunwhale's edge. He scrabbled hopelessly for a few seconds and then gave up. It was simple. He just desisted and listened in bitter relief to the sound of those boots ringing upward in the mist, rapping against the high bricks of the Herengracht and the muted night.

It was in him to get up, he had the will, the sheer idiot stubbornness in him to do it, he knew, but he heard the clonk of furniture beneath him and the flicker of light and it was enough to lie there alive in the cold and feel the hawser against his face.

WHEN HE CAME STIFFLY DOWN the steps into the tilting cabin, Billie held out the wavering flame of the cigarette lighter whose plastic was foggy and green, and let him see his way to a chair. She had her pack on the table and the phone in her hand. He blinked in the strange light and peeled off his socks. His whiskery chin shook a little, but his eyes were clear.

'Okay,' he murmured. 'Okay.'

Billie couldn't tell if this was a question or a command, but she hugged the receiver to her ear and kept dialling anyway. Tiny waves rocked against the furniture. She watched him open cupboards to find some socks. She tilted up her own wrapped feet and shook them at him. At the other end of the phone after the sound of oceans and the land and sky, a man said.

'This better be fooking good, then. Jaysus Mary and Joseph it better had!'

# VI

*For when the angel woos the clay*
*He'll lose his wings*
*At the dawning of the day . . .*

'Raglan Road'

## *Fifty-eight*

RAIN, GREAT UNRAVELLING SHEETMETAL SWATHES of rain fell as the old Transit slushed through the tunnels of hawthorn, through miry bends, past rows of poplars, of larch and oak. Curtains of mud rose at every turn and the wipers juddered across the glass. Through grey little towns of cold-pressed council houses they went, and onto pebblecast bungalows and mongrel Spanish haciendas with asphalt turnarounds in the strange pure green of land. They passed roadside camps of travellers whose miserable donkeys stood tethered to other people's fences in the rain, and everywhere there were ruins choked with blackberry and ivy, fallen walls, tilted crosses and mounds like buried cysts in the earth. Rain.

No one spoke. The three of them sucked carefully on the mints they'd been sharing since Dublin and rubbed at the misting screen with their mittened knuckles.

Peter Keneally steered carefully. It was like transporting bone china. He winced at every rut in the roads of the Republic and cast sideways glances at the two of them there up beside him. They were hollow-cheeked, you could say. Subdued. The little one's scars were like silky patches of sunlight. She had a queer notch in the front of her hair, right there at his elbow. The face of a saint, by God. Now and then the bush of her hair rested on his arm and he felt like singing. Scully had cut himself shaving, which was no surprise the way his hands shook. His eyes were bloodshot, raw as meatballs, and his clothes were clearly not his own. He looked like he'd seen the Devil, but he had a wan sort of smile on his face when they came into familiar country.

In the flat-bottomed valley before the long rise to the Leap, even before the road widened for the scarecrow of a tree that stood as a hindrance to traffic, Scully was pulling off his seatbelt and leaning over to touch his arm. Peter geared down.

Billie watched him get down into the hard icy rain where the van stopped, right there beside the funny tree with the bits of stuff in it. His hair flattened, his shoulders ran with water, but he didn't seem to hurry. The wipers slushed across in front of her and she watched him reach out for something in the boughs.

'Aw, now,' said the man beside her.

She saw the rag in her father's hands, watched it fall limp to the mud at his feet. She sucked her mint.

Out in the rain Scully held onto the tree wondering how it could happen, how it was that you stop asking yourself, asking friends, asking God the question.

## *Fifty-nine*

IT WAS THE FIRST NIGHT OF THE YEAR. Scully woke suddenly, kept his eyes closed and listened to the startling silence of the house. The quiet was so complete that he heard his own heartbeat, his breath loud as a factory. He opened his eyes involuntarily and saw, upon the boards of the floor, a curious light. It ran up the wall as well, like muted moonlight. Then he saw the empty impressed pillow beside him and swung out of bed completely, his naked skin shrinking against the cold.

Scully rushed to Billie's room and slapped on the light. The little bed was open and unmade. Her boots and papers lay spread on the floor, her toys lined up neatly. Down the stairs he felt his knees popping against the strain and he stumbled into the kitchen and the living room to find them empty and their fireplaces dead. He stormed upstairs again to check his bed once more and that's when he passed the uncurtained gable window and saw the world transformed beyond it. He rubbed it clear. A small dark figure trailed down through the bright miracle of the snow, and beyond the wood, beyond his own breath misting up the glass, he saw the lights coming from across the valley and the mountains that stood spectral and white in the cold distance.

BAREFOOT HE WENT with nothing but a bathrobe about him. The snow was soft and clean and cold enough to stop the pain in his feet after a while. He broke through to stones and gnarled sticks that snagged up in the ash wood, but he felt nothing. The sky was a mere soup bowl above him, his breath a pillar of smoke that led him on in Billie's footprints.

He found her by the old pumphouse in the castle grounds. Its ruined walls were rebuilt with snow, and snow joined it to hedges that looked solid as stone, a new settlement overnight. She was fully dressed and still, her black wellingtons gleaming in the light of the riders' torches as they stood bleakly before the keep. She turned and saw him, smiled uncertainly.

Billie looked at his bare feet, his shivering body as he pushed forward down the slope to the men and their tired horses. Their little fires crackled on the end of their sticks, and steam jetted from the horses' nostrils and you could see their streaming sides and tarry maps of blood. Some of the men were only boys, and there were women too, here and there, their round dirty faces shining in the firelight, upturned eyes big as money. Scully went down among them, putting his hands up against the horses and talking, saying things she couldn't hear. Questions, it sounded like.

Billie saw axes and spears and bandaged limbs but she was not afraid. The riders' hair was white with snow, and it stood like cake frosting on their shoulders and down the manes of their horses. Their shields and leggings were spattered with mud and snow and the shiver of bridles and bits rattled across her like the chittering of her teeth.

He looked like one of them, she saw it now – it was like swallowing a stone to realise it. With his wild hair and arms, his big eyes streaming in the firelight turned up like theirs to the empty windows of the castle, he was almost one of them. Waiting, battered, disappointed. Except for his pink scrubbed living skin. That and the terry-cloth robe.

Scully smelled them, the riders and their horses. He recognized the blood and shit and sweat and fear of them, and he looked with them into the dead heart of the castle keep whose wings were bound east and west with snow-ghosted ash trees and ivy, whose rooks did not stir, whose light did not show and whose answer did not come. He knew them now and he saw that they would be here every night seen and unseen, patient, dogged faithful in all weathers and all worlds, waiting for something promised, something that was plainly their due, but he knew that as surely as he felt Billie tugging on him, curling her fingers in his and pulling him easily away, that he would not be among them and must never be, in life or death.

It was only when they were high on the hill, two figures black against the snow, in the shadow of their house, that Scully's feet began to hurt.